STEERING TO FREEDOM

STEERING TO FREEDOM

BY

PATRICK GABRIDGE

www.PenmorePress.com

Steering to Freedom Copyright © 2015 Patrick Gabridge

ISBN: 978-1-942756-22-4(paperback)
ISBN: 978-1-942756-23-1(Ebook)

BISAC Subject Headings:
FIC032000FICTION / War & Military
FIC002000FICTION / Action & Adventure
FIC049040FICTION / African American / Historical

Address all correspondence to:

920 N Javelina PL
Tucson, AZ 85748
mjames@penmorepress.com

1.0

DEDICATION:

For Noah,
Hoping this story might shine a little light, as you navigate
towards your future.

ACKNOWLEDGMENTS:

This project was many years in the making, so it naturally ends up generating a long list of people to thank. I will endeavor to make to include you all, but so many other people are involved in shaping my life as a writer, every day. I am grateful to everyone who reads my books and comes to see my plays and makes the creative life all seem worthwhile.

Specifically, I would like to thank:

Kitt Alexander for helping me with my early research and provided an important biography—her work with the Robert Smalls Legacy Foundation has been important to preserving the history around this important man in our history.

Maxine Lutz at the Historic Beaufort Foundation was extremely helpful in providing me with information about the Robert Smalls house in Beaufort.

Boston's Museum of African American History happened to bring a traveling Robert Smalls exhibit to my home town at just the right moment—getting to listen to talks from scholars and see physical models of the *Planter* was invaluable.

Harvard's Widener Museum generously allowed me to conduct research as a visiting scholar, as I delved into the history of the Civil War and American slavery.

Lynn Ayers at the Wilberforce University libraries helped clarify some of the history around Wilberforce and Reverend Mansfield French.

My fiction group was instrumental in the development of this novel, providing me with much needed support and feedback, on multiple occasions. I am eternally grateful to Deb Vlock, Diana Renn, Eileen Donovan-Krantz, Erin Cashman, Greg Lewis, Julie Wu, Rob Vlock, Steve Beeber, and Ted Rooney, for their insights and friendship.

My dear friends, Jessica Maria Tuccelli, Dan Schreiber, and Mike Wiecek, read various incarnations of the book and were always ready to lend their friendship, in addition to providing invaluable comments about the book. Mike even enlisted his father, Bill, to give me some important information about Civil War currency.

Not many novelists end up thanking their playwright's groups, but I am indebted Rhombus, whose writers and actors have shaped me as a writer in myriad ways over the past dozen years and who patiently listened to my earliest explorations of Robert Smalls and his incredible tale.

My kids, Kira and Noah, provided me with powerful inspiration to delve into African-American history, as I searched for stories of America that included people of color. I stumbled across Robert Smalls while shelving books at the St. Patrick's school in Roxbury, while my daughter was just in first grade and my son was still a baby. In some ways, I feel like the story of Robert Smalls, and my attachment to it, has grown alongside my children.

And I especially need to thank my wife, Tracy, my favorite librarian. Without her, none of my work would be possible. I am grateful for every day we have together.

REVIEWS

Praise for Steering to Freedom:

"*Steering to Freedom* sweeps back the curtain on an extraordinary story of heroism and sacrifice. Escape is only the beginning. Robert Smalls doesn't just save himself: he brings out his family, his friends and his mates — and then he goes back, fighting not just the navies of the South but the deep-rooted prejudices and ignorance of the North. With a sure touch for historical detail and a mastery of the human condition, Patrick Gabridge brilliantly evokes the spirit of a time, a country in struggle, and the heart of a man at its center."

—Mike Cooper, author of *Clawback* and *Full Ratchet*.

"In Patrick Gabridge's meticulously crafted novel *Steering to Freedom*, we're treated to the gripping, true tale of Captain Robert Smalls, a South Carolina slave who, after seizing his freedom, risked his life in a series of nautical adventures to win freedom for all of his enchained brothers and sisters. This powerful and inspirational story is skillfully and dramatically rendered by a writer who not only knows how to steer a good story, but who does so without losing sight of the heart-breaking humanity of his players."

—Mark Dunn, author of *Ella Minnow Pea* and *Under the Harrow*.

PART I

CHAPTER 1

APRIL 30, 1862

Robert kept a tight grip on the wheel of the *Planter*. With the tide rising, she wanted to wriggle and twist in the current sweeping through Hog Island Channel. General Ripley was standing on the deck of the Confederate steamer, and the last thing Robert wanted was to nudge the *Planter* into the sand bar off Shutes Folly Island and fling the general into Charleston Harbor. Slaves didn't get second chances after mistakes like that, even those with precious navigation skills like Robert.

Officers and various hangers on lined the deck of the transport, all grateful to have been permitted aboard the general's flagship. With her tight teak decks, polished brass fittings, and double paddle wheels, Robert thought she was the finest ship in all of Charleston. Even though she was a hundred and fifty feet long, she was almost as fast as a racehorse. Robert had heard one lieutenant complain that it was a shame to see the General floated about the harbor in a converted cotton boat. Maybe the lieutenant didn't understand the importance of a ship that could haul a thousand bales of cotton, or a hundred men and guns, and still not get caught up in the muck of the twisting channels in these parts.

Captain Relyea stood down on the deck beside General Ripley, and from his inflated chest and proud lift to his chin, it was clear that he was plenty proud of his vessel. Every once in a while, Robert would see him run a slow eye back around the

1

ship, checking on each of the black crew members, making sure nothing was even slightly out of order. But Chisholm and Turno knew better than to risk the captain's wrath, which he would be happy to unleash upon them in the person of First Officer Smith, a man for whom the whip seemed made to fit in his hand. Even Johnny, slow and hulking as he was, knew he needed to be his most perfect self whenever the general was on board.

Right now, Smith stood a few steps behind Captain Relyea, balanced on the rail, hanging onto a guy wire to the signal mast, looking out with the rest of the crowd at the flotilla of skiffs, longboats, and small steamers arranged across the width of the channel, all trying to keep steady in the turbulent water. A fresh spring breeze out of the south broke the surface into chop, bringing in the scent of the marshes on Morris Island. The palmetto trees lining the shore of Hog Island swayed in the morning sun like gentle dancers. It would have been a moment of grand serenity, if they weren't loading so much destructive force into the water.

For the past week, they'd been pounding piles and logs down into the shallow seabed around the channel. Now the sailors on the longboats were stringing floating torpedoes across the deepest part of the channel. A munitions sergeant directed a crew of black slave laborers as they carefully slid a string of barrels into the water. Each was so heavy with gunpowder that it took two men to handle it. Pointed cones on each end kept them from rolling in the water, and contact switches stuck out of the side of the barrels. Once an invading ship pressed against the switch: kaboom!

Chisholm climbed up the ladder and joined Robert in the pilothouse, digging into the pockets of his mismatched uniform, searching for his pipe. He was brown as a coconut with tiny black freckles across his cheeks and big bushy hair, which always seemed a little out of proportion to his skinny body.

"What you doing up here?" Robert asked.

"Worried you might be lonely. Plus I wants to see better—all them army officers is blocking the view, not to mention Smith's big fat head." Chisholm lit his pipe and took a puff.

"He catch you up here loafing, he give you some new stripes," Robert warned, knowing that Smith would be happy to give some to him, too.

"We ain't doin' nothing besides watching. Look at Billy out there with those torpedoes. I thought you were gonna get him on the *Planter* with us."

"Maybe once you get whupped and tossed overboard, they'll have an open spot for him," Robert countered.

Their friend Billy was out on the skiffs, loading. Robert could always count on Billy to connect him with sailors on incoming blockade runners who might have a little something for a side trade, some lace or some tea. Billy was dark and strong, with an easy smile, and Robert had been trying to find a spot for him aboard the *Planter* for months.

Down below, General Ripley paced impatiently. He was like a larger version of Captain Relyea—bigger belly, bigger beard, bigger ego. "We'll be here all day if they keep moving at this pace," he complained loudly. "By the time they finish, the Union scouts will already be having dinner at the Mills House Hotel."

Apparently, the general's complaints carried quite well across the water, and Robert heard the sergeant bark at the laborers. And sure enough, they moved a little faster. Billy and his partner pulled another banded barrel over the side into the water and attached the stone weight that would keep it floating just below the surface. With the Hog Island Channel blocked, the Union would be forced to use the main shipping channel for any attack on the heart of the Confederacy, and the main channel was defended by half a dozen heavily armed forts, including Fort Sumter.

"Ain't nobody coming through Hog Island Channel 'less they wants to put on a fireworks show for all of Charleston," Chisolm said.

The scent of the air changed subtly, losing the flavor of

marsh, and Robert could feel the wind shifting to come from the northeast, maybe bringing a storm. He felt the *Planter* take a little step back, and he rang the bell to tell Alfred in the engine room to increase power just a notch.

Boom! Boom! Boom!

Three huge explosions rocked the *Planter* back on her haunches, as one of the laborers grounded a torpedo switch on the gunwale of his boat. A tower of water, wood, and bloody bits of men rose into the sky and splattered back down on the ships and boats all around. The men on the *Planter* lay flat on the deck, holding their collective breaths, waiting to see if the rest of the torpedoes would detonate, too.

Robert hung onto the wheel and straightened out the *Planter*, wondering what would happen next. Out in the channel, Billy's longboat had been completely pulverized, and the two nearest boats were in broken chunks, grasped by bleeding, sputtering men.

General Ripley and his entourage slowly stood, brushing themselves off. A detached brown hand twitched on the deck not far from Captain Relyea, who unceremoniously picked it up and tossed it overboard.

"Get a diver into the water and get that line reattached," General Ripley commanded. "And find some Negroes who are considerably less clumsy to launch the rest of the torpedoes. We just lost a valuable sergeant out there. Competence! War is won by boldness and competence. Let me see plenty of both. Now!"

The men around scattered to tend to the wounded and reconvene the torpedo party, all while General Ripley and Captain Relyea shook their heads and shared a look that seemed to say, "I am surrounded by idiots."

Chisholm rose shakily to his feet. "Sometimes I think Hell ain't nearly as far away as it supposed to be."

Robert smacked him on the shoulder. "Get down there now, or else Smith is gonna make you wish you was in Hell. At least go make yourself look like you's useful."

"But Billy—"

"Billy gone. And if you don't get down there, they might make you take his place on that crew. Go help those officers clean the blood off theyselves. Now."

Chisholm finally moved and slid down the ladder to the deck, joining in the swell of activity. Robert watched Smith and Captain Relyea carefully, waiting for orders.

Billy was gone. Eventually, the army would draft a list of the dead, even the slave laborers. The Confederate government would pay damages to their owners, but their women and children would never see a penny. One minute he was there, the next he was nothing but fish food. Sometimes life made no sense at all. Billy and the others blown to bits working for an army that was fighting to hold them as slaves forever. Robert had no idea what he could do about it, but he needed to do something.

CHAPTER 2

Every month it was the same. Robert waited in the doorway, hat in hand, head bowed. Mr. Kingman leaned over his ornately carved desk, working away at a ledger book. Robert waited and Kingman ignored him until just enough time had passed.

Surrounded by unruly piles of letters and bills, Kingman looked a little more hunched over his ledger than usual. He was a squat man with a bald head and bushy beard and smelled of the sweet cigars he smoked almost non-stop. There were rumors that his coffers weren't so full. Charleston was a city that lived on rumors, and the war bred them like mosquitoes. With the Union blockade squeezing Charleston, many businessmen were struggling to pay their debts. Kingman's gaze flicked rapidly from his pile of papers to his books, then he sighed out his despair with a long rattle.

Robert gently rapped on the door frame. "Excuse me, suh?"

Kingman finished inking yet another figure and looked up. His eyes weren't as cold as Captain Relyea's or Smith's, but that wasn't saying much. "Yes? Oh, Robert. Come in."

Last day of the month. Merchants like Kingman all across Charleston sat at desks just like this one, in homes just as swank, and collected their rents. Robert could feel the bills in his trouser pockets, but he didn't hurry to haul them out. A man like Kingman didn't like to rush business. Especially not with a slave.

Kingman lit a new cigar and looked him up and down. Robert wore his sailor's uniform clean and ironed. The jacket

6

was a castoff Hannah salvaged from some sailor who had left the hotel in a hurry after an unlucky night of cards. Robert had her cut off two of the decorative buttons from the breast, so it didn't look like he was putting on airs. In place of the missing buttons hung his slave badge, a stamped copper diamond, "Charleston 1862, Mechanic."

"Were you just down at the harbor?" Kingman asked.

"Yes, suh. We was steaming General Ripley on the *Planter*, suh." Robert tried not to think about Billy and the blood and bone they rinsed from the deck.

"He's a good man. Charleston is safe in his hands. Any ships arrive today?" There was a tinge of urgency to his voice.

"Nossuh. But maybe something coming tonight. The rain might give them cover."

"You have my money?"

"You know you can depend on me, suh." Robert reached into his pocket and hauled out a damp pile of mismatched paper bills. It gave Robert some satisfaction to pay with notes drawn from the State Bank of South Carolina. When he traded goods in the alleyways or on the docks, Robert never took bills, only gold or silver coins. But the Confederate Navy paid his monthly wages of sixteen dollars with Confederate money, which wasn't worth nearly as much as the bills claimed on their faces. Kingman could have asked for hard money, but he was on the board of the bank. It'd shame him to turn down his own currency.

"Four dollar from Hannah, for her hire out work." She earned five dollars a month as a maid at the Mills House Hotel, and she owed Kingman four dollars for the privilege of hiring herself out for wages. Kingman had enough slaves at home to care for him and his wife and dozen children, so he used Hannah to bring in cash. Robert had to pay his own master, Henry McKee, fifteen dollars a month to hire himself out to the navy.

"And four more from me, for Hannah." Robert added more money to the pile—the monthly levy he paid Kingman for letting him marry Hannah; a monthly reminder that his wife was just on loan.

"She still being a good wife to you, Robert?" Kingman smiled a winking smile as he picked up the pile of cash. "You getting your money's worth?"

"Oh, yes suh. I's very content." Some men wanted a soft, young pillow for a wife. But even though he was only twenty-three years old, Robert wanted a bear, with teeth and claws. Hannah was just what he needed.

Robert didn't like the leer that came with Kingman's smile. Hannah had lived a lot of life before she married him—she was a good fifteen years older than he was. Robert had no doubt that Kingman had an intimate taste of Hannah in the past.

Kingman counted the money with his thick, tobacco stained fingers. Some of the bukras didn't like to even touch money from a Negro, but Kingman wasn't squeamish—money was money. Once convinced it was all there, he handed Robert a receipt with barely a glance and returned to his ledger.

Robert shifted his feet nervously. Some of the crew, including Alfred, said he should wait to see how the war worked out. Maybe the Union would bring them all freedom. But from what he heard, the Southern generals were on a tear. If he didn't try now, he might never get the chance again. "Mr. Kingman?"

"Is something wrong?"

"No, suh." Robert took a deep breath. The book-lined walls of the office seemed to press down on him. The air felt thick and smoky. "I was just wonderin' if I can ask you something, suh?"

Kingman barely paused in his calculations. "I am very busy. What is your request?"

"You remember we talked a ways back, got to be two years ago, and we agreed on a price for me buyin' Hannah and Lizzie?"

This deal wasn't on the scale of some of what Kingman did,

but it wasn't exactly rent and body money, either. Kingman placed the pen gently down on the ledger and gave Robert his full attention, stroking his beard. "I remember."

"I been wonderin', suh, if the price we talk about, might have some..."

"Leeway?"

"Yessuh. Eight hunnerd is a mighty big pile of money."

Kingman looked Robert over again, his eyes lingering on the jacket and buttons. "You're making good money working for the navy on the *Planter*, yes?"

"Yessuh." Robert could almost hear the gears turning in Kingman's head, as he tried to assess what Robert wanted and how much he could pay for it.

"Well, patience then. Save up a little here and there. You and Hannah will both have to work harder. I know it's a hard concept to understand, but if you keep putting a little bit away, someday you'll have enough."

Robert could feel resentment stirring in his belly. He tamped down the urge to grab Kingman and shake him by the lapels. "Oh, yessuh," he said. "We scrapes and we saves. But I wonder if you might be willing to let me have them for seven hunnerd."

Kingman arched his brows. Wrinkles of surprise reached all the way up his bald head.

Robert continued, "With the blockade, you might want some ready cash. I could give you seven hunnerd, mostly in hard money." Blockade runners demanded only gold, not paper.

Kingman's surprise turned to annoyance. "My financial state is none of your concern."

Robert's heart fluttered. Maybe he'd gone too far. "I don't mean no disrespect, suh. I's only trying to know if you might be willing to let me pay seven hunnerd for Hannah, Lizzie, and little Robert Junior. I could pay you real soon." He held his breath and waited to see if Kingman caught the addition to the list.

When it came to deals, Samuel Kingman didn't miss much. His face flushed red with anger. "Now you want to steal from me, boy? We had a deal—eight hundred dollars for Hannah and the little girl. And that was a bargain, because you and I have dealt honorably with each other. We never said anything about the baby."

"He wasn't born at the time, suh."

"Well, he's born now, and he's mine. Just like Hannah and the little girl. I have faith in our generals. Robert E. Lee is a man of honor and intelligence. He will lead the South to victory. The disaster in New Orleans is a fluke. When this war is over, the plantations will need more hands than ever."

If Kingman was looking to the future, he could wait until the baby was almost a man and sell him for a thousand, two thousand dollars.

"Come back when you have eight hundred dollars. Bring an extra four hundred if you want the little boy, too."

Robert straightened up to his full height, which wasn't much. Being short was sometimes helpful, because he didn't intimidate, not like Turno. He raised his head all the way, just this once, and looked Samuel Kingman in the eye. A stupid risk. He searched for a speck of something human that might give Robert hope for his son. But Kingman's eyes were cold. Robert lowered his chin again quickly.

"You go on, now. I have work to do. I'll see you next month."

Robert stepped softly away, down the back stairs, into the narrow streets. At home, he had seven hundred dollars under the floorboards. Not enough. All the jobs and saving and planning. Not enough.

*****

Gas lamps lit the growing dimness on Chalmers Street just enough for Robert to see two dark figures in rags sitting with their feet in the stocks, a man and a woman. The woman moaned to herself. The man propped himself up on his elbows, to keep his back, all whipped to shreds, from touching the ground. He had the look of a field slave, and with the new "S" branded on his cheek, he'd never be much more.

When Robert was eleven years old, Master Henry brought him to Charleston to live with Missus Ancrum, Master Henry's aunt. Before Mama Lydia left to go back to Beaufort with the McKees, she brought him here, to see the slaves in chains and to hear the lash and crying from inside the workhouse. "Don't you end up here, Robert," she'd said. "Don't you shame me. In Charleston they want their niggers just so. You give them what they want, on the outside. Inside your head, you think what you want, but don't never let them hear it. Don't let them get a whisper. They happy to spare a dollar for the workhouse to whip you and twenty-five cents for salt to rub into your wounds, scar you for life, make sure everyone see how much they got to whip you. It up to you to be good and stay safe."

Now he understood that it depended on luck, too. Sometimes you got a master who felt it his duty to show you your place. Or you met someone like Samuel Smith, on the *Planter*. Robert tiptoed around the First Officer as carefully as he could, but Smith had a dagger in his eye for him. Robert took every pain to keep the ship off the shoals, keep the men working. That wouldn't work forever.

A few drops of rain spit down from the sky. The storm was finally here, and it would be a cold, miserable night for the two souls in the stocks.

"Halt!" The voice was louder than it needed to be. The authorities had stationed some boy with peach fuzz to keep watch on the corner, his grey uniform all patched and thrown together. His rifle pointed at Robert's chest, the barrel shaking a little.

"Show your pass."

Robert moved his hand slowly to show the copper badge on his jacket. "Number 712. Suh."

The boy fumbled in his pocket for a written list of the slaves who were in trouble, all while trying to keep the rifle from falling out of his hands. Robert stood very, very still. No sense giving him an excuse to shoot.

The soldier didn't find anything incriminating on the list and slid it back into his pocket. He scrunched up his face, trying to look tough. It really just made him look like a constipated child, but Robert kept that thought to himself.

"What's your business out here, nigger?"

"Jes' gon' home to my wife and chi'ren, suh. Been sailing General Ripley all around the harbor today. He be the pride of Charleston."

"Better hurry home. Curfew comin'. We don't want no black faces on the street after ten. You want to end up in the workhouse with the rest of them?"

"No, suh."

The boy looked at him again. You never knew what they might do. Two nights ago, the guard made Robert lie on his belly, face in the mud. Just to see him do it. Laughed at how close in color the mud was to his skin.

"Go on then." The boy stepped back into the darkness. Maybe he was looking forward to ten o'clock, with hopes of seeing a little action. Any trouble would come from soldiers letting off steam at the saloon. There was talk of martial law, the army taking control of everything. Hiding in the engine room of the *Planter*, Chisholm had read a newspaper article to them that the army planned to close the city's saloons and bars. Maybe that's why the soldiers drank harder every night, making sure they got it in before the doors closed.

*****

He trudged up the rickety wooden stairs that clung to the side of the stables, as the rain fell in cold, greasy drops. Their spot was never meant to be a home at all—it was just an attic above John Simmons' stables. Simmons owned three merchant vessels, all of which Robert had piloted in and out of Charleston

Harbor scores of times. In return for this unfinished space, Robert always dropped whatever he was doing to bring Mr. Simmons' ships safely through the shoals and snags.

Robert stood on the landing outside the door, wondering what he could say to Hannah. The cold water ran down his forehead, like a cascade of icy tears that would not be shed but should be. Finally, he opened the door, lifting it on its leather hinges so it wouldn't scrape against the rough planks.

The smell of home always hit him first—the scent of dinner, mingled with horses and manure, wood smoke, and the lye soap in the wash basin. Hannah stood at the stove, stirring stew in an iron pot he'd gleaned from the ashes of the Great Fire in December. Her house dress was pockmarked with holes and rips that barely withstood repair, but Robert liked the way it showed flashes of her skin, as if it revealed a bit of the inner Hannah. There wasn't much about Hannah that was soft. Her arms and legs were lean and muscled from changing linens at the Mills House Hotel, from long days on her feet, and from nights washing laundry she took in from hotel guests— Confederate officers and fancy ladies from Richmond.

Next to the stove, little Lizzie stood above a washtub and attempted to stir the steaming pot of laundry. She concentrated hard on the stick in the grey water, trying not to make Mama mad by splashing on the rough planked floor. In the corner, Robert Junior lay on his back in a pile of tattered blankets, tickling his own little brown toes. He squealed with delight, like only a one-year-old baby can.

He was a baby worth four hundred dollars to Kingman. They could find a way to save the last hundred for Hannah and Lizzie, but more than that seemed impossible.

What if Kingman didn't stay? Respectable Charleston families slipped out of town every day, for Columbia or Richmond. Their slaves were too valuable to leave behind.

"Daddy! I'm washin'." Lizzie proudly stirred harder. Even though she was only four years old, she knew it was important to be a good worker.

13

"Mama's lucky to have a helper like you."

Hannah turned to him, her eyes brimming with something close to hope. That small bit of optimism was dashed in the instant she saw the look on his face.

"Go give your Papa some sugar," she told Lizzie, who ran across the room and leaped into his arms. Junior saw his sister wrap herself around Papa and tried to untangle himself from the blankets, in order to join in. Robert dragged his leg, with his daughter clinging to it, across the floor and turned over his son, like flipping a stranded turtle. A tangle of little arms and fingers caught Robert, dragging him down to the floor.

"You hungry?" Hannah asked, finally breaking through the cloud of silence that clung to her.

"I feel like I'm just one big hungry." He growled at the children and said, "Maybe I'll just eat one of these chi'ren to tide me over."

Lizzie and Junior squealed and laughed as he tickled them and the sound was like pure, clear sunshine. Outside, it rained harder, and water started to leak through the roof near the stove. He hoped his patch over the bedroom still held.

"Lizzie. Come back and stir this washin' right now," Hannah called. She clearly wasn't in the mood for so much frolic. Robert set Junior back in the blankets and joined Hannah by the stove. She stiffened as he neared her. He'd raised her hopes up so high.

He put a hand on her waist, and she moved away. He saw a bruise barely visible right where her shoulder met her neck.

"Hannah? What's this?"

Even in a hotel as high class as the Mills House, sometimes men took what they wanted.

"I'm all right." The sound of her voice, the look in her eyes, the slight shake to her chin told him differently.

"Who?" It wouldn't be the first time. The younger women had it worse. Some of them didn't make it. Hannah had lived long enough to see that there would still be a tomorrow.

"I said I'm all right. Leave it." She dipped a bowl into the soup pot and set it on the table. "Your soup's ready. Lizzie, you stop now. Come eat your soup. Junior. Come on now."

The little boy toddled across the floor and into her lap. What Robert wanted more than anything was to take Hannah into his arms. He wanted to tell her it would be all right, that he would find a way to protect her, that he would find a way to free all of them.

But he didn't know how. Not yet.

CHAPTER 3

"Move that, so I can see."

Robert leaned forward with the lamp to give Alfred more light as he whacked the mallet against the blunt iron wedge. Without this adjustment to the port engine, the *Planter* wasn't going anywhere, and that meant more scolding and shouting, and maybe even a beating from Smith. Alfred gave five more thunderous whacks, but the metal key refused to slide into place.

"You gon' get it," Robert encouraged. Not many men in all of Charleston were better at fixing steam engines than Alfred, and that included Pitcher, the actual engineer of the ship, who was in his berth sleeping off yet another hangover.

"Come on, you tight little sow," Alfred growled. Sweat streamed down his face, and his scrubby grey hair glistened in the lamplight.

"No, she's a lady. You gotta sweet talk her." Robert stroked the side of the boiler lovingly. "Maybe bring her some flowers."

"I think she like to play rough sometimes," Alfred countered and gave another sharp whack with the hammer. The wedge slipped into place.

A crash of firewood erupted behind them. "You ain't done yet? Captain be back soon," said Turno, as he straightened the pile of wood, just in time to have Johnny, who nearly filled the room with his bulk, dump another load.

A white straw hat flashed in the doorway, and they all snapped to attention before seeing the wiry brown body of

16

Chisholm under it.

"Look what the wind done blew on my head," he said with a broad smile.

"Th- tha- that's the captain's hat," Johnny said slowly. Born a little on the slow side, he spent a good chunk of his day confused, and the world was more confusing than ever these days.

"You can call me Captain Chisholm."

Turno scowled. He was tall and muscled and serious as midnight. "He gon' to take it back and yo' head with it."

Chisholm took the hat off, spun it around on his hand, and tossed it onto Robert's head. "Perfect fit. Ain't that right, Captain Smalls?"

Robert laid down the lantern and puffed out his chest. He crossed his arms officiously in his best imitation of Captain Relyea, strode to the center of the room, and then boomed out, "Alfred, full speed ahead! Turno, cast off those lines. Smalls, put us on the sand bar again and I'll have you roasted alive."

The engine room filled with laughter. Alfred leaned his tired body against the boiler, wiping off the grease from his hands on a rag. "Suits you, don't it?"

Chisholm admired Robert, as if in amazement. "Dead ringer for him."

"Just order us out of the harbor, Captain. Right to the blockade," said Turno, still chuckling. It wasn't easy to make Turno laugh.

Robert stared out at the imagined horizon with a steely gaze. "Go straight for those Union bastards. Break on through."

"Straight to freedom," drawled Johnny, his stutter vanishing.

The laughter died abruptly, smashed flat against a glass wall. They didn't even dare look at each other. Such words weren't meant to be spoken aloud, only whispered in the dark of night.

"And the cannon on Castle Pinckney go BOOM!" Chisholm

pulled them back to fun.

The laughter returned, but tinged with the rusty taste of reality.

"Fort Sumter boom!" chimed Turno.

"Fort Wagner boom!" said Alfred.

"Fort Morris boom!" said Chisholm.

"Fort Moultrie boom boom boom!" drawled Johnny, trying to keep up.

"Our little speck a driftwood make good target practice for those Union gunners out there, huh?" said Turno.

"Thanks for the orders, Captain!" said Chisholm.

"You do as you're told!" scolded Robert. "Now swab those decks, stack that wood!"

The hoots rose again, bouncing around the room, until a head popped into the doorway. Robert snatched the hat off his head and cursed himself for being surprised. He didn't have the luxury of surprises.

It was just Alston, the steward boy, fresh and shiny in his uniform. "What you niggers laughin' 'bout?"

"Nothin'," said Turno. "Come on, Johnny. We need more firewood if this hulk gon' to carry General Ripley and his soldiers today."

With Turno and Johnny's bulk out of the room, it felt practically empty. Alfred shook his head and returned to his work.

"What you doin' with the captain's hat, Robert?" Alston was only fourteen years old and sometimes seemed as innocent as a baby. Robert never knew how much he could trust such a child. Maybe not too much.

"I was just looking for you, so you can give it to him." Robert handed the hat to the boy, who inspected it for damage or stains.

"Good thing you found it, otherwise I get a beatin'."

"Well, we don't want that. You run off and put it where it belongs."

As Alston scampered up the stairs towards the captain's cabin, Robert wondered what the other men had thought of him when he first started as a deckhand. Never figured he'd pilot a ship by the time he got to twenty-three.

What came next?

He caught himself. What came next? Slaves weren't supposed to think that way. The future was for white men to worry about.

"Robert. A little more light, huh?" Alfred was tightening bolts on the pillow block, the great chunk of metal that bore the shaft. Robert raised the lantern higher again.

"Think you can fix it?" Robert asked.

"Yeah, I can fix it." The lines on Alfred's face deepened. "How 'bout you? What can you do?"

Their eyes met and held, and Robert wondered if they were both looking for the same answer.

*****

Robert turned the wheel carefully as the *Planter* approached the walls of Fort Sumter. All along the channel, pilings had been sunk deep into the bed of the harbor and attached to logs and ropes to foul the screws of enemy ironclads. Torpedoes floated just under the surface, with enough powder to blow a hole through metal plates, let alone a wooden hull like the *Planter's*.

He gripped the spokes a little harder, fighting a dark urge. What if he nudged the ship out of the channel and found a torpedo the hard way? A half turn of the wheel would send a hundred Confederate soldiers and officers and General Ripley to the bottom of Charleston Harbor. Would that be enough payback for the lashes endured by every slave on this ship? For every shame visited upon Hannah, his children, on all their families? Justice for Billy and the others blown sky high? Would the Union think a slave had done them a favor? They'd probably just call it an unlucky accident.

It wasn't his place to make martyrs of every crew member on the *Planter*. Not today. He kept her steady in the channel.

Ahead, the walls of the fort rose straight out of the water, easily fifty feet high, twice as tall as the *Planter*. Though the fort still bore scars from the bombardment last April, Robert could see dark-skinned laborers replacing missing chunks of granite with hoists and cranes.

The whole city had been awake that night, the air electric with the buzz of approaching war. Hannah had served iced tea on the roof of the hotel to the lords and ladies of Charleston, as they observed the early morning cannon fire, like it was some grand display staged for their entertainment. Robert had been down at the docks, where the rest of Charleston—the shopkeepers and firemen and sailors and slaves—looked to the east, eyes glinting orange from the fire in the sky, their excitement magnified by the thunder of hundreds of shells.

Doom. Doom. Doom.

The whites had fired pistols into the air and cheered for a South Carolina free from under the thumb of the Yankees. The smoke from the batteries drifted over the harbor, a fog of destiny, pricking their noses with the sharp smell of gunpowder. Blacks and whites dreamed of very different futures that night.

"Officer Smith, signal Fort Sumter that the *Planter* requests permission to pass," commanded Captain Relyea from his perch in the front of the pilothouse.

"Aye, Captain," answered Smith. He pulled out a signal on the steam whistle: long, long, short, long. "Robert. Slow by half."

Robert pulled a lever to alert the engine room to cut their speed. "Slowing by half."

Captain Relyea stood in front of the open windows, arms crossed proudly over his barrel chest, his broad-brimmed hat parked just so. High on the fort, a reflection glinted off a telescope observing the *Planter*. Captain Relyea waved stiffly up at the sentries. He made the same formal wave every time they approached a fort, like he was above all this messiness.

They waited, and Relyea's eyes narrowed. He hated delays with General Ripley on board.

A voice finally shouted down from above, "Pass the *Planter*."

"Excellent. Robert, let's see if we can bring the general and his men to Battery Wagner without any further delays."

"Aye, suh."

"Officer Smith, tell Engineer Pitcher that the engines sound like a child with croup. Before we next have the privilege of transporting the general, they need to purr like a kitten."

Smith never minded giving Pitcher a hard time, and his lips curled in pleasure at the thought of passing along this message from the captain.

"One more thing, Mr. Smith," Captain Relyea called, still staring ahead at the approaching shore of Morris Island. "There is a broken chair in the ward room. General Ripley is currently being forced to sit on a stool, which is disrespectful to him and embarrassing to me. Find who is responsible and ensure it does not happen again."

Smith darkened at the scolding from his commander. "With pleasure, Captain." He disappeared below decks, and Captain Relyea strolled across the upper deck in front of the pilothouse. Did he know or care what Smith would do to whomever he decided to blame?

In title, Smith was both first officer and pilot of the *Planter*. Robert only received a wheelman's pay, because in Charleston only whites were allowed to be called "pilot." Everyone at the port knew who brought the ship home and kept her from running aground, and it wasn't Smith.

Robert took the *Planter* farther off the banks of Morris Island, knowing just where the sand tended to pile up after the ebb tide and a northern wind. Off to the eastern horizon, thin plumes of smoke and slips of white sails showed the ships of the Union blockade. All were careful to stay out of range of the guns of the forts.

*****

The leather strap snapped hard against Turno's back, the pain popping his head up. Smith jerked his hand back and the lash whistled through the air for another blow.

"Don't touch things that don't belong to you, nigger," Smith snarled.

This blow finally broke Turno's ebony skin, a trickle of red seeping from the raised welts. Turno sagged against the ropes holding his wrists to the deck pillars. Bystanders lined up along the wharf, taking in the free show.

"I think he's received the message, Samuel," called Pitcher. Engineer Zerich Pitcher was a doughy man, but stronger than he looked, and only just behind Alfred when it came to skill with steam engines.

"Don't you undermine me," Smith hissed.

Robert admired Pitcher's fearlessness. "I don't care what you do to him," Pitcher said. "But make sure he can load firewood and work the hoists tomorrow morning. We have two runs to make, and the captain will be displeased if we're short-handed. Experienced deckhands are scarce these days."

Smith tossed the strap at Robert's feet, where drips of red spotted the deck. "Clean up this mess," he told Robert. "And see that your crew stays in line, or I'll have you up there next."

Robert didn't doubt that his turn was coming soon. Smith's boiling spite could only be kept at bay for so long.

Smith climbed the ladder to the upper deck, each angry footstep like a hammer. As Robert stepped forward to cut Turno down, Pitcher pulled out his pipe and lit it, calm as a man on a picnic. Maybe the flask hidden in his vest pocket helped him ignore Smith's wrath.

Robert's hands shook as he reached forward to help Turno. At the other end of the deck, Johnny swept up the manure from the soldiers' horses, while the cook, Jackson, started mopping.

They looked up at Robert, ready to help.

"You boys keep cleanin' that deck," he told them. "It need to shine before the captain get back. You understand?"

They nodded, reluctant. Johnny always wanted to help, but there were too many eyes watching.

A lazy smoke ring from Pitcher's pipe drifted over toward them. Now that the show was over, the crowd on the wharf went back to loading and unloading cargo from the most recent blockade runner.

Robert pulled a knife from his belt and cut the ropes from Turno's wrists. He'd have to find a towel and clean water to wash the cuts. If Smith had been less agitated and more his usual ornery self, he would have instructed Robert to wash Turno down with salt water, to ensure the scars set up for everyone to see.

"You be all right," Robert said soothingly. "I take care of you."

"I didn't break that chair, Robert," Turno whispered.

"He don't care." It felt like being stabbed in the heart to see someone as strong as Turno suffer so much from the whip.

"I know. But I needed to tell someone."

"You just stay strong, all right?"

"Don't you worry about me. Samuel Smith ain't nothin'."

"That's right. That's right. You strong. You a man."

There was a whole war going on right now, and no matter what those Southern gentlemen said, this war was about white folks keeping their slaves, their power. Up in the North, some people felt different. Some of those folks were in ships off the bar, right now. Robert wished he could just fire up the *Planter* and sail it out to them, to a new horizon. Take everyone he loved and go.

CHAPTER 4

In the dark, Robert lay in bed with Hannah pressed against his side. This was one of the last cool nights left before summer started to blast away. On the other side of Hannah, Junior snorted in his sleep and twitched from dreaming of whatever babies dream about. Lizzie lay in the tangle of blankets, too, having snuck over from her little mattress on the floor in the corner. With her in the mix, there was hardly room to turn over.

"Hannah?"

She breathed in deeply, coming back from the edge of sleep. "Hm? What is it?"

"I been thinkin'."

"It's late. I'm tired. Let's talk in the mornin'."

She nestled against him, trying to find her way back to sleep. He hadn't been able to shake the feeling of Relyea's hat on his head. Johnny's voice: "Right to freedom." Turno's bloody back. The soldiers and guns moved by the *Planter* to make sure that owners stayed owners and slaves stayed slaves. He was getting paid to help them do it, paid to keep himself bound to Henry McKee. Paid to help Kingman own Hannah and Lizzie and Robert and sell them to anyone he wanted.

If Hannah said no to his plan, he'd be stuck on a leash for the rest of his life. He'd been trying to talk to her about it all night, but the timing never seemed right. Now she was sleeping, dreaming, in those few moments of rest between the hardness of life. If she said no, could she forgive him for making the offer? Could he forgive her for refusing?

24

If he didn't have courage to even talk to Hannah, then he was a coward who got what he deserved. He laid his hand gently on the bare skin of her shoulder, feeling her warmth, her life beneath his fingertips.

"I think we should go."

"Hm? Where?"

"I think we should escape. Get free."

Her body suddenly tensed, like she'd been struck by a little bolt of lightning. She rolled over to face him, but in the dark he could only see the vaguest outline of her. In the stable below, a horse chuffed, dreaming a dream of its own, oblivious to dangerous thought that had just been spoken aloud.

Hannah's voice was low and tight. "I thought we had a plan to buy ourselves free."

He put his hand on her hip, needing to have contact with her. "Kingman ain't gon' give you up easy. If he stay in Charleston, ships is havin' trouble getting through. The Union clip the wrong blockade runner, then he gon' come up short. Best way for ready cash is to sell a slave."

"But he said if we pay the extra money we can have Junior, too. We can save the money."

"There ain't no future here. Not for Lizzie or Junior."

"Sometimes families stay together." She was almost pleading, struggling to keep her voice low enough not to wake the children.

"You know anyone kinder than the McKees? Eleven years old they sent me to work in Charleston, made me say goodbye to my mama. See her once every few months. And when they ran outta Beaufort in November, they didn't bring her. Where is she now? Maybe she got herself free, because she knew freedom is worth more than any second-hand dress she got from Mrs. McKee, or a kind word, or a pocketful of candy."

Even in the dark, saying any of this aloud made his blood rush.

"You have a plan?"

"We go on the *Planter*."

"What?"

"Usually, Smith and Pitcher take turns sleeping on board at night. But twice, they all went ashore and put me in charge. They trust me. They'll do it again."

For a long moment, the room was filled only with the sound of children sleeping and a snort from one of the horses below, the rain tapping on the roof. Hannah's voice came back in an incredulous whisper. "You want to steal a steamboat?"

"That's right."

"And take it where?"

"Straight out the harbor, to the blockade. We sneak you and the chi'ren on board, and maybe the families of the other crew, too. Middle of the night. Wouldn't be the first time we brung passengers or cargo to the outer forts at night. No one knows the harbor better'n me, so I always get called to do it. We don't run. We walk out. We pretend like we's on a mission."

At first, her only answer was silence. Robert felt suspended over a cliff, with jagged rocks at the bottom. He listened for even a trace of a smile or appreciation in her voice and found nothing.

"That the craziest thing I ever heard."

"Exactly. That's why they won't see it coming."

She took a deep breath and held it. It was a horrible idea, and it was a brilliant idea. He could do it, but only if she believed in him.

"You gon' take us with you?"

"I don't want to live in a world where other men has their power over you and the chi'ren. And if I keep havin' to, it gon' kill me."

She slipped her hand into his. Their hands had always been a good match—strong fingers interlaced with strong fingers, working hands bound together in a hard world.

"What if we fail?"

"I ain't gon' let that happen."

"You talkin' 'about a lot of people doin' this thing. Any one of them talk, we all die. They won't just sell us off. Not even the chi'ren. They hang us all, tear us to pieces. Lizzie and Junior, too."

He'd thought of this a thousand times, but every time, he found the same answer. "If we stay here, we ain't never gon' live. They will take you from me, they will take our chi'ren. It just a matter of time. That tiny scrap of hope they give you, it ain't real, Hannah. It's just there to keep you in your place. The only way to life, to real life, is to take it for ourselves."

She ran her hand over his face, tracing his nose, his eyebrows, his lips, his jaw.

He could hear the hard smile in her voice. "I'm with you. They catch us, we all die together."

*****

Robert closed the door of the pump room, as Alfred and Turno looked at him through the tangle of pipes, confused.

"It don't take three of us to fix the pump," Turno said, as Alfred started rummaging through his tray of wrenches. Turno wore a ripped cotton shirt without sleeves that showed his strong arms and had a damp stripe along his back, as the stripes from Smith oozed on their way to healing.

"I got a question for both of you," Robert said. He trusted these two men as much as if they were his own brothers, but it's never easy to ask your brother to risk his life.

Alfred straightened as much as he could in the cramped room. "You been looking like you got something on your mind. Almost grounded us yesterday. Smith'd be glad to finally have an excuse to go at you."

"Someday, that man gon' have a serious accident," Turno said.

"I have an idea. A dangerous idea," Robert said. He stood absolutely still, knowing his future belonged to them.

"And it takes all of us?" Alfred asked.

"All or none. Together, we can take the *Planter* and steer ourselves right to freedom."

Turno scowled. "What you talkin'?"

"We wait 'til all the officers go ashore. Maybe for that big party at old Governor Aiken's house next week. Then we cut the ropes and put the steam to her in the middle of the night."

Alfred's eyes bored into Robert, as if trying to penetrate into his soul, to see if this could possibly be real.

Turno didn't look like he thought much of this idea at all. "You gon' sneak past six forts? The *Planter* ain't a canoe, Robert. It a hundred and fifty foot long steam ship, poppin' out flames and sparks and smoke. Some of them guards might be stupid, but they ain't deaf or blind."

Robert shook his head. "No sneakin'. We know the signals. We go out there lookin' like we got business at Battery Wagner."

Turno wasn't going to be easily convinced. "In the dark? If you beach her, we all die. They either shoot us to pieces or hang us. Depends on they mood."

"You know any better pilot in Charleston than me? You want me to drive blindfolded today, prove it to you?"

"He know how good you are" Alfred said.

"Sure, I know," Turno said. "But it just take one thing to go wrong. One thing."

Robert felt desperation squeezing around his heart. "Who put those stripes on your back, Turno? What gon' keep him from doing it again? They can do whatever they want to Lila and your chi'ren, too.

"My old mama, she took her chance. Maybe she's free in Beaufort right now. When the McKees run out of town, part of the big white skedaddle, there weren't no Mama Lydia to be found. Does my old mama got more steel in her than us?

"What it gon' take for us to be men? I pay rent every month, for me, for Hannah. 'Cause they own us. You feel like you part free, 'cause they let you hire out. We sail out on the water, and the wind blow across your face, the sun shine in your eyes, and you don't think 'bout them. For a minute, you don't feel it.

"We carry soldiers and guns to Wagner, Pinckney, Sumter, Moultrie. What for? To keep us in our place. You ain't part free. You a slave all the way. But we have a chance—there's a whole line of Yankee ships out there, and they be happy to add one more. We take the ship, the crew, and any wife and chi'ren we can sneak on board, too."

Alfred rubbed the stubble on his weathered face. "You done give this some thought."

"I have."

"The way you talk. It like you already free."

"Not as long as I'm here."

Turno kept looking at the other side. "What them Yankees gon' do to us? I talk to sailors who come from up North, they say the Yanks ain't exactly in love with the sight of black faces."

"It ain't gon' be worse'n what the white folks here do. They ain't gon' own you. There's Yankees dyin' out there to take you outta your master's hand. We need to show them we want freedom so bad that we can take it ourselves."

Alfred gave a firm nod. "You know I come with you to the end of the earth." They grasped hands, bound to each other with a promise. "They catch us, I say we blow this ship sky high and take as many of them with us as we can."

"They ain't gon' catch us." Robert turned to his other friend. "Turno?"

"You want to bring the whole crew?"

"That's right." He always knew Turno would be the hardest. Not because he'd be afraid, but because once Turno got going, he went all the way forward. If Turno came along, it would be to the very end, full bore.

"One Judas and we end up on the end of a rope, like Denmark Vesey."

"When I was just a child, I saw old Denmark swaying from that tree," Alfred said. "Long before you was born. The white folks made us all walk past, so we would see. And it worked. Put the scare in us for forty years. But if we do this, maybe we can be the ones to break that spell. Every black brother and sister in Charleston gon' watch the horizon where we left. Maybe we end up stealing more than just our own selves."

"You got a choice, Turno," Robert said. "Either be willin' to die like a man, or live like a dog. But if we three can't swear to make this happen, then it's off. If we stand solid together, the rest will come with us. We won't tell them right away. No secret can stay hidden that long. When we see the moment is right, we tell everyone we need."

Turno looked hard at both of them, and then turned to the pump. "This thing fixed now?"

"You know it," said Alfred.

Turno started working the handle of the pump. "I'm solid. But once we tell everyone, there ain't no turning back. If I even think they gon' make a whisper, I'll send them straight to hell. And when I get there myself, I'll whip them again."

CHAPTER 5

At Battery Wagner's dock, the *Planter's* crew worked with a gang of slaves from the fort to load horse carts with barrels of gunpowder, boxes of rifles, and cannon balls. Robert watched his men closely, trying to decide who was the weakest link in the chain that might haul them to freedom. Turno thought it would be the boy, because Alston was so close to Captain Relyea, his shadow, ready for any errand or chore, with a smile and a chirped "Aye, sir!"

But Robert suspected others were just as weak. Of all of them, he knew Jackson the least. He'd only been added to the crew a month ago, after the previous cook mistook hot pepper for cinnamon one time too many. Captain Relyea got him transferred to cook for a prison camp, where the palatability of food wasn't on the list of concerns. Did it make sense to trust the lives of Hannah and the children to a man he barely knew? Alfred had worked with Jackson on boats hauling rice up and down the Ashley River, and he vouched for him. Plus the man could really cook—they no longer had to make Alston taste the food first, just to make sure it was edible. Jackson played along with the other men when it was time to fool around, but Robert always felt he was holding back.

Robert heard the sound of Smith's boots on the deck behind him.

"Robert. The captain has requested you undertake a special mission. I'll take over supervising this bunch of tail draggers." Smith joined him at the railing and looked over the men.

Robert shifted slightly away—Smith carried the scent of the whip everywhere. "Johnny! Come on, you're twice as big as the rest of these slugs, you should be able to load twice as fast."

They all knew Johnny worked best if he was allowed to be slow and steady. He was stacking cannonballs in a careful pyramid, picking them up as if they were full of air.

"What's my mission, Mr. Smith?" Robert asked, hoping to distract Smith for a second and maybe spare Johnny a beating. Though if Smith was in the mood to beat someone, then someone got beaten.

Smith leaned in close, the rim of his hat brushing Robert's forehead. Robert resisted the urge to take a step back. "The captain understands that you know the purser at the battery's storehouse. Sergeant Mason?"

"Yessuh." Mason used to be stationed at the arsenal in Charleston, and he and Robert had traded many times.

"We heard they've been collecting strawberries. The captain has a sore spot for strawberries. See if you can get us a bucket or two. Go on, move. We're nearly unloaded."

*****

In the low-ceilinged room, almost more of a cave, Sergeant Mason hunched over papers on his desk, deciphering inventories and requisitions. The soldiers at Battery Wagner seemed to be half badger, the way they dug and dug. Supplies were kept down here in a bomb proof structure deep in the bowels of Morris Island. They were deep enough that the air felt cool, though it smelled stale and salty. A thin cloud of dust filtered into the air from the gaps in the plank walls and ceiling.

Mason was a small rat-faced man in a grease-stained uniform. When this war finally ended, Robert was sure Sergeant Mason would have enough cash hoarded away to buy a fancy Charleston townhouse with a fountain in the garden.

"Robert," said Mason, without looking up. "Are you here officially or unofficially?"

"Captain Relyea sends his greetings."

"What the hell does he want?"

"Strawberries, suh."

"The Confederate Army can't ascertain the movements of ten thousand Yankee soldiers, but they know the second my niggers find a few buckets of strawberries."

"Captain is partial to strawberries."

"All the officers like delicate fruit. What about the ladies in Charleston? What are they asking you for these days, Robert?" Mason never passed up the chance for a quick trade.

"Ladies is partial to English tea, for their sophisticated tea parties. Blockade making it hard to come by."

Mason raised his head and fixed his dark little eyes on Robert. "Captain Harrison would sorely miss his tea time."

Robert took two small bottles of amber liquid from his jacket pockets. Quinine. More precious than whiskey on this mosquito infested sand pit. He'd been saving them for just the right trade.

"What would some quinine say to you?"

"It would say that nigger Smalls is going home with strawberries and a bag of tea leaves. Washington!"

The curtain separating the office from the vast collection of stores moved aside slightly, and a grizzled old slave with a rheumy eye and a limp emerged.

Mason gave what passed for a smile. "We must satisfy Captain Relyea's sweet tooth. Get Robert what he needs."

Without a word, Washington shuffled back through the curtain and Robert followed, down aisles of boxes and bags and casks intended to keep the garrison alive through months of harsh shelling. The Confederates didn't forget that it was mostly fear of starvation that forced Anderson to surrender Fort Sumter at the start of this war.

Washington twisted through the supplies without hesitation. He knew exactly where everything was kept. He opened the box of tea, releasing the scent of a fancy drawing room into this dismal hole. Robert handed him a small cloth bag from his pocket. He didn't save seven hundred dollars without being prepared for any trade.

As Washington carefully filled the bag with the tea leaves, he whispered, "You hear 'bout the Yankee general? Hunter?"

"No."

Washington had been working for Mason for years and was one of the quietest men Robert ever met. But some people said his hearing was so good, he could hear a white man's conversation from two rooms away. "Black Dave, they call him. Gon' raise a Negro army. Says all slaves in Carolina, Georgia, and Florida is free now. Issued a proclamation yesterday. It like he kicked over a beehive, the way everyone buzzin'. Man came on a launch from Charleston this morning, and said the telegraph wires is 'bout meltin' with the news."

"Free? Can he do that?"

"I don't know what he can do. But you hear the officers talk, you'd think he come straight out the devil's mouth. 'Course, don't mean nothin' unless you can get yourself to the Feds. But this is news folks got to hear. Can you help spread the word?"

Robert nodded. This was the most he'd ever heard Washington say at one stretch. "I'll make sure of it." Almost none of them could read, and any slave getting caught reading a newspaper received a beating. News like this spread whisper by whisper.

Washington looked at him with serious eyes. If slaves started thinking freedom was as close as the front lines, that changed the secret set of calculations in every heart. "I know you will. Let's get them strawberries."

*****

Captain Relyea stood in the pilothouse and picked a plump strawberry out of a white china serving bowl. "Robert, be sure to thank Sergeant Mason the next time we're on Morris Island. This is food of the gods. Smith, don't you agree?"

"Yes, sir." Officer Smith took a berry from his own bowl. Alston had split the berries into three servings for the white officers, but Robert knew there was also a bowl hidden in the galley for the crew. He'd instructed the boy to do it, a test of his powers of deceit and obedience. If Smith found it, Alston would get a beating to remember. For now, the boy stood in the corner at attention, awaiting Relyea's next whim, no sign that he or any of the other slaves had tasted the strawberries. And they were sweet.

Robert raised an eyebrow at Alston, but the boy didn't flinch. Maybe he could keep a secret after all.

Smith glanced at a chart. "Bring us around ten degrees to port."

"Aye suh, ten degrees to port." Robert turned the wheel. They turned around the end of Morris Island into the main channel. He didn't need Smith to tell him how far to turn the wheel, or how to get to the mouth of the channel, but it was important to let Smith feel like he was good for something. Robert didn't need the chart—he'd brought hundreds of ships in and out of Charleston harbor. The mines and torpedoes made it tricky, as did the occasional snags from the stone fleet the Union sank at the head of the channel last year—old schooners from the North, filed with granite. They were supposed to block anything from getting in or out. Oh, how the Southerners had raised a cry about that. "Barbarism!" they'd shouted. "No honor in such a blatant act of commercial sabotage." It made Robert think maybe the Union was playing this war for keeps, and they didn't take too kindly to Charleston's pride at being first in everything—most refined city, most gallant men, most beautiful women, most slaves sold, most rice, most cotton, first to declare secession, first to fire a shot in the war.

But the stone fleet showed that the Yankees didn't understand the water here. The currents out of the harbor picked those ships to pieces in a few weeks. You couldn't just come from outside and pretend to understand this place. If the Union wanted Charleston, it needed to stop underestimating her.

A line of smoke rose from the water, just past Fort Sumter. Captain Relyea put down the strawberries and found his spyglass. "Blockade runner. The *Dauntless*. Made it past the blockade but now she's stuck in the mud. Bring us alongside, Smith."

"Aye, Sir. Robert, bring us around to starboard, skirt the edge of the channel."

Robert steered them into the channel, fighting the ebb tide, ringing the engine for more power. Finally he slowed the *Planter*, as she bucked in the current, and slipped her next to the *Dauntless*.

The blockade runner had probably been beautiful before they'd painted her grey to camouflage her from the Union cannon. She was a double-wheeled steamer, sleek and low to the water, heavy with cargo that lay carefully tied down in every spare spot of deck.

The *Dauntless'* push past the blockade clearly didn't go smoothly. The pilothouse hung in splinters. Her flag was full of bullet holes. The sailors on deck waved eagerly at the *Planter* as she pulled alongside.

"She'll want a tow," said Captain Relyea. "How bad do you think she's stuck, Robert?"

"The tide'll come back in an hour, and that'll lift her most of the way off. We got enough muscle to pull her the rest of the way. She didn't miss the channel by much."

"Shame to get all the way through the blockade and get stuck in a little mud," said Captain Relyea.

"She lucky. If she kept on her line, she woulda hit those torpedoes we laid last week."

Relyea looked out at the water in front of the *Dauntless*, as if now remembering the spot. "The General would have been greatly displeased."

"All of Charleston would have been displeased," added Smith.

"Absolutely right. Smith, have a line rowed out to them," ordered Captain Relyea.

On the deck below, Chisholm and Jackson stood on the starboard rail, assessing the *Dauntless*, watching their crew shifting cargo to make room for ropes. A couple of the *Dauntless'* sailors wore bloody bandages, including one black sailor, his ragged uniform singed with soot.

Robert knew what his own men were thinking: the Union shoots pretty straight. Convincing his crew to be part of the escape just got harder. General Hunter's proclamation would help, but that felt more like a rumor than a fact. The tattered ship in front of them was a concrete warning about the strength of the Union Navy. He would have to turn that power into a positive. If they could get past the forts and let the Union know they were friendly, well, then, they'd be protected. If Washington was right, there was no time to waste.

CHAPTER 6

In the purple twilight, Robert straightened the charts and logs in the pilothouse, while Alfred took apart the cabin lantern. Before stowing the map of Charleston Harbor, Robert traced a line with his finger on the route he pictured them taking, trying to imagine the water, the darkness, the wind, in front of each fort. Would they hear the order to fire before the cannons blazed?

Turno came up the ladder, carrying a bucket of water, and started wiping down the pilothouse paneling. If anyone glanced in their direction, they were working, not conspiring. And Turno's body always looked upright and solid, never a hint of waver or sneakiness in his stance. Even so, they needed to be quick about it.

"You know what you told us this mornin', 'bout General Hunter freein' slaves?" Alfred whispered carefully. The captain and Smith had gone ashore for the night, but Pitcher was in his cabin, not twenty feet away.

"Yeah." On the other side of the Union lines, freedom waited, but Robert needed the nerve and strength to bring everyone with him. He didn't know if he had either.

"I went to get parts for the lanterns this afternoon. Everybody's talkin' 'bout it. Real careful, 'cause they's afraid niggers start a stampede for the front lines if word gets out. Normally they don't pay me no mind, but the way they tripped over theyselves to make sure they didn't say too much—it were almost sweet of those bastards to notice. Wonder they didn't hurt their tongues with all the word dancing they was doing."

38

"So you think it's true?" Turno asked, not looking up from his scrubbing. Turno wasn't the kind of man who showed nervousness in a way that most would notice, but Robert thought if he scrubbed that brush any harder, it might go right through the deck.

"I do," Alfred said. "Now's the time."

Robert nodded. Alfred had spent more than forty years learning to bear being a slave. When he said it was time to go, it paid to listen.

"The ball, the big party at Governor Aiken's house, is in two days. We got to be ready," Robert said.

"You sure the officers all gon' go?" asked Alfred.

"Not one would rather stay on board the *Planter* with us than sip punch with the most beautiful ladies of Charleston. Not that I blame them," said Robert with a half-smile.

"What if we tell everyone, and then it don't happen?" Turno's was the voice of caution.

"Then we wait for another time," Robert said.

Alfred shook his head. "Then it's a secret with too many holders. Someone gon' slip if they have to keep quiet for too long."

"The officers is all going ashore," Robert insisted. "We gots to tell people the plan, starting tonight. We need to know they's with us." They would be rushing people to make decisions as it was. Panic was their enemy. People in a hurry make mistakes.

Alfred screwed the pieces of the lamp back together. "I think the boy will be solid."

"They all know better than to cross me," Turno growled.

"Need to make sure Johnny don't slip," Robert said. "But I think we can help him."

Robert still had one more piece of the puzzle to make fit, and he wasn't sure how Alfred even felt about it being part of the plan at all.

"I still haven't figured how to bring the women and chi'ren. I thought I had a hiding spot, but they just set up a new guard house there. We gon' need a different spot. I know some Negroes just vanish into the night and don't take nothing or no one. But I ain't gon' really be free if they ain't with me."

Turno grunted his agreement. Even though he didn't appear sentimental, a man would be a fool to put Turno's woman and children in danger.

"One whisper and we's all dead. One cry of a baby in the night," Alfred said. He had no woman no young 'uns, so maybe he couldn't understand.

"I trust Hannah more'n any other person in the world," Robert said. "And Lila and Mary got sense. They'll make sure the chi'ren stay quiet." Lila and Turno had two children. Mary managed to put up with Chisholm night after night. That meant she was more than tough enough.

"I don't like it."

Robert wanted real freedom, not the kind that still had a chain pulling him back down to the deep, the dark.

"They comin'," Turno said. "Been part of the plan from the start."

"How we gon' get them on board?" Alfred pressed. "Folks is gon' notice a little parade of women and chi'ren walking down Atlantic Wharf to the *Planter*.

"I think we can get them hid on another ship, upriver," Robert suggested. "Fire up our engines, then glide upstream. Send out a skiff for them."

Alfred looked skeptical. "Go upriver? That mean we be on the run longer, with twice as many chances to get caught. And where you gon' hide them?"

"There must be someone on a ship upstream we can trust."

"I know the steward on the *Etiwan*. Morrison. He got enough spine to do it," Turno said, tapping the scrub brush absently against the deck, as if running over every interaction he'd ever had with Morrison.

Robert knew Morrison. They both belonged to a secret mutual aid society that met every few months in the basement of First Baptist Church. It was a perfect breeding ground for co-conspirators, though no one ever spoke words of an actual plan there, for fear of spies. "Let's talk to Morrison tonight," Robert said.

"We got to tell the women 'bout what General Hunter said," Turno warned. "They gon' be scared to death. News like this could help. Otherwise they listen to what old master's wife say 'bout Yankees taking niggers and making them slaves for their own selves, or selling them to Havana and the sugar plantations."

"Every one of the crew gon' be worried 'bout that, too," said Alfred.

"We'll make sure they know the truth," Robert reassured them.

Turno smiled the smallest of smiles. "I've been wondering if freedom ever gon' come my way. This time I can almost taste it.'"

All three looked out, over the railing, into the thickening night, as the sea breeze carried the scent of the ocean, of possibility.

*****

Robert and Turno found Chisholm sprawled on top of an upturned crate in the crew quarters, grabbing a smoke before heading home. He drew a long pull on his pipe, his eyes half lidded like a cat.

"You two look so serious that if it ain't 'cause somebody dead, then we might jes' have to put on a funeral anyhow."

Chisholm always had a joke. This time they needed him to be dead serious. Robert could sense how tense Turno was and he hoped that Chisholm could contain his foolishness long enough so that Turno wouldn't punch him.

"You like bein' a slave, Chisholm?" Robert asked.

Chisholm cocked his head and rubbed his brown freckled cheek. "Well, I had the choice between bein' a slave or the King of England, but diamonds make me sneeze."

Robert saw Turno's hand clench into a fist.

"Me and Turno and Alfred got a plan to get us free. The whole crew. Wives and chi'ren, too."

Chisholm's grin vanished. He pulled himself upright. "That definitely as serious as a funeral. How?"

"We gon' take the *Planter*, with all of us on it. Two nights from now, when the officers go ashore for the ball."

Chisholm coughed and shook his head. "Y'all say I's the joker. I ain't never told a whopper big as that."

Robert laid out the whole plan. There wasn't much that could stop Chisholm's running line of jibes, but this time he was silent as the moon. When they finished, Chisholm took a long draw on his pipe.

"You in?" Turno asked.

"Do I got a choice?" Chisholm asked.

"You do," Robert said. "Maybe you ain't got to choose much in your life, but this time you decide. You don't want a part of it, then you stay here and live your life however you can."

In an ideal world, every crew member would buy in. If they didn't have a thirst for freedom in them already, then they would be a bad risk to have along. Better to tell them to go get lost in the city for a few days. Give Chisholm a jug of moonshine. Turno argued that every man had to be in, whether he wanted to or not. Robert wasn't sure.

"I's had my eye on every blockade runner heading out of Charleston for the past year," Chisholm said, "looking for a spot to stow away. But they pack those ships so tight with rice and cotton there ain't hardly room for the rats. And how's I gon' find a way for Mary on a blockade runner? But if we do this, she can help Hannah and Lila with the babies. You tell me what to do, I get it done."

"Think you can keep yo' mouth shut?" Turno asked.

Chisholm laughed. "You want me to be quiet like a mouse? I could do that."

"That'd give us away for sure," Robert said, finally smiling. "Keep on being your fool self."

Chisholm raised his hand in promise. "I swear I will be the best fool I can be. I knew you three was up to something, but I thought it was finding a way into the captain's liquor cabinet. I know where he keeps the key, by the way."

*****

They whispered the plan to Jackson in the galley, as he cleaned the pots and pans from dinner. He was quiet for a while, as if taking his time to picture how each step might work itself out. "Makes sense to me," he said. "The *Planter* is a good ship, faster'n anything around here. If I was ever going to steal one thing in my life, it'd be her. Her and myself. Count me in."

*****

It was one thing to huddle with the crew on the *Planter*, at least they all had an excuse for being there. Crouching below decks on the *Etiwan* with Turno and Morrison was a whole different kind of risk, and Robert didn't like it. Normally, he'd have taken time to arrange for an elaborate excuse, but there wasn't time. Turno said he could vouch for Morrison, but Robert couldn't risk the noose for fifteen men, women, and children without looking Morrison in the eye.

Morrison fidgeted under Robert's examining stare. The candle they'd brought was barely enough to see anything, but it was enough for Robert to judge what he needed to know. Morrison was tall and light-skinned and had to stoop in the hold to keep from hitting the ceiling. He was almost the same age as Robert, with a long thin nose, but a sharp, handsome look, good teeth. Blood from some master ran in him, not far from the surface. He kept his uniform sharp, a good steward being a reflection on his captain.

"Are you sure the ship will still be here Monday night?" Robert asked.

"We just ran for two weeks straight, but the engine started rattling and shaking so much the engineer was sure it was going to blow. Parts for boilers are scarce. They say we be here a week, so the crew is working all day, every day, fixing every little thing. She ain't as fancy as the *Planter*, but *Etiwan* ain't a bad ship."

It made Robert trust Morrison a little more to hear him stick up for his ship. Even if Morrison wasn't a true sailor, at least he appreciated the vessel he served.

"Your white crew goin' to the ball?"

"They fight every day 'bout which has to stay here and mind ship," Morrison said.

"Any chance they'll leave her without an officer on board?" Robert asked.

"The junior officers say it might be all right, since the engine don't work. What's the point? It ain't goin' nowhere. They all want to see the Aiken house. I was thinking, maybe the captain might want to paint the officer's cabins while we stuck here."

"Think you could suggest that to him?"

Morrison smiled. "I'll find a way so Captain Marshall will think it was his idea. Maybe we'll find some extra bugs in the mattresses, or a dead rat behind one of the bunks. Time to clean extra hard."

Robert liked the way Morrison thought.

Steps of hard-heeled boots tapped across the deck overhead. Morrison's eyes grew wide. Turno frowned at Morrison. "You sure you ready for this?"

Morrison nodded, as he listened carefully. The steps retreated.

"If Lila and her babies hide here, they need to be ready when we come with the skiff," Turno said, his eyes dark and hard. "You and me been friends a long time, but make sure you do your part."

"He get the message, Turno," said Robert. "Look, it's easier to get the women and children on here than onto our ship. The

44

guards don't watch so tight out here. You do what we need, Morrison, you can be a free man."

"I can do it."

They stopped by the boiler room on their way out and removed a few parts from the engine to guarantee that the *Etiwan* would still be there Monday night.

*****

Even with a mind as simple as Johnny's, no slave survived long under the hard gaze of white Charleston without knowing when to keep his mouth shut. But if the officers caught a whiff of a possible plot, they'd go straight to Johnny and trick it out of him. Words took a while to get into his head sometimes, and if they confused him in a cloud of language, they'd find the answers they wanted.

Robert chose to tell him in the long, narrow space between the two boilers. Chisholm stood guard outside, though he'd begged to be part of it. Johnny often bunked in here, sleeping on a thin bedroll on the deck. No bunk on any ship was long or broad enough for him, and hammocks couldn't last many nights with him straining their fabric. The thick air smelled of sweat, oil, and wood smoke.

Johnny sat cross-legged on the floor in a pile of his ragged bedding as Robert explained the plan. Alfred and Turno lurked in the shadows.

"Fort Sumter gon' be the last fort. Be almost daybreak when we get to it, but I gon' wear the captain's hat and gloves. We give the signal and then they let us pass. They think we takin' supplies to Morris Island."

"But we ain't."

"That's right. We just gots ourselves, and we taking us out to the blockade. The Yankees said that any slave who get to them will be free."

"Does we gets to keep the *Planter*? I likes the *Planter*. She my favorite ship." Johnny patted the deck fondly.

"Mine, too. But I think we might give her to the Yankees. Like a present."

Johnny grinned. "People likes presents."

"That right. So then they treats us extra nice. Maybe they give us a present back."

"Freedom sound like a pretty good present to me."

Robert nodded. "You know it. But the only way we gon' get that present is to keep our plan a secret. You know how to keep a secret?"

"I does. I never told no one that Chisholm stole the captain's tobacco."

Turno gave a worried moan from the shadows.

"You can't tell no one," Robert said. "You can't act like you goin' anywheres. You can't start telling people goodbyes. Nothin' like that."

"I ain't got nobody to say goodbye to. I want to come with you, Robert. I want to be free." Johnny had a master in Charleston somewhere, but mostly he stayed on board. He must have loaded a whole forest full of firewood over the years. But he also knew boats and how to use his strength in spots where it counted. In two days, who knew how much strength they'd need?

"You can come. But you got to promise not to tell."

Johnny sat up solemnly straight. "I promise."

The light of two candles suddenly flared behind them, and Turno and Alfred stepped ceremoniously forward. "We need more than just a regular promise, Johnny," said Alfred, his wrinkles showing deep and dark in the shadows.

"You need to swear a holy oath. That's the most serious promise there is," Turno continued.

Robert swept Johnny's bedroll out of the way to expose the bare deck. "Put your hand down here."

Johnny did as he was told.

Alfred and Turno handed Robert their candles. He waved them slowly in the air, as Johnny followed with his eyes. Then he held them over Johnny's hand and dripped wax in a circle, and then dripped an X right over the back of Johnny's hand. Their giant of a man did not flinch.

"Tonight, we call upon Jesus and his Holy Ghost to listen to Johnny's promise to keep our secret. Johnny—do you swear to Jesus and the Holy Ghost to never say nothing about our plan?"

His eyes wide, Johnny swallowed. "I does."

Robert held up in his hand and Alfred placed a small bowl in his palm. He dripped a dark red star within the wax circle surrounding Johnny's hand.

"What's that?" Johnny whispered.

"With this blood, do you swear that if you ever tells a word about this plan, that Jesus can loose his devils on you and they will pull out your tongue and eat your eyes and carry this hand with them down to the bowels of hell?"

Johnny blinked hard. "I won't never say nothin'."

"Swear it," Robert demanded.

"I swear."

"We all here as God's witness," Robert said, his voice deep and dark.

"Amen," chorused Alfred and Turno.

"Amen," said Johnny, his voice small.

Their group of conspirators was complete.

CHAPTER 7

"No one ever gets away with it," Alston whispered as he polished one of Captain Relyea's boots. Robert crouched next to him in the narrow corridor outside the captain's cabin. The officers were ashore trying to make sense of whether their cargo this morning was supposed to go to Fort Moultrie or Battery Wagner. A whole line of officer's boots waited for Alston.

"It happened just last week," Robert said. "Four slaves took a skiff and sailed right out to freedom." He watched the boy carefully and hoped the boy wouldn't conclude that last week's escape made their own plan a little harder to execute.

"I didn't hear 'bout that." Alston looked at Robert skeptically. In a world where crumbs were given to the rats most likely to squeal on their fellows, trust got beat out of you quickly.

"They keep it quiet, 'cause they don't want you gettin' ideas."

"Is that why they guardin' even tighter now? I got to show my badge ten times before I can fetch something for the captain." Alston had fine cheekbones and a light complexion, and if he'd been born in the right place, he might have worked himself up to being a butler. But instead life had brought him to the docks.

"They watching, but the guards is still lazy and stupid. If we slide this ship out of here, confident and quiet, they'll never sniff us out."

Alston absently rubbed the boot in his hands. "Who else knows about it?" Alston was a child, but he wasn't stupid.

48

"All of them. Alfred, Turno, Jackson, Chisholm, and Johnny."

Alston's unlined forehead wrinkled with surprise. "Johnny simple in the head, you know."

"He can keep a secret. You just got to tell him in the right way. They all men, and they want to be free. Even Johnny. How 'bout you, Alston? You gon' be a boy your whole life?"

Alston puffed himself up as much as any child could do while polishing another man's boot. "I'm a man already."

"Maybe to me. Not to them."

"I'm with you."

It didn't take a genius to see the fear in the boy. Turno was sure he was the weak link. Robert liked to think Alston wasn't far from what he'd been like as a boy. Or what Junior might be like in another thirteen or fourteen years, though Alston was a skinny wisp of a kid. Junior had some heft to him. "Listen. You don't want to come, we just tie you up and leave you on the dock. You be an innocent victim. You tell them you warned us it was a bad idea, that we all crazy niggers."

The boy set his jaw, trying to look deadly serious, which wasn't easy with the smudges of polish on his cheeks. His voice came out low and hard, the first time Robert ever heard such a sound out of the young pup. Like the growl of an attack dog coming from the mouth of a kitten. "I'm comin'."

Now it was Robert's turn to sound serious, and he put the sharpest steel in his voice. "Don't breathe a word. Don't look at me like you know something. Don't smile. Don't not smile. Nothing. You never had to hide a secret as deep as you gon' hide this one. Our wives and chi'ren comin', too. If Turno think you gon' cause harm to his babies, he'll be like a lion. When he done eating you, he'll crack your bones."

"You can trust me." The boy's eyes were steady. He didn't have to be a grown man to understand what scant rewards the future held if he stayed.

"I trust you. But we be watchin' you just the same."

Robert heard footsteps on the ladder leading up to the deck and quickly grabbed a rag and shoe polish and a boot. Smith stuck his head through the door, his face laced with its perpetual expression of annoyance.

"Robert, I've been looking for you everywhere. We're off to Fort Moultrie after all. Let's cast off." He gave a half smile. "Are you finally showing Alston how to polish a boot?"

"Yessuh. He learnin'."

Smith approached. He dragged his anger with him like a sack of steel chains, rattling and clinking around him. He looked down at the boot in Alston's hands. "He's a slow learner. Look at that. Polish that one again, you clod." He cuffed Alston's head with the back of his hand.

Robert joined Smith in the pilothouse, leaving Alston with the boots. Alston never raised his head to give him any sort of look, no acknowledgment of what they'd said. Which was good, because Smith's eyes didn't miss much.

*****

Robert stood at attention, as Captain Relyea, Smith, and Pitcher ate their lunch on china and a white tablecloth at the small square table in the wardroom. There was an extra chair, but Robert knew he'd never be invited to sit—it was reserved for visiting officers and men of importance. No matter how many times he kept them from running aground or from detonating mines, no matter how smoothly he kept the crew running, they would never break bread with him.

Would Yankee sailors be any different? Even on the ships from up North, the officers were all white, and the regular seamen, no matter their skill level, black or white, ate in the crew's mess.

One of the advantages of serving on a ship leased to the Confederate Navy was first dibs on food coming into Charleston. Alston carefully served Smith another steak from underneath a warming cover. On the table sat bread with jam, a bowl of fresh peas, and broiled potatoes.

Alston watched the officers, anticipating their desire for a new fork or more water. Not one extra glance came Robert's way. Perfect.

With a satisfied sigh, Captain Relyea leaned back in his chair and carefully wiped his mustache with his linen napkin. "Robert, make sure the crew is here early tomorrow. It will be a full day—we're to pick up a load of cannon from the battery on Cole's Island and deliver them to Fort Ripley."

"Yessuh."

"We leave at daybreak. We need to deliver the guns to Fort Ripley and be back here by four o'clock."

It was a nearly impossible request to fulfill, even if Robert actually planned to make it happen. "Yessuh. I'll make sure we got the engine fired up and ready to move by sunrise. We taking on a full load of wood right now."

Engineer Pitcher picked at piece of something stuck in his teeth. "Our main winch has a rattle. Could slow us down."

Smith crackled with annoyance. "You'd better fix it. Unless you want to spend tomorrow night here instead of at Aiken's house."

Pitcher never seemed to care whether Smith scowled or spurted words laced with acid. He mostly just raised his eyebrows. All three officers were eager for the party tomorrow night.

"We have an engagement tomorrow evening, Robert," said Captain Relyea. "I'll be counting on you to stay dockside overnight and supervise the ship."

Robert tamped down any excitement in his voice. "You can count on me, Captain."

"I know I can. You've done an excellent job with these boys."

"They could be better," said Smith, who was never impressed with anything the crew did. If they sailed him straight to the gates of Heaven, he'd still be complaining they were too slow to load wood or man the ropes.

51

"Given the raw material, we can only expect so much," said Pitcher.

"Officer Smith will ensure that things run smoothly tomorrow, won't you?" said the captain.

"Aye, Captain. They'll not shirk a minute." Or there would be blood. And salt to rub in the wounds.

"Make sure you leave yourself enough energy for Ms. Powell," Pitcher teased.

"Don't worry," Smith answered. Robert wasn't sure a man as hard as Smith could blush, but he came close. Smith had been courting the lovely Miss Powell for almost a year now, and Robert wondered what she saw in him. Maybe he was different when he wasn't on the ship. And some women, even the sweet ones, liked men with a mean streak.

"That will be all, Robert," said Captain Relyea, standing up from the table and brushing crumbs from his belly. "Our destination today is Fort Moultrie—prepare her to sail in fifteen minutes."

"Aye, sir." He left for the engine room, carefully keeping any hint of joy and anticipation out of his step. Tomorrow night was the night.

*****

Alfred stood on a ladder putting finishing touches on the last repairs to the winch. Since their return from Fort Moultrie, he'd been working on the pulleys and chains, making sure nothing would go wrong tomorrow. "Robert," Alfred called, as he climbed down to the deck. His eyes told Robert that something was up.

"You got it fixed?" Robert asked.

"It'll do."

"Because we don't want nothin' to go wrong." Out here in the open, Robert didn't feel safe asking what was wrong.

"Sometimes there's a weak link in the chain. And one weak link is all it take. Then the whole thing crash down."

Robert felt a sliver of ice in his heart. Something was wrong with their plan. "And people get hurt." Robert answered. "You think you found a weak link in the chain?"

"Was thinking about asking Jackson if he know anything about weak links."

What had Alfred seen? Robert climbed up to the galley, with Alfred right behind him.

Being a slave meant always having a mental map of where the white folks were at any given moment. If you didn't know where they were, you might get caught living life. Right now, Robert knew Captain Relyea was on shore, tagging along after General Ripley, and Smith was at the quartermaster's office, requesting a few extra hands for tomorrow's load of cannon. Pitcher was in the engine room, adjusting a pump.

He barely felt his feet on the ladder—it felt like his mind was some sort of octopus, always reaching out, touching each person in the plan, every spot on the ship, always touching, tapping, checking in eight different directions at once. In some ways, it was nothing new—he always needed to know the sandbars, the wind, the current, how much steam the *Planter* had and how much she could give. Had to know which ships were coming and which were going, and which had packets smuggled on board for trade, the names of sailors he saw only once a year, but who would perk up their ears to be recognized in a strange port, grateful to have someone who knew where to send them for a drink and a woman. It all mattered, all the time. There was an electric joy in the complexity, even living under the heel of the McKees and Captain Relyea. But that boot was always there, ready to push down on the back of his neck.

The smell of hot oil wafted to them as soon as he and Alfred entered the officer's mess. Beyond the swinging door, they could hear the chopping of vegetables. The officers would be back soon for supper. Alston was setting the wardroom table with the china.

Alfred looked at the boy and stopped, chewing on what sort of excuse to make. Robert didn't hesitate. "Alston, go down to the hold and look for a bag of apples. Don't you come up 'til you find them, or one of us come get you."

Alston set down the gilt edged plate and scurried away. They pushed into the galley, to see Jackson chopping onions. A pile of filleted fish coated in corn meal sat on the counter. Like everything on the *Planter*, the builders furnished it with only the best—mahogany paneling and a sturdy iron stove. Pipes carried steam from the boiler to help cook and keep the food warm.

Jackson looked up, knife in hand, relaxed. With the addition of two men to the room, the tiny galley felt much too small.

Robert kept an eye on that knife.

"What you two doin' here? I ain't got much to spare yet. But we'll all have fish later, there's plenty. Smith said to cook 'em, say he don't want no excuses for slow going loading them guns tomorrow."

When even Smith wanted to be sure they got fed, it meant the guns were heavy. Their first officer didn't want anything getting between him and Miss Powell.

Alfred's hand was in the pocket where he kept his own knife, but for now, he leaned against the paneling. Robert tried to figure out where this was heading, while still doing his octopus touches, his ears straining for sounds of footsteps, boots on the ladder, voices of the crew.

"I've been watching you, Jackson." Alfred said softly.

"That must be a treat." Jackson looked confused. He smiled reassuringly—his smile bright against his dark face. Not quite as dark as Johnny, but blacker than the rest of them. Robert watched his fingers, waiting for them to tighten on the knife, for any sign of guilt or nervousness.

"You and me go way back," Alfred said, his voice still calm. "Back to when you was just a boy."

"Sure," Jackson said. "We covered a lot of water together." A tinge of nervousness crept into his cheeks. A bead of sweat appeared at his brow, beneath his bushy hair.

"But I don't know why I seen you talking to Pitcher this morning, after breakfast. I don't know why I seen that man give you a coin."

Jackson took a half step back, but the knife still was loose. "What you saying?"

"Me and Robert got eyes on every nigger on this ship."

Jackson looked back and forth between Alfred and Robert, confused. "You didn't see nothing."

"I saw him give you a coin," Alfred insisted.

"Asked me to do him a favor." The fingers shifted on the knife handle. Robert wasn't sure whether Jackson was guilty and ready to fight, or afraid and ready to fight.

"Maybe he pay you because he want to be a hero for once. If he turns in the whole bunch of us, he would be the hero of Charleston, not just a souse of a washed up engineer. And you get something. Maybe more coins. I don't know."

"You and me. We know each other." Jackson's voice was just this side of pleading.

Robert finally spoke. "We trust you and Turno and Johnny and Alston and the women and Morrison. But we's only got so much trust to go around. It stretched real tight. If one little strand of it starts to fray, the whole thing might explode into a million pieces."

Robert avoided fights when he could. Some men itched for a fight, like Turno, whose blade was always ready. Robert guessed that Alfred had been in more than his share of scraps—he had scars that didn't come from whips or busted ropes.

If Jackson jumped, he'd let Alfred handle the blade work. Robert could hit him low and bring him to the ground, between the stove and cabinets. Jackson was on the thin side, not as strong as either him or Alfred.

Robert had never killed a man, but if Alfred thought this weak link was going to break the chain, this was the time. His octopus mind looked ahead to the corpse, the blood, how to clean up. This was the wrong time, the wrong place. They should have done this at night, on shore, near the water, a quick slip of the body over the edge into the harbor.

This was stupid. Stupid niggers killed other stupid niggers and then got hung or whipped or branded for it.

"He asked me to hide some bottles of whiskey. All right? There's talk about marshal law and closing the saloons. Pitcher's scared he'll come up dry. Asked me to hide bottles in the mess, in the stores, when no one was around. Captain got wise to Pitcher's hiding place in the engine room, so he can't keep it there no more."

The hand was tight on the knife. Alfred's hand was still in his pocket, his eyes fixed on Jackson's.

"Look, here, see, way back behind these pots, I hid one already." Jackson knelt down, and pulled out pots and pans, and there indeed was a stoppered liquor bottle.

"I'm not the one you got to worry 'bout. Not me. I want this as much as any y'all. I got a brother run off, three years ago, to Philadelphia. He a free man now. I got a place to go. I ain't gon' throw it all away. Alfred. Robert. You got to believe me."

Alfred should have been more patient. Beneath that grey hair, his wisdom was getting shaken by the pressure and the possibility.

"We don't got to trust you, Jackson," Robert said. The hope drained from Jackson's cheeks, the beseeching smile now gone cold. "We don't got to trust anyone. Alfred just doing what he's supposed to. Watching, trying to make sure we all ready. You ready, Jackson?"

"I'm ready."

Jackson's fingers gripped that knife, his eyes flashing between Robert and Alfred.

Robert held his palms up, almost a gesture of surrender. "I know you's telling the truth. Pitcher'd likely die without a sip. Alfred. Jackson's all right. You hear me. Jackson's all right."

Slowly Alfred pulled an empty hand out of his pocket, but his eyes still bored into Jackson, as if trying to see through his

56

flesh and bones, all the way into his soul. "Yeah. You all right."

The knife in Jackson's grip started to shake, as they all started to breathe again. Robert forced the laughter back into his own voice. "Alfred. Maybe you need to make sure Pitcher put that pump back together right. If he drunk, he might put the whole thing together upside down and pump the water into the ship instead of out. And tell Alston that we found those apples."

With one more discerning look at Jackson, Alfred left, his shoulders slumped like at the end of a long day.

With just the two of them, there was a lot more air. Enough for a long deep breath.

"We all got to stay calm," Robert reassured Jackson, who stared at the door swinging shut, before getting back to chopping onions.

"I'm doing my part," Jackson said. "You make sure you do yours."

I just did, Robert thought. Just kept you from getting filleted like those fish on the plate.

"You all right, Jackson. When we done, you gon' see your brother. All right?"

Jackson nodded. That was all Robert was going to get from Jackson. Now he needed to calm Alfred down, calm the whole bunch of them down, and keep them from slicing each other to ribbons before tomorrow's midnight.

CHAPTER 8

Meeting Street announced itself with light and noise. The whole block was jammed full of planters in their finest evening wear, soldiers in dress uniforms, and house slaves ready to carry home purchases from the final night of the Gunboat Fair. The ladies of Charleston had outdone themselves to raise money to build an ironclad ship to protect the heart of the South. Torches were tied along the wrought iron fence fronting Hibernian Hall, and its six towering columns were wrapped in red, white and blue stars and bars, and hand-sewn banners of white palmetto trees on indigo banners. All of Charleston society waited to pass through the gates to admire and buy donated quilts, silver plate, portraits, and furniture, all willingly sacrificed to uphold the honor of the South.

And to keep me in my place, Robert thought, as he stepped carefully through the edge of the crowd, looking for Mr. Henry and his daughter, Elizabeth Jane.

I shouldn't even be here. He told himself that it was far less of a risk than stopping by the Ancrum/McKee house, with some made up excuse. All in order to set eyes on them one more time. Better to just go.

"Robert."

He stopped at the sound of her sweet, familiar voice—Elizabeth Jane McKee Bailey. The nightingale of Beaufort. They said her singing is what drew her husband to her, but she was beautiful, too. Back when she and Robert were both children in Beaufort, she used to practice her singing in the mornings, while he and Mr. Henry went out to sail and fish on the river.

Maybe it was those shared mornings in the boat that made Robert and Mr. Henry move their hands the same ways. They shared the same way of sucking on their teeth when they were deep in thought and nobody was there to notice.

But some folks whispered that Robert, short and stout, and Henry McKee, the exact same height and build, had more in common than shared time outdoors. Robert and Elizabeth Jane and Mr. Henry all shared the same nose, same brow.

Mama Lydia never said who Robert's father was. He only asked her once, and the cold ice of her fingers on his arm made sure he never asked again. "You put that thought out of your head, boy," she'd warned. "Some things you got to know in this world, and some you don't. You know who your mama is and who your master is. You ask me that again, you like to stick a knife in my eye."

When Elizabeth Jane and Robert were both five years old, the two of them played in the yard together, hunting chameleons, while Mama Lydia hung out the washing to dry, like white sails in the wind. Together, Elizabeth Jane and Robert grew grimy with dirt and mud, earth.

Now she was grown and scrubbed clean, whiter than white, in satin and ruffles, auburn hair carefully pinned on top of her head, making a swan of her. Robert lowered his eyes politely, though she was definitely worthy of staring. And plenty of men in this crowd could barely keep their eyes off her. In private, she was the one white woman he could look in the eye, this woman who was perhaps his sister, a blood tie carefully hidden. But they were never alone anymore.

"Missus Elizabeth Jane. Lovely night. Mr. Bailey, suh." He nodded to her husband, who looked blankly at him. Edwin Bailey was a thin, shy man, with a bashful mustache, who was probably sick to his stomach at the thought of squeezing through the packed aisles of the hall.

"Are you going inside?" she asked.

He wanted to raise his head for one last look at her, to keep her image in his mind. But he didn't dare. "Oh, no, ma'am. Your mother and Missus Ancrum already brought their tea set. I's just on my way home."

"I heard the tea set sold twice. The first buyer donated it directly back to the auction. They're going to name the ship *The Palmetto State*. Which I suppose is technically perfect, but it lacks romance."

"Darling. Let's see if that quilt from Miss Ellsworth is still on sale." Edwin said, attempting to lure his wife away from Robert with shopping.

"Of course." She lowered her voice and leaned toward Robert ever so slightly. "Any word from Lydia?"

"No, ma'am. Not a whisper." At least she missed his mother a little. Mama Lydia had changed every diaper, made every meal, run every bath for the girl that became the splendid woman standing before them now. All those years left a mark. Elizabeth Jane had left a mark on him, too—his own Lizzie was named after her.

"I'm sorry. I hope she turns up. Oh, look, here comes father."

Henry McKee gently pushed towards them, a broad gray man in a gray suit. He'd looked a lot older lately, from the war and from fleeing Beaufort. But his eyes still lit up for his daughter, as he stopped to admire her. Robert felt invisible next to her, as he had a thousand times before.

"Clearly this crowd has been drawn here by the sight of you, my dear. You look positively radiant."

She put a gentle hand on his shoulder. "Oh, Father. You say that because you're required to."

"Wouldn't you agree, Edwin?" Henry McKee practically glowed with pride at his daughter, as if the light from her pale skin illuminated him.

"She leaves me speechless," said her husband, still looking nervously at the growing crowd.

"Oh, hello, Robert," said Mr. McKee, finally noticing him. Robert had seen Mr. Henry just a week and a half ago, when he'd paid his monthly hiring out fee. Robert could tell from the way he took the money that the McKees were struggling. With the Ashdale plantation in the hands of the Union, most of the McKee income had run dry. They would be forced to scramble with him gone, but white folk always landed on their feet.

"Are you here on a mission for the Navy?" Mr. McKee probed. "You have a certain look of determination."

Robert had spent so many hours of his childhood at Mr. McKee's elbow. Out on the water, you learn to read your partners. He was a fool to have come this close to Mr. Henry now. Would this moment of farewell ruin them all?

"Oh, nossuh. Just passin' by on my way home. Saw all the bright lights." A trickle of sweat formed at the edge of his scalp, and he resisted the urge to wipe it away.

"Yes, you always had a natural curiosity. Any news from the waterfront?"

Robert kept his eyes down, comparing the shape of his own hands to those of Henry McKee. If you changed the color, they could almost be the same hands. "Nossuh. I just tryin' to keep the *Planter* drivin' straight. General Ripley always have something new for us to do."

"Good. You keep working hard." Apparently satisfied that his slave was diligent and well-behaved and would keep bringing much needed money into the house, Henry McKee turned back to his daughter. "Elizabeth, would you mind if I accompany the two of you to the fair? Your mother is having a bout of the vapors this evening, so I am here on my own."

He held out his arm to his daughter, and she took it with natural grace. "Of course. We wouldn't want you to be lonely."

And with that, they started towards the hall. Elizabeth Jane turned her head to give Robert a goodbye smile. They disappeared into the whirl of men in coats and hats, of women bobbing along in their dresses, adjusting their shawls against the night air.

Maybe this is what it felt like to be free—to be able to look at all of this and decide to leave it. To leave the iron gates and cobblestone streets and piazzas. To leave the man who might be his father, without a word of farewell. To look at his secret sister and decide to never see her smile again.

All the people in this crowd would pay to keep him from making that choice. The women, delicate-boned birds, were willing to peck out the eyes of Yankee marauders, willing to sacrifice their finery to build a ship with guns meant to rip men to shreds, to drown them in the sea, to melt their flesh in fire.

He needed to be just as strong. For his children to be free, he had to be willing to burn this place to ashes and stretch the faces of these women with hunger and crease them with tears.

*****

In the dim candle light, laundry filled the lines strung across the bedroom, like flags of a surrendering army. Tomorrow, before dawn, Hannah would rise and bundle the clothes and deliver them for a few coins, just like any other day. Every movement, footstep, breath would need to appear absolutely normal.

Junior curled on the floor in a nest of blankets and rags, his thumb in his mouth, so still he could almost be dead. But then he breathed a small breath and snuggled deeper into the pile.

Lizzie slept on her belly on her straw mattress, covered with a quilt pieced together from scraps from a hundred mending jobs. Her arms and legs sprawled from under the blanket, as if she was in the midst of floating peacefully down from the sky. Kneeling next to her, Robert put a hand on her back, wondering if he'd ever feel her warmth again.

The planters acted like slaves didn't care about their children. *Animals don't care much for their pups*, was how they justified themselves when they split up families. But babies were insurance against escape. It was hard to run if you'd never been past the edge of the plantation, if you'd never read a map in your life, if you barely knew which way was north, couldn't read or write, and had never touched a coin or dollar bill your whole life. But babies made running almost impossible.

Whenever a woman escaped and left her children, the whites always sounded so self-righteous. *Just shows you*, they'd say. That meant: *Just shows you niggers aren't really human after all*. Robert knew it showed how hard that master whipped and raped his slaves. That master might end up choking on piss in his coffee or getting thrown by a spooked horse someday.

Mama Lydia wouldn't lay claim to any father for Robert, but Junior and Lizzie had a flesh and blood father, brown as mud, strong and alive. He couldn't give them much, but he claimed them as his own.

Robert ran over tomorrow in his head, imagining all of Charleston, every street, every step of all the people on the *Planter*, every person they might see, every stop they would make to eat, piss, shit, wave hello. The moments spread out like a nest of spider webs, each one connected at one or two sticky little points, all fluttering in the wind, waiting for some big dumb clumsy foot to crash through and finish them all.

Where was the weak link? The children? Bringing them put the whole plan at risk. Maybe it was Jackson. Alfred could have been right. How much would General Ripley pay for being spared another embarrassment?

Trust. That's what this took. Trust in Jackson, in the others, in himself to know he was right. A lot of slaves sported brands on their cheeks and limped on hobbled feet because they trusted the wrong folks. Forty years ago, right here in Charleston, Denmark Vesey trusted George Wilson, and that mistake sent three dozen men and women to the gallows. Some said you could still go down to Ashley Avenue, on a hot midnight in July, and hear the creak of those ropes.

Robert pushed through the sailors' underwear and women's traveling dresses and closed the makeshift door behind him. Hannah stood by the table in the lantern light, hands on her hips, staring at a neatly folded pile of clothes.

"What am I supposed to bring? I know we should pack

something. Who knows who long we'll be gone."

"Ain't like we's going on a trip. There ain't no coming back."

She frowned at him. "You know what I mean. Until we get wherever is next."

It was like the world ended right outside the blockade. He knew all about this world, here in Charleston, in South Carolina, up and down the coast, for miles in every direction. But the future wouldn't be anything like right here, right now. Could he even imagine a life so different?

"Don't bring nothin'. Only the children. Carry a bag that looks like you got something for the baby."

"I'll dress them up in a double layer, so they at least got something to wear. Wrap Junior in two blankets." He loved that she was always practical. "And a bag of food. Something sweet for Lizzie, to help her stay quiet."

"No bags. Just you."

"They catch us, I say I'm on my way to my husband, on the *Etiwan*. He workin' overnight and I bringin' him something to eat."

"Why you got your chi'ren with you?"

"Ain't got no one to watch them. My boy, he's been cryin' and fussing. A walk helps sometimes."

Robert frowned. If the guards suspected, they'd dig after a lie. "Don't let them catch you. The guards is twitchy these days."

She gave up on the clothes and turned to face him. "Don't worry 'bout us. I know how to stay out of sight."

"Don't go unless the lantern gets broke. If you don't see the signal, go back home. Don't let Mary or Lila come neither."

"I know."

He took her hands. His were thick and strong from a decade of hauling ropes and cargo on ships. Hers were thin, long fingered, but just as hard. Her eyes had seen plenty, but still looked for freedom.

When he married her, he was just a boy, barely done skipping around the docks, but he knew he didn't want to marry a girl. He wanted a woman. And she figured he could be turned into a man. At least that's what she said. *Why'd you marry me,* he'd ask her. *You work hard, your eyes are clear, and you make me laugh.* Not many ever saw Hannah laugh, but Robert knew the way. Maybe freedom would make her laugh come easier.

He kissed her. She wrapped her arms around his broad back, pulling him close to her. He held her head in his hands, wanting his hands on her, to feel her breathe, to feel her braids tied up tight behind her head, feel the skin of her back.

Her hands unbuttoned his jacket, pulling off his shirt. He tried to memorize her with his hands. *This is her breast. This is the space between them that I love. The curve of her hip. The tiny bit of a belly, the softness that no one else ever sees.*

He lifted her onto the table, his hands touching every part of her. Her ankles, her knees, her thighs, wanting to take his time. If tomorrow went wrong, he needed every memory of her clear.

Hannah wasn't willing to be so patient and pulled him into her, pressing her mouth against his, pulling his hips, grinding herself onto him. Her lips were as hungry as his. Her body tightened and moved even faster, harder, the table creaking and groaning. He felt he could devour her, her neck, her breasts, every bit of her and carry her with him, to sea, to freedom. He tried to keep his eyes open, to stay focused on her eyes, her eyes that said *keep moving, don't stop, please don't stop.*

They disentangled from each other and fell into each other's arms, their bodies slick with sweat, twisting together like two ropes coiled around the same mast.

He leaned back to look at her, but she clasped her hands tightly across his back and kept him close.

"Don't let me go."

"Never." They lay in the stillness of the night, the silence a cocoon against whatever was to come. "You know I love you. As much as I love the ocean and the bay."

"I'm too old to need someone like this."

"You ain't old." She smiled.

Risking never seeing that smile again was no small thing.

CHAPTER 9

He was awake, already dressed, as Hannah and the children slept. Over by the table, Hannah's dress still lay on the floor. Robert sank to his knees, moved the dress aside, and found the loose floorboard. He drew out the nail with the blade of his knife and lifted the board to reveal a pillowcase. Inside was all the money they'd saved to buy freedom for Hannah and the children. Seven hundred dollars in a pile of mismatched, worn Confederate dollars, South Carolina currency, and silver and gold coins.

With trembling fingers, he split the pile into halves, putting more of the Confederate money into Hannah's pile. If he ended up in the Union lines on his own, the Confederate money would be useless. He carefully laid the silver and gold coins in the pillowcase, and shoved it inside his shirt and ran his hands over his chest, trying to see if the cash made unusual bulges.

He stuffed Hannah's pile inside a sock and padded over to the bed. Hannah lay sleeping, mouth slightly open, long black braid snaking along the pillow. He kissed her gently on the forehead.

Her eyes popped open. "I'm ready," she said.

"Keep this money close. Don't leave the house until after dark, but get out before curfew."

"I know what to do."

"I got to say it anyways. I'll send Alston out 'bout nine o'clock to break the lamp on St. Michael's Alley. If you don't see no broken lamps, go back home."

She nodded. Her eyes were steady and fierce. With this talk of escape, she had more steel in her than ever. More than some of the men and boys on the *Planter*.

She reached her hand out for his. "If we get separated, where will I find you? What city?"

"Beaufort. If Beaufort falls, go north, to Washington. If Washington falls, won't be no freedom for nobody."

What if the Confederate generals really were as good as they thought they were? It was hard to tell how the war was really going from the scraps of news they could scrounge. If the South won, there wouldn't be a free spot of ground anywhere. Robert had heard there were no more slaves across the ocean, in England and France. It was English who finally made Frederick Douglass all the way free, when they bought his freedom from his master. That's what they said anyway. Which was bullshit, because Frederick Douglass took his own freedom. The man even wrote a book about his escape. One of the black deacons read a few pages to them last year at the secret society meetings.

Hannah pulled him down for a one final kiss goodbye.

He touched each child on the head, careful not to wake them. Junior stirred in his sleep, adjusted the thumb in his mouth, and continued on in innocence.

Robert took one more look through the gloom, at the ghosts of hung laundry, the bare, splintery floorboards, the cold cookstove, and the sturdy raw table. He listened to the shuffle of the horses below, swishing their tails. Smelled the mix of hay, manure, and laundry soap, one last time. This place had tried to be a home, but it wasn't so hard to leave behind.

*****

Robert approached the guard at the Atlantic Wharf, a man whose scarred face showed he'd already seen action in the young war. Most guards were just kids, and guard duty was punishment for getting in trouble. This man's face was bruised and his uniform tattered—it looked like they were resting him before shipping him back out. He'd been on duty every morning for the past week and waved Robert through.

Alfred was already in the engine room, making adjustments to the boiler. His body was slick with sweat and grease.

"She having a problem?" Robert asked.

"Making a noise I don't like. I want her to sing today. No bad notes for the Missus Planter."

Robert nodded. "You got everything you need? Nothin' we oughta send Alston for, case we run into trouble on the Stono?"

Alfred put down his tools, wiped his hands, and laid his palms on Robert's shoulders. "You been up all night worryin'?"

"Maybe."

"Take a breath. And then get everyone else to do the same. The engine gon' be fine. You just keep her ass out of the muck, right?"

"You know I will."

Turno came in to fire the boiler. He looked tightly coiled. The rest of the crew would arrive any minute.

"Turno," Robert said.

"Hey."

"Lila ready?"

"Scared to death, and there ain't much that scares that woman. Not even me."

Which was saying something, because everyone was scared of Turno. Even Smith, with the whip in his hand, paid attention to Turno.

"I had an idea," Robert said.

"Cain't we finish this one first?" Turno threw great chunks of wood through the iron furnace doors, the heat starting to flow out. Orange light began to glow in the grate, casting shadows against the dials and iron pipes.

"Today we's moving guns from Stono Inlet to Fort Ripley. Depending on how many guns, could be a lot to finish."

"They might have they own niggers at the fort."

"Right. But if we run out of daylight, our officers gon' want to get to the ball at Aikens. If that happens, maybe the guns stay on the *Planter* a little longer."

Turno was a hard man to make smile, but the idea of sticking it to the folks of Charleston always did the trick. "And maybe we have some presents to give to the Union tomorrow?"

Robert nodded. "Anything we can do to make them grateful is a good thing. I think generals is always happy for more guns."

"I'll find the right moment. Might need a partner."

"Don't ask Johnny. I don't want him thinking 'bout this too much."

"Nobody better at making a scene than Chisholm."

As if summoned, Johnny and Chisholm appeared, Johnny still chewing half a loaf of cornbread, which he stuffed nearly whole into his mouth. He joined Turno in throwing firewood into the boiler.

"Captain already looking for you," Chisholm said to Robert, laughing. "I think each one been to the barber last night. Must have been a line around the block of officers getting ready to peacock themselves for the ladies."

Robert hustled out of the hold, clapping a hand against Johnny's shoulder, just for the pleasure of feeling that much unmoving strength in one man.

"Mornin', Robert," Johnny called, spilling crumbs of cornbread out of his mouth. "Gon' be a good day."

*****

Captain Relyea paced on the deck outside the pilothouse, wearing his crisp white uniform and signature hat. A cloud of smoke belched from the smokestack behind the pilothouse, and swirled in the sinking breeze. Robert climbed the ladder to the upper deck with hands and feet that had climbed thousands and thousands of rungs.

"Where have you been?"

"Just checking on the boiler, Captain. Should have pressure

any minute."

"Is Engineer Pitcher down there?"

"Nossuh. Maybe having hisself some coffee, suh." Or else drinking a quick morning nip.

"Alston!"

The boy appeared. He was always waiting, just out of sight. "Yessir!"

"Tell Engineer Pitcher that I want him in that engine room in thirty seconds. And I want a full head of steam in two minutes. We have a very full day ahead."

"Yessir!" Alston vanished as quickly as he appeared, to be followed shortly by a clean shaven Engineer Pitcher, who for once didn't look like he was just roused out of bed.

"Jackson actually brewed a liquid that tastes like something resembling coffee. Ninety percent of the way there, I'd say."

"I want us to have left five minutes ago, Pitcher."

"Aye, sir. I'll see if I can get us enough steam to peel back time."

"Just get us moving," Captain Relyea spat, not in the mood for a chipper engineer. "Robert, prepare to cast off."

Smith emerged from the galley and strode into the wheelhouse, looking sparkling clean.

"Smith," the captain called. "Let them know I'm serious."

Smith pulled the bell, three short sets of double rings. Which in this case meant: *get your ass moving before I come down there and beat you with my whip.* Two bells chimed back. "Engine's ready, Captain. Full pressure."

"Robert, cast off," said Captain Relyea.

Robert descended the ladder and cast off the bowline, while Chisholm, Jackson, and Johnny loosed the other lines. As soon as they were clear, Smith engaged the giant paddle wheels on the sides of the ship, splashing and churning the water of the harbor. The whistle blew, warning smaller craft out of the way.

Robert climbed back up to the upper deck and took the wheel. The captain had settled in his favorite spot, just outside the pilothouse, standing with his chest thrust out against the coming wind. Smith stood next to Robert, ready to give instructions.

Robert knew every in and out of the harbor and every creek and the marsh between here and Beaufort. He knew how close he could pull to the shoals off Castle Pinckney, and that it was better to enter Wappoo Creek just to the port side. His mind saw water differently from most men—he didn't just see the surface, but all the way down to the muck and weeds underneath. He possessed an atlas of water and tides and shore and mud. If they planted pilings and mines, he just added them to the vision in his mind. He knew when the tide was about to flip, from the smell of the salt on the breeze and the cry of the Napoleon gulls.

They were already across the head of the Ashley River, approaching the mouth of Wappoo Creek. If the Union Navy hadn't been offshore with their blockade, the *Planter* could have just run out of the harbor and dropped south to the Stono Inlet. But now they needed to take the back door route, down Wappoo Creek and Wappoo Cut, past the fort at Elliott's Cut, and down the Stono River.

"Keep her steady, Robert," Smith called as he left the pilothouse for the lower deck. "I'll head us in the creek from the bow."

The ship motored past the dull green edges of the marsh reeds, and Robert smelled bits of swamp mud just uncovered by the ebbing tide—today it felt like a scent full of life and hope. They entered a rare straight stretch of the creek, and Smith waved them forward from the bow, signaling for them to gain speed, but Robert kept both hands on the wheel.

"Robert, Officer Smith wants you to speed up," said Captain Relyea, carefully drinking a cup of tea.

"I see him, Captain. But they sunk new pilings last week, about twenty feet ahead. We run past too fast, we gon' catch a paddle, and then we be here all morning."

Captain Relyea stepped forward to the map table, where he

could see a chart marked with the new obstructions. "Yes. Very good. Proceed with caution."

The banks narrowed, swamp grass only a few yards from each side of the *Planter*. At thirty feet in the beam, she was almost as wide as the Wappoo. But she drew less than four feet of water, so she could skip right over the bumps that would catch most ships. Robert thought of her as his big flat-bottomed woman.

At the hairpin, he reversed the starboard engine, spinning the paddle backwards to turn the *Planter* hard to the right, as she almost stood still. Not many ships capable of hauling hundreds of soldiers could pull that trick.

Captain Relyea raised the brim of his hat and squinted at the sun. "Can't you take us faster, Robert? The day's burning past."

"Tide's running low. We run on a snag, we lucky to make Stono Inlet by sundown. Goin' slower now will help us get home in time for the ball tonight."

"Don't you worry about the ball. Just get us to the inlet as quickly as you can." Captain Relyea took one more look at the map and left the pilothouse. Robert was tempted to show the captain just how fast he could get through this swampy maze. With a little help from the engine room and a quick flick of the wheel, he could throw Smith over the rail, right into the muck. But not today.

*****

"Pull! Pull! Heave that rope, you black bastards!" Smith shouted.

The gun rose a few inches off the dock, the lines creaking. The cannon, an 8-inch Columbiad, was no work of beauty, with its heavily banded rump, and a log hanging out its barrel to tie the rope around. Five tons of pitch black iron.

Robert wondered what it'd be like to be on the receiving end of that cannon. He'd watched the gunners drill down on the battery. Captain Relyea had even had the crew practice with the two guns that the Confederate Navy had installed on the *Planter*, one fore, a 32-pounder, and one aft, a 24-pound howitzer. Smith instructed them for a few days, back in February, but no one had touched the guns since.

A dozen sweating black slaves from the fort had joined the crew of the *Planter* on the ropes. Two other guns lay on the dock, waiting. The first two cannons had already been loaded and scooted across the deck of the *Planter* on temporary carriages.

"Heave! I'll feed your skins to the turtles. I'll fish with your balls for bait. Pull that blasted rope. Pull!"

The men sang out in rhythm, each beat reaching them forward with one hand, to carry the load a few inches higher, until it was finally high enough to clear the rail.

"I want to go to Canaan. I want to go to Canaan. I want to go to Canaan, to meet 'em at de comin' day."

Engineer Pitcher cranked the handle on the crane to rotate the gun over the deck. Smith jumped up over the rail onto the deck and steadied the gun. At the sight of him, the men stopped singing and listened to his commands.

"That's it. That's it. Easy. Come on now, hold it. Hold it."

Smith reached over his head to guide the massive iron cylinder towards the provisional carriage, a collection of roughhewn beams on wheels that would protect the deck from the gun.

The sun overhead had been pounding mercilessly on the men for hours. A grunt came from ashore, and suddenly a rope slipped, and the gun crashed down, flipping the carriage up against Smith, smacking him across the deck. The cannon smashed down, cracking one of the deck planks, before settling against the bulwark.

Complete silence filled the ship and shore. Not even the birds sang. And then Pitcher jumped from the crane to check on his fallen comrade. Smith lay face down on the deck, breathing hard.

When he finally pushed himself to his feet, he was red with fury. "God Almighty! You'll wish the devil got to you first. Hold that damn rope or I'll have you swing from it by your necks."

Every man on shore stared at the ground. No one dared be the first to catch Smith's eye.

Robert stood absolutely still. Waiting.

Smith looked over the men by the ropes, each one still puffing and breathing hard. Even Pitcher knew enough not to get too close.

"Turno. Johnny. Get over here and help me turn this over." Smith called.

They leapt onto the deck and helped him turn the carriage back onto its wheels.

Robert couldn't take his eyes off the busted plank. It wasn't easy to crack four inches of solid red cedar. And not easy to repair. They were lucky it wasn't much, much worse. If the gun had dropped from any higher, they might be trying to pull it out of the water beneath the *Planter*, through a hole in the deck. And there would be no fancy ball for the officers and no escape for any of them.

"Let's get this demon on the carriage and finish this job. Pick up that rope! Robert, get your ass over here and make these lines fast. Then get your hands on that rope and make sure these niggers don't slip again, or I'll slice the hide off your back."

Robert double-checked each knot, hoping this break would give much needed rest to the crew's blistered palms.

Pitcher stepped forward and put a hand on Smith's shoulder, which he smacked away.

"Don't touch me, Pitcher."

"Are you all right?"

"I'm doing a stupid thing in the heat from hell, with a bunch of shit-eating animals. Of course I'm all right. Let's get this piece of devil dung in the air and onto this carriage."

"It's hot. We have two more guns after this one. Get them

some water."

"Don't tell me how to do my job, you old drunk. And you'd better hope that winch doesn't crap out, or you'll be swimming home. Got me?"

Robert finished fastening the ropes to the cannon and joined the men on the line, between a sturdy blue-black skinned youngster and Johnny, who always pulled from the anchor position.

Smith picked up a cargo hook from off the deck and waved it at the men. Every one of them could picture the hook sticking in their throats.

"Let's go! Heave that rope. Heave!"

*****

Robert admired the dozen ways his crew found to delay. Jackson and Chisholm were masters—they swung their arms to make it look like they were moving fast, all while covering half the distance they should.

Everyone gave Smith a wide berth. No telling how much he got hurt when that carriage flipped over, but Robert was sure that unless his chest was caved in, he wasn't about to miss his chance to woo the lovely Miss Powell.

Once the guns were on board, they loaded the remaining ammunition. "We don't plan to leave them damn Yankees so much as a handkerchief," growled Smith to Pitcher, when Pitcher suggested perhaps they could just depart, seeing as the hour was getting late.

The captain returned to the *Planter*, with a frightened lieutenant on his heels. Captain Relyea looked at the young man like he'd look at a puppy annoyingly tugging at his pants leg. "We were sent for the guns and ammunition. Now we have business in Charleston."

The young man tried to calm himself, as he stood on the ramp. "With all due respect, Captain, I understand your mission. But I have only a few dozen soldiers." He waved at the stone and earthen walls of the fort behind him. It filled a small spit of land jutting into the Stono, on the border between the river and the sea. "If we're attacked, we have no way to respond other than a few rifles. If the Yankees come, a few bullets and rebel yells won't be enough to prevent absolute slaughter."

"Our orders are not to relieve you, lieutenant. We don't have the time to load the rest of your company. I will relay your concerns to the commander at Fort Pemberton."

The older man, though half a head shorter than the lieutenant, allowed no room for argument. He puffed his chest out one more breath broader, which convinced the young soldier there was no path off the island on the *Planter*.

"Very well. We will hold our position until we are relieved. Thank you for passing along our situation to command, Captain." And he said it without adding, *you old buffoon.* Robert admired his self-control. The lieutenant spun on the heel of his shiny boot and strode back into the fort, to break the news to his anxious soldiers peering through the rifle slits in the wall.

*****

Alfred adjusted dials and levers on the starboard engine. "I'd say we got off easy," he said. "Thought we'd see blood on the deck today for sure."

"There's still time," Robert said. "Do we have pressure?"

"Almost. Tell those lazy asses to throw more wood in the fire."

"I'll tell them to take their time. An extra five minutes, and maybe we'll be over the edge."

"You got somethin' planned I don't know about?"

"If we make it all the way through tonight, it'd be nice if we show up to the blockade bringing gifts. Like we's high class."

"And nothing says class like twenty tons of iron and gunpowder," Alfred said, smiling his broad smile.

Robert found Chisholm and Johnny, loading wood for the

port boiler.

"We's working. We's working," reassured Johnny, who had been getting yelled at all day. He had a welt on his head from a whack Smith gave him for loading shot too slowly. Robert had watched Johnny real carefully, not sure what was coming next.

"How's your head?" Robert asked.

"Thick. That's what they tells me. Thick and stupid. But I have a secret."

Robert shuddered. "We don't talk about secrets, do we?"

"No, Robert. You told me not to."

So Johnny still remembered. Robert wanted to say, "Don't worry about that knot on your head, because after tonight your head is gon' be your own. And if somebody tries to knock a dent in it, you can just pick 'em up and toss 'em in the river." But with Johnny, the less said the better.

"We all right?" Chisholm asked, as he chucked another log into the furnace.

"Not an easy day, but we all right."

"Shame 'bout that slip, huh? Almost managed to squash Smith before we said goodbye."

Robert looked at Chisholm's smirk and knew who'd let the rope go.

"What was you thinking?"

"I was thinking I hate that pig sucker and it'd be a shame to go without taking a shot. And you said to slow things down."

Robert backed Chisholm up against the boiler. "You almost crashed that gun through the deck. Then we woulda been stuck here all night, and no one goes to the ball. What do you think that means for the rest of us?"

"I'm sorry. I just..."

"Watch your hands and feet and your quick mouth for the next few hours, so we can get back. Got it?" His fists were clenched tight, and it took every ounce of self-control to keep from planting one in Chisholm's face.

"Aye, aye, Captain." Chisholm saluted him. Johnny just

78

watched them, confused.

"Load her up," Robert called, heading up the ladder.

*****

Captain Relyea paced on the top deck, in and out of the wheel house, as they steamed up the Stono. Robert wondered if the Yankees had any idea that the fort at the inlet was being held by twenty men with rifles. How grateful would they be for the information?

"What was the matter with those boys today, Robert?" The captain removed his hat and wiped his broad forehead with a handkerchief. "They're usually not a bad crew. But I've never seen niggers move so slowly."

"Hot day. Heavy guns. That slip spooked everyone. No one wanted the next mistake to be theirs." He didn't have to add *because they knew Smith would have gutted them.* Relyea didn't have much stomach for violence, but he never stopped it either.

Captain Relyea nodded. "That's the first rule of the military. Nothing ever goes as planned."

"Sounds like words of wisdom, suh."

The captain pulled out his pocket watch and checked it against the clock on the bridge panel. "It's late. When can you have us at Fort Ripley?"

"Before dark, not by much."

Captain Relyea looked at his watch again before snapping it shut. "By the time we get to the Ashley River, we won't be far ahead of sunset. Certainly not with enough time to unload all the guns. Get us through the Cut and take us back to Atlantic Wharf. We'll bring the guns to Fort Ripley tomorrow morning."

"Yessuh."

"I'll be in my quarters. Send Alston for me when we reach Fort Pemberton."

Captain Relyea left to freshen up for the big ball. Smith and Pitcher were in their tiny cabins doing the same—trimming, primping. They'd brought their dress uniforms aboard this morning, prepared for just this situation. Soon, they'd be calling out to Alston for hot water and towels and shiny boots. Robert was happy for them to spend the rest of the afternoon in there, getting as beautiful as they could possibly be.

He pulled the bell and picked up the speed just a hair. Now that they were going where he wanted, he was happy to push the *Planter* a little, to send the officers off to their revels as soon as possible.

*****

The three officers standing in front of the ramp couldn't have looked any more different from the assembled crew. Pitcher and Smith waited in their neat grey dress uniforms, bright double rows of brass buttons up the front, short-billed caps, beards perfectly trimmed. They stood gravely, arms crossed. Smith's leg twitched, making the tip of his dress saber wiggle back and forth. They knew they shouldn't all be going ashore. Orders were to never leave ships unattended, and unattended meant without a white officer on board. Robert drew himself up to look his very most trustworthy.

Captain Relyea stood with his hand on the grip of his saber, showing off cuffs decorated with a golden loop and double bars. Three serious grey peacocks in full display in front of a line of six humble slaves, dressed in patched clothes, hands worn and calloused, heads bowed. Robert watched each one carefully. No one had better even take a single breath that didn't seem meek and mild.

"You boys were a disgrace today. Slow and lazy. How am I supposed to explain to General Ripley that we failed in our simple mission? He will tell me to use you as chum, to toss you to the workhouse, and find a new crew." Captain Relyea paused to let his words sink in.

"You will have a chance to redeem yourselves. Tonight, I want the firewood completely restocked. There are stores on the wharf to be loaded—once we deliver the guns tomorrow, we have a list of additional stops. Make certain this ship is fully prepared to travel at daybreak. I don't care if you have to work all night. Look at me, Robert."

Robert raised his head to look in Relyea's grey eyes, which lurked under a determined frown of great import.

"Robert, I will hold you personally responsible for the state of this ship when I return. Any man neglecting his duty will be flogged. Is that understood?"

Robert tried not to glance at Smith, whose lips were twisting into a smile at the prospect of something going wrong. They all could imagine the whistle of the whip.

"Yes, Captain. I understand." He dipped his head in humble submission.

"Excellent. Gentlemen, the night is ours." With a nod, Smith and Pitcher parted to allow the captain to disembark, and they followed closely behind, their polished boots ringing against the stones of the wharf.

Seven black chins raised as Robert and the crew watched the officers walk into the fading daylight.

Robert hoped the officers drank champagne and rum and wine and beer until they felt like they were walking in the waves and settled down for a sleep so sound that even the tap of death's finger couldn't wake them.

Alfred seemed to be the first to breathe. "Praise God Almighty," he whispered.

"I thought they was never gonna leave. Never seen a man look at hisself in the mirror as much as that Smith," Chisholm joked. "Musta tried to see if he had covered up all the spite."

"What you all waiting for?" Robert scolded. "You heard what the captain said. We got a ship to load. Move your lazy asses."

"But, I thought that we..." Johnny looked confused.

"We gon' get that firewood and those casks of powder," Turno said, putting a hand on Johnny's shoulder. "You heard

Robert."

"I guess so." Johnny set himself in motion, the same lumbering speed as ever.

"Move!" Robert said. "Move, people. Jackson, we gon' need something in our bellies. Alston, you help him. The rest a you know what to do. Meet at eight o'clock, in the engine room."

They leapt into action, the cloak of exhaustion they'd put on for the officers suddenly removed. Robert was tempted to tell them to put it back on, to hide the energy of living on a knife's blade for one more night. But no officers were in sight, and the guards at the end of the wharf never bothered about what a bunch of crazy niggers did on the ships.

CHAPTER 10

Robert walked into the engine room carrying four lanterns and hung them from the steam pipes. Tonight, Robert wanted the men to look clearly into each other's eyes.

He heard a clank of metal on metal from the starboard engine and saw Alfred's ass sticking out of a nest of pipes. Robert felt ice in his heart. This was not the night for engine trouble.

"What you doin'? Looks like the *Planter* ate you for her supper."

Alfred grunted a laugh back at Robert.

"You gon' make her go faster?"

"She been making a sound I don't like."

"She got to run smooth tonight. Like butter on a hot pan."

"Don't worry," Alfred said, extracting himself from the engine. "She'll move when you need her to."

The smell of dinner accompanied Jackson as he entered the engine room, carrying pots of pork and beans and rice. Alston followed, with hands full of bowls and bread. Not far behind them, Johnny and Turno stooped through the door, rolling small barrels.

"Put those over by the port boiler," Robert instructed.

In a minute, they were all eating. "Jackson, where you get all this pork?" Chisholm called out between bites. "Since when we have beans with actual meat in it? You sure there ain't a ship's dog missing somewhere?"

"That's the captain's tomorrow dinner," Jackson said,

without even a hint of a smile. If the whole plan was suddenly abandoned, it was enough to land him a beating. Robert crossed Jackson off the list of potential weak links.

"Y'all eat up," Robert said to his crew. "Taste that pork, taste that bread. That ain't bread meant for slaves."

"Preach it, Brother Robert," Chisholm responded.

"That's a meal for free men. Tonight, that's who we are."

He let that sit with them, and they chewed it and swallowed it with light in their eyes.

"When you free, it starts in your heart. You free in your heart, Alston?"

The boy looked at him, his eyes wide with the prospect of what they were about to do. "Yeah, Robert. I think so."

"When we get our wives and chi'ren off the *Etiwan*, they be free, too. The masters, the navy, they might try to catch us, but they don't get to win tonight." The audacity of saying such words aloud made Robert feel lightheaded.

Turno stood, his head touching the ceiling. His eyes burned in the lamp light. "I ain't never going back. Not even if they catch us."

"They ain't gon' catch us," Robert said.

"I know. But if they do, we got to agree." Turno took the time to look at each man, a challenge.

"I ain't hangin' at the end of a rope," Alfred said.

"Me neither," Robert agreed.

Johnny looked worried. "They ain't gon' catch us, is they? Robert, you said we was gon' be free."

Robert smiled his best reassuring smile at their child-like giant. "They is not going to catch us. Don't worry."

"What do we agree to?" Chisholm asked, searching the men's faces, no longer the clown for a moment.

"They catch us, we light these casks of powder," Turno said, kicking the barrels he and Johnny had brought, "and blow the *Planter* sky high."

"That's right," Robert said. "We spike the guns. Don't leave

84

nothing for them. Don't give them us, not our wives, our children, not this ship or her guns. If we get boarded, we take the *Planter* to the bottom of the harbor."

He looked every man square in the face. The slightest waver in them now could lead to disaster.

"Johnny. Alston. Chisholm. Jackson. You men enough to be part of this plan?"

Jackson nodded.

"I don't wanna blow up, Robert." Johnny stammered. "B- b- but I don't want them to whip me and beat me no more neither. If you say do it, I do it."

"Chisholm?"

"Figure I gon' meet the devil one day or 'nother. Might as well be tonight."

*****

Robert stood with Alston at the gangway, looking up the wharf into the lights of town. Charleston was quieter than ever, with most of the officers at the ball drinking punch and eating frilly little foods. Maybe they were dancing with the ladies in their ball dresses, all puffed and laced and powdered. What was Smith like when he was away from the ship? Maybe he wasn't as ready to tear into someone, or maybe he was at that party right now, looking for a fight. Pitcher would find the other men like himself, clustered in the corner, raising flasks, mocking the finer folks. Captain Relyea would be with his wife, a little dark sparrow of a woman, trying to stay close to General Ripley, waiting for a scrap of praise, hoping not to be asked about the delayed guns.

He took the boy by the shoulder. "You know where to go, right?"

Alston looked up at him and swallowed, "Yes, Robert."

"St. Michael's Alley. There's a lamp right in the middle of the block."

Alston pulled a handful of small stones from his pocket. "Break the lamp. Don't let no one see me."

"Stay in the shadows. And don't take too long. The wives be looking for that broken lamp."

The boy looked even more scared than he had before. "I won't mess up."

"I know you won't. Here, take this." He thrust a rolled up map into the boy's hands. "When you see the guards, you say the captain sent a messenger for this chart, but we couldn't find it. Now you takin' it to his house, up on Church Street."

Alston nodded his head and looked out into the night, eyes wide.

"Don't run, but hurry."

"I will." And with that, he was scurrying up the wharf into the dim light.

Robert watched Alston pitch his story about the map to the first guard, who nodded and waved him through.

His family's freedom depended on one boy, so eager to be a man.

*****

Robert walked along the front deck, trying to think of something besides where the hell Alston was. Shouldn't have taken him this long. Glancing back over his shoulder, he almost tripped on an uncoiled line. The men had loaded the cargo, but it was haphazardly stacked. An empty sack, twine, pecan shells littered the deck.

He found Turno, Chisholm, and Johnny, perched at the back rail, watching the lights of guard boats puttering across the harbor.

Somewhere, far off, back towards town, Robert swore he could hear music from the ball. One of the regimental bands planned to play, and supposedly the finest musicians from all over South Carolina had joined up. From the harbor a breeze carried the scent of the sea. Six forts lurked in the dark.

"Quite a night," Robert said. "Don't you fret 'bout them guard boats."

"If you say so," Chisholm said, his eyes watching the water.

86

"Ya'll done good bringin' in the crates and cargo, but you left the deck a mess."

"Worried we gon' fail inspection?" Chisholm grinned.

"Who knows who might come this way? The *Planter* is our ship now. You need to make her look better'n any other ship in this harbor. Make every crate, every stack just right. Sweep and mop the deck, better'n if you thought the captain was 'bout to come on board any minute. You hear?"

"You're right," Turno said, looking upriver, to where the *Etiwan* lurked around the bend. "No sign of Alston?"

"Not yet. Go on now. Get that deck clear. Johnny, don't let these two slack. Got it?"

"Yes, Robert," Johnny answered, as he rose to his feet, towering high above Robert.

"And when you's all done, get some rest, but out of sight. Too many niggers on deck all night attracts attention."

They left, but he wasn't ready to go with them. He couldn't shake the feeling of dread about those forts out there, waiting. Castle Pinckney, just off to the left, was close enough he could almost hit it with a rock. They'd have to go by her twice, once to get the women and children, and again on their way out. Then Fort Pemberton, which was only half armed, since a good chunk of her new guns lay on deck of the *Planter*. They'd be far enough away from Fort Johnson, whose soldiers would hardly look towards the *Planter*. But they'd need to pass right between Fort Moultrie and Fort Sumter. And even if they did, Battery Gregg had enough power to knock her right to the bottom.

*****

Alston came back around ten. The guard didn't even question him, just waved him through. Robert and Turno were on him as soon as the boy cleared the rail, pulling him across the deck.

"Where you been, little man?" Turno growled.

"When I got to the alley, two soldiers was fussin' about

which whorehouse was best, and who drank too much from the bottle, and who was too drunk to put it to a whore anyways. I just stayed out of sight, and then I thought I'd better wait, 'cause I didn't want them hearing me breakin' nothing. Then my hands was shaking so much, I could barely hold a rock, much less throw it."

"Did you do it?" Robert asked.

"Yeah. But then there was more soldiers, so I had to go the other way, and I almost bumped into Hannah."

"Did you talk to her?"

"I didn't even look at her. I wasn't supposed to see her, right?"

"Did anyone see the two of you together?" Turno demanded.

"I crossed the street, soon as I seen her, and got round the corner, fast as I could. Hannah kept walking, trying not to look at the soldiers, trying not to be seen."

"They spy her?"

"Nah. I waited 'round the corner, just to be sure. Then I got out of there."

Alston looked up at the two men, still breathing hard. His wide eyes were full of questions, and one big one: *Am I still going to be free?*

Robert put a reassuring hand on the boy's shoulder. There wasn't much to him under that uniform, he was still all arms and legs, but he had plenty of heart, too. "You done good," Robert told him. "Real good."

"Lila and Mary was already goin' to be at your place," Turno said to Robert. "If Hannah saw what she needed, they be all right."

"They will. Now we just need the earth to turn a little faster, get us past midnight."

CHAPTER II

Turno held a crowbar in his hand and, at a nod from Robert, placed it against the locked door of Captain Relyea's cabin. The latch popped and the door swung open. Each step they took made it harder to turn back.

Inside, the walls were varnished fine-grained walnut. A built-in cabinet with pewter knobs filled the wall across from the comfortable bunk. Neither Turno nor Robert had ever sat on a mattress filled with down and cotton, let alone slept on one. A small swing-down table and two chairs barely fit into the wall by the window, which looked out towards the harbor.

Turno set down his lantern and pried open a locked cabinet. Inside was a pair of silver pistols with mother-of-pearl handles. Pretty to look at and still able to put a hole in a man. Turno looked them over closely, tracing a finger down the filigreed barrels, then stuck one in his belt and handed the other to Robert.

"You an outlaw now," said Turno.

Robert just smiled and opened a drawer. Inside was Captain Relyea's everyday uniform, crisply folded.

"They say clothes make the man," Robert said. "Let's see how it does on me. Go see if there's anything in the officer's cabins. Take what you need, but don't trash them. If we get ourselves out to the Union, those officers need to see we ain't savages. If we show 'em we know how to respect a ship and everything that comes with it, maybe we get them to treat us the same."

"Smith owes me something. We'll see if he left me enough to help settle his debt," said Turno darkly.

Once Turno was gone, Robert climbed into the second skin of Captain Relyea, keeping his little bag of cash strapped to his chest. Pants, shirt, jacket, all fit a little loose, but they would do for tonight.

The hat. He tucked his bush of hair inside and pushed on the hat. Flipped the brim up, just a tad, like Relyea would do. Thrust his chest out. Wished he had a mustache, to fill out the part. Though if anyone was close enough to see a mustache, the game would be over.

Turno pushed open the door, and Robert turned to face him, Captain Relyea's pipe in his hand. He bellowed, "What is it, Turno? Can't you see I'm dressing? I've got General Ripley coming any second and the ship is barely presentable."

Taking a step back, Turno shook with laughter. "Oh, man, oh, man. You is him. Crazy. Pure crazy."

Robert strutted across the small cabin, scowling his best captain's scowl, which sent Turno to the floor, and brought Jackson to see.

Hooting, Jackson said, "What can I get you for supper, Captain?"

"Pie, Jackson. At a time like this, all a man can think of is pie."

"Aye, aye, sir."

Robert took another imaginary puff from his pipe, then spoke in his own voice. "Brew us some coffee, Jackson. We need everyone sharp tonight. Turno, tell Alfred we leave in ten minutes. Get that fire hot."

*****

From the pilothouse, Robert surveyed the ship and the dock. Alston was lighting the port and starboard navigation lanterns. Chisholm, Turno, and Johnny were casting off. Down the wharf, the guard looked in their direction, as smoke drifted towards Charleston from their stack. It was just minutes after three a.m., and the guard had changed at two a.m., so the new man had no idea whether any of the officers were on board the *Planter* or not. At least, Robert hoped not.

With a deep breath, he pulled the bell line and signaled Alfred. The great paddles began to turn, chuffing and churning the water. He eased the *Planter* away from the dock, fighting the impulse to run. He needed to stay calm. He'd made a thousand tiny rebellions in his life, but almost all had been in his mind. This time it was real. He felt an electric thrill surge through his body. As of this moment he was no longer the same man. No matter what happened, none of them would be the same.

The lights on Castle Pinckney stared at him through the night, dead ahead, less than a mile offshore. The sentries on that fort were just some of the hundreds who all had the power to bring this night to a terrible and bloody end.

They cleared the end of the dock and he spun the wheel to shift her to port. He wanted a nice slow arc towards the *Etiwan*. The more routine and intentional this seemed, the better. Somewhere on the dark shore, Hannah and the children were hiding and waiting. Scared. As much as he wished he were there right this second, the only way he could help them was to keep his cool and get the *Planter* where it needed to be.

Chisholm climbed up to the pilothouse. "Turno said you wanted me."

"I need him down on the deck, in case there's trouble. But I need a wheel man. Try to be me, or Smith. Captain Relyea don't never steer the ship."

"Now?" Chisholm looked nervously at the wheel.

"No. You just stand here with me for now. No one's lookin' too close. When we's out by the forts, then you gon' have your hand on the wheel, and you do exactly what I tell you. Can you do that?"

"Yeah, I guess so." Chisholm's voice sounded thin and lifeless. In the dim light, his face looked almost that of a child.

"Try, yessir. With some snap to it." Robert demanded.

"What?"

"You think we's messing around? We driving a steamship through currents and torpedoes and sandbars. I know you got a joke for everything, but tonight, you act like a sailor. Got it?"

"Yes, sir!" Chisholm stood at attention, looking uneasily at Robert. Robert had never seen him scared before. As much as Robert liked Chisholm's humor, an edge of fear might serve him better tonight.

"We'll get this done. Let's see if your Mary had enough sense to get herself over to the *Etiwan*. She always seems smart enough, but then she's hooked up with you, so I don't know."

"She'll be there."

Robert set the *Planter* straight into the current and outgoing tide, steering halfway between Charleston and Hog Island. No guard boats in sight. No movement along the shore. Most of the edge of the water was pure black, as if instead of trees lining the shore, it was just concentrated darkness. The engines chugged and puffed, spitting out ashes and occasional sparks. Going upstream for the families was the craziest part of the plan—adding more time and risk. Sometimes crazy was the only way to live.

They heard a splash behind them. Turno and Johnny had loosed a dory they'd sneaked onto the *Planter* back at the Atlantic Wharf and were rowing towards shore.

"I'd rather be with them," Chisholm whispered.

Robert shared Chisholm's desire—if anyone was going to get Hannah and Lizzie and Junior, he'd rather it be himself. "They gon' have enough trouble crammin' everyone in that little boat without you takin' a seat."

Robert checked the clock. Every minute counted now. Once dawn arrived, the *Planter* would be missed.

Turno and Johnny had twenty minutes to retrieve the families. He might wait a little longer, maybe five, ten minutes more, if he had to. But after that, someone was sure to hear the

Planter hanging out in the middle of the river and wonder what was up.

In a few strokes, the rowboat melted into the darkness. Robert tried to stay steady in the current. He forced himself to keep breathing, keep paying attention to the ship.

Turno and Johnny had the two strongest sets of arms. With the current and an empty boat, they could be there in less than ten minutes. Getting back would be something else.

It would be all right. It would be all right.

Maybe.

From his palms on the wheel, Robert could feel the pulse of the ship, the steady turn of the wheels. She didn't like treading water like this. She liked to go. The *Planter* had a shallow rudder, so her nose tended to wander heading upstream, but Robert concentrated on keeping the bow pointed into the heart of the main current. He couldn't see much of the water in the dark, so he steered purely by feel. He'd spent so much time on this river that he could picture the surface of the water in his mind, as clear as if the sun were shining overhead.

Where was his family? He tried to stay focused on the water, the muck, but images of Hannah, Lizzie, and Junior flashed in front of him instead. He needed to jam all that deep down inside and keep the ship afloat and ready. He would see them soon. Turno would get them.

Why weren't they here yet?

Chisholm stood facing the rear of the ship, peering through the gloom.

"Any new lights?" Robert asked.

"Nothing."

"Try the glass."

He handed Captain Relyea's spyglass to Chisholm.

"Anything?"

"Not yet. It's awful dark."

They'd picked the *Etiwan* and the North Wharf for that very reason. It was dark as hell on the harbor end of the dock. The most of the lights in town were concentrated on the southern end of Charleston. No Yankees were going to come floating down the Cooper River. Any attack would come from the sea, or from the south through Wappoo Cut. Darkness was their friend.

Where were they? Breathe, breath, breathe, Robert told himself. *Feel the engines, feel the water.*

The clock read three forty-seven. Eighteen minutes gone. He was tempted to shut down the engines and drift, so he could at least hear the oars, even if he couldn't see the boat. But not hearing the oars also meant someone else not hearing the oars. If some guard suddenly noticed strange noises, their escape was finished. One wrong oar splash, one baby's cry, one groan of effort or gasp of fear. The guards on shore were listening and watching.

"Get down there," he said to Chisholm. "I'm going to spin her, so they're not trying to crawl up our wake. You and Jackson stand at the prow with a line. And a hook, in case it looks like we gon' run them over. If you see them, wave to me."

"Aye, Captain."

Chisholm sped out of the wheelhouse and down the ladder. Robert hit the bell line and pulled the lever, to spin the *Planter* counterclockwise. Twenty minutes and more. If the women and children had been ready, they should have been here by now. He needed to look down river, just in case. He could reverse both engines if he had to, in order to keep her from drifting too far downstream. Was it even worth going if Hannah and the children were lost? Or would it be better to embrace failure with the powder kegs and join them in oblivion?

The ship spun and turned to run with the current. They had a flare with them on the dory, just in case. The danger now was that he might plow over them in the dark. He hoped they had enough sense to light the flare if they heard the *Planter* bearing down.

If they were out there at all.

Robert watched Chisholm and Jackson at the prow. If they leaned any farther forward, they'd fall overboard. Every ear, every eye strained for the slightest confirmation that the plan had worked.

Jackson stiffened. Suddenly he jumped and grabbed the boat hook. Chisholm looked up at Robert and waved madly. Robert pulled the bell wire to reverse both engines.

In the dim red gloom cast by the running light, he finally saw the boat. Turno and Johnny had the main oars, and Morrison and Hannah were at the front oars, pulling hard against the current and the outgoing tide. The other women held the children close against the bottom of the boat, knowing the slightest cry could betray them. He should have known Hannah would be at the oar—she wanted her freedom as much as any of them.

At a command from Turno, they shipped the oars and Johnny caught the line from Jackson. They hauled the dory alongside, just fore of the paddle wheels. Robert looked back towards shore and saw a new light on the North Wharf. Had they gotten away cleanly?

He wanted to jump down and help everyone off the dory, but Jackson, Chisholm, and Alston had more than enough hands to get everyone on board. The last thing they needed now was to grind onto a sandbar. He focused on his mental atlas, trying to picture the bottom of the river at this very spot.

The light at the end of the wharf dallied, then retreated. He watched for a sign that word was spreading. If they'd been found out, maybe there was still one last chance. He could bring the *Planter* back to her slip at the Atlantic Wharf and sneak the women and children home. Deny everything. Get out bottles of rum and act like breaking into Captain Relyea's cabin was the result of a drunken party. Lashes for all of them, but not hanging. Not drowning in the harbor as the *Planter* sank, or burning as she exploded from shell after shell.

They'd be watched. They would never have another chance, but they'd live. They'd still have each other, still have Lizzie and Junior. Sort of. But as long as Kingman and Mr. Henry held their leashes, he and Hannah never really had each other. Even in the middle of the night, when it seemed like there was nothing in the world but the two of them, their bodies sweating under the sheets, their masters lurked in the shadows.

No. Tonight there would be no turning back. From this moment they were free of their chains, and no one could put them back on again.

The men hauled the dory onto the deck, straining to haul the long boat out of the water. Robert pushed the *Planter* forward again. No bells, no flares, no more lanterns from the shore. It was time to head downriver and test themselves.

On the deck, the men ushered the women and children to the store room in front of the port side paddle wheel—it was critical that they stay out of sight. Hannah looked up towards the pilothouse. Robert waved, almost a salute.

Turno climbed to the upper deck, Chisholm behind him.

"Glad you didn't leave without us," Turno said. His skin shimmered with sweat in the lantern light.

"Took your time, didn't you?"

"It's harder moving around in the dark than you'd think. And you can't rush chi'ren if you want 'em to stay quiet. You know how they is."

Robert had a hard time imagining Turno as the patient coaxing father. It was easier to picture him just gathering all the children and Lila under his arms and carrying them to the dory.

"I saw a light down there. You sure no one saw you?"

"Morrison said they's a guard down there who ain't as sleepy as he should be. Said he had to feed him a whole line of bull to satisfy him. But he didn't search the holds, and the babies didn't cry. If that guard had seen us, he'd of raised a cry." They all looked out at the far shore, making sure one more time, that there was no lantern lurking at the end of North Wharf. All was dark, all was quiet.

"Guess we's all in it together now," Chisholm said.

"All the way, to heaven or hell," Robert said.

CHAPTER 12

Castle Pinckney loomed on the far end of Shutes Folly Island, a dim shadow against a starry sky. It was no Fort Sumter—the walls of the circular fort were barely twenty feet tall, but its guns were plenty strong enough to sink any passing ship. A thirty-foot high wooden watch tower stood just outside the walls of the fort, lit by hooded lanterns. As the *Planter* approached the fort, the channel between Charleston and the island grew increasingly narrow.

"You can take wheel," Chisholm said. "I ain't no pilot."

Robert didn't move. "Eyes from Castle Pinckney gon' be looking our way. They know Relyea don't lay his hand on the wheel. I'll try to look like him and you look like me."

"I'm too good looking to look like you."

Robert was grateful for an excuse to smile. "Do your best to at least drive like me, all right?" He consciously unclenched his fists and flexed his hands. "You done a good job not hanging us up yet. Keep it up. Take us two points starboard—there's a rock off the tip of the island. We don't need a hole in the hull tonight."

Chisholm turned the wheel, bringing them closer to Charleston. Robert studied the shore anxiously. No sign of commotion. No whistles or bells, no lanterns running up and down the harbor front, searching for a missing steamship. Only three people would know for certain that the ship shouldn't be out and about. If they were lucky, Pitcher would be passed out in the barracks or on a park bench. Captain Relyea would be in his comfortable bed, next to his wife. Maybe Smith was finally falling asleep, after being tortured by the smell of Miss Powell's perfume on his hand, or the memory of a stolen kiss. He'd be ready to take out his frustrations with the whip tomorrow.

All of three of them dreaming soldier's dreams, white men's dreams.

Here on the *Planter* every dreamer was wide awake—hoping their collective dream would not blow into a nightmare.

A guard boat was running low and slow, just off Charleston's East Battery, not far from Atlantic Wharf. Looking for trouble, but not looking for them. Not yet. Its light moved slowly and steadily around the city's shoreline.

"Swing us to port," Robert commanded. "That's it. Stop. Back a bit to starboard." The shadows of sentries stood on Castle Pinckney's watch tower in dim lamp light. In less than an hour, the sky would begin to lighten. In two hours, the sun would break the horizon. If they weren't past Sumter by then, they'd better find the powder kegs and light the fuse.

Robert picked up Captain Relyea's hat from the chart table and pushed it onto his head. "How do I look?"

Chisholm shook his head. "Almost as much a fool as Relyea. Why he wear his hat in the dark?"

"I go without it, they gon' shoot my head right off my shoulders."

"Fine. Tilt it down then."

Robert tilted down the brim and puffed up his chest.

"Not so full," Chisholm coached. "They know he been out late to the ball."

"Relyea's a proud man. He don't want to show he's half hung over."

"Puff it down a bit, I'm telling you," Chisholm said.

A couple breaths, a shift of the hat, and Robert stepped out onto the deck, trying to imagine himself as Relyea. But he was as different from Relyea as a bear from a bird. Or at least that's what Relyea and all the white folks thought. But they breathed the same air, ate the same food, loved the same ship.

He called down to Turno, who was covering the dory with a tarp. "Turn the lamps up. We don't want to look like we's sneaking around. And send Alston up with some coffee."

Robert tried to look at the walls of the fort without raising his face high enough to betray the color of his skin. Castle Pinckney had twenty-eight guns on top of its circular stone face, though it hadn't seen or fired a shot during the whole war. He hoped tonight wouldn't be its first time.

In the pilothouse, he stood almost level with the guard in the watchtower, not more than a hundred yards away. The gunners in the fort would be sleeping, except for a skeleton crew. The officers would have been out at the ball, except for an unlucky handful. He stepped inside the pilothouse and pulled the bell to slow the engines.

"You sure you want to crawl by?" Chisholm asked.

"Just hold that wheel steady." Robert pulled the steam whistle, one long pull, one short—the signal requesting to pass.

They waited.

Robert stepped out onto the deck again, trying to embody an annoyed Captain Relyea. He crossed his arms and tapped his foot.

Finally the call came from across the water, "Pass the *Planter.*"

He heard Chisholm finally breathe again. "Give three short pulls," Robert instructed, "and push us ahead a little harder, but not too much."

They steamed past Castle Pinckney, now facing its front, where all guns lay pointed towards the mouth of the harbor. And now at their ship. It wouldn't take much effort for the gunners to put a hole in the *Planter.*

The channel was designed to funnel approaching ships past an enormous array of guns. Almost thirty cannon in Castle Pinckney lay behind them. And now the *Planter* was approaching Fort Ripley—half boat, half island, built as one more promise to the people of Charleston that no Yankee ironclad could make it to the Queen City's shores.

Robert raised the glass and spotted one guard, half asleep. The gunnery crews were bunked down for the night, saving their energy to unload the heavy guns that now lay motionless on the deck of the *Planter*, like sleeping demons of war. Keeping them off the battery might give a small bit of help to the Yankees, but it was hard to see how a Union ship could ever get this far. Fort Ripley could shell the channel all the way from Fort Sumter to here. Mix that with the guns from Fort Johnson, sitting off to the right on James Island, and it'd be a taste of hell for anyone who broke through.

Or who tried to get out.

He decided not to alert the guard on Fort Ripley with a whistle. No sense getting them excited about the arrival of the new guns, and then not deliver. Better to walk past, looking like they had other business entirely.

Off to the far right, it was too dark to tell if anyone on Fort Johnson was watching them. It was Fort Johnson that had fired the first shot to start this whole war. Those same soldiers would be happy to claim some glory for stopping runaway slaves stealing the best ship in Charleston Harbor. Better not to pay them too much attention, but instead look like they had a mission to Sumter, or beyond.

And they did have a mission beyond Sumter. Way beyond.

He leaned against the rail, feeling the wind against his face as they pushed ahead. He tried to smell the breeze—was there any shift in the wind coming, any change in the weather?

Alston appeared. "Turno said you wanted me."

"How they doin' down there?"

"They quiet. 'Cept for Lila praying and Mary telling her to hush herself."

Robert shook his head. Those two women couldn't get along for more than ten minutes. He imagined Hannah was about ready to throttle them both.

"Take 'em some food and see if that shuts 'em up."

STEERING TO FREEDOM

"Yessir."

"And then get your ass out on deck with Turno. I need eyes and ears lookin' for the edge of the channel."

He slid back into the pilothouse and gently shouldered Chisholm aside to take the wheel. "You doin' fine so far," Robert assured him, "but let me take us through the torpedoes and snags."

Chisholm eagerly surrendered the wheel. "You want me to go out there and wear the hat and fill myself with pomposity?"

"Stay right here. As soon as we thread through, you can steer us up to Sumter."

He slowed the *Planter* by half. They'd help sink the piles and chains, planting spike-covered logs lurking just below the surface. Long ropes ran out along the channel's edge, like tentacles of giant squids, waiting to snag a passing propeller or wheel.

Down below, Turno brought an extra lantern to the rail, and Alston followed suit on the other side of the deck. In the low tide, Robert could just make out the tops of the pilings, an extra splash in the gentle chop. The torpedoes were anchored just under the surface, waiting to put a fast end to their plan. He felt the current grab the *Planter*, and he fought to keep from slipping out of the channel.

On the port rail, Turno raised his arm high into the air, and Robert pushed the wheel to steer back into the channel, keeping an eye out for more splashes, trying to watch the sky, which wasn't quite so dark anymore. It was past five already, but there was no chance of rushing through the obstructions and torpedoes. Gunpowder was very unforgiving.

Alston waved wildly from his side, and Robert steered the ship away from the starboard edge of the channel. A bead of sweat slowly trickled down his back. Seemed like the *Planter* couldn't hold a line tonight.

Ahead, Fort Sumter grew more imposing by the minute.

"That's the last of this set of obstructions," Robert said to

101

Chisholm, stepping away from the wheel, and pulling a lever to speed the engines again. "Take her out toward the center of the channel, then we edge around the front of Sumter. Don't forget, we got more logs and torpedoes off the port side between Sumter and Fort Moultrie. You get too shy of Sumter, we end up blown to hell. You got it?"

Chisholm nodded and put his shaking hands on the wheel. Robert tried to be everywhere in his head at once—in the engine room with Alfred, watching the dials and adjusting the steam, shoveling the firewood with Johnny, at the rail with Turno and Chisholm, in the store room with Hannah and Lizzie and Junior, waiting and listening. He tried to be inside the two paddlewheels, feeling the water pushed by the blades, surging forward, tried to be inside the soldiers on the parapets of Sumter, watching the approaching steamship, wondering who was out so early.

Over the water between Sullivan's Island and Sumter, the line between sky and water was becoming visible, as the sky changed from dark nothingness to indigo. He was tempted to ring four bells and race for the coming sunrise. They could hope the gunners on Sumter were out of practice, or too hung over from their own night of revels.

Instead he slowed her to a crawl. Turno and Alston looked up at him, as he stepped wide of the pilothouse, doing his best to fully inhabit the spirit of Captain Relyea, a Captain Relyea who had every reason to be here, who had important business, and who followed protocol and would ask permission from Sumter to pass. He would be a Captain Relyea enjoying a cup of coffee and his pipe. Not in a hurry. Not intimidated by the walls reaching fifty feet above the water, or by the three rows of guns capable of reducing his ship to splinters.

Robert waved a hand at Chisholm. "They're watchin' close. You pull the whistle. Long, long, short, long."

"Aye, Captain."

Chisholm gave the signal.

"Slow her down one more notch," Robert ordered. "And

don't look so nervous. Turno, go coil some rope. Alston, tell Alfred to be ready. Get your black asses off my deck."

No signal from the fort.

The Yankees missed their big chance, Robert thought, as he looked at the repaired walls of the fort, soaring above the sea. The Confederates had been working every day and every night for a whole year, hauling stone and mortar, guns, supplies. Six months ago, she wasn't ready for a major assault. But now, it'd take the entire Union navy to blast their way past Sumter.

"Slow her one more peg." Robert could feel the fear creeping into him, like an icy fog starting at his feet and climbing towards his heart. If the men on Sumter took much longer, he'd have to back the engines, because the tide wanted to draw the ship out to sea. Fifteen souls on deck and within the holds and cabins all added to that push, wanting to draw her out past every last stumbling block. It was his job to make them wait.

"What taking them so long?" Chisholm asked.

Robert thought he saw the barrel of a cannon shift back from the top of the wall. Perhaps another in the middle row. Hard to say in the gloom. Were gunners cleaning the barrels of Columbiads, adding bags of powder, priming, loading? Would they get an offer to surrender? Or would the cannon just blast away? The dark eyes of the gun ports stared blankly back at him, threating to breathe to fiery life any second.

"Ring five bells," Robert said. Chisholm complied, puzzled. They never used five. But Alfred knew. Five bells meant: make sure the power kegs are ready.

"They should have signaled by now. I know I gave it right," Chisholm whispered, every trace of a joke long gone from his voice.

"Steady," Robert reassured him. "They been up all night. Shifts haven't changed for a while. Their minds move slower at daybreak."

"Turno and me know how to work the guns. They decide to shoot at us, we can shoot back." Maybe Chisholm was a little tougher than Robert had realized.

Robert saw Turno lurking in the shadows on the main deck, probably having the same thought. It'd take at least four men to load and fire the cannon, with a decent chance of blowing themselves up in the process. Not that it wouldn't feel satisfying to blast at the fort. Instead of blowing themselves up, they could just make Sumter do it for them and take out some of the soldiers with them.

In the time it would take for Turno to reach the forward gun, a sharpshooter on top of Sumter could put five holes in his chest.

Robert took a deep breath, watching the dark water at the edge of the fort, looking at the waves from their own wake breaking against hidden shoals just offshore of Sumter. "Keep your hands on that wheel. You ground us on a rock, we all finished."

"Yessir."

Robert crossed his arms again, keeping his hands well-hidden. No excuses. Puff the chest. What would Relyea do? Maybe the officer of the watch knew the captain, and just liked to make blowhards wait.

A double whistle blew from within the fort, and a voice called down from the wall, "Pass the *Planter*."

"Guess they like you after all, Captain Relyea," Chisholm said, his grin finally back.

Robert barely allowed himself a smile. "We ain't out yet. Let's speed her up, but not all the way. Head her straight through the channel. Once we out past the fort, take her a little bit to port, like we going to supply the batteries on Sullivan's Island. I'll tell you when to break."

Chisholm rang the bells and pulled the lever to push the *Planter* forward, riding with the current and tide into the main channel between Fort Sumter and Fort Moultrie. The channel mouth was a mile across, but the unobstructed space was only 50 yards wide. The two forts, plus the batteries next to Moultrie, Bee and Beauregard, could fill the space with shot in a heartbeat.

Robert resisted the urge to wave farewell to the guards on Sumter. The glow from the east was rising fast, and a sharp eye could spot their deception.

"Take her farther into the channel; they got a set of four torpedoes off the tip of that point. Don't get too close."

Sumter was receding fast, her eastern walls glowing pink from the light of the coming sunrise. He took a breath. Almost half a mile of water lay between them and the fort now, though Sumter's guns could easily blast a shell a mile or more. One direct hit would be enough to finish the *Planter*.

Three quick booms echoed from within the harbor. Robert ran to the starboard side of the upper deck, to check on Sumter, which lay directly behind them. No puffs of smoke. The shots had come from farther inside the harbor, maybe from Charleston.

"They shooting at us?" Chisholm asked, his eyes wide.

"Not yet. Just signal guns. Someone figured out we ain't where we supposed to be. Ring four bells. Give me the glass!"

A signal flag quickly raised above Sumter, and moments later was matched on a pole across the harbor mouth on top of Fort Moultrie. The batteries on Sullivan's Island were raising theirs, too.

Robert jumped into the pilothouse and grabbed the wheel from Chisholm. "Go down and shove firewood into that boiler. Tell Alfred I need every ounce of steam he can throw out of them engines."

He pressed the throttles forward, sending the wheels churning as fast as they could move. Chisholm launched himself down the ladder and ran to the engine room. Turno raced up the other ladder.

"What you need me to do?"

Robert couldn't answer for a second, as he turned the wheel hard, sending them straight out to sea, trying to remember where the last set of torpedoes lay in the channel. He hoped the masts of the Stone Fleet weren't hanging out here somewhere.

"Take the glass. Look at Battery Gregg. Tell me when her flag goes up."

Three more signal booms from the inner harbor.

"Flag's up."

Where would the first shots come from? Probably Sumter. They'd seen the *Planter* and maybe wondered why. The other forts wouldn't know what to expect and would be looking for ships approaching and attacking, instead of a ship heading out to sea. They'd get the message by signal flags soon, but it wasn't fast like a telegraph. There wasn't a simple signal for: *Shoot our own ship, she's an escapee.* But Sumter had a clear view to the city, and she'd send messages as fast as men could wave flags. Captain Relyea was probably standing at the empty dock in Charleston, jumping mad or about to hang himself.

"Can't he make this thing go any faster? "Robert asked.

"I ain't never seen her go this fast, ever."

"We'll see if it's fast enough."

A different boom, this one a lot closer. The hair prickled on Robert's scalp.

"What do you see?" Robert demanded.

"Smoke outta Sumter. Holy Jesus, here it comes."

A shell whistled overhead and exploded into the water fifty yards off to port.

Robert nudged the wheel, sending them to starboard. Then shifted again the opposite way. He needed to put distance between them and the fort, but moving in a straight line meant certain death.

Alston and Jackson ran out onto the front deck, and peered back towards the fort.

"Another one," Turno said, his face grim.

This time the shell came up short, but close enough to shower Alston and Jackson with water. Robert jammed the throttle lever as far forward as it would go, knowing if he pushed the engines too hard, they'd overload, or else the paddles might fly apart. She could go ten knots on flat water, but they were heading into deeper seas. He just needed a few more minutes, and he needed the gunners on Sullivan's Island to be slow to waken. The *Planter* could run almost a thousand feet a minute, especially loaded as lightly as she was right now.

He jammed the wheel hard to the right, knocking Alston and Jackson off their feet again.

"Get off the deck, you idiots!" he yelled.

Another twist of the wheel, as two more shells hit the water behind them and shoved the *Planter* forward, dipping her nose into the waves.

"Get below and start Morrison and Jackson on the pumps. You and Alston be ready with buckets of water and fire blankets, in case we take a hit."

"Yessir," Turno barked and slid down to the deck.

Robert looked over both shoulders. They needed to follow a thin line that led straight out to sea, equidistant from Battery Wagner and the Sullivan's Island batteries. The batteries still weren't firing, but once they noticed Sumter's attack and they'd catch on. The crossing fire between the forts would be deadly.

One minute. Three more shells from Sumter landed behind them, but not quite so close. Enough to splash her, but not to push her.

The sun popped over the horizon, hot and yellow. Blinding. The gunners would be shooting into the sun. For the few minutes the sun lay on the horizon, they'd have a hard time judging the success of their shots, especially from Battery Wagner. Robert steered the *Planter* right for the sunrise, for a chance at a new day like none of them had ever seen before.

CHAPTER 13

A splash off the port side caught his eye. But instead of erupting into a huge column of spray, the splash was followed by five, six, seven more splashes, as the cannon ball skipped across the waves, finally burying itself in the brine, twenty yards away. The gunners at Battery Beauregard on Sullivan's Island had changed tactics. They didn't have to be as accurate if they could just bounce their shots off the surface of water, like a flat stone thrown by a child. Except this stone would easily cave in the hull of the *Planter*.

The engine was running at her outer limits. A bell sounded from the engine room, warning Robert. She couldn't take it much longer.

He steered south, not as worried about Battery Wagner anymore, as its gunners faced the glare of the sun. Just a little more distance between the Sullivan's Island batteries, and they'd be safe.

Turno joined him in the pilothouse. "Alfred says you got to let up."

"We's almost there. Tell me what you see behind us."

Turno slid out to the edge of the observation deck and looked behind them. "Another skipper. Two more. Three more."

Robert waited. How would it feel to be smashed to bits? They'd come all this way. How could God let them come this far and then drown his children?

"Short. Even shorter this time. Our wake messin' with the

skips. One more... Not even close." Turno looked like he couldn't believe it. They were still alive.

Time to give the engines a rest. Robert dialed back the throttle two pegs. In a few more minutes, they'd be two full miles from shore. Robert finally took a breath.

The gunners at the forts gave a few last half-hearted attempts, then stopped wasting their powder.

Robert and Turno looked at each other, smiles slowly spreading across their faces.

"I think we did it," Robert said.

"Damn straight. Yes, we did!" Turno grabbed the rail and howled at the sky.

Robert grabbed Captain Relyea's hat and flung it out into the waves. Below, the deck sprang to life, as Alston skipped up to the prow and stood looking out into the wind. Jackson, Johnny, and Chisholm emerged from the engine room, whooping and hollering. Even Alfred came out on deck, followed by Morrison, Hannah, Mary, Lila, and the children.

"Look at that sky!" Robert shouted above the sound of the wind and the waves and the paddles. "Look at them waves. Look at yo'selves. No one ever seen you like this before."

Hannah held a squirming Junior in her arms and looked proudly up at her man. Lizzie stood next to them—her face full of sunshine, caught up in the joy of the crowd. *His* family. Not Kingman's anymore. Not belonging to anyone but themselves

White sails on the horizon froze Robert's smile. "Hey!" he shouted down. "Back to stations! Alston and Morrison, clean every mess. Johnny and Jackson, keep that firewood coming. Ladies and babies, go back into the store room. Chisholm and Turno, get up here." They'd had their minute of celebration and now it was back into the dragon's teeth.

The stars and bars still flapped from the flagpole over the pilot house.

"Chisholm, get that flag down. Who's got a white flag? We need to run a white flag up that pole before the Yankees blow us out of the water."

The blockading ships, some in full sail, others steaming under columns of smoke, were heading straight for them. They either thought the *Planter* was the head of an attack or a blockade runner. Either option meant shelling would start as soon as they were in range.

Chisholm came to the pilothouse with the Confederate flag from the rear pole. "I don't have a white flag."

"What?"

"No white flag. I don't think we brought one."

Turno's eyes turned cold. "We'd better find one."

"Look in the captain's cabin," Robert said. "Find a sheet, a blanket, something, and get it up on that damn pole."

Leading the Yanks was a three-masted clipper, coming fast, all sails in bloom. Four gun ports on each side stood wide open and ready. Robert raised the glass—it was the *Onward*. He'd heard her name mentioned by blockade runners—she'd captured the *Emily St. Pierre* in March, and drove the schooner *Sarah* aground at Bull's Bay, just two weeks ago. Under full sail, she'd be faster than the *Planter* and had a lot more guns.

Robert slowed her to a gentle stroll, rocking the ship in her own wake. The *Onward* sped closer.

"Is that flag up?" he yelled. Smith and Relyea would crow with vengeful satisfaction if he brought the *Planter* all the way out here and got sunk by the Union. He imagined all of Charleston lined up along the battery—Kingman, Mr. Henry, even Elizabeth Jane—laughing at the foolish niggers who thought they could get away.

The *Onward* turned broadside to the *Planter*, preparing to fire.

"Turno! Get everyone out on deck and wave every white sheet and baby blanket you can find. Everyone out on deck now! Alston, toss down everything you can find."

Two more ships closed in on either side, off the *Planter's* shoulders, to finish the job if necessary. Robert twisted the wheel, to present the *Planter* broadside to the *Onward*, in submission.

"Chisholm, get up here!"

Chisholm dropped the white dish towel he'd been waving and scrambled up to the pilothouse. "Take the wheel. Keep her steady," Robert commanded.

The *Onward* glided closer. Robert could see the figurehead clearly—a robed Goddess of Liberty, her right hand outstretched. Union sailors stood along the rail, mystified by the strange white-flag-waving spectacle of the *Planter*. Robert, still in Captain Relyea's uniform, strode to the edge of the promenade deck and waved over at the sailing vessel, the two decks nearly even with each other.

He finally heard magic words, "hold your fire" from the *Onward's* master of the deck. How long would they hold it?

A naval officer in blue coat and gold braids lowered his glass and shouted, "State your business, or we'll blow you straight to hell."

"We've come out from Charleston, sir. To join the Union fleet."

*****

In the new daylight, his men stood proudly at attention. Hard to say what the Union sailors would see—a bunch of Negroes in mismatched clothing, dirty from heaving firewood, exhausted from being up all night. Or strong men, brave enough to risk death for freedom. Alfred rubbed his scruffy beard, blinking hard in the sun, as if coming out of years living in a cave. Turno looked fierce, his brow furrowed, his hand pressed against his pocket, probably on his knife, ready for one last fight. Jackson had swiped a grey coat from Smith's wardrobe, but it looked out of place against his patched britches. Chisholm couldn't stop smiling—Robert never thought he was good for much besides making them laugh, but last night he stood tall when it counted. Morrison bumped Alston down to the end of the line, even though he wasn't properly part of the crew. Robert had to figure how to properly thank the *Etiwan*'s steward—without him, the women and children would be sitting in Charleston, trying to figure out how to get by without their men. And it turned out they didn't need to worry about Alston after all. The boy never missed a step last night, though he looked like he was about to fall asleep on his feet right now.

Hannah, Mary, and Lila stood just as proudly, outside the door to the store room, keeping a tight grip on the children. Tales were told in Charleston of escaped slaves being sold off, of children being taken to serve in houses up North, servants in name, slaves in practice. There were even stories about Yankees eating Negro children. Who knew what was true anymore?

What Robert really wanted was to grab Hannah and hold her tight, and stand with her and the children when the Union sailors boarded—to say, "This is my wife. These are my children. We are a family and belong to each other and no one else." But the only thing that was going to keep them all free and together was him making sure everyone stayed calm and in line. There would be time for holding Hannah later.

The crew had already tied the *Planter* fast to the *Onward*, and the two ships bobbed in the sea, linked by a dozen long lines. The *Onward* was still suspicious and didn't want to get too close. Maybe they worried this was a booby trap, and once they came alongside, the Rebels would blow up the *Planter* and take the *Onward* down with her, a fitting revenge for all the damage the *Onward* had done to the Southern cause.

A skiff was sent with four advance men, tough marines. They scrambled on board, guns strapped to their backs and chests—two took positions on the rail, and the other two quickly searched the ship, making certain no one else lurked on board.

The whole time, sharpshooters stood in the rigging of the *Onward*, sights trained on Robert and the crew, keeping a close eye on Turno and Johnny, since they were bigger than any of the marines.

Now, another boat was brought aside, this one full of

officers. The captain was tall and straight as a rod, with a wisp of reddish beard on his chin. Couldn't be more than a few years older than Robert himself. As soon as the captain was on board, Robert flashed a look to the crew, and they all stood a little straighter, eyes out front. Proud men.

The captain walked straight over to Robert. Robert saluted, as he'd seen men do for General Ripley.

The man smiled, maybe surprised at the formality of it all. "I am Captain Nickels of the *U.S.S. Onward.* Are you in charge here?"

"Yessuh. I's the pilot, Robert Smalls, sir. Now in command of this ship. I have the honor to present the *Planter* to you and the United States Navy. The *Planter* used to be the flagship for General Ripley. Besides her own two guns, we brung four cannon which was s'posed to be delivered to Fort Ripley this morning. We thought they might be of some service to Uncle Abe."

One of the *Onward's* men gave a snort. He was a proud looking fellow with a beak of a nose. Good for snorting. The man off the other shoulder of Nickels was looking around, giving the *Planter* a quick assessment. He had the leather face of a man at sea for most of his life. From his expression, he liked what he was seeing.

"Well," said Nickels, "on behalf of 'Uncle Abe' and the United States Navy, I would like to say thank you, Mr. Smalls."

It was everything Robert could do to keep his eyes on Nickels and not turn to look at the rest of his men. Never in his life had he been called "Mister" by a white man. None of them had even heard of such a thing, other than in jokes.

"You's welcome. We brung more besides. We got charts and maps, we know the signals, we helped lay the torpedoes and obstructions in the harbor. All these men is hard workers. I been sailing this harbor and these marshes since I was twelve years old. I know plenty about every inch of this coast, suh."

Nickels nodded, and Robert hoped that was a sign of him being impressed. He'd tried to think of every possible gift he could use to bargain for their freedom. None of them wanted to be shipped off to a labor camp somewhere. Who knew what could happen. "I think Commodore DuPont will be extremely interested in speaking with you, Mr. Smalls."

"I'd be real interested in talking with him, too, suh. But we got to take care of our women and chi'ren. They's tired and hungry."

Nickels seemed to notice the families for the first time. "Of course. We'll see that they're taken care of. McPherson, see that the contraband women and children receive what they require." A junior officer acknowledged Nickels with a "Yes, Captain."

Robert knew the word *contraband*, and it prickled his scalp. Stolen goods. Is that how they'd be treated—like stolen bales of cotton or casks of rum? Finders, keepers? Resold to help recover costs? Or as a prize bounty to be paid to the crew of the *Onward*?

"We will take the ship to Port Royal, immediately," Nickels said. "On arrival, we'll craft a plan for you and your families, Mr. Smalls. Final determination of this matter will belong to men of higher rank than me. You say you've piloted this ship up and down the coast?"

Going to Port Royal? Maybe home to Beaufort. Maybe his mother was there. Who knew what had survived the Yankee onslaught? If she was there, he would find her. Then his family would truly be complete. "Yessir. I growed up in Beaufort, sailing soon's I could walk. I've taken boats up and down every creek between here and there."

"Then you'll stay on board with Chief Packer here, and show us what you know. We'll take half your crew on board the *Onward*, and the other half can remain on board the *Planter*. Packer, arrange for a crew to assist you in the transit back to Port Royal."

"Aye, Captain." Packer, the old salt with the appraising eye, walked to the rail to holler for the men he needed.

At least Robert didn't have to leave the *Planter* quite yet. She'd brought him a long way. He'd helmed countless ships and boats, but none had ever meant as much to him as the *Planter*.

"One more thing, sir?" Robert said.

"What is it?"

"With your permission, my men would like to make a change to the ship."

Nickels agreed to the request, and in a few short minutes, Turno and Chisholm pulled the line on the flagpole and raised the stars and stripes high above the *Planter*, where it flapped happily in the breeze, a sign that Robert and his crew had completed the first step of their journey.

PART II

CHAPTER 14

MAY 14, 1862

The commodore's quarters in the *Wabash* were as fine as any plantation house parlor, with a plush Persian rug, polished mahogany paneling, and gleaming brass fixtures. Commodore DuPont, in his jacket with gold bars on the sleeves, rose to his feet when Robert entered. The commodore was so tall his head almost scraped the ceiling, and he towered over Robert. There weren't many times Robert had ever shaken the hand of a white man, and now here was one of the highest ranking men in the whole United States Navy, sticking his hand out and calling him "Mr. Smalls." The whole day felt like a bizarre half-awake dream. It didn't help that they'd spent all of yesterday sailing to Port Royal and then huddled together for a sleepless night, wondering what was going to become of them.

"Please, have a seat," offered the commodore. Half a dozen other officers were already seated in chairs arranged against the bulkhead walls, and a clerk sat at a desk, pen at the ready. Everyone waited for DuPont, who looked at Robert with great curiosity, his eyes bright under bushy brows. "I am told you delivered quite a gift to us yesterday, in the form of General Ripley's flagship."

"Yessuh." Robert swallowed hard. Would they see what he'd done as an act of bravery, or brand him as a thief?

"Tell us what happened."

That was the first time Robert told the story, still so fresh it seemed strange to be telling it. What would happen when he got to the moment they were at now? But Robert told it the best he could, and the commodore never took his eyes off him.

When he got to the part in the story where they met the *Onward*, he kept going, telling them about the forts in Charleston Harbor, where the guns were placed, the locations of torpedoes, how many men were stationed at each fort, the signals. He told them about Wappoo Cut and Fort Pemberton, and the nearly empty battery at the mouth of Stono Creek. He emptied his memory dry, hoping to share enough useful information to bargain for their freedom. The clerk at the commodore's elbow scratched notes with a pen, sometimes raising a finger for Robert to pause to let him catch up.

When Robert finished, DuPont leaned back heavily in his chair, stuck his pipe under his mustache, and puffed a cloud of smoke around himself. "That may be the most extraordinary story I have ever heard."

"Thank you, suh. Not quite so hard to tell it as to live it."

DuPont laughed dryly. "I am certain you will tell it a thousand more times before you are through. Your information about the Stono is highly interesting. A skeleton crew is all that's left?"

"The guns from that fort is sittin' on the deck of the *Planter* right this minute, suh."

DuPont puffed out another cloud, scenting the cabin with rich Carolina leaf. "Everything you've brought us is... well, quite extraordinary. The charts, the code book, the guns, the ship. The information."

Robert wondered whether people were going to be included on that list of useful items. Items to be used or discarded.

"It's a spark, you see. Sparks are important in a war, to set people's imaginations on fire. You, Mr. Smalls, have the potential to bring a little light into this conflict. You are not what people think of when they think of a Negro. But maybe we can change that."

"I'll take him to General Benham's office, sir," said DuPont's chief assistant, a slim young lieutenant in a crisp uniform.

"Nordhoff is already there, hoping to talk to Mr. Smalls before the *Atlantic* steams out."

"It's as if you read my mind, Lieutenant Maxwell."

"Suh?" Robert had no idea what was going on.

"General Benham will be most interested in your information," explained Commodore DuPont. "Tell him exactly what you've told me. And Charles Nordhoff is a reporter. They're a bit like rats, but sometimes they can be useful. The ones stuck here are jealous of their fellows who have been reporting the action from New Orleans. They're practically ready to hang themselves with boredom. They need a surprise. Don't worry, they may be hungry, but Lieutenant Maxwell will ensure they don't bite."

"What about my peoples, suh? What you gon' do with us and our chi'ren?" Last night he'd wondered if they could sneak ashore and fade away. But they wouldn't last long in the swamps with the children. Maybe he and Hannah could buy passage north on a passenger ship, but he wouldn't have enough money to pay for the crew. He couldn't just leave them stranded. And where should they go? Jackson had family in Philly, but that was a thin thread. Robert and Hannah didn't know a soul outside of the Carolinas.

"I've already sent the families ahead to General Stevens in Beaufort, sir," Maxwell said. "The *Planter's* crew are still aboard the *Onward*."

"You what?" Robert tried to conceal his panic. He'd thought they were all waiting just a few slips down. Every risk he'd taken had been to keep the families together, and now they'd grabbed them. It couldn't have been done without guns pointed right at Turno, or at Hannah, for that matter. "No one said nothin' 'bout takin' my wife and chi'ren." He tried to calm himself. Panic was a sign of weakness.

"I promise they are absolutely safe," Commodore DuPont reassured him. He had a peaceful way about him, the calm of a man who had been under fire from guns and hurricanes and the heat of the public eye. And he could press that calm down on you, if he wanted. That's what the best ship's captains did—give a stillness to the crew so they could function, even as pirates fired cannon or waves threatened to capsize the ship.

"We didn't have the proper food or berths for them here. I assumed that Beaufort would be more suitable," Maxwell explained.

"I been livin' under the thumb of a man 'bout to take my family my whole life," Robert explained. "You can't just... Please, suh. None of us knows what to think about you. The women and chi'ren been told the Yankees like to take them and sell them off to Cuba, or worse."

"None of us have any such intentions," said the commodore. "You have done us a great service, Mr. Smalls. I will do everything in my power to see the United States Navy and government show proper appreciation to you and your people. Once you speak with General Benham, Lieutenant Maxwell will take you to your family, along with all of your men."

What Robert wanted was to grab a gun off one of the guards and force them to take him to Hannah and the children right this minute. But instead, he just said, "Thank you, suh."

"And I will personally write to Senator Grimes in Washington and insist that you are awarded a prize fee for the *Planter*." The commodore nodded at the clerk, who took out a fresh piece of paper for the letter, as if he was prepared for it to be dictated any second.

Prize money? Robert almost slipped out of his chair. In times of war, victorious naval captains and crews were usually awarded a portion of the value of the captured ship. None of his crew would have dreamed of getting prize money for the *Planter*.

"And you can continue to be of service, if that's what you choose," the commodore continued, looking at him a bit hopefully.

"Service, suh?" Back in Charleston, the white folks often called their slaves "servants." He had no intention of being anyone's servant, ever again.

"Talk to the reporters. Help us with our efforts against the rebels. An experienced guide to these waters is exceedingly rare. I'm not sure how we'll use the *Planter*, but you already have a crew who know how to work her. Would you be willing to sail for us? Would your men be willing to continue working on the *Planter*?"

Robert liked that word: *willing*. As if he had a choice.

"I knows this coast better'n any man in Charleston or anywheres. I been sailing since I was twelve years old. I can help get yo' ships where they needs to go."

DuPont nodded, pleased. "Expect us to call on you. Get settled with your families today. General Stevens will find space for you, somehow. Beaufort was your home, yes?"

"I was born there. My mother might still be there, I don' know what happened to her. Ain't heard one word since November."

"I hope you find her. I would ask, as you search, that you don't stray too far. There will be many men, generals and captains alike, who will want to hear from you."

"Yessuh." If there was ever a moment when it was important to be recognized as useful, this was it.

DuPont rose and extended his hand one more time. "It's always a pleasure to meet another man of the sea, Mr. Smalls."

*****

General Benham made Robert tell him about the fort at the Stono Inlet three times, pressing for every small detail. By the third time, the general's face was flushed and he was pacing around his office, his leg jiggling with excitement. He was approaching middle-age, with the start of jowls and wings of hair jutting out from the edge of a wide, bare forehead—not the sort of man Robert would expect to seem so gleeful. "They don't think we have the nuts to go through by land. Wait until General Hunter hears about this. Lieutenant, where is the general?" he asked Maxwell.

"At one of the plantations, sir. Taking his wife on a tour."

General Benham turned back to Robert. "This is what we've been looking for. Every star on a man's shoulder seems to multiply the number of enemy troops he estimates are lying in wait. Where are you going to put him, Maxwell? I need this man."

"We'll keep good track of him, sir. Right now, Nordhoff is waiting." Lieutenant Maxwell hadn't let Benham's excitement get to him, and Robert wondered if the young officer consciously mirrored the calm of Commodore DuPont.

"Fine. But Mr. Smalls, I will want to see you again. Think of any detail that might tell us more about the troops on James Island. With your help, we might find a way to get you back to Charleston."

*****

Another office, another retelling of the story. This time Charles Nordhoff scribbled notes as fast as he could write, as they sat in a shipping clerk's office that Lieutenant Maxwell appropriated for them right on the Port Royal harbor. It was filled with careful stacks of papers in a hundred different filing slots, labeled with names of outgoing ships and docking slips. Nordhoff was a burly man with small spectacles that made him appear deadly serious. He spoke with a touch of a German accent, though it wasn't nearly as heavy as on the German sailors Robert had met in Charleston. "When I was a young man, not that long ago, I was also a sailor, so I know what it is you have done," Nordhoff said, casting an appraising look at Robert. "It is not so easy, this escape of yours. Some will doubt it."

"We done it. Go out and look at the *Planter*. Look at my men. Don't matter how we done it, or whether folks believe us." What Robert wanted more than anything was to find Hannah and the children. Every hour spent talking to these white folks meant another hour that he didn't know where they were. Back in Charleston, even if he was working, he could always conjure an image in his mind of where he thought they were. But now it was impossible.

Nordhoff looked up and pointed his pen at Robert. "I will tell you why it matters, Mr. Smalls. The North has been sold a lie about slaves, a lie they choose to believe. That you are weak, lazy, and dangerous. Four million of you. Only the truth will wipe away this lie, but the truth is easily hidden. When mothers bury their sons, they need to know the truth of why. I have seen for myself, the black men and women and children on these plantations. But we need a story to grab their imagination. You have that story. I will write it, and my readers will believe. I am good at what I do. You will see. No one wants to read about the horrible boredom of war. Battles are short, marches and sieges are long, and tedious. They want heroes. And surprises. They will certainly be surprised to discover a black hero."

"I's just a sailor, tryin' to help my family."

"Not anymore. Once they read my story, you will be much more."

*****

Beaufort wasn't what he remembered. The same buildings were still there—the fine summer houses for the planters and the shops along Bay Street. But soldiers in Union blue were everywhere, working, parading, standing guard on every corner. Gunboats, launches, tugs, and supply boats jammed the wharves full. On the docks, black workers rolled barrels and toted crates, but there was no boss and no crack of the whip. Clumps of escaped slaves lolled in the shade of live oaks, looking dirty and thin.

Robert followed Lieutenant Maxwell down Bay Street to John Joyner Smith's house, a white mansion with six columns supporting double porches meant to catch the sea breeze. Instead of fine ladies in hoop dresses hiding from the sun and drinking lemonade, the porches now held Union officers, issuing orders and taking notes, handling the business of a standing army and a flood of escaped slaves.

The corporal at the door directed them inside. It felt strange to come and go through the front door, instead of coming in through the back. Black folk in Beaufort never went through front doors.

In an almost barren parlor that was now an office with half a dozen mismatched desks, a captain was concentrating hard on the letter he was writing. The place smelled of cigar smoke and sweaty wool uniforms.

"Lusk," called Maxwell, "doing some actual work, or writing love letters?"

The serious young captain flushed beneath his scraggly beard. "I was indeed writing to Mary, about the extraordinary events. This must be Mr. Smalls."

"How do, suh." Robert tried to be patient. But he needed to find Hannah. Now.

"You must be looking for your family," said Lusk, as he carefully folded the letter he'd been writing.

"Yessuh."

"He hides his anxiousness well," said Maxwell. "But it's obvious they haven't left his thoughts all day. Promise me you've put them somewhere good. The commodore and general have a personal interest in their comfort and safety."

Lusk shrugged his narrow shoulders. "The town is overrun with thousands of contraband, not to mention all our troops. There's barely room to fit another man, let alone a group of fifteen Negroes."

"Where are they?" Maxwell demanded.

"They're fine. I'll show you myself."

The dozen blocks down King Street were the longest Robert had ever walked. Some of the houses were boarded up, some full of soldiers, some now hospitals, giving off the foul odor of rotting limbs and death. They walked past the Beaufort Baptist Church, with its thin white steeple pointing a finger straight up at God. He'd spent many long Sundays there as a child. He'd been born and raised just one street over, in the McKee House on Prince Street. He could go reminisce there another day. Right now all that mattered was finding Hannah and the children.

Lusk led them straight to Dr. Berners Barnwell Sams House, one of the biggest and most solid mansions in all of Beaufort. Its red brick walls and smooth concrete columns made it seem squatter and more substantial that most of the planter's houses in Beaufort, as if they'd designed it to be the last one standing, no matter what might come.

"They here?" Robert asked.

"Out back," Captain Rusk answered. "We tossed out a few pockets of other contrabands, to make room. It wasn't easy to find even a few square feet, but at least we've got you a roof."

They walked past the cook house, past the smithy and barn, to the mansion's slumping slave quarters, low wood buildings that needed a fresh coat of whitewash and new siding. Out on the dusty ground, Junior stood smacking a stick against a stump. Lizzie was playing a clapping game with Donna, Turno's daughter. Lizzie saw Robert and smiled as wide as he'd ever seen her. "Daddy! We's playin' nice, just like mama said."

He picked up both his children in his arms, just to feel them. They squirmed and protested and he set them back down to their spots in the sun. Hannah was already out the door, with Chisholm and Mary not far behind her.

"They found us a palace, Robert," Chisholm called. "We's just stayin' here until they get it ready for us."

Hannah came and pressed herself against him. "I was gettin' worried."

He savored the warmth of her flesh beneath her dress, the life that was as precious to him as his own. For an instant, he just pulled her close and forgot about the soldiers and crew all around them and held her. He felt his knees start to shake, as all the tension of the last two days threatened to burst out of him. Not yet. He took a deep breath, and another, and finally loosed his hold on Hannah. "They treat me fine. You all right?"

"We will be. Turno and the others left to find some food."

She took Robert inside the rickety cabin. They had two rooms for the fifteen of them. Robert and Hannah hadn't lived in slave quarters since they were children, and never in anything as cramped as this. He could tell Hannah seethed at the thought of staying in this place, and he couldn't blame her. They'd just delivered an entire ship to the Union Navy. They'd be better off sleeping on the *Planter*. But he tamped down his frustration. He needed them to keep helping them, even when a thousand other outstretched hands were begging for aid.

Captain Lusk stood smiling, arms crossed, proud of his accomplishment. Lieutenant Maxwell looked skeptical. "This is it?" he asked.

"It wasn't easy finding this. They're slaves," Lusk answered. "They're used to far worse. They've got a floor and a roof, which is better than half our soldiers."

Hannah spoke, her voice low and steady. "We ain't slaves no more. Not ever again."

Lusk didn't seem to appreciate the correction.

Robert knew that this situation couldn't last, but at least it was a start. "Thanks, Captain Lusk. We's glad to have a place to sleep tonight. This will do fine, 'til we find something with a bit more leg room."

"Can you at least have someone get them some blankets, Lusk?" asked Maxwell.

"The missionaries should arrive any minute. They've heard of the whole episode." Lusk had given all the help that he intended to give. He turned to go and waited for Maxwell to join him.

But Maxwell wasn't quite ready. "Commodore DuPont will do more to help you," he said earnestly to Robert and Hannah. "I will send someone back with supplies, as soon as I can. Whatever you do, don't leave without sending word as to where you're going."

"I'll let you know, suh," Robert promised. "Tell the

commodore I thank him. And you tell him we countin' on him to do right by us."

*****

Robert stood on Laurens Street in front of the Sams House trying to make a plan. Hannah and the women were busy solving the puzzle of cramming their party into two small rooms and filling hungry bellies with the meager supplies that the other men had bought. Alfred said the general store on Bay Street wouldn't even let them in the door. And the sutler wagons were run by the lowest kind of crooks he'd ever seen.

Right this second, it was time to answer the question that had plagued him every day for the past six months: Where was his mother?

Since the white folks skedaddled out of Beaufort, he hadn't heard a single word. Black folk, and the information they carried, moved in only one direction—out of Charleston, to the Union lines. Every time he saw Mrs. McKee, she practically wept with worry for her faithful servant. And Mama Lydia had been faithful, for more than sixty years. Never spoke a bad word about any of the McKees. Raised their children. Cooked their meals, cleaned their house, did everything she was ever asked. Except one.

More than sixty years a slave, and then one day she took her chance. That's what he hoped anyway. She could have been snatched by rebel soldiers. There was a time, before the Union army came ashore, when the town had no law. Just a few thousand slaves, suddenly free, ready for the biggest celebration you can imagine. Not a safe place for an old woman, though Mama Lydia had a way about her that could reduce even the most hulking brute to a plaintive little boy.

And then the soldiers arrived, with their rough ways and strange diseases. How did she feed herself? Where did she go? Everyone she knew lived in Beaufort or Charleston.

He'd have to search the entire town. He would walk down to Bay Street and start asking. Cover one street at a time, covering

127

the whole grid. Though he was grown now, people would still remember Lydia Polite's boy, the one who liked to sail. Or, they'd remember that he was the one who looked so much like Henry McKee.

He was tempted to visit the McKee house on Prince Street, but instead he turned onto Pinckney Street. The breeze carried the scent of magnolia blossoms, mixed with the salt from the marshes. He'd lived in Charleston for half his life, but Beaufort still smelled like home.

An ambulance wagon stood with its rear flaps wide open and its tailgate down, and two men carried a wounded soldier up the front steps of the Edward Means House, a fine red brick mansion, with careful square corners on its wraparound porches and narrow pillars. Its lush gardens now stood ragged and untended in the strong May sunshine. The men stepped carefully up the front steps, around a small black woman sitting on the stairs. If this war went on much longer, they'd have to keep turning these grand old houses into hospitals, until there were none left. What would the planters think of all the Union blood staining their polished floors?

The woman stood and looked at him, arms crossed, eye brows arched.

"Robert," she said in an annoyed voice. "What took you so long?"

"Mama?"

He ran to her and wrapped her in his arms. She was a bird of a woman, more compact with each passing year. Her skin was darker than his, just one generation from Africa. She pushed him away and took a good look at him.

"You grown up the rest of the way now. I heard what you done."

She'd always been lively, but now she had a whole new brightness to her. She was never easy on him as a child, and the look of pride on her face now made all the risks they'd taken seem worthwhile.

"You heard 'bout that, huh?"

128

She smiled. "Beaufort ain't talked 'bout much else all day long, black or white. You done got everyone's attention, no doubt about that. Didn't I warn you to keep your head down?"

"Yes, ma'am."

"Well, I'm glad you had the gumption to ignore that advice," she said with a low chuckle.

"What you doin' here, Mama? You safe? You got food? A place to sleep?"

She shook her head and clucked at him. "I been takin' care of myself and many more since Thomas Jefferson was president. I still be doin' the same, just right here. I help cleans and takes care of the soldiers, poor boys. They's all shot to bits. The army gives me food to eat, and I sleeps in the corner."

"They got you sleepin' on the floor?"

"Ain't hardly 'nough beds for these boys. I be fine. This war won't last forever."

She was right about that, but he wasn't so sure that the end of the war would end up in their favor. He wished he had her confidence.

"But you done it. Made yourself free."

"We quite a pair, huh?"

CHAPTER 15

The next morning, Robert followed Turno, Jackson, Alston, and Alfred to the sutlers' wagons parked behind the stores on Bay Street. They left Johnny and Morrison at the Sams' slave quarters to guard the families. Chisholm and Mary had found old friends in the night, old friends with a jug of homebrew. They'd come back reeking so strongly of liquor that Hannah and Lila wouldn't even let them in the cabins, but sent them to sleep it off under the rhododendron bushes.

The first wagon already had a line of soldiers waiting to spend their pay on any bit of luxury they could find: oranges, lemons, candy, cakes, pies. Even some books. Pots and pans. Canned meat and vegetables. A few contraband hovered around the edges, but there was never room to squeeze to the front. Alfred just shook his head, and they walked over to a tattered wagon that didn't have nearly the selection or sense of order. The soldiers here appeared down on their luck, and the items for sale all looked like they'd had hard journeys.

An old field hand approached the proprietor, a grey-skinned man whose snaggle-toothed mouth looked like it had never even tried a smile. "Suh?" asked the old farmer, "How much dollars I gots to pay fo' one them fryin' pans?"

"This pan right here?" Snaggle-tooth held up a cast-iron fry pan with a skim of rust on it "Well this would be five dollars. Think you got five dollars, boy?"

The old man pulled some coins from his pocket and looked at them, uncertain.

"Why, yes, that one right there. That shiny silver one, you give me that, and I give you this frying pan. And I give you a bit of this chewy candy to take back to your pickaninnies." The sutler reached forward eagerly to pluck the coin from the old man's palm.

Robert put a hand on the old man's arm, pulling it out of reach of the trader. "That's a ten-dollar coin, old man. You give him this, he s'posed to give you back five dollar."

The old man looked back and forth between Robert and the sutler, confused. "That so?"

"My mistake," the sutler growled. "I meant to say that this frying pan is seven dollars."

"What he say?" the old man asked Robert.

"He testin' to see how much you want this pan, and how much you know how to count," Robert explained.

"I knows how to count. I just don't know so much how to figure. All these coins looks the same to me." The old farmer's skin was burned to black leather from a lifetime in the fields, and most of his teeth were long gone.

"How bad you want that pan?" asked Robert.

"Cotton agents stripped just 'bout everything from the plantation. Even the pots and dishes. Mooma say she need somethin' to use to cook for us."

Robert took the man's coin and handed it to the sutler. "He'll take the pan. For five dollars."

The sutler handed the old man the pan and three one-dollar coins. "The price went up to seven dollars. Thanks to short fella here."

"The price was five dollars," Robert insisted. Turno and the rest of the crew stepped forward. The sutler didn't even flinch.

"You must be new to town. General Stevens values order. Especially from Negroes. I'm sure his soldiers would be happy to maintain order right at this very spot, if things get out of hand." His face looked like a snake about to bite. "Who's next?"

Alfred dragged Robert and Turno away from the wagon,

into the shade of an oak. "Don't do it," he counseled.

"Cheating him in broad daylight," Turno seethed. "Maybe I can knock a few of those teeth out and see if he learns to deal straight."

"We got to feed your little young 'uns," said Alfred. "If we roust this sutler, none of the rest will sell to us. And I'm sure the general's soldiers be happy to send to you a cell, but only after they take turns beating on your faces."

Robert looked back at the ragtag little market. The black folks waiting patiently in line couldn't make more than a few dollars a week digging ditches or unloading ships, but they all needed to eat. No one escaped with more than the clothes on his back. He and Hannah had brought a fortune with them compared to these folks, but even they would have to be careful.

"Sutler didn't have to cheat the old man. Coulda made plenty without it," Robert said.

"He don't care," Jackson said. "We ain't no more than rats to him."

"Where else they gon' go?" reminded Alfred.

"That the magic question, ain't it?" said Robert, an idea slowly dawning on him.

"I ain't sure I like that look," grumbled Turno.

*****

It took three days of scouting before Robert finally discovered a spot that might work for his plan. And even then, it might not come without a fight.

Early in the morning, while most of the town was still half asleep, Robert led the entire crew down to the far western end of Bay Street, past the main businesses and sutler's tents, to a two-story wood-framed store that sat boarded up, paint peeling, listing to one side. Probably wouldn't make it through the next hurricane. He wondered whether the bunch of them might be able to just give a strong breath and blow it over.

But raggedy as it might be, Robert wanted this building.

At Robert's nod, Johnny ripped the boards off the back door with his bare hands. Robert banged the door open and stepped into the gloom of the store. Warm yellow light shone through gaps in the siding, casting rays of morning through the dusty air. Men and women lay scattered across the floor on piles of rags and filthy blankets—squatters. A dozen sleepy faces looked up at him.

Turno coughed and swore at the stench. "You sure you don't want us to find you an outhouse for this, Robert? Might smell better."

An ebony-skinned man rose to his feet. "What you want?" His eyes were bloodshot and his teeth were so crooked and mismatched, it was like they were from a dozen different mouths. He held a broken chair leg in his hand, ready to defend his claim on this place.

"I want this store," Robert said, firmly.

"Cain't have it. We's here. Go find yo' own place." He looked like he'd been strong once upon a time, a field hand, but lack of work and food had sapped him. He was a good half a foot taller than Robert, but not in the same league as Turno and Johnny. His companions began to assemble behind him, and more faces poked around the stairs coming down from the second floor.

"This is the place for what I aim to do. It'll help everyone. Even you and yours. You'll see."

The man hacked up a gob of mucus and spit it at Robert's feet. "The devil take you, little man. Ain't no landlord here. You turn things ugly, you'll see plenty ugly."

"We see all the ugly we can stomach just in your face," chirped Chisholm.

The man remained focused on Robert. "The general don't like commotion on his streets. You make commotion, you find yo'sef behind bars and with the lash at yo' back."

The man might be right, but Robert was getting used to taking risks. "What your name?" Robert asked.

"Sampson."

"That a strong name. A good name. Come stand with me, Sampson." Robert moved to the wall, stepping over piles of rotten plaster and lath. The man followed nervously, and Robert leaned towards him. "There are two ways we can do this, Sampson. I know this ain't fair. There's a lot that ain't fair in this war and in this life. We got no claim to this place, no more than you. But I aim to take it. If we take the first path, I pay you some coin. I'll give you five dollars." Robert flashed a coin in his palm. "And I'll pay every other man in this place two dollars, to move on out. You all go find a tent in the missionary camps."

"What the second path?"

"You see those big men over there? They gon' throw you out through that door. Then the rest of my men gon' clean this building out of every one of your peoples. They gon' use yo' heads to open up every window and door. Get some light and air in this place."

Turno and Johnny gave their most ferocious glowers. Sampson shifted his feet nervously. "General Stevens..."

"The general need something from me. Him and Commodore DuPont both. You want to see which one of us they likes better, go ahead."

Robert flipped the coin up into the air and closed his fist around it.

"When?" asked Sampson.

"Now."

The man looked up at Turno and Johnny, and behind them at Alfred, Jackson, Chisholm, Morrison, and Alston. They all stood with their arms crossed, looking as intimidating as they possibly could. Chisholm belched a big belch. Alston struggled not to laugh. But Turno and Johnny were big and strong enough to end the discussion.

Robert placed the coin in Sampson's open palm.

*****

The crew and family of the *Planter* set upon the store like a swarm of bees trying to establish a new hive. Johnny and Jackson unboarded windows, and the rest of them threw every bit of broken junk into the weedy yard behind the building. Hannah and Lila didn't want a single vermin-infested rag left inside.

Upstairs they found two bedrooms, as trashed as the downstairs, smelling of mold and piss. The roof clearly leaked whenever it rained. But it all could be repaired.

Robert surveyed the upper floor. He and Hannah and the kids and Mama Lydia could stay in one room, and Turno, Lila, and their children would stay in the other. The rest of the crew and Mary could keep the two rooms at the Sams' slave quarters, and everyone would have space to breathe. Robert had been trading on the side in Charleston since he was a boy, now he could use his skills in an actual store.

"Hey, Robert. Someone down here for you," Jackson called up.

Robert carefully picked his way down the wobbly stairs. A large round white man, with a big round bald head, stood at the front door. He looked almost like a picture Robert had seen of a snowman, big white balls all piled up on each other. Yankees did strange things like that.

The man extended a soft, beefy hand. "Reverend Mansfield French. God bless you. You must be Robert Smalls."

"Yessuh." Robert shook the man's hand. The reverend sweated in the heat, but the oppressive humidity didn't fade the smile on his face.

"The whole town is abuzz with talk of what you accomplished with the ship in Charleston, Mr. Smalls. I see you've already put your industrious nature to work here in Beaufort. Do you have plans for business?"

"I might." Robert wondered what this man wanted from him.

"I've brought something that might be of use." The

Reverend gestured at two buckets filled with cakes of soap and scrub brushes. "If the outside is anything like the inside, you might need these."

"The inside is worse," Robert said. "Hannah!" She came to the door. "This is Reverend French. He come to lend us some tools."

She lit up at the sight of the buckets. "Thank you, suh. Can't do much without strong soap and water. We put it to good use and get them right back to you."

"They're a gift. In appreciation for what you've done to inspire the Negroes of these Sea Islands." He lowered his voice. "And to show the ignorant white officers that Negroes possess the same kernel of heroism as every other man created by God. Many have not yet had their eyes opened to a true understanding of the Divine."

"Thank you, suh," Hannah said, taking the buckets inside. She gave Robert a puzzled smile.

"I hear the commodore is quite taken with you, Mr. Smalls."

Robert looked down at his shoes. Mr. French seemed to have ears all over town. "That's kind of you to say so. Is there something I can do for you, suh?"

"It's I who should be asking that of you, Mr. Smalls. I am here from New York, on behalf of the American Missionary Association, attempting to provide a path to salvation for the wretches who find themselves here, adrift, escaped from bondage, but unclaimed by a nation at war with itself." Reverend French peered around Robert into the store. "Have the Bostonians or Philadelphians been here yet?"

"No, suh," answered Robert.

Reverend French smile shifted to reflect a sense of satisfaction, perhaps at having been first to reach them, though Robert still didn't understand why they might be considered such a prize.

"Being favored by the commodore can be to your great advantage, Mr. Smalls. Beaufort is no longer a sleepy little town

—there are generals and commodores and majors and captains here, each with a different vision of the future for this place and for your people. I fear that they do not always keep the will of God in mind, through their machinations. Let us pray on their behalf."

The Reverend bowed his head and put a sweaty white palm on Robert's shoulder. "Lord God, we thank you for granting success to Mr. Smalls and his crew and family and for bringing them to safety, past the forts, and to the protection of our gallant navy, and now to the security of Beaufort. We ask your help in leading us all down a more righteous path, according to your will, Oh Lord. Amen."

"Amen," Robert answered.

"My wife, Austa, and our daughters, will return with food for your families. I know it's hard to arrive with nothing. We do our best to help the needy and educate the ignorant. I hope you will allow me to be your friend. I'm sure we can both help each other."

"Well, yessuh, Reverend."

"If there's anything I can do, you must let me know."

They shook hands. "Actually," said Robert, "There is something."

*****

Reverend French waddled up to the store as Robert worked with Jackson and Morrison to put the newly arrived supplies on the shelves. The reverend waved a newspaper at Robert. "Robert!"

In two weeks, they'd cleaned out the building enough to make a home and a store out of it. At Robert's request, Reverend French had used his New York connections to order two crates of pots, kettles, pans, brushes, brooms, knives, forks, spoons, soap, candles, sewing needles, sacks, canned food.

The reverend paused to catch his breath, completely pink from exertion. He was known more for leisurely breakfasts and long prayer meetings than jogs up the street. "Commodore

DuPont has had some success on your behalf. See for yourself."
He thrust the paper at Robert who took it and glanced at it.
He'd never be able to read all those words. He looked up at
Reverend French, who quickly grasped the situation and took
back the paper.

"Why don't I read it to all of you?" the reverend asked.

"I's sure we all wants to hear it," Robert said, unsure what
the papers might have to do with them.

"Senator Grimes from Iowa has sponsored a bill on your
behalf, directing the Navy Department to appraise the *Planter*
and its cargo and to pay you and your crew one half the value. It
mentions you directly—An Act for the Benefit of Robert Smalls
and Others—they've paid attention. You will receive prize
money after all."

Robert steadied himself against the shelves. Prize money to
a Negro. The *Planter* was worth maybe fifty or sixty thousand
dollars. Serious money.

"Guess we is the 'and others,'" Jackson said.

"They can call me Mrs. Morrison, if it means I get a piece of
that prize," Morrison laughed.

"Amen, brother. Robert, you done good with old DuPont,"
said Jackson.

"Let us praise the lord for sharing his bounty and mercy
upon us," said the Reverend. Jackson and Robert and Morrison
bowed their heads.

Robert hardly knew what to think. The world didn't make
much sense anymore.

CHAPTER 16

As he and the crew walked down the dock, Robert felt his pulse quicken. The *Planter* lay in her berth, as if she'd been waiting for him this whole month he'd spent stuck on land. Now they were finally going to be reunited. He and the all the crew, including Morrison, were being hired to sail the *Planter* on a new mission.

Workers were using a small crane to lift a half-inch sheet of iron from the dock to the side of the *Planter*, where more workmen bolted the armor to the outside of the paddle wheel housing.

"Looks like we's expecting some excitement," Chisholm said under his breath.

"Don't look beautiful, but it might help," said Morrison.

"Maybe 'gainst muskets," Alfred said, not exactly pleased. "Half inch of iron won't stop even the smallest shell. Where they sendin' us, Robert?"

"I don't know yet."

He'd missed his ship. Not just the sight of her, but the smell of her oily engines and the wood smoke from her smokestack. He'd missed the sound their feet made on her deck, and the quiet music of the waves lapping against her hull.

On the gangway, they were met by a group of naval officers. The one in front was a big strapping fellow with bright eyes and a bushy red beard, a captain. He stepped towards them. "Are you Robert Smalls? Is this your crew?"

"Yessuh. Is you the new captain?"

"No, I'm Captain Rhind of the *Crusader*," he pointed over at a three-masted steamer, with half a dozen guns on each side and scars that showed she'd seen her share of action. "We'll be bringing firepower, and the *Planter* will carry troops. This is my first officer, Lieutenant Forrest. And these are the two new officers of the *Planter*, Captain Johnson and Engineer Wilson."

Forrest was young and intense looking. Johnson was a soft man, past middle-age with sleepy eyes and limp tufts of hair sprouting from his scalp. Engineer Wilson was a yellow-skinned beanpole of a man, who didn't look like he'd have the strength to lift a wrench.

"It's an honor to meet you, sirs." Robert introduced the crew to the officers. All his men did their best to stand at attention, though Chisholm's best these days was unacceptable to just about anyone. Lieutenant Forrest's nose wrinkled in disapproval at Chisholm's slouch. Robert hoped that he couldn't smell the whiskey on him.

"I've given instructions to add musket-proof bulkheads around the machinery and wheel housing," said Captain Rhind. "No sense having the small stuff slow us down. The big things, well, that's what the *Crusader* is for. We'll give back as good as we get. Mr. Smalls, I'm told by Commodore DuPont that you're well versed in these shores and that your intelligence was extremely helpful in the action on James Island. If the army had spent a little less time dithering and acted as soon as you'd arrived, they might have avoided the debacle there. Apparently, it will be our job to remove the bad taste from that recent failure.

"Gentlemen," he said, turning to the *Planter*'s new officers, "prepare this ship and yourselves as quickly as possible. We leave in two days." Rhind looked curiously at the *Planter*'s crew one more time, turned smartly on his heel, and left the ship, with Lieutenant Forrest trailing behind him.

Captain Johnson looked over his new crew and nodded sleepily. "Well, boys, you heard what Captain Rhind said. Let's get her ready. We don't have a first mate right now—Robert, you seem like you know everyone well enough, I'll need your help getting things organized until the navy staffs us properly. I'm going to my cabin. The air down here is thick as molasses. It seems more suited for drinking than breathing."

He climbed the ladder and disappeared, leaving them with Engineer Wilson, who looked at them skeptically. "You have all been on this ship before?" he asked.

"Yessuh. We knows her as well as we knows our own families," Robert answered, still wondering about the new captain.

"You. Alfred. Why don't you show me what you know about this engine? Robert, direct these boys on what to do to get us ready."

Alfred followed the man towards the engine room, while Robert looked at the rest of the crew. "What are you waiting for?" he barked. "Get her loaded. There's wood down there. Find the station master and ask for supplies. Jackson, make sure we got somethin' to eat. Chisholm and Morrison, check the moorings and lines."

They didn't exactly leap into action, but they moved anyway. They'd already been ashore too long. That much was obvious to Robert. They'd worked hard on the store, which was good, but it didn't take the kind of discipline you needed to run a ship. He'd have to get them back in shape fast, before getting back in the line of fire.

*****

Robert followed Captain Johnson down the wharf to the *Crusader*. Behind them, in the dim light of dawn, a line of soldiers were boarding the *Planter*. They looked a lot like the Confederate soldiers back in Charleston, young and scrappy, except these seemed better fed and less interested.

The deck of the *Crusader* swarmed with activity, as the crew prepared for battle, piling ammunition and powder. Dark black coal smoke rose from the tall smokestack just behind the center line.

They met Captain Rhind and Lieutenant Forrest in the captain's stateroom. Another nervous-looking white man was there in suit jacket and ill-fitting tie. A pilot, but not someone Robert had ever seen before.

Rhind didn't waste any time. "Gentlemen, we need to sail as soon as possible. We're heading up into Wadmalaw Sound. The Rebels have set up a new camp, and there is concern that they're planning to sneak beyond James Island onto Edisto Island. The 55th Pennsylvania will ride aboard the *Planter* and land after we soften up the rebel camp. Once established on the ground, the 55th will move north and cut the railway line to Charleston."

"The troops are boarding the *Planter* as we speak, sir," said Captain Johnson. This was the most Robert had heard out of him for the past day. Apparently, Captain Johnson had a lot of sleep to catch up on, because he spent most of his time napping in his cabin. Rumor said that he had a history of crashing ships onto rocks and reefs, so they'd given him a choice between a tugboat and a transport.

"Excellent. Mr. Taylor here will serve as pilot aboard the *Crusader*. Mr. Smalls will pilot the *Planter*. We will use these maps, based on charts and information provided by Mr. Smalls after his recent escape from Charleston." He stepped back to reveal his map table, with a chart of the Wadmalaw River that Robert had worked on with the Navy mapmaker more than a month ago. The shape of the sound always made him think of a Chinese dragon, long and twisting. And dangerous.

Robert took another look at this new pilot. "Nice to meet you, Mr. Taylor," he said. "Where do y'all hail from?"

"I been sailin' these parts most my life. Fishing and haulin' and pilotin'." Taylor chewed on his thumbnail.

"That so? You spent a lot of time on the Wadmalaw?"

"All over. Lifetime of knowledge."

The man had rough hands. Scars on the fingers. Probably a fisherman. But not a pilot. Robert would have heard of him. It was one thing to steer a fishing boat up the river, and another to navigate a 170-foot steamer drawing more than 12 feet of water. Taylor gave Robert a bad feeling in the pit of his stomach.

"The tide waits for no man. Does everyone understand the plan?" asked Captain Rhind.

"We'll follow your lead, Captain," said Johnson, and the meeting adjourned.

On their way out, Robert called out to Captain Johnson. "Suh? I has a question for Captain Rhind, suh. Mind if I ask him, then run over to the *Planter*?"

"Be quick about it."

Robert weaved back through the busy deck and spied Rhind talking with Lieutenant Forrest up by the wheelhouse. He was taking a risk, but Rhind seemed like a man more interested in facts that niceties. He'd see if that was true.

"Captain Rhind, suh, I hates to interrupt. But, I wonder if I might have a moment of yo' time."

Rhind raised a skeptical brow. "We're about to cast off."

"'Bout the mission, suh."

"Speak."

"In private. Just a moment of your time, suh." He stepped away from the wheelhouse, hoping the captain would drift his way, out of hearing of Taylor.

"Make it quick."

Robert kept his voice at a whisper. "Suh, I been pilot 'round these parts for years, and I ain't never heard of no Taylor. Has he already been a pilot for you up toward James Island?"

"He's new to us. But I have word that he's suitable."

"We'd heading into tricky waters, up the Wadmalaw. A ship as deep as *Crusader* won't have much room. There ain't many white men left around here who might be pilots."

"Are you implying the man is a fraud?"

What was the word of a black man worth against any white man? Robert knew the answer. He needed to tread carefully. "I's sure he's a good Christian man. But..."

"You'd better hurry back to the *Planter*. Mr. Taylor has been vouched for. Would you propose I replace him with you? How's my crew going to listen to a Negro pilot?"

"Commodore DuPont don't seem to have no trouble with it."

"Sadly, they're not all as good men as the commodore. Hell, I am certainly not as good a man as the commodore. I applaud your escape with the *Planter*, Smalls, but you can't trade on that to land a larger assignment."

"Aye, suh. I beg pardon, Captain."

Robert took one last look at Taylor. Local white man? Not many would be willing to waste a ball of spit on a federal ship, let alone pilot her up on a raid. The *Planter* might not want to follow too close.

*****

They reached the mouth of the North Edisto River by three o'clock. The troops stretched out on the main deck and slept or played cards. A few got sick over the rail. Maybe they were seasick, or else nervous about rebels firing at them. Robert was nervous, too. Thanks to Nordhoff's articles, everyone seemed to know about him and the *Planter*, and that meant the boys on the other side might take special joy in shooting at her. Getting stuck in the mud and captured was not an option for him and his crew. There were prices on all their heads back in Charleston.

He was glad Hannah didn't know where they were heading. She might chain him up to the counter at the store. But the only thing keeping him and Hannah and the children free was the war and the Yankee army. If they lost the war, life was over.

He still wasn't sure about that white pilot. The good news was that the mouth of the North Edisto was wide and pretty deep. Wouldn't take much skill to keep them all afloat. And the light was good, just the right mix of sun and clouds to give a sense of what lurked under the water. But if it kept clouding up, Taylor was going to be guessing when they hit the shoals off Bear Bluff.

Captain Johnson stood on the observation deck drinking tea with the officer in charge of the 55th troops, Captain Bennett. Bennett was a small, dark man who kept a sharp eye on his men below.

"Any orders, suh?" Robert asked, as the *Crusader* steamed in front of them, up the river.

"Match their pace and keep us out of the muck. We'll let them lead the way." Johnson turned to Captain Bennett. "Have you seen much action?"

"Not yet. We were spared the misery of the James Island disaster. My boys are ready for a fight. Maybe today they'll get it. Quite a crew you've got. They didn't have any white sailors left?"

"Fresh out. They're better than you'd think, don't worry."

Robert was tempted to give a ring down to Alfred for a quick surge ahead to tip those teacups, but he restrained himself. Today was about getting the job done and getting his crew back in shape. After their escape from Charleston, they'd always be his crew, no matter who tried to run the *Planter*.

*****

It happened at Bear's Bluff, just as he'd expected.

One minute they were steaming along, twin columns of smoke twisting peacefully down the river, and then suddenly, the *Planter* was gaining on the *Crusader*. Fast. Taylor had shoved the *Crusader* straight into the sandbar off the point. Idiot.

The distress flag rose on the *Crusader*. He could hear the engine straining to reverse her out of the mud, but they'd had a strong head of steam when they hit the bar. That was Taylor's other mistake.

"Oh, that's not good," said Captain Johnson.

"She won't get off there on her own," Robert said. "But she ain't so deep that we can't pull her out. Won't be the first time we've hauled a steamer out of the mud."

145

"Full stop," Captain Johnson ordered. "Send over a boat for a cable from the *Crusader*."

"Aye, suh." Robert rang the engine room to stop, and called out, "Alston! Get Turno and Morrison!"

Soon Turno and Morrison rowed over to the stuck *Crusader*. Robert spun the *Planter* in place, so that the engines would be pulling forward with maximum power.

When the skiff returned, Turno, Morrison, Chisholm, and Johnny wrapped the sturdy rope around the *Planter's* Sampson post. The soldiers on deck stepped back and watched as the crew of the *Planter* efficiently executed their duties. Robert was glad they moved quickly—too much time sitting idly in the river was an invitation to rebel pickets to try a little target practice.

As soon as the lines were fast, Robert gave the signal to the engine room. He shifted her slowly forward. The cable pulled tight, but the steamer stayed put. He tried again, easing the *Planter* as slowly as he could. One jerk would snap the rope. He backed her slightly to the port, then starboard, giving the *Crusader* a little wriggle in the muck. The screw on the *Crusader* wasn't useful at slow speeds like this. This was when paddles could save your life.

The bow of the *Planter* lifted ever so slightly, as the hull of the *Crusader* fought being moved. One more inch. Then suddenly the *Planter* surged forward and brought the *Crusader* with her. Cheers rang out from the *Crusader* and from the men on deck of the *Planter*.

"Nice sailing," said Bennett to Captain Johnson.

"That's why we're here," said Captain Johnson.

"Captain Bennett, suh," Robert said, "Once we start moving, it's less than a mile 'til we'll be in sight of Simmon's Bluff. You might want to warn your boys."

"Right." Bennett climbed awkwardly down the ladder and assembled his troops.

A boat from the *Crusader* rowed quickly over to the *Planter*. Lieutenant Forrest called up to the upper deck. "Captain

Johnson, we offer our immense gratitude."

Johnson gave a small bow. "My pleasure, sir."

Robert wondered what he'd have to do for a single officer to notice that it was he who actually knew how to use the *Planter* to free the stuck ship. Sometimes the Union didn't seem so different from the Confederates.

"Captain Rhind requests that Mr. Smalls accompany us on the *Crusader* for the rest of this trip, sir. We would like to avoid a repeat performance as we approach the rebel camp."

Someone had noticed, after all.

"Right away." Johnson turned to Robert. "You heard him. But this can't be permanent. We need you on this ship."

"Don't worry. Me and the *Planter* go way back. I ain't in a hurry to be rid of her."

*****

"Pleasure to have you on board, Mr. Smalls," said Captain Rhind, as Robert hurried up to the wheelhouse. "We need you to instruct quartermaster Hingham here on how to get us to Simmons Bluff with a little less mud on our keel."

"Aye, suh."

"Mr. Taylor, or whatever his name is, appears to either be an impostor or a saboteur. We will determine which at a later time. He's been assigned to the brig for now, though my first impulse was to merely chuck him overboard. I am clearly not the first to underestimate you, Mr. Smalls. I will attempt to avoid it happening again."

"Thank you, suh." Robert didn't dare smile, but it wasn't easy to keep it in. Now was the time for business. The afternoon was aging fast, and the tide was beginning to ebb. If these soldiers took too long in their mission, it was going to be a lot harder getting out than in.

"Ten degrees port," Robert called to Hingham, who turned the wheel. On a ship like the *Crusader*, there were more men to handle each task. "How fast you want us there, Captain?"

"As fast as you can, while keeping her clear."

"They gon' see us coming once we get 'round that bend." Robert pointed to a line of low trees running out on a raised spit of land that stuck out into the river. "We gon' take a hard turn to starboard out here, then we be facing straight into them. Won't be two miles off."

"How much room will we have to maneuver?"

"It's tight. Won't have much use for the starboard guns at first."

"Bring us there. Now." Rhind turned to Lieutenant Forrest. "All guns primed and ready, but especially the port guns. Extra hands to every port side station. Fire as soon as we're in range." Forrest called out and the drums called the men to their guns.

Under Robert's direction, Hingham steered them around the bend, and they surged up the sound. A tiny wisp from a camp fire gave away the position of the enemy. A few rowboats lay scattered on the shore below Simmon's Bluff, more a big pile of sand with pine trees than a proper bluff, but in the South Carolina low country, it was high ground. Robert swung them to the right, to give the port side of the ship a straight view of the bluff.

"Fire" ordered Rhind. Thunder exploded across the deck as all six guns let loose. Shells exploded over the Rebel camp, raining down fire and metal. "Keep it coming!"

Robert straightened out the *Crusader*, and moved her closer. By the time the next volley was ready, they were only a hundred yards off the bluff. More shells arced over the camp. A tree caught on fire, another shattered.

A whistle of a musket ball whistled overhead. Another, this one closer, splintered a spar on the rear mast.

"Give them another taste," called Captain Rhind.

Robert saw men running away through the trees.

"If they had artillery, they would have used it by now," suggested Lieutenant Forrest.

"I think they haven't got much of anything, and we've

interrupted their supper," said Rhind. "Make sure the landing is clear for the 55th," he called out to the gunnery officer.

After two more salvos, the *Planter* pulled close to shore and the 55th Pennsylvania loaded into longboats and rowed to the bluff. The woods were oddly quiet. On reaching the beach, the men jumped into the water, muskets at the ready, and ran for cover of bushes along the shore.

A few more shots rang out from above as the soldiers pushed up the bluff. The rest of the men followed off the *Planter*, and soon the entire company was ashore. Smoke from the camp intensified.

Robert focused on the water. It was already close to seven o'clock, and the tide was ebbing fast. The *Crusader* was a fine ship, but she was no riverboat. Getting out past Bear Bluff wasn't going to be simple if they were stuck here at low tide.

"Captain?"

"Yes, Mr. Smalls."

"The channel gets real narrow at low tide."

Rhind understood the problem. At his instruction, Lieutenant Forrest fired a flare over the burning rebel camp. In less than five minutes, soldiers filed back to the longboats. Captain Bennett drew his boat close to the *Crusader*.

"Good hunting?" asked Captain Rhind from the rail.

"They scattered. Your shells did the trick. But the path to the railroad is too thick. We'd get bogged down and have to spend the night. Who knows when they'll be back and with how many. They're gone for now, though. Victory for our boys. And not a scratch on them."

"We'll celebrate back in Port Royal. Tell them to hurry back. The tide is our enemy at the moment."

The battle was over. White men shooting at other white men. Fire and sand. It was hard for Robert to make sense of it all. But he'd done his bit. Maybe next time, they'd get to take a harder strike at the men who wanted his children to remain slaves forever.

CHAPTER 17

Robert stood outside the store, sweating in the August heat, looking at a pile of salvaged lumber. The siding on the building started falling off a month ago, letting in the insects, the heat, and the rain. Now they had a few days off from the *Planter*, so it was finally time to tackle this chore. But no one else was here to help yet. Putting up siding by himself in the August sun seemed like a bad idea.

Chisholm was probably sleeping off yet another drunken night. There had to be some way to dry that man out. Mary was no help—she had a nose for liquor and a way of making friends, at least for a night, with anyone who had it. The two together could drain a jug so fast you'd think there was a hole in the bottom.

Robert sat in the shade of a moss-draped live oak to wait. The lack of breeze made the air press wet and heavy against his skin.

A few plantation Negroes walked up to the store across the yard, carrying a bushel of beans, and waved to him before going inside. They'd make a trade with Hannah for soap or a pot, and maybe some candy for the little ones back home. Word had spread that black folk could get a fair shake at Smalls Supplies, and customers flocked through the door from sun up to sun down. Hannah, Mama Lydia, and Lila took care of everything when the men were gone to sea, which hadn't been so much lately. General McClellan's failure up north had led to ten thousand troops being reassigned northward from Port Royal to help rescue him. That meant less need for transports around Port Royal, so the crew of the *Planter* was often idle. It also made everyone nervous. General Hunter had ordered the plantations on Edisto Island to be abandoned, because the army could no longer protect against raiders.

Johnny and Alston slowly walked up the sandy street. Alston had his bag slung over his shoulder—maybe he was going to try to talk Hannah into doing some wash for him.

"Mornin' gentlemen," Robert called. "Where's the rest of the shirkers?"

"Chisholm wouldn't move," said Johnny.

"He ain't dead," chirped Alston, who had an extra bounce to his step. "But he smell so bad I almost wish he was, so we could just bury him." They all laughed.

"At least you two is here. Where Alfred"

"At the *Planter*. Said Engineer Wilson called him to work on the boiler," reported Johnny.

"I can't stay, neither," said Alston. "I got a berth as a steward on the *Albatross*. Heading to New Orleans and Texas. Their steward got sick, so they need a new one, and I had my name on the list. I have to be there in an hour."

"You're leaving us?" Robert said.

"It make me sad," said Johnny glumly.

"You ain't seen enough of the world from the deck of the *Planter*?" Robert teased. The boy had grown at least two inches in the three months since their escape. And now he was off to the Gulf of Mexico. Robert felt a pang of jealousy—Alston had no cares in the world, no wife, no children, just the open sea and the possibility of adventure.

He wrapped an arm around the boy's shoulders and led him into the store. "Well, brother Alston, we can't let you head into the big world empty handed."

Hannah was at the counter, finishing trading with the customers. "Hannah, Alston's shipping out on the *Albatross*," Robert called.

"No. Well, I am sure sorry to see you go, Alston. Junior's gon' be beside himself when he find out. You like a big brother to him. Once you out there, you find someone to help you write us some letters."

"Yes, ma'am. And I've been learning some on my own from Miss Towne, too. I might be able to write some all on my own," said Alston. The classes led by the teachers up north often filled the tent, so many contraband crammed in to better themselves.

"We get Chisholm to read them. Or Reverend French. Reverend's a real good reader," said Johnny.

Robert rooted around in the wooden bins and barrels and shelves and found a reasonably sharp knife with a leather sheath and a bone handle. He grabbed a whet stone, too, and put them in a small cloth bag with handfuls of the candies that Alston liked. He tossed in a bar of soap. "Might need to clean yourself up when you go into port, hoping to meet a fine lady. Soap is just the thing. You might want to look like a sailor, but no need for you to smell like one. Just ask Hannah."

Alston smiled bashfully.

Robert handed the bag to their promising young man and pressed a twenty dollar gold piece into his palm. "You never know when you might need this, son."

"Robert. Thanks. It's..."

"It's yours. They supposed to tell us 'bout the prize money any day now. That could mean hundreds of dollars for you, maybe more. You take this for now, and then you come back and get the rest. Or we send it to you. Just make sure you keep writing to us, so we know how to find you."

"I will."

The door burst open with a wail. Morrison's sister, Vera, pushed her way inside, weeping and staggering.

"They took him! Came right out of the swamp and stole my brother."

Morrison had gone out to visit her yesterday, trying to convince her to leave the Edisto plantation she'd been farming.

She and a group of others had refused to evacuate, unwilling to give up the cotton crop they'd been nursing all year.

"What happened?" Robert asked.

"They came at sunup. You know Morrison don't like to be out in the fields, but he said he'd help us. Went out early to beat the heat. Soon as we saw them, we ran. I hid in the wood shed. They must have come by boat. Didn't have horses but they had guns. Shot big old Mama Delilah right in the leg. They grabbed Morrison and the boy, Daniel, and two of the hogs. Disappeared back into the swamp."

"Did you tell the federals?"

"Told one of them officers, a colonel, or some such thing. But all he say is that we not s'posed to be out there anyways, 'cause we know they ain't got the soldiers to protect us. Nothin' they can do. They took him, Robert. They took my brother."

She sobbed onto his shoulder and he patted her awkwardly on the back. Morrison was gone, back to slavery. He'd be taken to Charleston and sold to work in the city, or shipped off to labor at a Confederate fort, or sent to work in the fields to feed the Confederate army. If they did take him to Charleston, he needed to hope he wasn't recognized. If he was, he'd be lucky if they stopped whipping him while he was still alive.

Morrison a slave again. The world seemed like a dark, dark place. The raiders could strike at any time, grab any of them. Even a man like Morrison, who had done everything right, who had done his part to get Hannah and Lizzie and Junior free. Without Morrison, Robert's family would still belong to Samuel Kingman.

Hannah led Vera over to a chair behind the counter. "He got hisself free once, Vera. He can do it again. He a good strong, brave man. And smart. This war gon' end, and when it do, he gon' come back home here to find you."

Hannah knew what to say. She always knew. Robert just wished there was something he could do, but the soldiers were right. There was no going after him. The swamps were a dense maze of reeds and creeks and channels with countless hiding places. The raids kept every black man, woman, and child on the Sea Islands on edge, as if the hand of the devil might suddenly reach up from hell and pluck them out. And there was nothing Robert could do about it.

*****

Two weeks later, Robert found himself on Hilton Head Island, sitting on the deck outside General Hunter's seaside headquarters. At the table with him sat General Saxton and Reverend French, both looking comfortable and relaxed. Being at ease was Reverend French's specialty. General Saxton was a narrow-shouldered man with intense eyes but a warm smile. He was in charge of the whole Negro problem and the experiment to try to turn Sea Island contrabands into independent farmers. There was no sign of Admiral DuPont, who had just been promoted to admiral a week ago.

A strong breeze shook the branches of the oak trees that lay on the other side of the beach house, and Robert looked out at the rising clouds over the ocean. The wind carried the scent and promise of a summer thunderstorm.

The invitation had been brief. "General Hunter requests your presence at his headquarters tomorrow, at 11 am. A launch will be sent." No word of what the meeting was about. He'd hoped it would be about getting the Department of the Navy to reassess the value of the *Planter*. The appraiser had valued the *Planter* at $9,000. Robert and every other sensible person knew it was worth at least $60,000. Sure, even at $9,000 he would get $1,500, and the crew $450 each. Some folks said that he should be happy to get anything. Who ever knew a black man to have $1,500?

Who ever knew a white man to let a black man have his fair share? That's what Robert wanted to know. His share should be $9,000, and the crew $2,700 each. Real money. Barely free for three months and already he wanted the world to treat him fairly. No wonder even the Northerners weren't so sure about emancipation.

General Hunter finally emerged from the house. They didn't call him "Black Dave" for nothing—he wore a constant frown and his big droopy mustache gave him a dour expression even in the best of times. An angry pink scar ran across his cheek and neck, a battle wound from the Battle of Bull Run. They all stood at his approach.

"Please have a seat, gentlemen. All is quiet in Beaufort, I trust."

"It's been a good week," answered General Saxton, taking another sip of his coffee. "Mostly petty squabbles among the missionaries. And the superintendents always have some complaint or another."

"You're too close to them, General. A little distance might serve you well."

"I can't get this whole endeavor to work without getting my hands dirty."

"I suppose not. Now, explain to me again about your Washington scheme," asked General Hunter.

Saxton tapped the tabletop to emphasize his frustration. "We can't farm the plantations if they're subject to constant raids. As Washington continues to siphon off troops, our defenses grow weaker. All of us here know the importance of this project. If we can show the success of independent Negro farmers, we can allay some of the concerns around abolition."

"Easier said than done, of course," said General Hunter. "I've already had my hand slapped on emancipation. Lincoln is not our ally."

"But with God's help, he may be," interjected Reverend French. "And he is a practical man." The Reverend helped himself to another biscuit and slathered it with jam.

"Exactly," said General Saxton. "Lincoln knows we don't have the troops to continue to hold this area. But we do have men here, we just need permission to use them."

"Yes, black troops. Train them, arm them, have them defend

their own farms and families. You don't have to sell me on the idea," said General Hunter, with a note of impatience.

Robert liked the sound of black soldiers. He knew Turno was eager to get a rifle in his hand and take a few shots at the white Southerners. Plenty of others would be, too.

"We will sell it as a matter of necessity," said Saxton. "First to Stanton, then to Lincoln. We could raise 50,000 troops in the Carolinas alone. Every Negro in uniform is one less pair of hands feeding the rebel army."

"I know Secretary Stanton from our time together in Ohio," said Reverend French said. "I would be happy to serve as your emissary."

"Stanton's as prickly as they come," General Hunter agreed, looking unsure about whether Reverend French was the right man to avoid those prickers.

"That's where Mr. Smalls comes in," said General Saxton, with a wave of his hand toward Robert.

Robert sat up a little straighter, surprised and a little confused. No one had mentioned anything to him about this.

"He's a perfect Negro Hero. The perfect argument for the full humanity of the black man, for Emancipation. Right here in the flesh," Reverend French clapped Robert on the shoulder. "Robert's story can soften the hardest heart, even Secretary Stanton's."

General Hunter twisted his mouth, considering whether this could possibly work. He ran a finger along the puckered line of his scar. "What do you think, Mr. Smalls? Could you do this for us? For your people?"

"I ain't quite sure what you all want from me," Robert said. He knew it wasn't piloting a ship or running a trading post, and those were the things he was good at.

"General Saxton and I will write a formal request to the Secretary of War and the president, to allow us to arm and train Negro soldiers," said Hunter. "You and Reverend French will deliver it."

Washington? He'd never been outside of South Carolina. "I's just a ship's pilot, suh. I don't know nothin' about talking with politician folk."

"We could bring Hannah with us," Reverend French volunteered. "Show her the capitol. You'd be doing your duty, and she'd get a bit of an adventure. You could find someone to cover for you at the store. I'll ask some of our teachers if they can help."

Robert wasn't sure he wanted Reverend French meddling in his store or in his life. And he wasn't sure Hannah would leave the children. Though it would be something to sail with her on a voyage to somewhere new.

General Saxton leaned forward. "We need to stop the raids. Every day, another man is stolen back into slavery. Every time a soldier is shipped up to northern battlegrounds, we grow weaker. If we get too weak..."

Hunter filled in the final threat: "If we get too weak, we will be forced to move to a base in Savannah or Florida. If we cede this ground, your people will not come with us. The Rebels will return and enslave every black soul in sight."

"But the conditions under Confederate control will be ten times as harsh as life in the old days," said Saxton. "The blood they've shed in this war will be repaid from the backs of every black man, woman, and child."

"We need you to join Reverend French and argue for the resources to win this war. Can you do this for us?" asked General Hunter.

Robert hated to leave the children and Mama Lydia. But he thought of Morrison, off in Charleston or who knows where, being chained, whipped, and sold. The same thing could happen to any of them. Not just could, would happen, to all of them, if the Union pulled out of Beaufort and the Sea Islands. He was being given a chance to try to stop that from happening. There wasn't much point to risking everything on the *Planter* if he wasn't willing to keep fighting to keep free.

"Yessuh. I go with Reverend. Just tell me when we leave."

CHAPTER 18

The slightest hint of a breeze drifting off the bay made the night air behind Smalls Supplies at least somewhat breathable. The men sprawled on benches they'd slapped together from old boards, sweating through their shirt sleeves in the August heat, while the women carried food out from the kitchen and clucked at the children. Robert looked over the wobbly table spread with their feast—plates overflowing with fried turtle meat, chicken, corn bread, beans. His friends knew how to wish a man good luck and make him wish he wasn't leaving.

Jackson raised a cup of beer. "A toast to Robert. Go show those gov'ment folks what a real man is."

Half a dozen hands raised their mugs in the light from the bonfire and lanterns. Chisholm said, "Hope they don't fill his hero head any more full, or else they likely to capsize on the way home. If they can even load him on the boat."

"That okay," Alfred joined in. "He can just walk on water all the way back from Washington."

They all laughed, and Robert harder than any of them.

Turno clapped a strong arm around Robert's shoulder. "You rub them worry lines right off your forehead. Me and Alfred and the boys, we gon' take care of the store."

"Just make sure you always got two eyes on this place, Turno." Robert was serious now. "We got to stay dependable."

"Who can you count on better'n us?"

"And you keep an eye on my mama, too, yeah?"

"Maybe I'll keep an eye on Turno," came Lydia's voice from

behind them. She set down a bowl of string beans on the table. "You just go and talk those big mens into doin' what's right. You tell them to let a man be a man. If Turno wants to be a soldier and fight for his peoples, then why they say no? You tell them. But you do it respectful, now."

"You sure you ready for the young uns, Mama?" Robert asked.

She swatted him on the arm. "I might be old, but I ain't too old to steer Lizzie and Junior right. 'Sides, I have Lila to help me."

Robert smiled at her. He'd made her promise to stay in Beaufort—no trips out to the Ashdale plantations to visit old friends. It was easier to worry about the store and the children and Mama Lydia, instead of what Washington would be like. What he was supposed to say to all the important people there? His friends here acted like he was something special, but that was just Beaufort. He'd rather stay here, steaming out on the bay, steering the *Planter* in and out of the channels.

Hannah came out of the kitchen with another plate of fried chicken and Junior attached to her skirts. Funny how he seemed to know they'd be leaving soon. Lizzie was keeping a close eye on Robert, even when she was playing with her little friends.

"You can't stay away long, Hannah," Alfred said, helping himself to a drumstick. "What we gon' do without yo' chicken?"

"He's got a point, Robert. How can I leave your crew here to starve?" Hannah pursed her lips, teasing Robert.

It had taken gentle but relentless pressure from Reverend French and Mrs. French to convince her to go on the trip. But the navy was willing to pay Hannah's way, and this was a chance for them to have an adventure together. Robert had used every bit of charm on her, the same charm he'd used to get her to walk with him down at the Battery back in Charleston, when he was still barely eighteen and she was a grown woman. He was glad it still worked.

"Lila, Mama, and Jackson all knows how to cook just fine,"

Robert assured her.

"So now he sayin' my cookin' ain't nothing special," Hannah answered, her hands playfully on her hips.

"Maybe too special," Alfred said, his voice suddenly low and serious. "Keep it down."

A group of half a dozen soldiers walked unsteadily around the corner, drawn by the light and the smell of good food. They were enlisted men with a bottle, probably smuggled in by one of the sutlers.

We should have done this indoors, Robert thought, cursing himself for being so shortsighted. It was his job to think ahead. Sure, they would have almost melted in the heat, but they could have avoided this.

"Now there's some real Southern cooking," said one of the soldiers, a pistol on his hip. He was a big man, practically bursting out of his uniform, and sloppy drunk.

"Does it come with that famed Southern hospitality?" said another, this one with a mop of red hair sticking out from under his blue forage cap. "The only Southern hospitality I've seen is minie balls and shrapnel."

"Hail, good Negroes. We are your protectors. Your guard dogs against the evil Rebel Raiders." This one wore wire-rimmed glasses and raised his arm in greeting, as the band of men staggered confidently over to the tables of food. The leader.

Robert felt a wave of dread flood into him as Turno moved to confront the soldiers, with the other men behind him. Lila was already pulling on the tail of Turno's jacket, trying to pull him back from the coming fight.

"The hell we are, O'Neil," growled a stout man through his black bush of a beard. "You got your head up your ass if you think I'm getting my head blown off for a bunch of niggers."

"I'm just suggesting that these lovely contraband might condescend to sharing some of their feast with the warriors tasked with keeping the Rebels out of Port Royal," said O'Neil, whose eyes seemed plenty sharp behind those glasses. His devil-may-care grin seemed to promise a lot more trouble than they needed tonight.

"This our dinner," said Turno.

Turno's hands were in fists, which Robert thought was good. The flash of a knife would lead to a bad outcome for everyone. Each soldier had a sidearm, and two had rifles. And at least one of the soldiers with a rifle wasn't quite so drunk—he'd planted his feet and had his weapon in his hands, scanning the group, paying the most attention to Turno.

"Ours now," said the bearded one, as he stepped forward to put his hands on a plate of chicken.

Turno was faster than Robert expected, and his big hand swallowed the man's wrist.

"Put it back," Turno said, as the other soldiers reached for their weapons. The man didn't move, but Robert saw his eyes twitch in pain. Turno's grip was like a vise.

"Turno," Robert said. "Let these men have some chicken."

"You got two seconds to get your hand off me, nigger," said the soldier.

"Turno." There was pleading in Robert's voice now. "You know no man can help himself around Hannah's cooking. Turno."

Hannah gathered Lizzie and Junior behind her. Everyone else was frozen, waiting for disaster.

Robert fixed his eyes on the soldier with glasses, O'Neil, hoping one of them might see a way out of this.

"See," said O'Neil. "This is what happens without manners. Misunderstandings. Say please, Metzger. He meant to say please."

"Screw," said Metzger.

"Metzger," said O'Neil again, an edge of steel in his voice. "Please."

Turno released his grip on the soldier's arm. The man quickly pulled the plate of food to his chest. Robert knew that wrist was practically crushed, but there was no way the man would dare rub it in front of any of them.

The others still stood with their sidearms drawn, but now hanging loosely at their sides.

"Maybe you fellas should take some corn bread, too," Robert offered, without a hint of friendship in his voice. A plate of chicken wouldn't be enough now. But a little more might salvage something for the rest of them.

"Why, thank you," said O'Neil, reaching forward to take the basket. "You've done the Union army a great service tonight, Mr. Contraband."

"Watch yourself," said the bearded one to Turno.

Turno's only answer was a glare hot enough to light a man on fire.

"Where's the bottle?" called O'Neil, as he led the soldiers down the alley. "I need something to wash down this cornbread."

"You enjoy your picnic," said the sloppy, sweaty one bringing up the rear, as if nothing had just happened.

Once the soldiers were out of sight, the buzz started, curses and threats and soothing and pleading. Hannah didn't let go of the children until there wasn't even a sound of the soldiers.

Alfred stood close to Robert, far calmer than the rest. "Nice work," he said under his breath.

"Can you keep things quiet while we's gone?" Robert asked.

"I can. But you get the job done up there in Washington, all right? Put our man Turno in that same uniform. Then they got to look at us different."

Robert hoped Alfred was right. He picked Junior up into his arms, just to feel his warm squirming son. There was a whole world of people out there, on both sides of the war, determined to force him and his children to live like animals. How was he supposed to convince them otherwise? This trip to Washington seemed hopeless. And absolutely necessary.

*****

STEERING TO FREEDOM

The *Massachusetts* blew a farewell blast from her whistle and slipped from her berth, a coil of coal smoke twisting over the heads of the well-wishers on the dock. She was more than 200 feet long and no wider than the *Planter*. The *Massachusetts* had already seen action in Florida in attacks on Ship Island, and despite repairs, her battered armor gave her charm, but certainly not beauty. Nowadays, she was running up and down the coast as a transport and supply ship. Her upper deck featured two masts, a central smokestack, and not much else. She was designed strictly for business.

Robert gripped Hannah tightly around her waist, as they looked down at the dock and waved to the children and Mama Lydia and their friends. Lizzie smiled brightly, caught up in the excitement of the crowd. Junior was already squirming in Mama Lydia's arms and starting to cry, reaching his little arms out for his mother.

"They gon' be all right," he reassured Hannah, while they soaked in one last glimpse of their family.

"I know. But I don't like it."

"They got a whole hive of folks to watch over them. Even the admiral and the generals."

"They don't care two shakes for us, Robert."

"Long as I's useful, they keep helping us."

He gave her a handkerchief and she wiped at her cheeks. He hoped bringing her was the right thing.

Next to them, Reverend French waved regally at his own wife and children and the assembled faces of his band of New York missionaries. The Boston and Philadelphia missionaries were nowhere to be seen, but that didn't surprise Robert. They complained that the reverend was too holy and ignored everyday practicalities. But, like Reverend French always said, sometimes you have to take time to keep God in the room. They could complain all they wanted about Reverend's lackadaisical schedule, but who made this trip happen? Who had the connections close to President Lincoln, to men who could actually make the decision to turn contrabands into free soldiers? Only Reverend French.

"I know it's hard," Reverend French said gently to Hannah. He had seven children of his own, though they were mostly grown. "Leaving them and Austa never gets easier. But we leave them in the care of our friends, and in the protective hands of our Lord and Savior."

He put one thick, well-manicured hand on Robert's shoulder and another on Hannah's, and bowed his head. His ample belly pushed towards the center of their little prayer triangle. "Let us pray. Lord, as you looked over Moses and the Israelites in their journey through the desert, we beseech you to watch over our families in Beaufort, and ask that you protect and guide us on our journey ahead. We seek only to do your will, to bring ourselves, our families, and our nation to a more holy and perfect state of being. We ask for your grace and patience, and to give us good cheer as we pass over the depths of your seas, under the heavens you created. Bless this ship and fill her sails with the winds of divine Providence."

"Amen," said Robert quickly, with a touch of finality. There was always a chance with Reverend French that the breath he took was merely preparation to keep the blessing running a few more minutes. Sometimes a strong "Amen" would stop that train in its tracks.

"Amen," agreed Reverend French. "You'll be fine, Mrs. Smalls. Once we hit open water and the cooling wind is in our faces, you'll see. We'll have a chance to breathe. Your children are well-loved and well-guarded. You will worry, of course. But not too much, I hope."

The *Massachusetts* steered down the Beaufort River, building speed. Robert watched Hannah lift her head and look back towards the rear of the ship, hoping for one last glimpse of her babies, but Port Royal was already blending into the dark green rim of the Carolina marshes and pine forest.

*****

STEERING TO FREEDOM

Robert stood a few paces outside of the pilothouse, watching the wheel man guide the *Massachusetts* through the waves. They were offshore of Saint Helena Sound, and in a few hours they'd pass Charleston Harbor and the blockading fleet. What would Captain Relyea think if he knew Robert was passing so close to Charleston? Word was that Pitcher, Relyea, and Smith spent a few days in jail after the *Planter* vanished. Hard to imagine Relyea ever finding work near Charleston. Maybe Smith would never hold the power of the whip again.

The pilothouse lay low on this ship—she wasn't built to hold six or seven layers of cotton bales and still be able to twist through the catfish channels of the marshes like the *Planter*. Here they had proper holds, now overflowing with furniture, cotton, and bags of rice from seized plantations, and cases of letters from lonely soldiers. And a few coffins, too.

He'd love a chance at the wheel. The *Massachusetts* was long and lean, an extra fifty feet longer than the *Planter*, but only a few feet wider. Her great iron propeller slid her smoothly through the water and with the two masts loaded with sail, she could really move.

He was tempted to climb the foremast for a bird's eye view of the ship. Maybe he'd ask the engineer to let him take a look in the engine room, too. The crew weren't sure what to make of him and Hannah. The other passengers were a handful of returning missionaries, merchants, a paper pusher or two, and a few regular army officers. Thanks to a request from the admiral, Robert and Hannah had a small stateroom to themselves.

The ship's steward, a brown-skinned boy with big ears and bright eyes, climbed up from below decks and looked at him curiously. His uniform was clean, though it was missing a few buttons and was a size too big, maybe to give him some room to grow. Robert couldn't help wondering where Alston was now.

"Better ask your question before someone call for you," Robert said.

"You really the one that done took the 'Secesh ship?"

"Me and the others and the hand of God."

Those bright eyes got a little brighter. "I'm glad to know you, suh. You need anything, you jes' ring. I git it in a snap."

A voice called impatiently from below, "Speck!" and the boy vanished with a friendly wave.

It felt strange to be recognized. Back when Robert was that boy's age, he would have felt awfully shy. It took nerve to approach a stranger. Maybe young Speck had a future.

"Should have known I'd find you here." Hannah's voice came from behind him. "You said you'd be back in five minutes."

He turned to face his wife, who stood with her arms crossed, her blue and cream patterned traveling dress fluttering against her in the breeze. He liked the way the cloth pressed up against her strong legs and hips.

"Well, I—"

"That was more than an hour ago."

"I just wanted to take a look around the ship."

"Oh, I know you, Robert. You 'bout ready to grab that wheel or haul a rope." She was almost smiling. "So, will she get us to Washington without sinkin'?"

"She ain't exactly the *Planter*, but she'll do."

Hannah shook her head. "You and that boat. I'm surprised you was able to leave it behind."

He grinned guiltily and took a step towards her. "Not easy. She's solid built and ready to ride. But look who I didn't leave behind." Slipping both arms around her waist, he pulled her close.

For an instant, she relaxed and let herself be drawn to him, but then she stiffened and pushed him back with a hand on his chest. "Robert. People can see. You got to act proper. They watchin' us, every minute."

His smile deepened. "Mrs. Smalls," he said in his most proper voice, "may I request the honor and privilege of a tour of our cabin?"

And now he got the smile he'd been hoping for, one that often got lost in the sea of work and worry in Beaufort. "Why, Mistuh Smalls, I would be delighted."

*****

The instant the cabin door was closed, his lips were on hers. He always loved the way she tasted. "I think I'm gon' like the rest of this tour," he said.

"Hush. We gots respectable ladies for neighbors" she whispered, as he ran his hands up her back, bringing her close. With every new kiss he undid another button. The dress had too many damn buttons. Front and back and all over the place. She was just as hungry for him as he was for her, and she reached back and undid the last fastenings herself. Then her hands moved on to his jacket, tie, and shirt.

She arched her long neck and cinnamon shoulders as he kissed his way down to her bare breasts. His fingers were rough from years on the docks, but he knew how to use a gentle touch. He liked her hands on him, her own hands toughened from hard labor in the hotel and from steaming tubs of laundry. But now those hands were just for him, on his chest, his hips, everywhere. She knew what to do with those hands.

Robert moaned and pushed her back half a step. "Let me see you," he said, his voice hoarse with desire. "All of you."

She let her slip fall to her feet and stood naked before him. For the whole time they'd known each other, he'd shared her. With Kingman, with the men at the Mills House Hotel, in more ways than was even thinkable. Husbands of slaves weren't allowed to be jealous the way a free man was. The ones who couldn't control their jealousy ended up sold or dead.

And he shared her with the children. There wasn't an ounce of privacy in the old rooms over the stables, or the new ones crammed above the store. But here in this little cabin, not much bigger than a prison cell, they were alone. And free. A man and a woman, a black Adam and Eve. These four walls, rocking in the waves, could be their Eden.

He made her wait for him, as he admired every inch of her body. The gentle curve of her breasts and her dark nipples, begging to be caressed. The curve of her hips, a woman's hips, the lean muscles of her belly, sturdy thighs, thighs she'd wrap around him in two more heartbeats. Knees worn hard from scrubbing floors. Five freckles on the flat lovely space between her breasts and chin, dark little stars on a sky of brown.

"You seen enough?" she asked, shyly.

"I almost never get to see you, all of you," he said, his voice low and thick. "You's so beautiful, Hannah. No man ever been as lucky as me."

"And now I'm all yours." She closed the gap between them again, her breasts grazing his chest. "So maybe you better take me."

He did. They took each other in every way possible in that small box of a cabin—on the bunk, on the floor, against the wall, against the door. They moved to the rhythm of the rocking waves and the pulsations of the giant iron screw beneath the water. Every ounce of pent-up longing, for freedom, for release, for a world that could make sense, was channeled through their bodies, until they had nothing left.

They finally lay on the bunk, bodies sticky and spent. He floated on the edge of consciousness, his fingers drifting lazily against her back, tracing her spine, feeling like he'd been hollowed out.

*****

The stars glimmered overhead, the Milky Way a smear of bright infinity, as Robert and Hannah leaned against the rail, looking up past the billowing sails.

"Something, ain't it?" he said.

"I can see why you like being out here, on the water."

The world beyond the ship seemed empty and blank, either full of possibility, or full of dread.

"This as far North as I ever been. From here on, it's all new ocean to me." Every turn of the propeller pulled them closer to Washington and the strange, unfamiliar world that lurked here.

"You nervous about meetin' all them fancy folks?"

"Trying not to think about it."

"You be fine. They all think you's a hero. They won't have much use for me."

He grasped her hand in his. "You be with me. You put all them families on the *Planter*, just as much as me."

"I ain't no society lady, Robert. I's good at doing. Even right now, I feel like I should be doing something. This the first time in my whole life I don't have to do nothing for nobody. Even since we been to Beaufort, we got the store, the chi'ren, customers coming through the door. I knows how to do that."

Her face looked troubled in the dim light, and he reached a hand up to her cheek. "Ain't a sin to rest, Hannah. When we get back, it all gon' start up again. If we don't take this chance to breathe and look up at those stars, we ain't never gon' do it."

She leaned against him, allowing him to put his arms around her. He felt her breathe, deeply, and start to relax.

"If you really need to do for someone, maybe when we get back to the cabin..."

She laughed. "I knew it wouldn't be easy marrying a younger man. Don't you never get tired?"

"Not of you."

"You just use that charm on those white folks in Washington, and we all be okay."

The prospect of the meetings seemed a little more real, now that they had sailed north of Charleston. He looked out into the darkness ahead. "You think they really might listen? Might let us fight? I'm just a sailor."

"You a man. That's what they need to know."

CHAPTER 19

Washington was like Charleston and hell, mixed together. Some of the buildings were grander than anything he'd ever seen before, crafted in towering white marble. And then, between the government edifices and fancy hotels and mansions, encampments of black refugees sprouted out of the stinking earth. Little black girls and boys, no different from Lizzie and Junior, stumbled in the mud, wearing rags that would have shamed even the most humble slaves on Edisto plantations.

The carriage driver, a white man in a dusty brown suit, pulled over to the side of Pennsylvania Avenue to make way for a column of soldiers marching in dusty uniforms, trying to keep in line as a rooster scooted through their ranks, squawking and crowing. A soldier finally gave a sharp kick, sending the bird into the middle of the avenue. It flapped its wings, releasing a cloud of tattered feathers, its comb blood red in the hot sun. Then it was grabbed by a black teen-aged boy in a busted straw hat and shoved into a burlap bag, the squawking silenced with a quick snap. Above the din of the marching soldiers, a voice could barely be heard: "Hey! That's my rooster. Boy! Come back here, boy!"

The boy ran and a bearded white man stumbled down an alley after him.

"That's the Capitol building, right over there," called the driver. Reverend French, Robert, and Hannah rose off their seats for a better look. It was a building on a whole different

170

STEERING TO FREEDOM

scale from anything Robert had seen before. The front columns alone would have made for a splendid building in Charleston, but then there was a whole other set of columns at the base of the dome, and then another. The rest was covered in scaffolding, with cranes and beams and workmen scrambling over the building like insects.

"The old wooden dome had started to rot," Reverend French explained. "The new dome will be iron, designed to last for centuries. Just like, God willing, our restored Union, once this war is over." He mopped the sweat dripping off his own bald, white dome with a handkerchief. For as far north as they'd come, it seemed hotter here than back home.

Hannah nodded appreciatively. "Looks important. Majestic. That's the word."

Robert wished he could come up with words like that when he wanted them. Majestic. This whole trip wasn't about sailing, it was about words. What were the generals thinking, sending him up here? Reverend French knew the words. Hannah could find them. Robert could tell you all the words for any part of a steamboat or sloop or schooner, but what words were he supposed use with the Secretary of War of the United States, to convince him to let black men be soldiers?

"Yes," said Reverend French. "The presidential inauguration is held on the capitol steps. The grounds are filled with a sea of people."

"Wish I could have been there to see that," Robert said.

"They don't allow niggers at the inauguration," the cab driver chimed in, spitting a great spurt of tobacco juice as he clicked at the horses to start up again. "Never have."

Robert wondered how a country that wouldn't let colored folks get a glimpse of a new president could ever let them be soldiers? Or voters? Big ships didn't turn easy. If the generals were right, time was running out for their freedom in Beaufort.

"You've got a reservation at this hotel, right?" the driver asked. He took a plug of tobacco from a pouch in his pocket and put it in his cheek. "Most hotels are packed to the gills these

171

days, with the war, and with the government and army growing so fast. Isn't hardly anywhere to put people these days."

"We certainly do have a reservation," Reverend French assured all of them.

A breeze stirred, but rather than bring relief, it carried the stench from the latrine ditches dug close to the river. From hospital tents drifted the odor of rotting flesh. If Robert succeeded in his mission this week, his friends would have a chance to be part of that stink themselves.

*****

They passed the elegant Willard Hotel, the one where presidents stayed, and turned north a few blocks, to the Baltimore Hotel. The four-story building with peeling brown paint probably hadn't been much to look at even when it was new.

The inside of the Baltimore was dark and smoky, and the red-patterned carpets needed sweeping. The closeness of the lobby, with its elaborate woodwork, multiplied the heat. Hannah produced a fan to keep herself from fainting from heat stroke.

A clerk with pock-marked cheeks and a thick round nose sat behind the front desk, reading a newspaper. He looked up at their arrival, but that was about all the greeting he seemed capable of extending.

Beyond the desk, three hallways extended in every direction, and a set of carpeted stairs rose in front of them.

"Good afternoon," the reverend said. "We have a reservation for two rooms. I wired ahead from Port Royal. The telegram may have been sent over from the War Office, perhaps a day ago." He was puffing from the heat, but still managed to use a tone that insisted he was someone important.

The clerk slowly produced the registration book, frowning slightly at the new arrivals. "Name?"

"Reverend Mansfield French, and Mr. and Mrs. Robert

Smalls."

"Hm." The clerk looked over the writing in the book. "I see the names. Smalls. That seems familiar."

"You're obviously a reader," Reverend French said, "Perhaps you saw Mr. Smalls mentioned in the newspapers in May, for his heroic exploits in Charleston Harbor."

"Oh, yeah." The clerk broke into a grey-toothed smile, pleased to have a real live famous person in front of him. "You're the nigger that stole the boat. It's all anyone talked about for days and days. Way to stick it to the Rebs."

"Mr. Smalls is a hero," continued the Reverend. "Commended in an Act of Congress."

"Good for you. If a couple thousand more do what you done, then the Rebs will have to head back home, and this damn war could be over. Beg your pardon, Reverend."

Reverend French smiled. "We pray to God every day for the end of this war, and for freedom for all of God's children, and an end to the scourge of slavery that's been festering in our country."

The clerk wrinkled his nose at the mention of slavery. "One of those abolitionists, huh? We get all kinds here. Watch out. Not everyone with a brother or nephew marching through the mud is keen on you fellas."

"Thanks for the advice," the reverend said. "We've been traveling for a long time and would greatly appreciate the keys to our rooms."

Robert inched his fingers towards his jacket pocket, ready to present cash for the room. He wasn't sure how much it would be, but he intended to pay his own way.

"Rooms?" the clerk said.

"Yes, we have a reservation for two rooms."

"Who else is coming?"

"No one. It's just us three, here on official business of the United States Army, on behalf of Generals Saxton and Hunter." Reverend French's voice rose just a notch.

"We don't rent room to niggers. I thought they was here with you."

"We're together, yes." Reverend French shifted nervously, irritated.

"Sometimes, people bring their servants. There's two servant's room in the attic, one for men and one for women. Only two other niggers there now, so there's bunks enough. But I couldn't give them a room."

"I have money," Robert said, his hand out of his pocket presenting a wad of bills. "Maybe a little something extra, for the special hospitality you'd be givin' us."

The clerk's eyes widened at the sight of the cash, and he picked nervously at a scab on his cheek. "Well, I... It's just not allowed. I couldn't. Times is hard, and I need this job. Much as, you know, you being in the papers and all. The other guests wouldn't understand. My boss won't even hire Negro maids, even though I tell him that they use them over at the Willard, and that's the most high-class place in the city. He brings down Irish girls from New York, fresh off the boat. Says they work harder, cheaper. I can register you as Reverend Mansfield and servants. But just the one room."

Robert felt a fire rising in himself, burning far hotter than the summer heat.

"What if I pay for two rooms?" Reverend French asked.

"Sir, I know you're trying to be clever, and all, but—"

"We don't want to be clever," Robert interrupted. He was tempted to unleash Hannah on this boy. She was keeping everything bottled up for now, but her fan was beating faster and faster. He could imagine her using it to beat the clerk senseless. After all her years of working at the Mills House hotel, emptying chamber pots and changing dirty sheets, she'd been looking forward being a guest in a hotel. To being treated as fully human. "We just want a room. And we've got cash money, right here."

"The hotel don't want your money."

"This man and woman are just that," said Reverend French, his face getting red, "a man and woman, created by God, just like you, just like the rest of your guests. He's served his country in time of war."

The clerk's sympathy shifted to annoyance. "Look, Reverend, do you want a room for yourself or not? They can stay in the servant's quarters, like the rest of them. And don't look all high and mighty at me. Go try your argument at the Willard and see how far God and sympathy gets you."

"You don't understand who these people are," the Reverend protested.

"Reverend," Robert said. "That's enough." There was no sense unleashing his inner fire on this clerk—the flame would only burn him and Hannah and accomplish nothing. He'd spent a lifetime learning when white folks were going to change their minds. It was a skill that kept him from having a back full of scars. He had hoped that once he was free, it was a skill he wouldn't need so much. He should have known better.

Robert looked at Hannah, who quickly turned and walked out towards the street, her head held high. He grabbed their traveling bags and followed behind her.

*****

They waited in the hired cab until a lady wearing a fine silk hoop dress and shimmering pearl earrings emerged from the dress shop, accompanied by a black servant carrying a gown shrouded in muslin, as carefully as if he'd been transporting a holy relic. The woman watched him with sharp eyes, making sure he kept her new acquisition far from the dirty street. The driver helped the lady mount the carriage with careful grace. She disappeared from the street, just as the horses dropped a load of dung to the cobblestones and pulled the carriage out of sight.

Reverend French instructed the cab driver to wait, and they knocked gently at the front door of the shop. Hannah tried to straighten her traveling dress, which bore stains from a day on board a steamer, carts, and carriages, and was damp from sweating in Washington's never-ending heat. Robert liked her that way—a little rumpled and sweaty.

"I's a fright," she said. "What she gon' think of me?"

"You look fine," Robert tried to reassure her.

"You say she tells the fanciest ladies in Washington what they should wear, making they gowns."

Reverend French patted her gently on the shoulder. "You have never met a woman with more understanding and compassion that Mrs. Keckly, I promise you."

The door finally opened and they were met by a short, sharp-chinned, brown-skinned woman in a perfectly fitting black work dress, one that seemed more fashionable because of the ribbons and buttons she'd sewn on it. Her face broke into a genuine smile at the sight of them.

"Reverend French! I'm so sorry you had to wait, but Mrs. McClean can't bear to be disturbed during a fitting. Usually the summer is our quiet time, but all the ladies are trying to beat the rush for the autumn galas. With all I'm doing for Mrs. Lincoln these days, I can't keep up. Even with the three extra girls I've hired, it just isn't enough. But I'm prattling. Please, come out of the sun."

She led them into an elegant parlor filled with a row of dress forms lined along the back wall, and a triple set of full-length mirrors for ladies to admire their full beauty.

The way she stood, so straight and proper, reminded Robert of some of the undertakers' wives in Charleston, part of the whole group of free blacks who didn't have much use for him when he was a slave, though they bought smuggled sugar and tea whenever he had it. She was light-skinned like them, too, coffee with lots of cream.

The reverend took a step back and admired her. "You look absolutely lovely, Mrs. Keckly. I can't tell you how happy it makes me to see you thriving. If anyone deserves it, after all you've been through, it certainly is you."

The "all you've been through" took the light from her eyes for a moment. "You're very kind, Reverend French. I so appreciated your letter after George... Many other mothers have had to sacrifice for the Union. I can only hope the war will end soon and help dry our river of tears. But I am being rude. You must be Mr. and Mrs. Smalls."

She extended her hand in a genteel fashion, and Robert took it, not quite sure what to do with it. Kissing it didn't seem quite right, though he'd seen a few dandies in Charleston do it, so he just shook it. "It's a pleasure to meet you, Ma'am."

Hannah took her turn as well, and gave a little bow, maybe like she'd done at the Mills House Hotel as a maid. The two women weren't far apart in age, with Mrs. Keckly just a few years older.

"Thanks for welcoming us," Hannah said.

"I'm sure you've had a long trip. Betsy! Please bring some cold lemonade for our guests. Sit, please. I'm so flustered by seeing you, after all I've read in the papers. I'm forgetting my manners." She led them over to a pair of burgundy velvet covered couches near the carefully curtained bay windows.

A dark-skinned girl in a simple frock emerged from the back, carrying a tray with lemonade and cups. The cold drinks felt like a taste of heaven after a long day in the heat.

"I am so sorry to intrude on your workday, Mrs. Keckly," said Reverend French. "But we have something of a challenge. We've come on an important mission from Generals Saxton and Hunter, but have had trouble finding a place to stay. We tried the Baltimore Hotel, but–"

Mrs. Keckly shook her head. "The hotels are worse than ever. With so many newly freed Negroes on the streets, white folks almost can't bear to see a black face anymore. And the poor people truly are horrifying—dirty, smelly, ignorant, with absolutely no idea of how to improve their situations. And almost no one seems interested in helping them."

Helping poor Negroes was Reverend French's mission in life these days, and his face always lit up when he talked of it. "We confront the same problems in Port Royal, but our experiment on the plantations will show that with freedom, faith, and the right guidance, the Negro can be completely self-sufficient."

With a laugh, Mrs. Keckly waved towards herself and Robert and Hannah. "You don't need to tell us."

"If we want abolition to move forward nationwide, we must prove it on a broad scale. This year's harvest will show what can be accomplished."

"There are many possible examples, aren't there?" said Mrs. Keckly. "I've read all about your exploits on the *Planter*, Mr. Smalls. I've gone over the newspaper clippings so many times, I feel I've memorized your entire adventure. I run a dress shop, I tell well-respected ladies how to appear fashionable and beautiful. But a story about me won't capture anyone's attention or imagination. What the two of you have done is entirely different. Adventure on the high seas, danger, darkness, the churning river, mines and torpedoes, the dreaded Fort Sumter."

Robert happily soaked up her admiration. "It was quite a night."

"You must have been so frightened," Mrs. Keckly said to Hannah, "with your children in tow. The thought that if something went wrong..."

"It was a good plan," Hannah said. "Robert had it all worked out. As long as everyone did their part, I knew we could do it. You know how it feels, to need to be free so much that it's worth any chance."

"I do. And I know how it feels now. My heart is sometimes very heavy. Very heavy. My son, George, I saw him to freedom. Even saw him to college, to Wilberforce University. I give thanks to God every day for helping Reverend French and his friends found a school that would admit Negroes. But George was light skinned enough to pass for white, and he left college to join the Missouri's First Regiment. He was killed at the Battle of Wilson's Creek, almost exactly a year ago." She paused, eyes down. "Even when my heart feels black as coal, missing my son,

I know it's no longer bound in chains."

If Robert's dispatches convinced the president, Mrs. Keckly wouldn't be the only black mother mourning a fallen soldier. But without the grief of mothers like Mrs. Keckly, a whole race of men faced a bleak future.

How would he handle such a loss? He didn't like to even imagine life without Lizzie or Robert Junior. He wished they weren't hundreds of miles away, so he could find them for a quick touch and a laugh.

"I'm so sorry," said Hannah. "We's all grateful for your sacrifice. No mother should have to bear it." Robert knew the absence of the children weighed heavily on her.

Mrs. Keckly took a deep breath and tried to force the smile back on her face. "Thank you. We must carry on."

"Your faith in the Lord will bring you comfort," said Reverend French, "I pray for you and all the mothers who suffer in this war."

"Victory will bring us the relief we need," said Mrs. Keckly. "But you did not come here to hear my woes. What brings you?"

"We're desperate for a place for Robert and Hannah to stay," said Reverend French. "I hate to impose, but my resources are proving to be useless. I hoped you might be able to help."

"Of course!" She brightened at an excuse to leave behind her grief and do something actively positive. "I rent a room from Walker and Virginia Lewis, right across the street. Mr. Lewis is a steward at the Capitol and one of the finest men you'll ever meet, and Mrs. Lewis is a lady. I'm certain that Walker's brother, Daniel, has a room that's just come empty. I will write you a note of introduction. Daniel's wife, Martha, is a dear. She cooks for Senator Sumner. She'd be delighted to have you take a room in their house."

Robert nodded. "We're much obliged, Mrs. Keckly. It's hard to be a stranger so far from home. Not knowing the ways things is done."

"You could pay me back by calling me Lizzy. The both of you. I'd be delighted to be able to call you friends."

"I'd like that, Lizzy," said Hannah, though Robert could feel her holding back. Was it hard for Hannah to be around a woman who'd been free for a few years already, and who appeared so polished and put together? And whose wide dark eyes would definitely be considered beautiful?

"And I have a favor to ask, one that would put me in your debt."

"Anything," Robert said. She was the kind of woman who made you want to perform favors.

"I am not the only one to notice the disastrous plight of our dark brothers and sisters, newly crawled out from under the pressing burden of slavery. Though I see the finest white ladies throwing balls and raising money for wounded and sick Union soldiers, and for their widows and orphans, not a penny is going to clothe and feed the least among us, those scraping for crumbs in the muck."

"Something must be done," enjoined the Reverend.

"Done by those who have more experience with freedom and have made something of ourselves. With the help of other ladies at the Union Bethel Church, I have just formed the Contraband Relief Association. We will gather donations of food, blankets, clothing, and money, to help our suffering brothers and sisters."

"You're a godly woman, Mrs. Keckly," said Reverend French. "How many white hands withdraw their largess, ignoring our Savior's words, 'For it is the one who is least among you all who is the greatest?' How many ignore Christ's sermons about helping the poor, giving the cloak from one's back?" The reverend had made this point around Beaufort many times, though Robert had noticed that the reverend himself always had a full table and a soft bed.

"I'm sure we can give a little something," Hannah said, though they were already working hard back home to help the newest escaped slaves whenever they entered Beaufort. Every time an order of blankets arrived on an incoming ship, they set aside some for the new arrivals. There were always leftover greens and corn from the farm trade saved to feed the hungry. It was the Christian thing to do, and it was smart business. Those newly escaped men and women, if they stayed, would find work on the plantations or the docks. If they treated them right to start, any money they spent would be spent at Smalls Supplies.

"Though I would appreciate any donation, I have a greater request. We are having our first fundraiser in two days, a dinner with music and speeches at the Fifteenth Street Presbyterian Church. Nothing would excite our guests more than hearing you tell your story, Robert. Hearing what you've done in the heart of the South will stir them to have hope. And hope will cause them to be generous to our unfortunate cousins living in the mud."

How was he supposed to speak to a crowd and not sound like an ignorant slave? It was one thing to talk to the crew in the engine room, another to stand on a stage like the Reverend did every Sunday.

He looked at Hannah, hoping she'd offer a way out. But she looked as determined as ever and nodded. "You want to be a captain someday?" she said. "Time for you to start thinking about how to be a captain to your people, and not just on the water."

All three of them looked at him with such expectation— Reverend French, who treated him like a man from the first moment they met, his wife who never doubted him in anything, and this dark-eyed woman with the compelling smile, with her skill with words and the sewing needle, who used her charm to get all the way into the White House itself.

"I guess I could say a few words." But he was sure he was going to regret it.

CHAPTER 20

A knock on the door jolted Robert upright from a deep sleep. Light spilled through the shuttered windows. "Mr. Smalls," called Mrs. Lewis from the hall. "The reverend has arrived and is asking for you."

Hannah stirred under the sheets with a low moan. Robert was already on his feet, splashing water from the basin onto his face and giving his body a quick sailor's shower. "I'll be right down," he called. "Thank you."

Lizzy Keckly had come through yesterday, as she'd promised, and found a room for them with the Lewis family. Daniel was a barber with a shop on U Street. "No matter how poor folks are, sooner or later they need a haircut," Daniel had told them. "And if they wants to serve in the fancy homes round here, they need to look right, not like they cut it themselves without so much as a mirror."

When Daniel and Martha heard that Robert and Hannah were part of the *Planter*'s liberation team, they refused to take any money for the room. "It's an honor to have you stay with us," Martha had insisted. She was a thick-waisted, light-skinned woman with bright green eyes—who seemed to know just about everyone. "Lizzy says you will speak at our gala tomorrow, which is absolutely perfect. Some of those fine-dressed Negroes only get that way 'cause their grip on a dollar is so tight. Maybe you're what we need to loosen those fingers a little. They see them wretches on the street every day, but sympathy don't make a man give. Hope and heroism might make them feel like they's part of something important. You do that, and they'll reach into their wallets."

"Don't get up," he told Hannah, as he quickly tossed on the new suit Hannah and Mama Lydia had made for him back home. The cloth hadn't come cheap, but if he was going to meet important folks, he needed to look proper.

"Get that tie right," she said, brushing her hair out of her face and crawling to him across the bed. "And eat something 'fore you go, or else your stomach be growling right through that meetin'."

"You gon' be all right here?" He knew how much she missed Lizzie and Junior. It didn't seem right for her to spend all day here by herself, feeling lonely.

"Mrs. Keckly told me to come by her shop. I can pretend to be an assistant and listen to whether the nonsense talked by fancy ladies in Washington is any different from what they say in Charleston."

He stood in front of her, and she dusted off his shoulders. "I look all right?"

"You look like a real gentleman, but not so much we can't see the sailor in you."

*****

In the carriage, Reverend French put down his Bible and greeted Robert. "I know it's far too early to be up and about," he said, as he nodded to the driver. Reverend French was well known in Beaufort for his leisurely morning prayer service and long breakfasts. This was probably the earliest he'd been out of his robe in a long time. "But the reception room at the War Department fills up fast with beseechers, office holders, widows, orphans, and soldiers. The office opens precisely at nine, and we need to secure a spot as close to the door as possible."

"I thought Secretary Stanton was your friend. You goes way to back to Ohio and all that."

Reverend French scrunched up his face, like he'd just chewed on a lemon. "Oh, yes. But Stanton is... how shall I put it, a challenging personality. And he's more cautious than any official I've ever met in taking care not to show favoritism. Our friendship could almost be a hindrance in this case. We will speak cautiously and directly."

The reverend lapsed into silence and looked a lot more worried than seemed promising.

*****

As the Reverend had predicted, the hallway outside the War Department reception room was far from empty when they arrived. Over the next half hour, the corridor filled with people determined to talk to Secretary Stanton. Robert's was the only black face among the crowd. Across the carpet from them, a soldier in blue uniform leaned against the wall, supporting himself and his one leg with crutches. A frail woman with wrinkles upon wrinkles constantly dabbed at her teary eyes with her kerchief. Lawyers in suits and long mustaches held leather cases of papers, preparing to make their arguments to Stanton, who, the Reverend explained to Robert, was once Attorney General, head lawyer for the whole country.

How were they supposed to make an argument to a sharpie like that, even with papers from Generals Hunter and Saxton?

The air in the hallway soon grew hot and moist with the breath and sweat of dozens of people in various states of anxiety and desperation. Was he as desperate as the rest? Success meant freedom for him and Hannah and Lizzie and Junior and Mama Lydia. Failure meant a possible return of slavery to the Carolinas. The Union soldiers might get tired of this war, but no soldier born a slave would shrug off his duty and let the South win.

General Hunter's big proclamation from last year, the one that stirred up Robert and the crew, didn't last four weeks before a nervous President Lincoln took it all back. Robert wasn't sure a man who could yank out the rug of freedom like that would change his mind, no matter what the generals back in Beaufort said.

At exactly nine o'clock, the door opened, and a colonel with a dark cloud of a mustache and beard stepped forward and looked over the assembled throng. His voice, tinged with a touch of Scotland, rang above the hum of the crowd. "Good morning ladies and gentlemen. Welcome to the War Department. I am Colonel Hardie, and I will assist you today in bringing your request to Secretary Stanton. You will be orderly and well-behaved. There will be no pushing, cutting in line, or spitting on the floor. Violators will be removed and not be readmitted.

"As you pass through this door to the reception room, you will state your name, your place of residence, and a brief summary of why you need to see the Secretary. If you begin to relate your entire tale of woe, or your brilliant plan to save the Union Army, you will go back to the end of the line."

He looked around, catching the eyes of people he suspected might cause him the most trouble. But for as much complaining as he was likely to encounter, Colonel Hardie wore a broad smile and stood with an energy that made it seem like he was glad to get out of bed every morning, just to hear about these people's problems.

Thanks to Reverend French's determination to arrive early, they were close to the front of the line. Ahead of them, an old man wobbled on a cane and held a horn in his free hand, to overcome his poor hearing. At the very front stood a sharply dressed man with slicked back hair and a practiced smile. Robert had seen enough of his kind to know that trust would be a dangerous option with such a man.

The colonel sat behind a writing desk with a sheet of paper and pen, blocking passage through the doors of the reception room. "Name and business," he said efficiently, but not curtly.

"Mansfield French and Robert Smalls, from Beaufort, South Carolina. We carry a written request from Generals David

Hunter and Rufus Saxton, regarding the raising of Negro troops." Anyone in Beaufort would have fallen over to hear Reverend French speak without a Bible verse and the start of a sermon.

"Why didn't this request come through normal channels?" queried Hardie with the raise of an eyebrow.

"The generals wish to have the request be personally made by Mr. Smalls. He's well known for his bravery in the incident involving the steamship *Planter* earlier this year. Providence has given us a man with a unique—"

Hardie gave Robert an assessing look. "Yes. I've heard of you. As has the Secretary. May I see the dispatch?"

Robert handed it to the colonel. He read it quickly, and his mouth twitched. "Interesting. Go inside and take a seat."

With that, Hardie was already on to the next supplicant. Robert and Reverend French found a comfortable settee on which to make camp. At the front of the room, near another set of double doors, stood a tall desk, suited for standing rather than sitting, flanked on either side by a collection of more traditional desks, already occupied by clerks converting ideas, favors, and questions into ink on paper. Windows along the left side of the room looked out across a parched lawn towards Pennsylvania Avenue and the White House. Dozens of chairs and settees and couches and stools were arranged into rows with plenty of legroom and a central aisle. It reminded Robert a little of the Tabernacle Baptist Church back home in Beaufort.

The room seemed split evenly into thirds—ordinary citizens, soldiers and veterans, and businessmen and government officials. A buzz of commiseration and excitement grew, as partners conferred about strategy, and strangers made new friends, looking for advice or sizing up the competition. Many of them glanced over at Robert suspiciously. Slavery had only been abolished in Washington a few months ago, and any dark face was still supposed to be kept in its place.

Reverend French leaned toward Robert. "When we knew each other back in Ohio, Stanton was a model of sociability. But when his wife, Mary, passed, he took it hard. Almost killed him. And then his brother cut his own throat, not two years later. To bear so much while keeping a good humor is too much to ask of any man. Did Job ever smile?"

"I imagine not."

"Stanton found himself a second wife, Ellen. A woman of expensive tastes. But now they've just lost their son, poor little James, in July. Just a baby."

"Losing a son's more than any man can stomach," Robert said, wishing Junior wasn't so far away, wondering what he and Lizzie were up to. Toddling around the store? Out in the yard, chasing chickens? Keeping Mama Lydia busy, that was for sure. As scared as Robert was of talking to Stanton, Junior and Lizzie were reason enough to try.

"We'll make no mention of it. Not even in sympathy. Nothing personal here. Edwin possesses the most curious combination of integrity and ambition. He's managed to add a bit of ruthlessness and steel to the mix, which has gotten him where he wants to be. Fortunately, the Lord has given him a natural dislike of slavery."

A bell tinkled three times, somewhere on the floor above. The clerks at the desk suddenly sat at full attention, pens scratching furiously at their papers. The double doors boomed open, held by uniformed orderlies, and Secretary Stanton entered the room. He wore a fine dark suit with a high white collar, and his beard cascaded halfway down his chest, stopping at an ample belly. His balding head and shaved cheeks at first gave the appearance a harried bookkeeper, but Stanton's gaze was something else entirely. He stood in the doorway of the silent room and looked at each petitioner with sharp eyes and an assessing frown. Robert knew plenty of other short men like this one—ready for a scrap, willing to take on any comer and lay him flat on the ground. This one did it with the law and power instead of with his fists, but it was all the same.

No one in the room could keep his eyes raised when Stanton looked at them full on. Even the battle-hardened soldier in the corner ended up studying the lint on his own trousers. Robert met Stanton's eyes for just long enough to both catch his attention and let him know this might be something important.

The entire room watched as Colonel Hardie, still wearing his broad smile, approached Stanton. The colonel showed Stanton the list of petitioners, telling him in a low voice which ones had the most possible merit and were least likely to try his patience.

Stanton reached into his suit pocket for a handkerchief and wiped his small, steel rimmed glasses and then looked at Hardie's list once more. "Corporal Flint?"

The young man in the middle row with crutches and a missing leg started to stand. "On my way, sir," he called.

"Stay where you are, soldier." Stanton left his desk and quickly stepped over to the corporal. Two clerks shadowed his every move, ink and paper at the ready. "Looks like you've already made a great sacrifice for your country, Corporal," Stanton said, his voice gentler than Robert had expected.

"Yes, sir. Lost my leg at Bull Run."

"Why are you here today?"

"They lost my promotion paperwork, so I'm getting my pension as a private, but I'm a corporal. When I showed them my stripe, they said anyone can buy one for two dollars. I don't know what to do. I used to farm in Maryland, near Frederick, but I can't get around much. And the land has been passed over twice by armies. My children are hungry."

"But you have no documentation?"

"Just this stripe," said the soldier, pointing to his uniform. "And a letter from my wife. She wrote it to me, answering after I told her about it. We're just simple folk, it ain't literature or nothing." He handed Stanton the letter, which the secretary read quickly but carefully.

"Some say an army runs on its stomach. But they always forget to add the paperwork," Stanton said. He turned towards one of the clerks. "Alert the Paymaster General's office to establish Corporal Flint at his proper pension and disability pay, back dated. Corporal Flint, the army will attempt to deal with you in a slightly less idiotic fashion from this point forward, but given the nature of the beast, I won't make any promises."

"Thank you, sir." Corporal Flint stuck out an eager and deeply scarred hand and shook Stanton so hard the man almost fell over. Stanton quickly retreated to the podium.

The next half dozen applicants didn't fare as well as Corporal Flint. One woman, who'd come looking for the War Department to compensate her for broken windows in her house after a nearby battle left in tears. Another man, the slick one, stood absolutely still as Stanton took his letter of introduction from Mrs. Lincoln and tore it to shreds. Stanton's nostrils flared with disgust as he sprayed the torn papers in the man's face. "Tell Mrs. Lincoln that when I need to fill a post, I am perfectly capable of finding people who are actually qualified, rather than hangers-on barely acquainted with the concept of a day's work."

As the man weathered a string of abuse, Robert could see the heel of his boot shaking. The secretary finally paused for breath and mopped his forehead with his handkerchief and wiped his glasses. He returned the spectacles to his nose and squinted in disbelief. "You're still here? Hardie!"

The man broke his own paralysis and scurried down the center aisle and out the doors, schooled on the perils of looking for patronage from the War Department. Or at least from this particular office. Robert had seen plenty of loafers and thieves operating under cover of Union business back in Beaufort.

"Mansfield French and Robert Smalls," came Stanton's voice. He peered curiously over the rim of his glasses as they approached the desk. Would they escape his wrath? The reverend didn't look nervous, but maybe he felt their old friendship would insulate him from the fire. Robert's palms and the backs of his knees were sweating.

"State your business." If he and Reverend French were ever

friends, there wasn't any sign of it from Stanton.

The reverend smiled a familiar smile that seemed to ignore the fury that had been spit out by Stanton just minutes before. "We've brought a written dispatch from Generals Hunter and Saxton in Port Royal. In this case, the messenger is as important as the message itself. This is Mr. Robert Smalls, recently of Charleston, who, through a careful plan and great bravery, delivered a valuable rebel steamship and guns to the Union Navy, and brought his crew and family out of bondage, with a flourish worthy of Moses himself."

"General Hunter knows how I feel about stunts. I would expect you to, as well, Mr. French."

Reverend French swallowed hard. "His bravery has been publicly recognized by Congress."

"True valor is not a political act. Perhaps Congress would do better to keep their grubby hands off it. The letter?" Stanton held out his hand impatiently.

Robert produced the letter from General Saxton and they watched Stanton read it. Robert wasn't so good with his own reading yet. Hannah was making progress, and little Lizzie was already mastering her ABCs and reading little books over at a school run by Ms. Towne. But Reverend French had read him the contents of the letter enough times that Robert knew much of it by heart:

> I respectfully but urgently request authority to enroll a force not exceeding 5,000 able-bodied men from among the contrabands in this department. The men are to be uniformed, armed, and officered by men detailed from the Army.
>
> My reasons for asking this authority are the following: Along the entire coast occupied by our forces, the people suffer greatly from fear of attack by their rebel masters, in the event of which they expect no mercy at their hands. This fear contracts their individual labors, as well as paralyzing their efforts for

social and moral improvement. The rebellion would be very greatly weakened by the escape of thousands of slaves with their families from active rebel masters if they had such additional security against re-capture as these men, judiciously posted, would afford them.

The letter went on to detail the evacuations from the plantations and the loss of valuable crops and the difficulty housing all the refugees. Stanton read it all carefully.

The secretary folded the letter and slipped it back into the envelope. "And are you the type of contraband they intend to uniform and arm, Mr. Smalls?"

"Suppose I is, sir. I's ready to do whatever it takes to protect my family and my freedom."

"You've already done quite a bit, if what they wrote in the papers is true."

"I haven't read them myself, sir. Been busy piloting ships for the Union against the rebels and starting a business, sir."

Stanton smiled a half smile. "Then you're the only man in Washington who doesn't read his own press. You had a plan?"

"Yes suh. Just started as an idea, almost a joke. But every one of us always wanted a chance. And when we heard General Hunter was freein' any slaves that escaped, we knew it was our time."

"General Hunter's reach far exceeded his grasp."

"The promise of freedom made it worth a try," Robert said.

"Despite the risk. You even brought your family, yes?"

"I couldn't leave them behind. None of us could. How I gon' leave my babies behind, belonging to some other man, and I out there, breathing the free air? Woulda tasted like ashes. Nossuh. We all was ready. Every one knew the hangman would be waiting if we failed. It was a plan, all mapped out. Takes a lot of trust to put the life of your wife and chi'ren in the hands of a crew, but no man ever let slip a whisper. Every one is a man today, suh, ready to do his bit to help the Union, to get his brothers out of slavery."

Robert hadn't planned to say much of anything, but the words just came pouring out. It wasn't just the secretary who was listening, but the whole room had gone silent. Every eye was staring at him. The blood rushed to his face. Would Stanton feel he'd been grandstanding?

"There will be many heroes from this war, Mr. Smalls. You might just be one of them," Stanton said. He stepped squarely behind the desk and scribbled something on a piece of paper, blotted it, stamped it, folded it. He gave it to Robert, along with Saxton's dispatch.

"The War Department is not currently in the business of arming Negroes," he said loudly enough for the entire room to hear. "Though we appreciate your efforts on behalf of the Union, Mr. Smalls, I cannot grant your request."

*****

Both men blinked hard in the bright sun, as Reverend French led the way down the sidewalk to the shade of an elm tree. A group of soldiers slowly walked down Pennsylvania Avenue, kicking up a cloud of dust. Carriages passed back and forth, spiriting officials to meetings, while an ox cart driven by a black man in a floppy hat gradually hauled a load of firewood, headed for the kitchens and restaurants feeding the men holding the reins of power.

"It's a long way to come for a quick no," Robert said. "What am I supposed to tell everyone back home? He didn't even give a reason. 'We ain't in the business of arming Negroes.' Ain't they in the business of winning the war? The generals say they need more men, and we is more men."

Reverend French rubbed his temples with his thumbs, trying to make some sense of what just happened and what to do next. "There must be a way to circle around Stanton. He's not the only Ohio man in Washington. Salmon Chase and I were both present at the start of Wilberforce. No one has given our Port Royal experiment more support. I don't know what he can do from Treasury, in terms of raising troops. But perhaps I could convince him to speak to Stanton, or even the president."

Robert looked out across the sun baked avenue. The colors all looked dusty and faded from the heat and his own disappointment. "Stanton seems like a man who's dangerous to play games with."

The reverend nodded in agreement, and they both watched the traffic move past. Robert wondered if they could catch an earlier passage back to South Carolina. He didn't believe in giving up, but this wasn't anything like back home. Even if he wasn't a slave up here, he still didn't count for much.

He realized he still had the envelope and folded piece of paper in his hands. He opened the paper, but had a hard timing deciphering the pen scratchings. He showed the note to Reverend French.

"What it say?"

French looked at it, shook his head, read it again. Then he smiled and whispered, "Bless you, Lord."

"What it say?"

"It says: *Go to the White House and see Lincoln tomorrow, 11 am. Not for public consumption. Edwin Stanton.*"

CHAPTER 21

From the outside, the White House was as grand as any Carolina plantation house. The great columns on the front made Robert think of the Hampton Plantation, up on Wambaw Creek. He'd heard that the men who started the whole United States were mostly planters anyway, so he supposed it made sense that they wanted to put the boss man in a big plantation house.

He and Reverend French walked up the large circular drive and presented themselves to the guard at the gate. The guard looked skeptically at Robert, but allowed them to pass. Union soldiers in dress blues paraded over the front lawn, long rifles and bayonets pointing up at the overcast sky.

As they climbed the front stairs to the main entrance, messengers passed them at a jog, both coming and going. Inside, clerks scurried back and forth with armfuls of paper. Men in suits, lawyers and legislators, talked in low tones, raising them when they hoped to have their message overheard by just the right person.

Reverend French had seemed perfectly calm during yesterday's visit to Secretary Stanton's office, but today he kept wiping damp palms on the flaps of his jacket. So far, Reverend French had found a way to use his special touch with prayer or gentle voice, to get what he wanted. But this was a visit to a different kind of man.

Robert had been over his head for so long, maybe it didn't matter if the water was getting deeper. If his feet couldn't touch the bottom, it didn't matter how deep he was going to sink.

The uniformed guard inside the door gave them a quick assessing look. One side of his face was longer than the other, making him seem lopsided. "Secretary Stanton sent you," he said, in a baritone voice, barely above a whisper.

"Yes," said the Reverend. "We're here to see Mr. Lincoln at eleven o'clock."

"We'll see how the timing works out." He nodded towards a group of civilians in slightly worn suits and carrying notepads. Reporters looked the same here as they'd looked in Port Royal, a little threadbare, a little hungry. "Since they're here at the moment, we'll take you up the back way. This meeting is meant to be discreet." The guard sent them back out the door and downstairs to the servants' entrance.

"You told me he met with other black folks just last week," Robert complained to Reverend French as they went back out into the wet heat, "and they came in through the front door. I ain't as good as them?"

"That meeting was for show. The first time a president ever met with Negroes in the white house. Perhaps concealing you from the public means we have a better chance of him taking you seriously. Mr. Lincoln shows great caution when it comes to the Negro question. No matter which door we enter, what matters is that he hears your voice."

*****

An usher in a dark suit waited for them at the servant's entrance and led them through a maze of hallways, offices, kitchens, and storerooms, up a flight of stairs, to a long, carpeted corridor. No sign of reporters.

They entered an office with two military officers at desks. A thick-necked man with short red hair stood by yet another interior door and beckoned them over.

"I'm Ed McManus. Sorry about the back door, but them's the orders. He should be finished in one minute. We'll keep this short, all right? The hall out there is busier'n ever." He had a lilt of Ireland to his voice, and Robert wondered how long he'd been here. The newspapers said that Mr. Lincoln was talking about shipping all the free Negroes to South America after the war, to some new colony. He wasn't talking about shipping all the Irish back to Ireland, though there were plenty of people who wished he would.

*****

President Lincoln seemed twice as tall and half as wide as Robert expected. He was looking over some papers on his desk when they entered, and he walked over to them, slowly, his legs like some skinny old horse stepping through a rocky field. The Commander-in-Chief couldn't look any more different from carefully attired Secretary of War Stanton, with a suit that was too short in the legs and starting to fray at the end of the sleeves.

His eyes were deep set and dark, and the lines etched on his face showed he understood how hard this war was for everyone. But he managed a smile of greeting and extended a giant hand, first to Reverend French and then to Robert.

"Reverend French, Mr. Smalls, thank you for coming. Secretary Stanton said you carry a message from Port Royal."

The words stumbled out of the reverend's mouth. "Oh, yes, of course, Mr. President. It's an honor to meet you. I've been a supporter, and I want to let you know that everyone in Port Royal sends you their very best wishes. Our little experiment will show everyone that freedom is not just an option for the Negroes, but a necessity. One that will help the entire nation come to peace with our essential problem."

Mr. Lincoln cocked his head in patient puzzlement at Reverend French, waiting for the nervous greeting to play itself out. He had no idea, Robert thought, how long Reverend French could go on. Robert reached into his pocket and produced the letter from the generals and handed it to the President.

Reverend French took a fluttery breath, and Robert could swear the man seemed dizzy from the surroundings of the office. Maybe he should be ready to catch the reverend in case he swooned from excitement.

Lincoln read the letter and placed it on his desk. He gestured towards some chairs for them, though he himself perched on the edge of his desk, exaggerating the height difference even further. Robert found himself wanting to shove the chair backwards, to give himself some space between him and the looming legend.

"Reverend French, I'm happy to hear about the positive progress on your project. Seward and Stanton assure me it will bring important results. For now, most of my time is occupied with thoughts of battle and trying to understand what makes my generals tick. Some of them don't seem to keep very good time, no matter how much I try to wind them up." He smiled at his own small joke. Maybe learning to smile with the weight of the world his shoulders is what got Mr. Lincoln through the dark days. "And then I try to understand how to answer questions like this one. They sent you here, Mr. Smalls, in hopes of persuading me."

"I told them I'd do my best, suh."

The great man stared at Robert for a moment, evaluating him. He'd be an impossible opponent in a poker game—he'd just look at you and you'd want to lay down your cards. "I have heard tales of your exploits with the Confederate ship. What was it called?"

"The *Planter*, suh. Double-wheel steamboat. Transport, now a gunship. Shallow draft, fine fittings, strong enough to haul a thousand bales of cotton."

"Or guns and troops."

"She took plenty of rebel soldiers and cannon all around Charleston Harbor, that's for sure. But she's working for the Union now."

"Thanks to you."

"And my crew, suh. No one can run a ship all by theyselves. We made a plan and stuck to it. If we got caught, we was ready to send her straight to the bottom."

Lincoln leaned forward, and the attention of those eyes, fully fixed on him, drew Robert to tell his story, the whole story. Lincoln's attention never wavered. Finally, Robert finished with them being boarded by the officers of the *Onward*.

"What made you do it?" the president asked.

"No man wants to be a slave, suh. Every one of us spent a whole life wishing, waiting. I gots me a wife and daughter and little son. But they wasn't mine. Their owner could of taken them any time he want, to settle a debt, to trade for a new horse, didn't matter.

"They tell me, back when these states was formed, a soldier with Massa Washington said, 'Give me liberty, or give me death.' I know what that man meant. When I heard that General Hunter said escaped slaves could be free, if they got to the Union, I knew it was time."

Lincoln got to his feet and walked away from them. He looked out the window, over Washington, maybe over the whole nation. What did he see out there? Did he see the miserable escapees in the mud? Slaves on the plantations all the way down South, waiting for their chance to be free? Or did he just see problems, annoyances, a thorn in the side of a nation, a thorn that was causing an infection likely to destroy the whole body?

"Hunter's proclamation helped, did it?"

"Yessuh. We was ready to risk everything, but we needed hope that it weren't for nothin'. You want to know how to keep men slaves, year after year, from father to son, to sons after that? Just take away all they hope. Every dark face in Beaufort, they tell me, 'You tell Massa Lincoln to give us hope that the sun gon' shine freedom on us.'"

The president didn't exactly look like a shining ray of hope at the moment. His brow was furrowed, and he rubbed his fingers together. He paced in front of the desk, his mind clearly churning.

The reverend had remained silent for longer than anyone back home would have thought possible. He added his voice now. "Mr. Lincoln, if I may. I know many wonder whether the contrabands will work, will they fight. They work as hard as any other man, in the blasting heat and swamps, even though they still live on plantations where they've suffered for generations, waiting for their Moses. But what you'll see, more importantly, are their own little gardens, scattered amongst the fields, a thousand carefully tended little Edens. These people are stewards of the land. No one needs to tell them to water or plant their own gardens. You have it in your power to give them a stake in this country, Mr. President. Give them that, and you'll find no better gardeners, no better soldiers."

Mr. Lincoln stopped pacing and looked Robert right in the eyes. His gaze was strong enough to set Robert back in his chair. There was power in this man, and Robert was certain most of the time he kept that power carefully under wraps.

"If I give Hunter and Saxton permission for this, will the Negroes fight?"

"I give you my word, suh. If they free men, they gon' fight to protect they freedom. I'll go out and recruit them my own self, go plantation to plantation, getting them to sign up. Won't be easy, because they had a whole lifetime of learning not to trust any white man. But they got hope in you, suh. They wants to trust you, want to trust in someone who won't throw back on the chains and haul out the whip."

Mr. Lincoln resumed motion again, his voice low now, almost muttering to himself.

"There are some to whom Negroes in Union blue will be an affront, enough to turn their stomachs. As much as I may dislike it, I am sometimes the nursemaid to such throngs. I need to keep their digestion and hearts intact, if there is any hope of preserving this Union. Is there any hope? What does Edmund say in King Lear? "The wheel is come full circle." Where does our fate lie? So many plans, so many thoughts. The horse won't go back in the barn. Some would like to keep the door closed, but maybe it was half-broken to begin with."

Robert let silence fill the room before he gave one last plea. "Mr. Lincoln. Please. Give us a chance to show the world we's really men. We won't let you down."

Lincoln looked at Robert and then examined his own weathered hands. "In my youth, I spent time as a riverboat pilot, on the Sangamon. I'm sure I never had a fraction of your skill, but you and I both know that even the best pilot sometimes runs onto a sandbar. There are ways to get unstuck, but the best solution is to avoid running aground in the first place. I must navigate these treacherous currents with utmost care. I wish it were simple." He gently led them towards the door, the meeting over. "I don't have an answer for you now. See Stanton on Monday, and he'll relay my decision."

CHAPTER 22

Robert leaned against the back wall of the 15th Street Presbyterian Church, watching more than a hundred brown and black ladies and gentlemen crowded around the edges of the pews helping themselves to plates of stewed beef, chicken, bread, greens, beans. They wore their finest dresses and best suits, all on display for each other. Most of them were light-skinned—not many as dark as him.

Hannah walked down the aisle to Robert. "Lizzy says we got more food coming. Can you and Mr. Walters set up another board?"

She wore an indigo satin wrap around her shoulders, which brought out a glow in her cheeks. It was elegant, probably something she borrowed from Lizzy Keckly. She'd been so nervous this afternoon, fretting about her dress. He'd wrapped her in his arms and told her that every woman would be jealous of her. But he knew how she felt. The people here had been living free for years, some even born free and educated. Did the odor of slavery linger on him and Hannah?

Hannah guided him over to Solomon Walters, a tall young man with a flashy smile. They walked out behind the church to a pile of lumber.

"Lots of lovely ladies here, tonight, eh, Mr. Smalls?" said Walters. He had a cocky tilt to his head—no doubt he was used to women admiring his broad shoulders and high cheekbones.

"Hard to argue with that. Though, of course, I's married."

"Don't mean you're blind."

They each picked up one end of a wide pine board. "Naw. But you'll see," Robert said. "Wives have a powerful sense of hearing. When you's married, you learn to appreciate works of beauty silently."

Walters laughed a big laugh. "I intend to appreciate tonight every which way. These ladies ain't just beautiful on the outside, but on the inside, too. I likes a woman with a big heart. And other places, besides."

As they set up the makeshift table, Lizzy Keckly scurried over with three more ladies behind her, each carrying a covered platter. "Thank you, gentlemen. Mr. Smalls, as our honored guest tonight, I'm embarrassed to see you moving tables."

"Sometimes it's easier to do something useful, instead of drinking tea and shaking hands."

As the ladies set down their platters, Walters steered himself over to a fine young woman in an emerald dress that matched her eyes.

Lizzy Keckly remained focused on Robert, almost leaning into him. "It warms my heart to see so much compassion for the poor wretches flooding into our city. Though I suspect many have come solely to hear you speak."

His heart started beating faster, and he wasn't sure whether it was the prospect of going on stage, or the scent of Lizzy Keckly's perfume. "I gon' try not to disappoint. But, you know, I's just a sailor."

"Oh, you're far more than that." She looked at him in a way that made him feel that no matter what she said, there was something she wanted from him. Or was that just what he wanted her to be thinking?

"At some point, you'll just have to accept it," she continued. "For all our people, and even for the white people, what you've done goes far beyond Charleston Harbor." She looked at the door as another group of people entered, carrying food. "Oh, Mrs. Lovely has arrived. Please excuse me, Mr. Smalls."

She brushed his hand as she left, a gesture more familiar than he would have expected. His skin tingled where she'd touched him. She was so refined. Before the war, she'd worked for Mrs. Jefferson Davis and had even been asked to accompany them to Richmond after secession. Now she dressed the wives of senators and the president. A woman of dignity and beauty, but he could see the sadness behind her smile. Lost husband, lost son, hard times as a slave. She could hide it from the fancy white ladies, but he could see it, like a ghost behind a mirror.

Would she ever marry again? Maybe she'd fall for one of these men here tonight, though not someone as young and fresh as Walters. What caught the eye of a woman like her? Did she look at other men the same way she looked at him? He could imagine her looking at him from very close, close enough to touch anywhere and everywhere.

He shouldn't even be thinking about her. Not with his own fine wife over by the tables, looking a little lost.

He'd been in a haze all day after meeting President Lincoln. Lizzy Keckly and Hannah and all the assistants from the dress shop spent the day cooking breads and cakes and cookies. Robert mostly tried to stay out of the way. He couldn't stop thinking about the president, the man with eyes like deep pools of sorrow and death that could drag you right down.

He'd had the president of the United States sitting on the desk right across from him listening to every word of their story. He talked to Mr. Lincoln like a man. But what had he left out? What combination of words, stories, or facts, would have convinced the president that black men would stand and fight for the right to be free, that they cared as much about being Americans as any white soldier?

Maybe he should have pressed harder for total abolition. He could have stood up from that fancy chair and demanded freedom for every slave on American soil.

It was easier to wallow in doubt than to think about standing in front of Lizzy Keckly's friends and neighbors and giving some sort of speech. He was no preacher like Reverend French. And he was certainly no orator like Frederick Douglass or Reverend Henry Highland Garnet, black men who traveled around the world, just because of their words.

He pushed through the thickening crowd to Hannah, and she reached for his hand. "This is Reverend Palmer. Reverend, this is my husband, Robert."

A bald yellow-complexioned man bowed in greeting. "You have a charming wife, Mr. Smalls. It's a delight to meet you. When I saw the story of your exploits in the newspaper, I must have read it five times." His voice was deep and melodious, like it came from the deepest bellow of a pipe organ.

Robert smiled uncomfortably. When he was steering the *Planter* through the channels, or even when he piloted the *Crusader* for Captain Rhind, the sailors listened to him because no one wanted to be stuck in the muck. He was good at looking at the water and knowing what was underneath. It was a lot harder with people.

"I was glad it turned out like we planned," he answered Reverend Palmer.

"I hear you've been having important talks with people high in the chain of command," said Palmer. "I heard a rumor you were in the White House today."

"The Reverend French and me, we, uh, we been talking to people." How did the news spread so fast? He looked at Hannah, wondering if she'd said something to Lizzy Keckly. But Hannah seemed to know exactly what question he was thinking and shook her head, almost imperceptibly.

Washington wasn't different from anywhere else, he supposed. It didn't take five minutes for word to spread across Charleston or Beaufort about anything out of the ordinary.

"Let's hope these people find it in their minds and power to listen," said Reverend Palmer. "If they won't listen to a man like you, what hope do we have?"

*****

Robert sat up on the dais and looked down at the sea of faces. Could he and Hannah and Lizzie and Junior ever fit into a group like this? Maybe Lizzie and Junior could, someday, if they kept studying at Reverend Peck's school in Beaufort, with Miss Forten, Miss Towne, and the other abolitionist ladies. Maybe if they sent Junior off to Reverend French's Wilberforce University. Imagine: Robert Smalls Junior, educated man sitting in the pews with all these high-class Negroes.

Mrs. Keckly stood at the lectern, the smile on her face so full of happy sunshine that Robert couldn't see a trace of the sadness that usually lingered behind it.

"Ladies and gentlemen, welcome to the first festival of the Contraband Relief Association. The mere existence of this gathering is a ringing testament that the colored ladies and gentlemen of this city have a moral and social understanding of the world. When I brought the idea for this association to the ladies of my church and the other colored churches in our city, I was pleased by the response. But tonight, I know there was more to their answer than good manners. We have a feast at our disposal to provide ample proof. Thank you to all the ladies of the association for their hard work."

The crowd burst into applause. A man raised a turkey drumstick high overhead in tribute, and his wife quickly dragged his hand back down.

"As you know," Mrs. Keckly continued, more serious now, "the streets and alleys of our city are rapidly filling with men, women, and children newly escaped from bondage. They've come here hoping for flowery paths, days of perpetual sunshine, and bowers hanging with golden fruit. Instead they've found mud and cold shoulders.

"Many of you have offered a meal and a kind word. Maybe a blanket. Or a bed. Or a job. But the vast need overwhelms any single person. Which is why we band together, as the Contraband Relief Association.

"Times are hard, even for those of us in this room tonight. But I ask you to open your hearts and give as generously as you can. But not yet. If you do it now, after just listening to me, that's one thing. I am merely a dress maker. Before you give, listen to our special guest. Robert Smalls has proved himself a hero for his bravery and daring. Those ignorant people who question whether members of our race can join America as full citizens have been shown the answer, in the person of Mr. Smalls. Many of you have read of his exploits in the papers, but tonight he's here to tell you the story in his own words. I present to you: Mr. Robert Smalls."

There was another round of applause, and she signaled for Robert to replace her at the lectern. "Don't worry," she whispered as she passed him on stage, "They'll love you."

Robert took his spot in front of the crowd. Looking out into the sea of brown faces and clapping hands was like looking up at the wall of Fort Sumter, each expectant pair of eyes like one of those cannon barrels, ready to blow him to smithereens.

But Hannah gave him a smile, a real smile, not just "do a good job," but she smiled like she loved him as much as any person anywhere on earth. That smile brought him enough strength to at least grab onto the podium, so he wouldn't fall over.

He thought of Alfred, Turno, Jackson, Johnny, Chisholm. He thought of Alston, off in the Gulf of Mexico. Of Morrison, snatched away. They deserved to have their story told.

"I don't talk as smooth as Mrs. Keckly," he said, trying to get the quaver out of his voice. "If she can't get you to open your hearts and your wallets, I don't know why my story should. But I promised I'd tell it, so I will."

He looked around at the faces again. They seemed willing to listen, for now. A few had gone to the back of the room to refill their plates with more bread and chicken. He wished he were back there with them. "I won't take long, 'cause I know there is cookies and pie for when I's done."

A little laugh, but not much. They were waiting.

"This ain't just my story. The *Planter* is a hundred fifty feet long, thirty feet wide, made from live oak and red cedar, finest brass fittings. Double boilers for the side paddle wheels. Took all of us to run her, whether we was moving cotton for the planters, or soldiers and guns for the rebels. Or running ourselves to freedom."

He told them the whole story, starting from messing around with Captain Relyea's hat. Finding Morrison to hide the women and children. The dark of the night, the crickets and the owls in the darkness, the slick black muscle of the Cooper River. Thinking he might never see his family again. The torpedoes and what they can do to a ship. How it felt to wait for the signal at Fort Sumter, the way time stopped as they teetered on the edge between life and death, standing in a borrowed hat and uniform, needing to be someone else for just a few minutes longer. For his whole life he'd had to be someone else, to pretend to be obedient, scraping and bowing. Freedom meant a chance to finally be himself. It meant loving his wife and his children all the way, not holding that little bit back, in case master decided to sell them off.

Chicken legs and biscuits sat untouched on their plates. The ladies' fans grew still. Every ear listened, every eye saw the image of Charleston Harbor.

"Finally, a thin voice called down from the edge of the fort, high above the water, almost like an angel from the clouds. "Pass the *Planter*." And I turned the wheel, and steered us out towards the rising sun.

"And just then, we heard the signal guns from the harbor. Flags raised up on all the forts. Boom! Boom! Boom!" Robert shouted, and the audience jumped in their seats as Ft. Sumter sent the shells arcing towards the *Planter*. He drew the picture with his words, all the way to the *Onward*, the frantic search for a white sheet, and the tense uncertainty over what sort of barbarians comprised the Union Navy.

"We made it through that dark night, to find what had been promised for us. Safety. Freedom. A whole new day."

The crowd leapt to their feet, hands pounding applause, a sonic wave of appreciation. Blood rushed to his face. They kept going, hollering and hooting. He tried to keep the emotions from spilling out through his eyes, trying not to shake.

They finally simmered down. "Thank you. You's too kind. But since you is, I want you to do two things. First, show some of that love for my wife, Hannah. She led all them wives and precious children out from shackles to a new life."

Hannah stood reluctantly as the crowd stood again and clapped. She was a hard woman to make blush, but Robert had managed it.

"And last, I want you to think about what Mrs. Keckly and the Contraband Relief Association is tryin' to do. I's a contraband, but I got some luck and some skill. A lot of these folks got nothin'. They making a harder journey than we did in the *Planter*. They walkin' alone through woods and swamps. Hungry and cold. And when they get here, they don't get nice folks like you giving them applause. They find a city overflowin' with other poor Negroes, just as desperate, just as friendless. Ain't none of it their fault. They didn't pick to be slaves. They didn't pick this war. The one choice they got to make was to be free. But freedom ain't fillin' their bellies, or giving blankets to their chi'ren, or keeping them dry at night. They's a lot more of them than there is of us. But if everyone tonight gives a little, we can help. Thanks. Thanks for listening."

He stepped away from the podium to more thunderous applause. The energy he'd had when telling the story was fading fast. There was nothing he'd like better than to find a spot under one of the tables and hide, to collect himself. But Lizzy Keckly already had him by the elbow and was steering towards the throng. He noticed collection baskets making their way through the crowd, and people were opening their wallets and purses. Yes, he would rather have been out on the water under full steam, but tonight, they'd made something happen. The feeling surprised him—a sense of power and satisfaction, not so different from when the *Planter* finally reached the *Onward,* or when the *Crusader* returned from the raid on Simmon's Bluff without a scratch.

Maybe there was something to this speechifying after all.

208

CHAPTER 23

"You made quite an impression on the president," said Secretary Stanton. He hadn't looked up from the letter he was writing as Robert and Reverend French were shown into the office and took their seats in armchairs. It was a small room, the walls lined with books from floor to ceiling. In each corner were desks covered with official looking papers and documents. A uniformed messenger stood at attention by Stanton's elbow. Stanton wrote his careful, controlled script, barely pausing for thought, taking care to keep his beard out of the ink. He finally finished, blotted it, and handed it to the messenger, who left at a trot.

"It's been quiet for a few days, but wars never sleep for long." He took off his round little glasses and rubbed his eyes. "The stamina required for managing a war is more than I expected. But we must see it through to the end."

He put his glasses back on and studied them with his piercing eyes. "You've been down there nearly a year now, Mansfield. Lived with them, seen them in new freedom. Do you think this makes sense?"

Reverend French relaxed a little at the mention of his name. Without an audience, perhaps Stanton wouldn't be so hard on them. "It's been an illuminating year, and I thank God for bringing me to Port Royal. They are a people interested in salvation and freedom. Do they sin? Do they lie, cheat, and steal? Yes. But no more than any other race. Do they require assistance to bring them from bondage to be fully included in society? Yes."

Stanton shook his head. "The question is: will giving arms to five thousand Negroes start an unquenchable wildfire of violence?"

Reverend French shook his head vigorously. "I've never heard any freedmen express interest in revenge against their former masters, or against white people in general. Quite the contrary, actually. Unlike Shakespeare's twisted tragedies, or even the Hebrew kings and armies from the Bible, there is no lust for vengeance."

Secretary Stanton frowned, unsatisfied. "You've always had a soft heart, Mansfield. Sentimentality is barely permissible in university presidents, and completely useless when attempting to create national policy."

"They're used to following orders. They'll make good soldiers, Edwin." His no-nonsense tone was one Robert had never heard from him before.

Stanton shifted in his seat to fix his gaze on Robert. "What about you, Mr. Smalls? If you'd followed orders, you wouldn't be here, would you?"

"Hard to argue with that, suh."

"Every escaped slave who reaches the Union lines has proved he is something of a scoundrel. He has lied and deceived any number of people, to put himself out of reach of his master."

"People is willing to go pretty far to do what's right," Robert said, careful not to challenge Secretary Stanton. He seemed like a man you could never best in an argument straight on. "Just like the Union is willing to put up an army and kill the soldiers on the other side. You ask those men to do what wouldn't seem right in any other time. Slaves escaping ain't doing nothing but what they can, for what is right. Reverend French tells me you believe in abolition. Slaves didn't start this war. They ain't out there killing and slicing people up. They just want to be free."

"You're asking us to allow you to recruit freed slaves to go out and kill people. Blow them to pieces with cannons. Drown them in burning ships. Any number of unpleasant ends for white soldiers at the hands of black men, who once were slaves."

"They is men who is willing to die, just like white soldiers. For the Union, for freedom. They be brave enough, you give 'em a chance."

"Would you kill your master if you had the chance, Mr. Smalls?"

Robert sat back in his chair at the blunt force of the question. The McKees had owned him, sure. But they never laid a hand on him. They'd let him hire himself out and build a life. They could have sent him to the plantations, but they kept him in the house and on the boats. Mrs. McKee never said more than five unkind words to his mama. And Mr. Henry... *You want me to kill a man who might be my father*, he wanted to ask Mr. Stanton. *What kind of man would that make me?*

What kind of father keeps his son a slave?

Of all the ways Robert was different from Mr. Henry, that was the biggest. He could never do that to Junior. He'd risked his life to set his son free, and would do it again, as many times as it took, to keep him that way.

"No, suh. The McKees been like part of my family. My escape is making life hard for them, and I'm sorry it is, but I didn't do it to bring harm to them. No, suh. I did it for me and my family. I don't want to kill nobody."

"What about your crew? Perhaps they're not as charitably minded as you."

Robert could guarantee that Turno had a list of every man who had ever cracked a whip against his back. Samuel Smith was high atop that list. If they ever met on the battlefield or on the water, there would be no holding Turno back until Smith was on his way to Hell. In pieces. That might not be what Mr. Stanton needed to hear.

"If we wanted to kill white folks, we coulda killt the captain, first mate, and engineer, on any night. Slit their throats, dumped them in the harbor and made a run for it. The *Planter* had two guns on her—we could have shot soldiers at the fort, blown up the dock, gone hunting for small boats on our way out the harbor. We didn't want blood. We wanted to cut off the chains from around our necks."

Stanton smiled, an expression that made him look briefly like an entirely different person. For an instant, Robert could see who he might have been before the death of his wife and brother and son and so many other people's sons.

"I heard you spoke with great eloquence at the 15th Street Presbyterian Church Saturday night. You're a man full of surprises, Mr. Smalls."

Secretary Stanton reached to the top of one of the many piles of papers covering his desk, and pulled off a single sheet with lots of words on it. He handed it to Robert, who looked at it but couldn't make it out. He handed it to Reverend French.

"Go ahead," said Stanton. "Read it."

Reverend French scanned the orders and cleared his throat. "The population of African descent that cultivate the lands and perform the labor of the rebels constitute a large share of their military strength, and enable the white masters to fill the rebel armies and wage a cruel and murderous war against the people of the Northern States. By reducing the laboring strength of the rebels, their military power will be reduced. You are thereby authorized to arm, uniform, equip, and receive into the service of the United States such numbers of volunteers of African descent as you may deem expedient, not exceeding 5,000, and may detail officers to instruct them in military drill, discipline, and duty, and to command them. The persons so received into service to be entitled to the same pay and rations as are allowed by law to volunteers in the service. You may turn over to the Navy any number of colored volunteers that may be required for the Naval Service.

"By recent act of Congress, all men and boys received into the service of the United States, who have been the slaves of rebel masters, with their wives, mothers and children, are declared to be forever free. You and all in your command will so treat and regard them."

Robert's heart felt like it stopped beating. *Declared forever free.*

Reverend French looked up at the secretary. "This is exactly what we—"

"Were looking for?" Stanton interjected. "I hope so. It's a risk for everything and everyone. I'm not sure how we're going to sell this to the public."

"We'll prove ourselves," Robert said, not worried about meeting Stanton's eyes anymore.

"We need this war to end. Soon. This isn't about debate, it's about getting the job done. But, for now, get the job done quietly. Tell General Hunter and General Saxton this is not a matter for the press. I'm giving them the men they want, and they need to give us time to mold public opinion."

"We'll find our path to glory with a whisper, if need be," said Robert.

"In the end, I doubt that will be true or necessary. But do your best for now." Stanton returned to the papers on his desk, already prepared to move to the next matter at hand. They were dismissed.

Robert patted the dispatch in his jacket pocket. A few thousand black men in the South would get chances of their own.

CHAPTER 24

It was warm for New Year's Day, not a cloud in the sky. The mist that lay on the river when they started the *Planter* out of Port Royal at daybreak had burned off most of the way, only a few small tendrils hugging the shore. Robert couldn't imagine a better day to start a whole new era of freedom.

From the looks of the crowd at the Beaufort docks, there were plenty of other folks who agreed. After his time in Washington, Robert had been sent to New York to give more speeches in front of packed churches and auditoriums, but even the New York crowds were nothing compared to this.

"I thought General Saxton was exaggerating when he told us every Negro in ten miles would be here," Captain Eldridge said to Robert, as they steered the ship into the docks. Eldridge was the latest captain of the *Planter*, a older navy man running what was now officially an army vessel, after General Saxton had requested her from Admiral DuPont. Eldridge seemed to like the *Planter* and her crew well enough. Robert wasn't sure what to make of him yet.

Below, Johnny and Turno readied the mooring lines. As the ship turned broadside to the docks and the name of the steamer came into view, a cheer rose from the hundreds of black folks waiting. "The *Planter*! Take us to freedom, Robert!"

He'd known it was going to be a big day, because fabric had been selling like crazy at the store over the past few weeks. Every man, woman, and child wore their best clothes, even if it was just a cleaner set of rags. It was like Sunday, Easter, and

Christmas, all rolled into one.

Beyond the docks, a handful of white soldiers and merchants watched the crowd, trying to decide if the growing throng was likely to be a problem. White guards in uniform tried to push the people back a few feet, so that the ship's crew could put out the gangway.

Robert finally spied Hannah, the children, and Mama Lydia, beyond the front row of eager passengers, carrying baskets and blankets for the picnic that would follow the speeches.

People surged onto the ship. "Keep moving to the back," Turno bellowed. "Plenty of room for all y'all. Spread out. Keep moving to the back."

Robert climbed down to the deck to his family. "Daddy!" squealed Lizzie, throwing herself into his arms. Not to be outdone, Junior squirmed out of Hannah's arms, and grabbed Robert's other leg. "Mama," he said to Hannah, "I told you to bring the children, not the monkeys."

"These was all I could find," Hannah said, laughing. In the yellow dress she'd made, she looked like a sunny day. Every soldier in the First South Carolina would notice her, no doubt.

Mama Lydia waved to a handsome couple boarding the ship. And to another young mother, and to a limping old carpenter. "You know every face here?" Robert asked Mama Lydia.

"Oh, naw. There's peoples here that never been a hundred feet away from they's plantation." She nodded towards a few tight knots of coal-black people, dressed poorer than most. They looked a little lost in all the hubbub.

There weren't many young men in the crowd. No, they were already at Camp Saxton, in uniform, preparing to show themselves off. As soon as they'd returned from New York, Robert had gone out to the plantations, asking the men to sign up and defend their families and their freedom. It hadn't been an easy sell. Everyone worried how the cotton would get grown. Who would watch over the women and children and old folk? Then he started to talking to the women, too. "I know you just

215

got the first breath of freedom in your whole lives, and now, here we is, saying, 'Let your men sign up.' But what if the planters win? If we let massa win, you ain't never gon' have a free breath the rest of your lives. They gon' take every one of your chi'ren and sell them off."

An old woman hobbled across the deck, leaning on a stick, not a tooth in her mouth. "Yo' mama raise you right, Robert. God bless you, son. You show 'em you a man. You show all the mens."

"Thank you. Hey, Johnny. Find Miss Grandmamma some place to sit."

Johnny's massive form parted the waters of the crowd, and he gently led away the old woman to try to find a bench.

The people kept coming in a jubilant wave of hopeful faces.

*****

From the pilothouse, Robert had the perfect view of the Old Fort Plantation, now known as Camp Saxton and home to the First Carolina Volunteers. From the river bank a great lawn spread towards John Joyner Smith's decaying mansion, surrounded by rows of live oaks, festooned with drapes of Spanish moss. Behind the mansion, he could make out the tip of the slave quarters, and the start of the fields, where more than a hundred slaves used to plant cotton. Now the fields were trampled flat, used to train newly recruited Negro soldiers. Up near the big house, row after row of white tents stretched out into the fields, so regular it was like they'd set them up with a tape measure.

The grounds were crawling with people and the air rang with the song of their excited voices. General Saxton's little steamer, the *Flora*, had made three trips to carry people here, and long boats and skiffs and rafts from plantations on every creek and sound for miles around had floated to the riverbanks in front of the plantation, crammed full of people. The docks were full now, and every tree near the shore held a web of lines

216

to craft of every size, held tight by the flow of the Beaufort River. On some, men and boys who had started rowing early in the morning now lay sprawled on benches, faces under their hats, sound asleep. Robert wondered if they were dreaming about the feast set to follow the speeches. They'd roasted ten oxen for this afternoon, and the smell of barbecued beef wafted across the field, mixed with the scent of tobacco from a hundred pipes puffing up clouds of sweet Carolina leaf grown by their own hands.

In the middle of the lawn, workers had constructed a platform for the important folks— the high-ranking officers, head teachers, a handful of ministers. The black folk rested on the lawn, their children playing and dancing to music played by a band from the New Hampshire Third Regiment, with their trumpets and drums and fifes. Along the left side of the lawn, the First South Carolina stood at loose attention, in neat lines. Eight hundred men, their bright scarlet pants and blue jackets making them look like a field of flowers from far off. A closer look showed young faces, full of pride. No one had ever seen a collection of black soldiers like this. A year ago, they were beasts of burden, and now they had guns in their hands and steel in their spines.

Robert wished all of Charleston could see this sight. The whole of the South needed to learn what they'd had under their thumbs all this time.

Mr. Lincoln should see these men, as a reminder that they were real. They'd been a hidden part of the war, and now they were standing with their buttons shining like stars in the winter sky.

"Robert, come on. They's gon' start soon. Let's get our seats. Johnny gon' watch the ship." Chisholm waited impatiently on shore.

With one last glance at the view, Robert slid down the ladder to the deck. Johnny was perched on a barrel, working a fishing line over the side.

"You sure you all right to stay?" Robert asked.

217

"They gon' talk too much for me. I stay right here. You go get all those words, Robert."

The crew of the *Planter* secured a space in the shade of an enormous live oak, not thirty yards from the speakers' platform. Captain Eldridge and first mate Ensign Hallet and engineer Barger stood in a clump with the other white folks not important enough to have seats on the platform, but who couldn't be expected to sit with the black folks on the lawn.

Robert had hoped there would be a seat for him up on the platform. Not next to General Saxton and Admiral DuPont, or the white officers of the First Carolina, like Colonel Higginson and Captain Trowbridge. But maybe towards the back, in front of the abolitionist teachers, like Ms. Towne, or maybe near Reverend French and Reverend Brisbane. Or maybe they could have found a chair for him near the two black soldiers sitting proudly in their seats, Corporal Bob Sutton and Sergeant Prince Rivers. Even in this huge crowd, Robert could sense eyes being drawn towards Prince Rivers. Men and women alike, and even the folks on the platform, Colonel Higginson, Ms. Towne, all glanced at the handsome black soldier. They said he was a natural leader. Robert couldn't help looking at him either. Skin like the darkest cherry, and a smooth, strong jaw.

Prince turned his head a little, and their eyes met for a moment. They'd known each other for years. He used to be a coach driver for Henry Middleton Stuart in Beaufort, and Stuart dragged him off to Charleston when the war started. But when the Union forces set up camp in Port Royal, Prince stole a horse, and rode through the lines to freedom. He was one of Robert's first recruits for the new regiment.

Prince Rivers was all right. Though stealing a horse wasn't the same as making a plan to take a full-sized steamship out of Charleston Harbor, keeping it secret, sneaking women and children on board, and having the nerve to steam past six forts bristling with cannon. Now *that* was something. Something that might land a man a seat on the platform. Or maybe even earn a chance to say a few words. The folks gathered here today might want to hear from a man who had met with the Secretary of War, who had met with President Lincoln himself, and pressed for change. And actually helped get it. Maybe they'd want to hear from a man who had experience talking to crowds, in churches and auditoriums around Washington and New York City. A man with a gold medal from the black citizens of New York, with a proclamation of appreciation. All of that might be enough for an invitation, recognition as someone who had done a part to make all this possible.

Or maybe not. Robert spit on the ground, as if that might help take some of the bitter taste from his mouth.

The blare of a trumpet quieted the hubbub, as the new chaplain of the First South Carolina, Mr. Fowler, stepped up to the front of the platform. He was a young white man, maybe the same age as Robert, and he looked over the crowd, beaming with enthusiasm. Robert thought the new black soldiers would be lucky to have him guiding their souls as they leaped into battle.

"Lord, Heavenly Father, we beseech you this day, to guide our nation in this most difficult time. We ask that you bless all those assembled here today, as we go forth into not just a new year, but a new era of freedom. May your heavenly grace show us the light, through all the years of darkness and toil. We ask this in Jesus' name, Amen."

"Amen" rumbled across the ground like thunder. That thunder broke into a rainbow of song, as the chaplain started them off on a hymn.

Then General Saxton's chief lieutenant introduced an old man with a halo of grey hair, though the planters in Charleston wouldn't consider him any kind of angel. Dr. W. H. Brisbane once owned a Beaufort plantation, but then caught abolition fever, moved to Ohio, and freed all his slaves. Robert wasn't the only slave who'd fantasized about having an owner like Dr. Brisbane.

Though he was ancient, Dr. Brisbane's voice was still young and strong, bouncing off the trunks of the oaks. "Good day," he said.

Someone in the crowd called out, "Welcome home!"

Dr. Brisbane smiled. "As many of you know, this was my family home. But slavery was poisoning my life, and I determined to do something about it. I prayed to God every night to return me to the land of my birth. Sometimes my faith was weak, because it seemed impossible. But here we are. And in my hand, I have this remarkable proclamation, which General Saxton has asked me to read to you today."

He cleared his throat and began to read in a strong clear voice. The crowd grew absolutely still. "Whereas, on the twenty-second day of September, in the year of our Lord one thousand eight hundred and sixty-two, a proclamation was issued by the President of the United States, containing, among other things, the following:

"That on the first day of January, in the year of our Lord one thousand eight hundred and sixty-three, all persons held as slaves within any State or designated part of a State, the people whereof shall then be in rebellion against the United States, shall be then, thenceforward, and forever free."

He continued reading, while the crowd soaked in the complex language that made them free, but left many others still enslaved. Under all the words lay a promise of freedom for all black men and women.

When Dr. Brisbane lowered the paper, the crowd leapt to their feet and raised a sound up to the sky, a cry, a laugh, a howl, all mixed together, five thousand voices strong. Robert was on his feet with the rest, tossing Junior into the air. Hannah stood next to him, eyes closed, her face raised to heaven. Mama Lydia sang a hymn of praise, lost in the din.

"Forever free!" Robert yelled. Junior, now perched on his shoulders, echoed the cry of his father and the gathering. As the sound subsided, General Saxton's lieutenant stepped forward and waited for silence. "Today we have the privilege of being at the headquarters of the First South Carolina Volunteers, the first freed slaves to become soldiers in defense of the Union.

Steering to Freedom

Reverend Mansfield French is here to present the regimental colors to their commander, Colonel Higginson."

Reverend French carefully unfurled the regimental flag, a bright blue banner, with a fierce eagle clutching a green wreath of peace. A collective breath was drawn at the sight of it—this was a flag for them, for their sons and husbands, for freedom.

And then French untied the cord from a fresh new American flag, the banner bright in the sun, and handed it to Colonel Higginson, who looked out at the crowd and waved the flag, to show every star and stripe.

It was like seeing the flag for the first time. It had hung on a pole in Beaufort, and on the *Planter*, and even in Charleston before the war, but they were dingy rags compared to this one. As of today, it was their flag, too.

The silence was broken again, but this time not by a cheer, but by a deep, strong man's voice. "My country,' tis of thee, sweet land of liberty, of thee I sing."

More voices joined, pitched in harmony. "Land where my fathers died, land of the pilgrim's pride, from every mountainside, let freedom ring."

Verse after verse, the song continued to its end, all of them joined into one. Every eye fixed upon the flag Colonel Higginson proudly held aloft.

The song ended, leaving the air full of a fog of something almost not quite real. This was the day they'd all been waiting for.

Through the celebration that followed, the song kept echoing in Robert's ears: "Long may our land be bright with freedom's holy light." All his travels had led to this point, which no longer felt like an end, but a beginning. The only way to keep the freedom proclaimed to them today was to fight for it, no matter what the cost.

PART III

CHAPTER 25

JANUARY 23, 1863

Robert looked down from the pilothouse of the *Planter*, scanning row after row of black faces under blue caps, trying to catch sight of Turno in his new uniform. He had thought about signing up for the regiment himself, but when he'd hinted to General Saxton that he was thinking about joining, Saxton told him, "We won't take you. I will issue a direct order to every recruiting officer to refuse your papers. Our best pilot will not be allowed to sign up for the infantry. If you want to help the war effort, you can't do it by digging ditches, peeling potatoes, and standing guard duty."

As pilot for the *Planter*, Robert was one of the few who knew their destination—the St. Mary's River, between Florida and Georgia, to raid lumber, brick, and salt mills. Seeing action was a grand idea, but sending the *Planter* a hundred and twenty miles along the coast wasn't smart. The port engine was having trouble keeping pressure. The new chief engineer, Barger, had all kinds of ideas, but none of them worked. The two new officers, Captain Eldridge and Mr. Barger, were quite a pair. Real smilers. When Colonel Higginson was looking for ships to take the First South Carolina down the coast, they raised their hands right away. Reverend French called them enthusiasts. Chisholm called them roosters, because they were always crowing about how ready they were to leap into action.

At a command from Captain Trowbridge, a young, lean army officer with a goatee, a company of a hundred Negro

223

soldiers marched on board the *Planter*. They stepped in close unison, each carrying a rifle and heavy pack, while Colonel Higginson watched proudly. Some of the other Northern officers lined up along the docks looked at black soldiers like they were strange beasts.

Robert finally spotted Turno, still back on the wharf. He gave a glance over toward the *Planter*, and Robert gave a quick salute. Turno was all soldier now—no smile touched his lips. A raised eyebrow was his only greeting.

*****

The *Planter* limped into St. Simon's Sound well after dark, flashing the signal to the sentry boats. Today had been a long stretch of trying to guess every sandbar and mud hump on the inland side of the Sea Islands, hoping the smoke from the stack wouldn't attract attention from rebel pickets. They'd scraped bottom half a dozen times, drew a long line on the hull from a submerged log, and grounded only once.

Right now, it was everything Robert could do to stay standing. His hammock in the engine room called to him.

Captain Trowbridge appeared in the lamp light outside the pilot house, looking as fresh as the breaking of a new day. "Gentlemen. Better late than never. Is there anything we can do to make tomorrow better?"

"Not a thing," answered Captain Eldridge, still smiling.

"Firewood, sir," Robert said, injecting reality into Eldridge's little cloud of optimism. They'd burned a good portion of their firewood, as Alfred and Mr. Barger wrestled the port side boiler into submission.

"Good. The soldiers need some useful work," said Trowbridge.

Trowbridge slid down the ladder to the main deck. The sergeant called out, "Attention!" and the men, who had been dozing after a long day in the sun, jumped to their feet, scrambling for caps and weapons. "Form ranks!"

Steering to Freedom

By the time they glided alongside the *John Adams*, a converted ferry from up North, the men looked like a collection of actual soldiers again.

On the deck of the *John Adams*, Colonel Higginson stood with his arms crossed, like a disapproving father. "I was about to give up on you," he called. "Trouble with the Rebels?"

"Just the engine," answered Trowbridge. "But Mr. Barger managed to supply us with steam, and Captain Eldridge has kept us afloat."

Barger had mostly shouted useless suggestions to Alfred over the noise of the engine. And it wasn't clear how much time Captain Eldridge had spent on Southern rivers, but he wasn't exactly a wizard when it came to judging the currents and twists of the island waters. Robert thought maybe they should try running the *Planter* without him and Alfred for a day and see how far they got.

*****

Inside the thick brick walls of Fort Clinch, flavorful smoke rose from bakeries and kitchens, lines of men drilled in formation, and officers conferred in offices in the two story brick headquarters. Captain Trowbridge and Captain Eldridge were inside there now, debating with Colonel Higginson on the fitness of the *Planter* for upstream sorties.

Robert and Alfred walked through the bustle of the fort towards the outer edge of the parade ground where a hundred white tents sat, pitched in groups of ten. In front of them, black soldiers from the First South Carolina lounged in the thin January sun, smoking their pipes. Across the open ground, a group of white privates and corporals rocked their camp chairs back against the brick walls of their barracks. One white soldier grumbled loudly, "Union army's going straight to hell, with all these monkeys in uniform."

Robert and Alfred found Turno sitting on a log, sharpening his bayonet. His eyes were fixed on the white soldiers. He didn't even look up when Robert and Alfred sat next to him.

"Planning to do some bayonet practice on them bukra soldiers?" Robert asked.

"They got it coming."

"They all got it coming, brother," said Alfred "But you might want to start on the ones in the Confederate uniforms first."

Turno finally smiled. "What took y'all so long? We got here yesterday."

"Alfred kept trying to get the boiler to heat his coffee instead of making the paddle wheels go 'round," Robert said.

"Ha! If Robert hadn't kept knocking us into logs and rocks and sand bars, we would of beat y'all here."

"Port engine again?" Turno asked.

"The relief valve is shot, but Barger's afraid to ask for the whole part, knowing it'll lay us up for weeks," said Alfred.

Turno tested the sharpness of the bayonet on his thumbnail. "Much as I love that old barge, I don't want my company getting nailed when she can't make steam."

Turno looked the same as ever, tall as a tree and strong as a bull, but he wasn't part of their crew anymore. Weeks of drilling and practice and firing guns and training had tied him to the other soldiers.

"Lila says you better come back in one piece," Robert said. He, and just about everyone, suspected that black soldiers might be sent on missions too dangerous for white soldiers.

"And she want you to bring her back a real paycheck," added Alfred.

"They doin' all right?"

"She down at the store every day. She and Hannah got each other to complain to. The chi'ren all runnin' wild, like a pack of puppies," Robert said.

A few more insults floated across the grounds. The white soldiers had taken off their jackets and were playing with knives. Robert could see Turno contemplating possible next steps.

"Make you wish for Camp Saxton?" Robert asked.

"Makes me wish it was dark. Lot you can accomplish in the night. But they just jealous. They been stuck here for months and never seen action. Then here we comes with Colonel Higginson ready find some Rebs, and he brought the boats to do it."

"We'll make sure the *Planter* gets you there," Alfred said.

"Hell. You just make sure she gets us out," said Turno.

*****

Despite many reassuring smiles from Eldridge and Barger, Colonel Higginson could not be convinced to let the *Planter* carry his men up the St. Mary's for their scouting mission. That night, limned by the rising moon, the *John Adams* steamed upriver with a hundred men, including Turno, to get a taste of what lay out there.

Alfred and Robert returned to the boiler room to repair the failing relief valves, grateful that Barger and Eldridge had joined Captain Trowbridge for dinner on shore. With those two off the ship, it felt more like home again. The new steward boy, Cesar, was busy cleaning and prepping officers' quarters. Jackson was off with Chisholm searching for better rations for the food stores. Johnny was sacked out on the deck after a full day of loading firewood.

"Ever feel like casting off and settin' sail again, just us and the crew?" Robert asked.

Alfred cranked hard on a wrench. "Even after they paid us for it, she still feels like ours, don't she?"

"Paid us? Ha! Cheated us. Paid a quarter of what it worth. I say it's ours 'til they cough up the rest."

"You itchin' to make more headlines?"

"Naw. Wishin' we was out with Turno. All them brothers in arms, ready for action, and us running the ship."

"They ain't gon' let a black man be captain any more than they gon' let a Negro be called an engineer." He pulled down on the wrench and finally removed the valve. He stuck his finger inside, clucking his tongue in disapproval, then reached for a steel file.

"I still wish we was going with 'em," Robert said.

"Hannah and your chi'ren like your face just the way it is. Why don't you work a little harder to keep your head attached to yo' neck?"

Robert pulled on the pipes around him in frustration. "I want to be a part of things. The 'Secesh say it all about honor, and the Union soldiers don't give a damn about you or me. But all this is about puttin' the chains back on you and me, on every black man. I want to be part of the fight."

Alfred put down his tools and shook his head. "Ain't you noticed how many of them fine houses in Beaufort been turned into hospitals? When we get back, listen to the moans coming through the windows. Smell the rotten flesh coming from the piles of arms and legs. You already put in your piece of this puzzle. And I'm working my fingers to the bone to get this ship where she need to be, so our new black soldiers can join other soldiers in the hospitals. It don't make you special to get killed by some cannonball. Any idiot can stop a bullet. What you done already, that make you special."

"I guess you right." But Robert wanted the *Planter* to play her part. It was embarrassing to have her dragging along, covering up her name in mud. She was once just a cotton transport, he was once just a slave. He needed to keep proving that they were more than that now.

*****

The *John Adams* floated back around the bend late in the afternoon of the next day. A cry went up from the watchmen on top of Fort Clinch, and every member of the First South Carolina ran through the massive brick gates to the waterside, forming a patchwork line of red trousers and white shirts and blue jackets, like a stretched and distorted American flag.

As the ship glided next to the *Planter*, the new bullet holes on the bow showed they'd seen some action. The soldiers on board hooted and hollered, "Success!" and "Victory!" under the watchful eyes of Colonel Higginson and Sergeant Prince Rivers. Corporal Bob Sutton wore a bloody bandage around his head. Half a dozen privates sat on top of an enormous packing crate, their legs dangling three feet above the deck.

As soon as the *John Adams* was made fast, Sergeant Rivers called the soldiers to attention. The colonel and his two captains left the ship first, followed by Rivers and Sutton. The officers stopped on shore to watch a detail of men carry out a canvas-wrapped corpse to the fort.

A whisper ran quickly through the crowd. The dead soldier was Private Bill Parsons, a former field slave from the Tombee Plantation. He'd been one of the first men Robert had recruited. "Fell right by Colonel's side," they said. He died in the moonlight, shot by Rebel cavalry surprised near Township Landing. But new Union recruits killed and drove off the rebels. A first victory for these black warriors.

Not for Bill Parsons. Robert tried to remember his wife and children—she was a little bitty woman, with a dull look in her eyes, like she couldn't keep up with all the changes going on around her. Would she blame him for Parsons' death?

The rest of the soldiers marched silently off the *John Adams*, but there were still smiles poking through at the thoughts of all they'd accomplished. Turno was with them, not a scratch on him. His eyes seemed full of a new wisdom.

*****

Robert and the *Planter's* crew stood on the deck of the *John Adams* next to an enormous crate. Hurley, the chestnut-hued fireman from the *John Adams*, stood with them. His forearms and hands were stained black from all the coal he'd shoveled over the past days, weeks, and months. "You know what's inside?" he asked.

"We heard about it. But we wants to see for ourselves," said

Robert.

"Captain and the Colonel won't like that."

"We ain't gon' hurt it," Alfred said. "They's having a meeting up in the brick house, making plans for us all to end up like Parsons."

Robert slipped a small pry bar from his sleeve and set it to the edge of the crate. All his crew had grown up on the docks of Charleston and could uncrate a stray box in the blink of a cat's eye. They pulled off the top and front panels to reveal an ornately carved piano-forte, made of polished rosewood. Chisholm reached forward and flipped open the front lid to reveal the keys, glowing impossibly white on the gritty deck of the *John Adams*.

"They brought this all the way back?" Chisholm asked.

"Colonel couldn't bring hisself to burn it," Hurley explained. "Gon' send it to a colored school in Fernandina. It was sitting in the grand parlor, with the packing crate half-built and waiting. Maybe they was planning to ship it out today."

"Well, it got shipped out all right," Alfred said.

Robert reached forward and pushed and held a key, and the note rose into the air like an element of pure birdsong. "Chisholm. Can you play us something?" he asked.

Chisholm's master's wife had trained him to play when he was a child, but his master thought he was better suited to work on the docks. He could play just about any instrument you put in his hands.

"I might remember a tune or two." Chisholm looked at the keyboard with something close to hunger.

Big Hurley shuffled nervously. "Them officers gon' hear and then we all gon' catch hell."

"We ain't gon' hurt it," Robert said. "We gon' play it."

"It get so much as a scratch, Colonel gon' scratch you all over."

Johnny grabbed a half barrel of gunpowder and rolled it over for Chisholm to use as a seat. "Play."

"Don't play too hot," Jackson cautioned, "or you blow us all straight to hell."

Chisholm began to play, the notes drifting on the breeze down the river and out to sea. He played marches they'd heard on Emancipation Day and songs full of missing home. Heads poked out from the other boats lining the shore, and refugees camped in the shadow of the fort glided over. Someone joined in with a fiddle, and another with a harmonica, as darkness floated off the inland swamps. Chisholm leaned into the keys, pounding out a hopping dance tune. The men clapped their hands and stomped their feet on the deck, calling out. The worries of tomorrow disappeared into the deepening night.

Lanterns appeared at the gate to the fort.

"Concert's over," Robert said quickly.

The box went back together with four quick strikes of a hammer. The men faded into the gloom as if they'd never been there. All of them had spent their entire lives finding and hiding secret moments just like this.

*****

Captain Eldridge was just as eager to be part of the next excursion as Robert. With Barger by his side, they convinced Colonel Higginson to trust the *Planter* on a sortie up the Crooked River.

The *Planter* moved slower than Robert would have liked, but she was steady and steerable. He assessed the flow of her engines by the vibrations coming through the wheel and through the soles of his feet. Today, he could still feel a slight shake, a halt somewhere in the rotation of the port wheel. Did Captain Eldridge pay attention to the ship through the soles of his feet?

Using a crude map from the scouts, they chugged to Crab Island, where the river widened before fracturing into dozens of channels. Low flat marsh, brown from the winter chill, stretched out on either side. The sea was a mile off to the starboard, separated from them by the swamp and grass-covered dunes.

The Crooked River soon earned its name. West, then north, west again, then into a bay facing south. Army Captain Trowbridge looked anxiously out over the dull, featureless marsh with his binoculars. "Everything looks the same out there."

To Robert, the marsh was a maze of possibilities and traps. "Suh, look for one channel a little straighter than the rest. The rebels probably bringing out the salt on boats half our size."

"Slow her down a notch," Captain Eldridge ordered. Robert focused on the water, looking for mounding mud and sand beneath the surface, while examining each creek mouth for some sign that it was used as an access route for the salt works. Armies ran on food preserved with salt. No salt meant no food, no army, no victory.

"I see it!" Captain Trowbridge hopped with excitement. He was only a year or two older than Robert, and sometimes his enthusiasm made him seem even younger. "It's quite a ways off, but I see a few buildings, up this stream off to the right. More than a mile through the eel grass. Can you wait for us here?"

"Of course," Captain Eldridge answered with his usual smile.

Trowbridge turned to Robert for his opinion. Trowbridge was one of the few white officers who didn't require a white man's answer for something to be true.

Robert nodded his agreement. "Tell your men to row as fast as they can. We's almost at high tide. In an hour or two, those bars and snags we passed gon' be ready to grab us."

Captain Trowbridge practically hurled himself down the ladder to the main deck. "Move, move, move!" he yelled, sending the men to their feet. Robert held the *Planter* steady in the main stream, trying to keep from getting pushed against the bank of the creek. With help from Johnny and Chisholm, the soldiers slid two longboats, each with five pairs of oars, off the front of the *Planter*.

Soon they disappeared into the tall marsh grass, only reappearing for brief moments when they crossed a section of open channel. Captain Eldridge kept close watch on them while Robert focused on keeping the *Planter* in the main stream.

Chisholm climbed up the ladder to join them. "Can you see them, Captain?"

"I've lost them. Those boys might not know how to row straight, but they do row fast," Captain Eldridge answered.

"Straight don't count for much in these little creeks anyways. Channels out here weave like a drunk on a bender," said Chisholm.

Johnny boosted Chisholm onto the roof of the pilot house. Robert could hear the creak of his steps overhead.

"Don't come crashing on my shoulders, you and your big feet," Robert called.

"Yo' big ugly head strong enough to take it," Chisholm answered.

"You see 'em?"

"I see where they headed. But no sign yet."

Cracks of gunfire snapped across the marsh. And again.

"Musket fire. No large guns. That's a good sign," said Eldridge. "See anything?"

"Nothin'. Wait. See there. Oh, they must have done something," Chisholm answered.

"What?" asked Captain Eldridge.

"Smoke. And that ain't just the captain's pipe."

A dark plume rose from above the marsh.

"Well, everyone knows we're here now," said Captain Eldridge nervously. "Robert, signal Alfred to make ready. Johnny and Chisholm, make sure we've got fire. We might be in a hurry."

Robert anxiously watched the Crooked River ebb towards the sea, sinking the steamer closer to the river bottom, inch by inch.

*****

The longboats finally reappeared. Two canoes followed behind them, paddled by soldiers who'd given up their places in the long boats for barrels of salt. Every man at oars had his jacket off and pulled hard, muscles straining.

Robert looked downstream at the narrow passage they'd need to pass through. If they grounded her, they'd test the balky port engine to her limit.

The longboats reached the *Planter*, and Captain Trowbridge leaped onto the deck with a helping hand from Johnny. "Are we back in time?"

"The water's draining fast," Eldridge answered. "Unless we want to spend the night as target practice, we should hurry that boat on board."

Trowbridge was red-faced with joy when he came up to the pilot house to watch Robert slip the *Planter* through bottleneck after bottleneck. "There were twenty boilers, a pair of storehouses, and more barrels of salt than we could take. The pickets knew they were overmatched and ran at our first shots. Might have clipped one of them, but it was better to ensure the destruction of the works than chase after geese with guns. The men were fantastic. Focused and strong. Masters of destruction. The Rebels won't recover the works after what we've done."

Robert listened to the growing tales of success and looked down at the deck to see strong black men in blue Union uniforms. Their smiles were as broad as the horizon, and they slapped each other's backs and howled victory at the sky. They were fighting for their own freedom. For his freedom. No one could say they weren't men. Not anymore. Not even President Lincoln.

He just wanted a chance to be closer to the action, to feel more like a part of the fight, just like them.

CHAPTER 26

Robert stood outside the command headquarters in the spring sunshine, waiting patiently to meet with the admiral, watching the comings and goings of Port Royal harbor. The water was dotted with dozens of ships of all sizes, bringing supplies for troops, carrying wounded soldiers to the hospitals in Beaufort, hauling loads of coal and lumber. He could just make out the *Planter*, lingering at the north end of the wharves. Alfred and Barger were taking apart the starboard engine, trying to ensure she could keep up with the increased demands of moving soldiers up the coast. In the months since the trip to St. Mary's, life had grown calm, with few raids for the *Planter*. But now something was going on. All kinds of ironclads had been spotted offshore, with a few steaming into Port Royal for repairs. The *Nahant* had laid up for nearly three weeks on Station Creek, getting her gun carriages repaired and a new coat of black paint. Robert couldn't help admire and wonder at the strangely shaped vessel. How could it possibly stay afloat?

From what the newspapers were saying, most folks around the country were looking west towards Vicksburg, where General Grant couldn't seem to break the rebels. Nobody was paying attention to South Carolina right now. Maybe that was about to change.

Lieutenant Maxwell led Robert to the Admiral's office. It felt strange to see DuPont on land. Robert always imagined Admiral DuPont was one of those men who lived every moment at sea, in the flagship. And now the *New Ironsides* was the new flagship, a great iron-plated rigged steamer with massive guns.

The admiral stood at his map table with Captain Rhind, studying charts of Charleston Harbor. They both smiled when they saw Robert.

"I'm glad to see you, Robert," the admiral said. "I heard from General Gillmore that he's been keeping you busy with the *Planter* ferrying every sort of cargo."

"That's right, suh. Keeping her floating as best we can." Robert wondered what Rhind was doing here. Last he'd heard, Rhind had gone up north for some important mission.

"I have asked the general for permission to borrow your services from the army. It comes with a chance for glory, but also bears a risk of great danger."

"I's ready to go wherever you need me, Admiral," Robert answered, trying to stand as tall as he possibly could.

"We're going to take Charleston," Rhind blurted out, unable to contain himself a minute longer.

"I always wanted to sail the *Planter* back through that channel." Robert knew Rhind would be angling at the front of whatever battle was about to occur.

"The *Planter* might join us later. But we need your skills on the way in, to spearhead the attack," said the admiral.

"We've assembled a fleet of nine ironclads. You'll be with me," Rhind said.

"If you're willing, of course," Admiral DuPont added quickly. "Captain Rhind has specifically requested you for his pilot on the *Keokuk*." At times like this, Robert felt his freedom more than ever. DuPont could ask General Gillmore to let him go loose from his contract, but they still had to ask Robert what *he* wanted.

An ironclad was a long way from a riverboat full of cotton. Robert had piloted big ships in and out of Charleston Harbor, including enormous steamers headed across the Atlantic. But an ironclad. He'd never even been on board one of the water-borne fortresses. Now he had a chance to ride back to Charleston in an iron warship, and not pretending to be someone else this time. He'd go back like a man.

"I'd be happy to help bring the stars and stripes back to Fort Sumter," he said.

"The rebels' greeting will be hot. Our own response will be skillful, but lacking in finesse. The danger cannot be minimized," warned the admiral.

"I been watching my friends and neighbors joining up, guns in they hands. Let me do what I do best. I'll make sure the fleet gets into the harbor and we take our licks at Sumter."

"You know he has the best knowledge of the channel that we'll ever find," Rhind jumped in, apparently resuming an argument that had been running for a while.

"The honor of leading the attack is the privilege of the senior captain. Captain Rodgers has earned his position and knows the ironclads as well as any sailor alive. The *Weehawken* will go first. The *Keokuk* is too untested, too unlike the others. You will have plenty of chances for glory from the rear."

"At least ask Rodgers to take Robert as pilot. I'm willing to find another, if we can have Robert at the point," Rhind already sounded exasperated.

"He won't take a Negro pilot. Even Secretary Welles would agree with him. Too many eyes will be watching this battle."

"If we succeed, then those eyes will see—"

"And if we fail, the blame goes in the wrong direction. There's too much at stake."

"What's at stake are the lives of more than a thousand sailors and officers."

For the first time, Robert saw Admiral DuPont's face redden with anger. His voice was low, cut with steel. "Are you questioning my commitment to my men?"

Captain Rhind bowed his head quickly, knowing he'd gone too far. "Not at all. I apologize. I trust your judgment completely, Admiral."

Robert knew enough to keep his mouth shut. He'd rather serve with Rhind anyway. Even then there would be plenty of white sailors on board the *Keokuk* who wouldn't like seeing him in the pilot house, no matter what Captain Rhind had to say. Didn't matter. They'd do their jobs and he'd do his.

The admiral took a deep breath, expelling his anger and frustration through a mere exhalation. "There's no point forcing this issue, Rhind. Much of what happens in this war defies logic. War is fought both by cannons and politicians. The press has already gotten sniffs of what we're about to do. The pilot of the *Weehawken* will lead us into the channel safely. And to ensure that he's probably coached, you and I will go over the charts with Robert now."

*****

Hannah watched from the doorway as Robert quickly packed his seabag with clothes, underwear, socks, trousers.

"How long will you be gone?" She looked so worried, Robert wondered if she was thinking of blocking the door to keep him from going.

"Hard to say. Could be a few weeks. You know how they do. They have a plan, then a storm blows in, or there's a battle in Mississippi that changes which ships need to go where."

It was one thing to pilot transport and cargo ships, and it was another to take a 700 ton hunk of wood and metal into battle against the toughest forts ever built. The *Keokuk* ran with a crew of ninety men. Some had wives just like Hannah, wondering when they'd be home, praying. It was up to him to help get them home safely.

Hannah circled her arms around his waist, and he stopped packing and enjoyed the feeling of her pressed against him. It seemed like they hadn't touched much lately. She worked so hard in the store downstairs that she was tired most of the time, and Lizzie and Junior were constantly underfoot. He was off in the *Planter* at all hours of day and night, often for days at a time. When he'd get home for a few hours, he'd need food and a bath and sleep.

He turned to face Hannah and stroked her cheek. When she

worked down in the store, she could sometimes still be the fierce lioness he'd known in Charleston, but she'd lost her razor sharp edge in the past year. Freedom agreed with her. There was a new softness to her chin and jaw. He kissed the line where his finger traced her face.

"This time's different, ain't it?" she asked.

He kissed her on the lips, taking the time to remember how she tasted. "Maybe."

She pulled his hips close to hers and he could feel himself growing hard. Rhind was leaving for the *Keokuk* on a sloop in a little more than an hour. Plenty of time.

He closed the bedroom door, by the time he turned around, she'd already slipped out of her dress. She reached forward and unbuttoned his jacket, the speed of her fingers increasingly urgent.

"This one's dangerous," and she wasn't asking. How had he given himself away? His eyes, his step, the way he needed to have a hand on her waist when he told her about this new assignment?

"It's an ironclad. One of them new ships."

"Is it any good? Where you taking it?"

"Can't say, even if I knew. But I'll be back."

"You'd better be."

He pushed her back onto the bed and she pulled him with her. Every nerve ending seemed alert, his mind recording every sensation, every thrust, every kiss, every moan. No matter what happened on board that ship, he'd find a way back to Hannah, to this moment, this place, this feeling.

*****

She lay cradled in his arms, still naked, as he stroked her chest, gently moving a finger from one nipple to the other.

"Give you enough reason to come back in one piece?"

"You always do. But keeping you and the chi'ren free, that's the reason to go."

"They gon' ask a lot this time."

"I'm willing to take my turn. You know me, I'm gon' be all right."

Her sad smile made it clear that she was not convinced.

*****

"Give me full-port engine, hard right rudder," Robert called down to quartermaster Anderson who manned the wheel in the pilothouse below them.

"Full-port engine, hard right rudder," echoed Anderson.

"Back off starboard engine to one-third."

"Backing off starboard engine to one-third," came the response.

The heavy ship began to turn to the right in a graceful arc, splashing water over the anchor assembly that jutted off the tip of the *Keokuk*'s prow. Robert glanced aft to get a look at her wake, trying to understand how this ship would steer when they needed to avoid oncoming fire.

Captain Rhind stood next to Robert, just inside the safety lines circling the top of the forward casement. The *Keokuk* had two hexagonal casements, stationary turrets, each housing an 11-inch Dahlgren gun. The pilot house was molded onto the rear of the forward turret, a room five feet wide and ten feet across that housed the wheel and a hatch down to the berth deck. When in battle, Robert would stand on a small metal shelf in the pilothouse and stick his head in the foot-high bump that provided a lookout. Somehow he was supposed to navigate by the view provided from thin slits cut through eight inches of armor, all while the *Keokuk*'s own gun was firing just on the other side of a wooden barrier.

"Could be a challenge," Robert had said, when Rhind first showed him the set up.

"You might not be able to see very well, but at least you're less of a target than the pilots in the monitors," Captain Rhind had said. He had a point. On the new *Passaic*-class monitors that would be joining the fight, the pilot house sat on top of the main turret. Every shot fired by attackers would be directed right at the pilot.

At least for this test run they could stand in the open air on top of the turret and not in the cramped pilot house.

"What do you think?" Rhind asked, his red beard whipping about in the wind.

"Don't exactly spin like a riverboat, but she can move." She moved like a pig in the water, but Robert wasn't sure how much Rhind loved this ship, and he didn't want to start with any bad feelings. *Never insult a captain's ship*—every pilot knew that rule by heart.

The *Keokuk* was about the same length and width of the *Planter*, and maybe a little faster on the straight line, if she could actually hold a straight line, which she couldn't. She swam like a goose with a gimpy leg. She weighed more than twice as much as the *Planter*, and Robert could feel every ton of it when she tried to turn.

"Be glad you're not on one of the monitors," Rhind said. "They're fifty feet longer and twice as heavy. And half as fast as the *Keokuk*. They're like driving a brick."

"How her engines been holding up?"

"No major problems. They did pretty well on the trip from New York. You know how new engines are. But the Engineer O'Malley seems good at keeping her up to speed."

Robert called down to Anderson, "Both engines half, all ahead."

"Both engines half, all ahead."

The *Keokuk* straightened out and slowed. Robert tried to imagine easing into the channel leading into Charleston Harbor. For the battle plan, he had convinced Admiral DuPont to enter through the South Channel, then they'd skirt slightly to the north, to provide a little distance from the guns of Battery Wagner, before heading into the main channel, smack between Fort Sumter and Fort Moultrie. The idea wasn't to speed past the forts but to batter Fort Sumter into submission.

If they were smart, they wouldn't be having him test the most maneuverable ship of the armada, which was going to be at the rear as they entered the harbor in single file. Instead they should have had him on one of the other monitors, which had drafts at least two feet deeper, at around ten feet, or even the *New Ironsides*, which drew about sixteen feet. Those were the ships that would have problems with the channel, and if he knew how they handled, he might give them a better path. Instead, he'd be following whomever they decided to have pilot the *Weehawken*. Probably some Irishman like Anderson who never spent a day in Charleston.

"Why she so much lighter than the others?"

"New type of armor. The *Keokuk* has alternating one-inch layers of iron and wood. The monitors have eight inches of plate, and that costs a lot more. The government needs this fleet of ironclads to stop eating so much of the treasury. If the *Keokuk* is a success, we'll see a lot more like her."

"Think her armor will hold?"

Rhind winced at the question and gave a quick look around. They had the top of the casement to themselves. "I hope so. There's only one way to find out."

So they were the experiment. Smaller ship, less armor. When the *Nahant* had been in Station Creek for repairs, Robert saw how the flat deck of the monitors overhung the main hull by several feet on either edge. On the *Keokuk*, the deck was rounded, like the back of a whale, so there was no overhanging ledge. With any luck, the rounded body of the *Keokuk* would deflect any shots that hit her. The regular monitors had fared well in the attack on Fort MacAllister last month. Now they'd be bringing the most powerfully armed and armored line of ships ever assembled against Fort Sumter. When they pounded her into submission, their names would go down in history.

"Starboard engine full, left full rudder," Robert called out.

Anderson repeated the order from below, and turned the ship hard to the left. The ship wasn't the straightest he'd ever steered, but her engines felt strong and smooth. She was definitely capable of bringing them into harm's way.

"If you keep her out of the mud, I might get my first visit to Charleston," Rhind said, squinting into the April sun and wind with an expression of delight and anticipation.

"I promise to show you the sights, sir."

The *Keokuk* rolled gently as they turned in a full arc, no longer headed out to sea, but now pointing towards the mouth of Charleston harbor, and towards the two dozen Union vessels anchored at regular intervals a few miles off shore, as part of the blockade and in preparation for the coming attack.

"I'm ready to lay out them buoys, if you is," Robert volunteered. "Give me a chance to try her out at a slower pace."

"Excellent. Forrest!" Rhind called down to first lieutenant Forrest, who was on deck with a crew of sailors. "Signal the *Bibb* and the *du Pont* that we're ready to lay the trail. Mr. Smalls will guide us to the chosen line."

Forrest quickly barked orders to the ensign in charge of the aft signal flag. Robert had Anderson slow the ship, so they could meet up with the survey vessels to lay out the path they'd take into Charleston Harbor, marking the watery road to their destinies.

CHAPTER 27

The *Keokuk* and the entire group of ironclads lay at anchor just outside the harbor mouth, not more than a mile and a half from Fort Sumter, waiting for the signal from *New Ironsides* to begin the attack. It was like standing in front of someone pointing a loaded gun at your heart.

Captain Rhind, Robert, and Lieutenant Forrest stood on the top of the forward turret, watching the signal pole on the flagship, but there was no change. In front of them, Fort Sumter poked its head out of the fog. Battery Gregg and Fort Moultrie lay invisible behind the mist, as completely hidden as the rows of obstructions and torpedoes lurking under the waters.

The stench of rancid pork meant they were ready to go. Yesterday, as they'd prepared for battle, all the ironclads, including the *Keokuk*, had slathered their decks with slush, barrels of grease collected in the galleys over the past weeks. Slush was supposed to make the enemy shells skip off the hull. But it stank and tracked itself inside the ship, and the ship's boys were constantly on patrol with buckets of soapy water, trying to stop the grease from defiling every inch of the ship's below decks.

The top deck of the *Keokuk* lay black and slick under the weak sun. Anything sticking above the surface of the deck had been stowed below, even the galley smoke stack—until this was over, their diet would consist of corned beef and stale bread. Every hatch had been tightened and sealed. Other than the two turrets, the anchor assembly and the central smoke stack were the only interruptions to the Keokuk's smooth round back.

Without the vent stacks, the air below grew stuffy and foul, and the crew looked for every possible excuse to crawl onto the top of the turrets where they could breathe.

"Think you could take us in, even with this fog?" Captain Rhind asked.

"Maybe in a smaller ship. And if I was standin' on the bow, us inching along, with Anderson watching my every sign. But not looking through them little holes." They all looked at the top of the pilot house, which rose just a foot above the top of the front turret.

"Nothing for it but to wait," said Rhind.

"The men are on edge," Lieutenant Forrest said, quietly.

"Have them double check everything, for the third time," Rhind suggested. "And rest half of them in hammocks. Whether it happens today or tomorrow, it'll be a long day."

They all looked out at the top of Sumter again. The rebels knew they were coming. It was just a matter of time.

*****

That night, Robert lay in a cot suspended over the wardroom table, visualizing the path he'd laid out for the ironclads. The forts boasted more guns than the ironclads, but the ships' guns were larger, especially the monitors' 15-inch Dahlgrens that could lob shells weighing more than 600 pounds as far as a mile. The monitors were hard to hit from the forts, with their flat decks barely rising above the water. The *Keokuk* showed a lot more hull. Robert didn't sense that Rhind had much confidence in its strength, though he put on a good show for the men. This was the ship they'd been given, and they were going to make the most of it.

Unlike the monitors, whose turrets swiveled, the *Keokuk's* turrets each had three portholes for firing, and the guns rotated inside the turrets. The ship needed to be properly aligned towards the target and the current would make it all tricky.

Snoring came through the door of Lieutenant Forrest's state

room. He was a vigorous first lieutenant, either awake or asleep. There were ten staterooms surrounding the open wardroom, but all were claimed by the ship's officers, so the stewards had rigged this visitor's cot for Robert.

Where he should dine had been a question. The captain had his own mess, in his forward cabin, and the officers all ate in the wardroom. The crew either ate topside or in the berth deck. But Robert wasn't an officer or crew member. On most ships, pilots were invited to eat with the officers, but most pilots weren't former slaves. At their first dinner, the chief engineer, a big tattooed Irishman, O'Malley had sat at the wardroom table and stared at Robert, not touching his food, not saying a word.

"Something wrong, O'Malley?" asked Forrest. Robert had met O'Malley on his first tour of the ship, following Captain Rhind, and even then O'Malley had kept a wrench in his hand rather than shake Robert's.

"If I wanted to eat with niggers, I would slop with the crew."

The other officers around the table hushed, their eyes moving back and forth between O'Malley and Robert. Ensign McIntosh, a young officer with a fuzzy blond beard and big ears, sat with his spoon of stew poised above his dish.

Robert waited to see what Forrest would do. They all needed O'Malley to be at his best over the next few days. But if the crew hesitated for a second to execute Robert's commands, they'd end up blown to pieces.

"Do you know who this is?" Forrest demanded of O'Malley.

"A nigger pilot. Don't know how we got stuck with him. Navy run out of real pilots?"

"Mr. Smalls ran the *Planter* out from under the noses of six Confederate forts without ever touching the bottom of that ship to the sand, past every torpedo and obstruction. At the personal request of Captain Rhind, Mr. Smalls has agreed to take us back to where he started, so he can risk getting blown to bits in the company of the entire crew of the *Keokuk*. Do you think Captain Rhind is an idiot?"

"No."

"Captain Rhind personally selected you, O'Malley, because he thinks you can keep this hunk of junk moving. He requested Mr. Smalls because he saw him at work on the *Crusader* and knows he has the knowledge and bravery to take us to the gate of hell and back. I don't care if Mr. Smalls is black, green, or purple. I want someone who will help reclaim Fort Sumter for the United States of America. Captain Rhind thinks he can do that. If you have a problem sharing the table with him, go explain your objections to the captain."

Forrest waited, his gaze steady on O'Malley, who finally lowered his watery blue eyes and took up a fork in his meaty, scarred hands and helped himself to a scoop of stew. Once he'd taken the first bite, everyone else finally breathed again.

*****

The break of the next day brought more mist, laying heavy over the glossy surface of the sea. Robert watched a steady parade of officers, sailors, boys, cooks, and gunners climb to the top of the turrets to stare out at the collection of ironclads and at the signal pole of the *New Ironsides*.

A mid-morning zephyr carried the tatters of fog out to sea, mixing with the sun to create a perfect spring day. Launches moved between the ironclads, carrying dispatches from the flagship. The boys brought up cups of coffee made using hot coals from the main boiler firebox, since the galley smoke stack was still out.

Fort Sumter lay ready and waiting, like an open mouth full of teeth, waiting to bite. Every soul on top of those turrets wondered whether their collection of ships had enough muscle to knock those teeth out.

*****

Finally, the *New Ironsides* signaled for all ships to get underway. The water hummed with the stoking of massive engines, punctuated by the staccato clanks of hatches slamming

247

shut. Robert and Captain Rhind stood side by side on the narrow shelf inside the pilot house, peering through the slits in the armor.

"Raise anchor," Rhind instructed Lieutenant Forrest, who repeated the order, and then shouted it into the speaking tube that led to below decks. The ship creaked and rolled as the great chunk of metal was raised from the seabed. "Keep her steady," Rhind instructed quartermaster Anderson who stood at the wheel, unable to see anything other than the wall separating them from the gun turret. "We must remain patient. She'd rocket to the front of the line if we let her, but we'll stay where we're told."

The ratchet of the armada's anchor chains made a clacking chorus, signaling their approach to Sumter. Flags raised over the fort, signaling the other forts. Hundreds of eyes trained spyglasses on the nine ironclads and their flotilla of support steamers and schooners, gun boats, tugs, and tenders.

They waited breathlessly for the *Weehawken* to move, but she stood still, drifting ever so slightly, as the other ships tried to maintain their places in line. A new flag raised over the *New Ironsides—Wait*. Robert and Rhind had their spy glasses up to their eyes in a flash, scanning each ship, settling on the front of the line, the *Weehawken*.

"It's that damn raft," said Rhind, under his breath. "Rodgers was the only one who thought it could work."

In order to try to deflect and disarm torpedoes, the *Weekhawken* had been fitted with a forty-foot raft made of heavy beams, bound together by chains. It was supposed to intercept the explosives and keep them from detonating close to the monitor.

"Caught in the anchor chain," Robert said, watching sailors and engineers crawling out of the tall turret of the monitor and scrambling down the deck, trying to keep their footing in the coating of grease. A steam-tug was already scooting over towards them, tools and winches at the ready.

"Blast it all. What do you think? Doesn't look like a quick

fix."

"No, suh."

"Lower anchor," Rhind ordered. The sound of other chains showed that the other captains shared the same thought. A thousand men in floating iron cages went back to pacing like tigers, hungry for a piece of meat dangling just out of reach.

*****

They waited an hour and a half before the signal finally came to resume the journey. Lieutenant Forrest called the men to quarters—each man had a specific station, whether it was the gunners in the turrets, the engineers tending the engines, or the boys hauling empty powder buckets back to the magazine. The surgeon, Doc Spencer, waited below at the canvas-covered wardroom table, ready for whatever bloody repair and salvage business came his way.

The *Weehawken* fully raised her anchor, but the raft slowed her well below her usual crawl. "They ought to just take a gun and blow that cursed raft off the bow. Then maybe we could reach the channel before sunset," Captain Rhind growled.

"Think we should volunteer?" called up Forrest, saying exactly what Robert had been thinking.

"Don't tempt me," Rhind said.

They waited for the line to form properly. The order of battle was to keep each ship a hundred yards apart. Going last meant that by the time they even got to move, the front ships would be engaged with Fort Sumter and Fort Moultrie. Each ship slowly steamed past the navigation buoys they'd placed the other day. Robert hoped the pilots on the front ships had some idea where they were going. Otherwise, they could end up in a great iron knot.

The ships surged forward, as the pilots tried to keep the ungainly vessels in the channel. *Weehawken* limped ahead in the lead, followed by the *Passaic*, *Montauk*, and *Patapsco*. In the center, the *New Ironsides* loomed high above the turrets of the ironclads on either side of her. Next in line came the *Catskill, Nantucket*, and *Nahant*. The turrets on each ship rotated back and forth, as the gunners sighted their weapons in preparation. Each rotation caused the vessel to slow and then lurch forward, as steam was diverted to turn the heavy gun towers. The top-heavy ships rocked back and forth in the water with each turret adjustment.

"Mr. Smalls has the controls," Rhind instructed Anderson.

"Aye, sir. Smalls has the controls."

Now their fate lay upon his shoulders.

The faint sound of "Dixie" wafted across the water from Fort Sumter. The Rebel band was playing a song to greet them. And then thunder rumbled, as the *Weehawken* came within range of both Fort Moultrie and Fort Sumter. Fire blasted from the gun placements on the face of Fort Sumter. Water erupted all around the *Weekhawken*, which continued to steam ahead, and returned fire of its own.

Stay to the left, stay to the left, Robert thought, wishing he could send his thoughts to the pilot on the *Weehawken*. It was hard to stay left in the channel, because it put you closer to Sumter, but otherwise, you'd run aground. The *Keokuk* was closing on the *Nahant* in front of her.

"A hundred yards between us and *Nahant* ain't gon' be possible, captain."

"Give her as much room as you can."

A huge stream of water erupted into the air near the *Weehawken*, as she tripped a mine. Robert and Rhind both watched her for signs of damage, but she merely rocked, and then rotated her turret to send another six hundred pounds of iron hurtling towards Fort Sumter.

"Guess she proved there are mines in there, after all," Rhind said.

Robert kept an eye on the water as well as the battle. They were close to Crab Shoal. So far, everyone had managed to skirt it. He didn't want to be the one to lay up on her.

The forward ships were clumping together, the *Passaic* moving close to the *Weehawken*, all of them purposefully shifting back and forth in the water—moving targets were harder to hit. The fire from the forts blasted non-stop. Every ten seconds, another shell let loose. The range was long enough Robert could see the great deadly balls arcing through the air. The water near the *Passaic* churned into foam from the shells hitting all around it, and then the Sumter gunners found their range and the iron started smashing against the armor of the warship. Two hit the bottom of the turret, sending sparks and shards of metal flying.

"Not good," Rhind said. "She can't spin her turret. Must have jammed the plates. She's out."

They'd pulled the *Keokuk* within five hundred yards of the first group of monitors. The *New Ironsides* floundered in the channel. She'd sent off a single broadside at Sumter, but none since.

"She's warped in the channel, in the current," Robert said. "Can't bring herself to bear upon the forts. She draws too much water to play on the edge of the channel like that."

"They're still too far from Sumter," Rhind chided. "They ought to leap in. Shot from that distance will barely scratch those stone walls. They need to put the pistol up to her face and pull the trigger."

The first half of the line was smashed with shell after shell. A set of objects floated in the channel, too high out of the water to be mines. Mines were meant to be hidden.

Range markers, Robert realized. The Confederates had laid range markers for their gunners all along the channel.

"They buoyed out range markers!" he shouted to Captain Rhind. "That's why they never seem to miss."

"Son of a bitch," Rhind growled. "Ah, finally!" he exclaimed, lowering his glass. "DuPont has signaled to disregard the position of the flagship. We'll get our turn to fight now. Give her four bells, Forrest, and sing out to the engine room to give her all the steam she can take."

"Aye, sir."

Rhind turned to Robert, his eyes alight with desire for battle. "Now's our chance. Can you bring us close to her north face? If we can come within five or six hundred yards, we can actually do some damage."

"Wherever you want us to go, I'll get us there."

*****

Robert steered them into the narrow south branch of the main channel, but they weren't the only ones with that idea. The *Nahant* was just as eager to move into the action. The water got shallow that close to the fort, and the two ships were so close there was hardly room to keep from running aground.

"Cut the starboard engine," Robert instructed Anderson. He wanted to bring her around, so the gunners would have a chance to make something happen. She swayed in the current. "Starboard engine one quarter, half left rudder."

Captain Rhind shouted to Forrest, "What are they waiting for? Tell them to start firing."

As if the message had flicked through the ether, the pilot house shook as the front turret fired off a salvo, followed closely by a shot from the rear casement. It would take close to three minutes to reload. The cramped space in the turrets made for slow firing.

The air was full of fire, smoke, and flying metal. The sound rolled on, louder and louder, never a spare moment between shots.

From the observation slit, Robert could see not just the water, but also cannon balls hurtling towards the *Keokuk*.

"Here comes another!" he shouted.

The men braced themselves, as a chunk of iron crashed against the forward deck. In the time it took to reload the forward gun, two more shots hit the deck, one right in front of the turret, rocking the ship.

Robert shouted to Anderson, "Shift her forward. Slow now."

And they crept even closer to the face of Sumter. Rhind grinned at the sight of a one of their shells hitting the face of Sumter and sending up a cloud of rock and smoke.

Two more shots hit the *Keokuk* right at the waterline, one after the other, sending up spray and making an enormous cracking sound. Robert didn't like the sound of that crack.

"McIntosh, get me a damage report from the berth deck!" Rhind shouted. "Keep us steady, Robert."

Robert struggled to keep the *Keokuk* in deeper water—the foamy sea was full of ash and smoke and spent powder. The sound grew loud enough to vibrate the armor surrounding the pilot house. It was as if they were within the roar itself, in the throat of an infinite dragon.

The *Nahant* was getting nailed almost as hard as the *Keokuk*. Three shots hit the *Nahant's* pilot house on top of the turret, smashing the whole assembly. Robert hoped the pilot survived.

Below Robert, sailors hauled powder and rolled shells to the *Keokuk's* guns. The forward Dahlgren let off another salvo, but Rhind's smile was gone now, as they took another succession of hits—one, two, three, four. Water rained down on the deck, as if they were in the heart of a hurricane.

A soaking wet Ensign McIntosh stuck his head through the hatch. "The pumps are holding for now, captain. But we've been holed up and down the water line."

"How much water are we taking?" Rhind demanded.

"The engineers are trying to patch it, but it's not good, sir."

"Tell them to work faster. We're not done yet."

Another shot from their own forward gun nearly shook them off the pilot house shelf. "That's the way!" Rhind shouted.

The *Nahant* loomed closer, too busy trying to turn her turret to pay attention to where she was going.

Robert hollered at Anderson, "Half reverse, both engines. Don't lock horns with the *Nahant*. Rudder sixty degrees."

"How come the rear gun isn't firing?" Rhind called to his

officers. "What's the point of sitting here if we're not trying to kick them in the teeth? Forrest, find out what's the matter."

Forrest disappeared through the hatch. Robert and Rind peered through the aft slit in the pilot house armor, trying to see why the Keokuk's rear cannon was silent. The armor was dented, with gaping holes from rifled shells. They couldn't see whether the *Keokuk's* doors on the firing portholes were open or shut.

Hundreds of yards behind them, now anchored to keep from getting fully stuck in the muck, the *New Ironsides*, stood bravely as shot after shot bounced off her thick armor.

The *Nahant* scraped past the *Keokuk*, heading back out of the harbor with her smashed turret—if she couldn't return fire, she was just clogging up the channel for the rest of the ships.

Forrest poked his head up through the hatch. "Captain, every officer and man in the rear turret is either dead or wounded."

Dread filled the pilot house. Seventeen men had manned each turret when they entered the fight.

"Watch out!" Anderson leapt up from the wheel and grabbed Captain Rhind from the observation shelf just as a shell crashed into the top of the pilot house. The force of the blow knocked loose bolts holding the armor onto the walls, sending them flying like bullets around the tiny cabin.

Robert flew off the shelf onto the deck, in a heap with Anderson and Rhind. His eyes blazed with pain, and when he reached up to clear them, his hands came away slick with blood. Iron dust and smoke clogged his eyes and he couldn't wipe them free.

"Water! Give me some water to wipe my eyes!" Robert shouted.

He found a leather bucket and splashed the water over his face, cooling his eyes, and scrabbling fingers across his eyelids, searching for metal splinters. Finally, he was able to open his eyes enough to see.

Forrest climbed into the pilot house and rolled Anderson off Captain Rhind. "Captain? Captain? Are you all right?"

Rhind sat up and appeared uninjured though he was clearly dazed from the explosion. "I think so. Thanks to Anderson."

A sharp chunk of the wheel had broken off and was embedded in Anderson's back. "Can you reach it, Smalls?" Anderson asked. "Get it out of me. Get it out."

Robert reached forward and withdrew the long slice of wood from Anderson's back.

"That would have been me, Anderson," Rhind said quietly.

"Saw that shot coming just in time," Anderson answered, already standing up and reaching for the wheel, the back of his jacket covered in blood. Captain Rhind and Robert gingerly climbed up on the shelf to look out of the observation slits, though the metal of the turret bowed inward now. Robert could barely see through the blood dripping into his eyes. His face felt like it was on fire.

The forward gun went off again, booming against the thin wall between them. An enormous crash came from behind the wall. Not a good sound.

The air between them and Fort Sumter looked like it was full of bees leaving a beehive that had just gotten a sharp kick. The *Keokuk* felt the sting of those bees again and again and again. Robert tore his gaze away from the approaching swarm of missiles and concentrated his attention on the *Keokuk*'s position in the channel. Anderson stood strong at the wheel, despite the spreading red stain on his back.

"Bring her ten degrees to the starboard," Robert ordered. "Slow both engines." It couldn't get much worse.

Captain Rhind looked out the observation slit and then promptly ducked, as the shadow of another shell passed over them and smashed into the rear turret.

"Forrest! Why isn't the forward gun firing? Get me a damage report."

Whatever report came back, it wasn't going to be good news.

Robert could see where a three foot section of armored plate had been ripped off the underlying layers of wood and metal. One solid hit in that spot and the *Keokuk* would be resting on the bottom.

Forrest's head popped back up the hatch. He was coated in a mix of seawater, gunpowder, and blood. The din of battle drowned out his voice.

"What? Repeat that," Rhind ordered.

"The forward gun has been thrown off its carriage. They're trying to raise her with the shot winch, but they can't get it to budge." Robert knew it was futile—the 11-inch Dahlgren weighed almost 16,000 pounds and the shot winch was only meant to load shells weighing 160 pounds.

"Damnation."

"We've got every hand on the pumps, but we're taking water fast. I don't know how much longer we've got."

Captain Rhind looked at Forrest, and then back out at Fort Sumter and its fiery cloud. He shook his head in frustration and shouted into the din. "Get us out of here, Robert. Follow the *Nahant* to safety. We'll have to come back and fight another day."

"Aye, sir. Anderson, full starboard engine, full reverse on the port engine. Rudder full left."

In the way she turned, Robert could tell the *Keokuk* had already taken a lot of water. Every rip and dent in the hull made her harder to steer. A long groan rumbled from the bottom of the ship, as she scraped past a shoal, now that she lay two feet deeper in the water. The engines strained and huffed as Robert steered the *Keokuk* away from the steadfast face of Fort Sumter.

CHAPTER 28

Though she left the battle before the others, the *Keokuk* was last to arrive at the anchorage. Robert didn't dare push the engines any harder. When they finally bobbed in the group of ironclads clustered around the *New Ironsides*, he gave the order to lower anchor. Captain Rhind was already below, directing the engineering teams, trying to fashion patches for the holes in the hull.

At first, it seemed like all the support vessels were afraid to approach the flotilla, as if the poisonous stink of defeat was contagious. But as soon as the anchor chain rang out on the *Keokuk*, a tug steamer, the *Monarch*, drove up to her. Lieutenant Forrest was already on deck with one of the engineering teams, trying to open hatches that had been clamped shut by Sumter's shells.

Robert climbed the ladder inside the pilot house and unscrewed the hatch, but it wouldn't budge. The assistant quartermaster, Abe Hunter, stood at the wheel in the dim cabin, replacing Anderson, who had finally been dragged to see the surgeon by Captain Rhind.

"Get me a bar or post, to see if we can get this damn thing open," Robert called. Fresh air would be welcome—the pilot house was filled with coal smoke and iron dust and flakes of paint and ash. His eyes were swollen to slits from shrapnel wounds.

Hunter returned with a two-foot long iron rod. Robert braced himself on the ladder and pounded up on the hatch. Nothing. Through the slits, he saw the legs of one of the repair crew who'd climbed onto the turret. "Try again," the sailor said.

Robert gave a few more whacks with the bar and the hatch flew open. He climbed out to see 3rd engineer Emanuel, a wiry young officer, holding a pry bar. "Watch your step," Emmanuel warned. "It's a mess out here. And the slush just makes it worse. Makes us stink so bad that we're all going to have to burn our uniforms when we're done, otherwise no one will ever want to be near us again."

Calling it a mess was an understatement. *Keokuk*'s armor had been a complete failure. For the first time, Robert had a true sense of the damage done to this young ship. The whole bow was dented and splintered. One of the shells had punched a hole through to the captain's cabin. Two iron plates in the midsection were completely dislodged, and half a dozen sailors strained to pry them back into position, but the sheets were too heavy to be moved and too bent to ever fit again.

"How bad is it below?" Robert asked Emanuel.

"Hard to believe we'll make it until morning. On the plus side, it'll be easier to catch fish for dinner—they're already in the galley. But O'Malley is a clever guy. He might get her patched enough to steam her back to Port Royal."

A sailor on deck caught a line from the tug but slipped on the black grease and fell into the water. Instantly, three crew mates dropped their tools and threw him another rope.

"Get the stanchions and lines up," Forrest ordered. "How can we save this ship if we can't even stand on deck? Get every available boy up here with soap and hot water and have them start scrubbing."

Robert looked out at the other ships. The *Nahant* looked the worst, with a big dent at the base of her turret, and the *Nantucket* didn't look much better. But none of them seemed to have been actually pierced by shots like the *Keokuk*, whose rear turret looked like a cheese grater.

Launches and cutters scurried between monitors and the *New Ironsides*. Captain Rhind emerged onto the deck and leaped from the *Keokuk* into a waiting boat. He looked back, grim-faced, as two sailors rowed him to the flagship.

Lieutenant Forrest joined Robert in surveying the ship and the fleet. The pock-marked face of Fort Sumter stood serenely above the smoke from the battle. They'd been unable to even make her flinch. Robert's fantasy of raising the stars and stripes over her ramparts seemed more distant than ever. The rebel flag waved defiantly over Fort Sumter, Fort Moultrie, Battery Wagner.

"You look like hell, Mr. Smalls," said Forrest.

"I'm better than most. How many hurt down there?"

"At least twenty injured and one dead. McIntosh."

Forrest yelled at the newly emerged repair crew to move farther down the deck. They crept carefully over the slippery surface, carrying wrenches and buckets of bolts.

"You should have Doc Spencer look at those eyes. We're going to need your vision to get this wreck back home." Forrest was right—even in tow, they'd need someone on board who knew the reefs and channels.

"I'll get us wherever we need to go, don't worry. I'll even take you by the best fishing holes." Though if the damage to his eyes was real and permanent, how could he keep piloting? How could he do anything?

"At least let him clean you up, before your eyes swell shut the rest of the way. That's an order, Smalls."

Robert reluctantly climbed down to the wardroom, which was filled with the smell of blood and burnt flesh. Thick black water sloshed above his ankles. In the lantern light, he could see through the open hatch into the berth deck, where the wounded were slung in hammocks, waiting to be carried up the ladder.

A sailor sat on the edge of the table, his shoulder covered in a red bandage, a thin drip of blood plinking into the water. His eyes stared down at the rising sea gradually invading the *Keokuk*. Every wounded man in the room knew that when the seep turned into a flood, there would be no escape. Every one knew about the fate of the ironclad *Monitor*, which had floundered on her way under tow off Cape Hatteras. Sixteen of her crew had drowned. With most of the hatches on the *Keokuk* smashed shut, she seemed like a giant metal coffin.

The surgeon waded over to Robert. "Hurts pretty bad?" he asked.

"Kind of stings," Robert said.

"Stay still."

Doc Spencer took a rag from a bucket of pinkish water and rubbed it around Robert's eyes, trying to see what was stuck in there. They both felt the cloth snag, and Spencer took a pair of forceps from his vest pocket and pulled out a long sliver of metal from Robert's cheek. It felt like fire coming out.

"Just missed your eye," Doc Spencer said. "The swelling will get worse for another day or two, but if we keep it clean, you might not lose your sight."

Something, at least, to be grateful for.

"If you see Lieutenant Forrest, tell him I've got twenty wounded men who need to get out of this crate."

"I'll make sure of it," Robert assured him. Spencer wrapped some clean gauze around the top of Robert's forehead and wound a strip across his nose and around the back of his head.

"This might keep some of the junk of out of your eyes. When we get to Port Royal, we'll get you to the hospital and have them clean and bind it again."

Robert nodded and left, eager to get into the fresh air, away from the rising water.

*****

Captain Rhind returned from the flagship shortly before dark. His launch was followed by another tug, a small steam tender, and a repair ship. Rhind gathered Lieutenant Forrest, engineer O'Malley, and Robert into his cabin. Anderson's wound was still bleeding too heavily to even think about including him in the meeting—they left him under the close eye of Doc Spencer, waiting to be evacuated.

"What's the word from the admiral?" Forrest asked as soon as the cabin door was shut.

"He had planned to try again tomorrow, but it seems impossible. All the ironclads are to return to Port Royal. This attack wasn't his idea, but he'll end up taking the blame for it." Rhind's face looked like he'd aged ten years in a day. "What's the latest report?"

"Eighteen holes at or below the waterline, sir," Forrest stated formally, still standing straight at attention, despite being soaking wet and filthy. "One section of armor is entirely dislodged. We're taking water faster than we can pump it out. If the wind rises, the topside holes will let in every swell."

Robert looked above the captain's head and could see right through a gaping wound in the hull and watch the legs of the engineering crew struggling to repair yet another smashed panel of wood and iron.

"Can you keep her afloat long enough to have her towed to Port Royal?" Rhind asked O'Malley. O'Malley shifted on his feet, impatient to return to the engine room and his crew.

"We'll be lucky to keep her afloat long enough to carry out the wounded, Captain. Have you got someone to take them? I've got all hands on the pumps and firemen feeding the coal as fast they can shovel, but if the water gets much higher the *Keokuk* will turn into a great boiling kettle."

"Do the best you can. I have a repair crew waiting to plug the holes in the waterline. Just keep those pumps working."

"Aye, captain." With a nod, O'Malley opened the door and strode back to his impossible task.

Rhind turned to Robert. "If we can keep her afloat, can you steer her back to Port Royal?"

"The rudder and controls is workin'. But she gon' be harder to steer than a bathtub full of rocks. If O'Malley can dry her out a little, I can get us home. As long as the sea stays calm."

Rhind seemed determined not to give up on their iron beast. "Let's find a way to give you a chance. Forrest, work with the crew of the tug to evacuate the wounded. I'll direct the engineers. Robert, you stay with me. If we can get ahead of the water, we'll run a line to the *Passaic*, in hopes of a tow."

A giant groan came from the hull of the ship, as she shifted and settled against her anchors, straining to contain the ever-rising water.

*****

At midnight, they carried the last wounded man, Anderson, off the ship. Robert paused from his work with a crew of crowbar wielding men, trying to pry loose a piece of twisted iron off the oak beneath. The dark and the slush and the odd camber of the *Keokuk*'s deck made the work nearly impossible. Since Rhind had returned from the flagship, they'd repaired only two holes close to the waterline. The loose plate of armor had been removed, but the repair tender didn't have a replacement of the right size. It didn't help that the *Keokuk* was unlike all the other vessels. They tried to improvise with planks and caulking—on a wooden ship they could have driven spikes into the hull to temporarily fasten them. Here that wasn't an option.

A light touch on the back of his neck raised Robert's head. The wind was rising.

*****

A wave swept over the deck of the *Keokuk*, which no longer stood out of the water. Instead the casements were like two iron islands, with a tiny spit of a smokestack between them. Lamps hung from the iron stanchions on top of both turrets, in an imperfect circle, thanks to dents and pockmarks from the Confederate guns.

Forrest and Rhind stood atop the forward turret with Robert, watching the watery tentacles grip at their vessel.

"Captain?" Forrest said, gently.

Rhind turned his face into the rising wind and looked along what could be seen of the ship in the twilight. "Call them out.

And hurry."

Forrest disappeared quickly down the hatch. They heard his voice coming up from below, echoing like at the bottom of a tomb. "Abandon ship. All hands out. Now, now, now! Drop what you're doing and go. Abandon ship!"

"Let them know we're coming," Rhind ordered Robert, who picked up a signal flag and waved it towards the waiting launch. Half a dozen lanterns lit in reply, and crewmen ran to the rail, lines in hand.

Men swarmed out of the *Keokuk*'s main deck, so covered in grime and soot that in the half light of approaching morning, they barely looked human. They were followed by O'Malley, who dragged his exhausted bulk away from the station where he'd fought a hopeless battle.

The ship creaked and shook violently, as if in response to her bowels being suddenly emptied of life. Forrest scrambled out of the hatch, as another wave swept over the deck and disappeared into the open hatches and holes. The men reached for lines and each other.

The next lurch almost shook Robert and Rhind off the turret. Forrest clambered up the iron ladder and joined them.

"All clear?" Rhind asked.

"Aye, sir."

The three men looked out over the black silhouette of the *Keokuk*. The men had been pulled to safety, and now they called for Robert and the officers to join them. Robert wondered how long Rhind would wait.

Another wave. Another shake and the bow began to dip and this time it didn't stop.

"Down we go, boys!" Rhind said, and they all quickly slid down the ladder—Robert first, then Forrest, followed by the captain. Rhind patted the side of the casement fondly. "You gave it your best."

The aft of the ship suddenly shifted down to match the bow and they found themselves waist deep in the sea. Robert grasped a line and held tight. Behind them, with a great gushing of sea and air blowing through every gaping hole, the *Keokuk* sank, leaving only two small swirls of black iron breaking the waves.

CHAPTER 29

Robert rode in the back of a cart with three other wounded black sailors to Hospital Number 14, which had been the Baptist Church of Beaufort before the town fell into Union hands. They'd practically driven right past Smalls Supplies, and he'd considered just hopping out of the cart and walking home. But Captain Rhind had made him promise to at least visit the doctors at the hospital. His exact words were, "These drivers will come back and tell me whether you went to see the doctors, and if I don't like the answer, I'll get them to drive me into Beaufort and I'll drag you there myself."

Robert's body hurt like hell. On the day of the battle, he hadn't paid attention to the splinters all over his body, how his face and eyes ached, and how he could hardly hear anything. Now it felt like his whole body had shut down.

The boy from the *Keokuk*, the one who served dinner in the wardroom, didn't look so good. Burns covered his face and bloody bandages laced across his chest. One of the others was from the *Nahant*, a sailor wounded when a bolt inside the turret flew off. Didn't look like he'd ever use his hand again. The other one was Sam James who used to sail for the Ellis plantation, hauling cotton. It was hard to tell exactly what was wrong with him, but he had a bandage around his head, and his eyes didn't seem to see much of anything.

The driver clucked his tongue at the horse, and they pulled in front of the soaring white columns of the church. At the sight of the carts, two black orderlies taking shade under a catalpa tree pulled a last few draws on their pipes and picked up the stretcher at their feet.

Robert waved off any thought of riding on the stretcher—he was perfectly capable of walking on his own two feet. A white nurse with a kerchief covering her hair scurried out of the church, giving instructions to the orderlies. She glided over to Robert and put a gentle hand on his elbow as he swayed.

"You don't want a stretcher, but perhaps I can give you a hand inside," she offered. She was young but something about her eyes said she'd already seen enough horrors to last a lifetime.

"I'm fine, ma'am. Captain just said I needed to get a doctor to look at my eyes and get the papers signed."

"We can do that. Let's get you inside, out of the sun, and into a chair."

The front doors stood wide open, but he hesitated. It wasn't the sight of bandaged men stretched out where the pews used to be, and it wasn't the smell of rotting flesh, or the buzz of flies that gave him pause. When he was a boy, living in the McKee house, he used to come here with Mama. But back then, the front doors and sanctuary were for white church members only. He and Mama entered through doors on either side of the main entrance that led up to the balcony. The separate doors ensured that white and black members wouldn't get in each other's way as they entered the house of God.

They'd all cram shoulder to shoulder in the balcony, as the hot air rose, fanning themselves, hoping a breeze would blow through the open windows. Reverend Fuller was pastor back then, a native of Beaufort who'd gone off North to Harvard to study law and returned to become a minister. Every Sunday he preached about how God set up places for them in this world and the next. In this world, God had placed the whites as the masters and the blacks as the servants. But that didn't mean that God loved them any less.

The only time Robert ever walked through the front doors was for the fellowship parade. Every year, Reverend Fuller had the Negro members line up in single file, down the steps, down

Charles Street, all the way to the river. At a call of "Alleluia" they would sing hymns and clap and march down the center aisle, past the white members, who sat in their pews, singing and clapping along, shaking hands with the dark-skinned members of the church, in Christ's fellowship. Even Robert, as a child, could shake a friendly white hand that day, before heading up to the galleries to hear Reverend Fuller preach about how even the black man had God's grace in him. The white planters were supposed to pay attention to that grace, but not so much that they'd invite a Negro to sit in one of their pews. Or set him free.

Now here he was, going in through the front door, and there weren't any planters sitting on velvet cushions, listening to how God made them masters of men. Some folks in Beaufort worried that once this war was over, life would go back to how it was. Stepping over the broad threshold, Robert knew they were wrong. He didn't know what the future had in store, but it was never going back to the old ways.

*****

Laying on the polished wood of the pew, he waited hours for the doctor, staring up at the vaulted ceiling, lost in memories, his ears still ringing from Ft. Sumter's roar. It was better to think about old Sundays at church instead of walls of fire and men screaming on the *Keokuk*. Or the red stain spreading across Anderson's back. The black water gurgling up through the hull of the *Keokuk*, like a cold starless midnight, empty and hungry.

The doctor, a half-bald white man in a blood-stained suit jacket, looked him over, poking at the cuts and swollen bruises around his eyes. "I don't think there's any metal left in there. I'd say let's leave it alone. I'll give you some ointment for it. I'll put you down on the disabled list for a few weeks—you need to let those eyes heal. Keep away from the sun and the salt water for at least two weeks."

Robert nodded, though the idea of staying on land, out of the sun, for two whole weeks, seemed impossible.

He was ready to head home, but the memories conjured by this place sent him onto Prince Street instead. Down past the magnolias and soaring live oaks, he stopped in front of the McKee House. Though the McKees sold it to the de Treville's in 1851, everyone still called it the McKee House. Store deliverymen used to ask old mister de Treville where he lived, and as soon as he gave the address, they'd say, "Why don' you tell me you'se live in da McKee house?"

Hard to know who it belonged to now. There was a sign on the boarded up front door: "Seized by Order of the United States Government." It wasn't as grand as most of the hospital mansions, but it was still a fine two story house, with black shutters over tall windows and a broad front porch. The paint was starting to peel. Most empty homes were being taken for taxes. Many of the plantations were auctioned off just a few weeks ago. Some said maybe the government would sell the houses, too. How much would they want for it?

He'd been born in the small slave house in the back yard. That was usually where George, the carriage driver, slept, and Robert and Mama Lydia, too. Though Mama often slept on a blanket inside the house, near the foot of Mrs. McKee's bed. When he was a little nub of a boy, he and Elizabeth Jane used to play hide and seek in the big manicured garden. Now weeds choked the yard. It only took a few months of neglect for the wrong things to start growing in Beaufort.

He imagined Lizzie and Junior running on those paths, instead of crammed into their apartments over the store. He could practically see Hanna tending the little kitchen garden out back.

He was supposed to return home a hero. Not just the hero of the *Planter*, but on the winning side of the Battle of Charleston. Instead, he was the pilot of the only ironclad sunk in the attack. Their losses were nothing like Antietam or Shiloh, but they carried the same stink of failure.

He dragged his feet down dusty streets lined with hospitals. The closer he got to the waterfront, the more people he saw. His bandages hid his identity, and he hurried his steps, not eager to talk with anyone right now. They'd all want the blow-by-blow of the battle, want to know what went wrong and who was to blame. It would be impossible to bear.

Dusk was settling in from the sea, the sky clear and purple to the east. Inside the store, Hannah was sweeping up for the night. At the sight of Robert, she flung down the broom and wrapped her arms around him. Her cheek against his was wet. She stepped back half a step, to get a better look at him. "How bad is you hurt?"

"Not as bad as most."

"Doctor looked at you?"

"Yeah. Real army doctor. I might not be much to look at now, but I'll get back to my normal beautiful self in no time."

She ran her fingers over his bandaged face, so light he could hardly tell they were there. Most folks would never think Hannah knew how to be so gentle.

"You had me worried. I heard every kind of rumor, but then they started saying your ship sunk. I prayed you didn't go with her."

"The rebels had their chance with me last year. If they wasn't going to get me then, they wasn't going to get me this time." He tried to smile, but it made his whole face hurt.

"Maybe you don't have to give them any more tries."

"I'm gon' keep doin' my part. We lose this war, we lose everything. Long as I breathe, I's gone be part of it."

She looked like she was thinking about putting up a fight about it, but instead gave him a long look, her eyes filled with sorrow. "Can you at least heal first?"

"Doc said I had to take two weeks away from the sun and water, to rest. By then, you'll be picking up that broom and sweeping me out the door and down to the docks."

"I might not be in a hurry to be rid of you."

"We'll see."

"And when the swelling goes down around those eyes and the fog clears from yo' head, you might see something else, too." She took his hand and placed it on her firm belly. He knew her body as well as he knew the *Planter*. There was a new roundness, just barely perceptible. A new child was on its way, and this one meant to be born free.

"That's the best welcome home any man ever had," he whispered.

CHAPTER 30

Reverend French brought the news.

Robert and Alfred were behind the store, perched on wobbly chairs in the shade. "There will be another property auction next week," the reverend said, after taking time to look at Robert's swollen face and say a prayer of thanksgiving to God for returning Robert home alive. Another prayer beseeched the Lord to watch out for the souls of the men who died in the battle, and yet another asked the Lord to guide the generals and admirals in their attempts to break the rebel defenses.

"Do you know which houses they's gon' sell?" asked Robert.

"It's a smaller sale than last time, one or two plantations, and perhaps a dozen homes. Philbrick is trying to convince some of the freedmen on the plantations to pool together their money to buy land, but the wages have been slow in coming. The Negro workers are understandably nervous."

As much as Robert admired Revered French, it seemed like he was deliberately teasing it out right now. The reverend was always thinking about the big picture, and Robert just wanted to know about one particular property.

"They sellin' the McKee house on Prince Street or not?" he demanded, unable to control his impatience.

"Yes. That's on the list. I wondered if you would consider it."

"I ain't just gon' consider it. I gon' buy it."

"It's a fine house. Though it's easy to wonder if it might come with a certain bitterness, given that you were born into slavery there, and your mother lived there as a slave. Some

271

wonder if Negroes who buy these homes might just tear them down, out of spite."

"Tear it down?" Robert never ceased to be astonished by the foolishness of white men. "That a fine house, built by the hands of carpenters darker than me. That roof was put up by black men. That garden was dug and shaped by slave hands. Spite? I'd be grateful to have something so fine end up in the right hands."

"Let us pray on your behalf." Reverend French sent up more words to God. Robert wasn't sure God was always a good listener, but learning that the McKee House was for sale made him think that He might actually listen sometimes.

Reverend French casually poured himself some tea. "I might also partake in the auction. I'd love for Austa and the children to have a little more room."

"What place you got in mind?"

"They said the Fuller House on Bay Street, the "Tabby Manse" will be on the boards. It would suit us perfectly. I'm assuming you have no interest in it, since you have your sights set elsewhere."

Folks said Reverend French wasn't practical, but Robert wasn't so sure. He bet the reverend would converse with everyone in town, making sure they wouldn't bid on the Fuller house. And the reverend was tight with Mr. Brisbane, chair of the tax commissioners, the ones who decided which houses got sold when.

"We'd be situated just right to visit for an after dinner stroll, won't we?" Robert said, with a smile. "It'd make me feel right civilized."

*****

It seemed like every black man and woman in Beaufort made an excuse to come buy something at Smalls Supplies that week. Or at least to look over the merchandise and track dirt onto Hannah's newly swept floor. Really they came to see Robert's wounds and hear him tell the story of the Battle of

272

Charleston. Every twenty minutes, he had to start the tale all over again—the waiting, the order to proceed, the nervous dread of waiting for the firing to begin. Boom, boom, boom. Thunder from Sumter, thunder from Moultrie. The shuddering of the ship with each new explosion. Hole after hole pounded into the hull. The never ending noise, the spray of metal, wood, and blood.

After every round of the tale, the listeners would be left in awe by the enormity of it all, and Robert would casually ask if they'd heard about the Direct Tax sale coming up. "Oh, yes," they'd say. Maybe they were thinking about pooling their money to buy a few acres. Maybe they had an uncle or cousin thinking about buying a house.

Robert made sure each and every one of them knew that he intended to buy the McKee House. They'd better know enough not to bid against their hero who had fought against Ft. Sumter and lived to tell the tale.

*****

With all of the prospective buyers packed into the parlor of the Rhett House, it was clear they should have found a ballroom in one of the bigger mansions or used a church, though Robert thought buying and selling people's homes wasn't something you should do in a church. Jesus was pretty tough on those old money lenders.

Mama Lydia stood next to Robert, on his other side was Hannah. Alfred had come along, too, though he wasn't planning to buy yet. "First I gots to find me a woman. Ain't no point in having a house 'less you gots a woman to clean it for you. And anyways, I still got my sea legs. When this war's over, who knows where I might go. Always had an interest in seeing me a Chinaman. Maybe I'll ship out to Shanghai someday."

A few other Negroes were there, like Deacon Harris, wearing the sharp hat he always wore to preach at Tabernacle Baptist on Sundays. Sergeant Prince Rivers stood on the other side of the room, tall and strong, but even he had trouble making elbow room for himself in the press of white missionaries, teachers, merchants, speculators, government appointees, and army and navy officers. Some might be looking for homes, like Reverend French, who stood near the front of the room, talking softly with his tax commissioner friends. Others couldn't pass up a bargain.

If the Union lost the war, the planters would come back and drive everyone out. William DeTreville would be sure to come back for his house on Prince Street. And even if the Union won, sooner or later all these Northerners would hear the call of their own home places again. Maybe the teachers from Boston and New York and Philadelphia would stay. The way they cooed and mooned over their students at the schools, you'd think they were their own children. Miss Towne, Lizzie's teacher was just like them. Robert and Hannah always made sure the teachers got some eggs and jam whenever they walked by the store. But the lady teachers couldn't buy any property today—only men could buy land at this auction.

Not long before all the air in the room was about breathed out, Dr. Brisbane rose from the chair behind his desk and called the room to order.

"By the power vested in me by the Congress of the United States and Secretary of the Treasury Salmon Chase, I will now begin the sale of seized property within the environs of Beaufort, Port Royal and Saint Helena Islands."

Robert wondered if there might be a little glee in the old doctor's voice as he started to sell off the property of his old slaveholding neighbors. He looked even livelier now than he did when he gave his Emancipation Day speech.

The bidding started on a small house on Duke Street that Deacon Harris wanted. He started out strong, but an army colonel pushed the price over five hundred dollars. Then to six hundred. The Deacon looked over at Robert and scowled. "They never let us have nothin'," he murmured.

Reverend French bought the Fuller House, but the price went all the way up to a thousand dollars, under pressure from another white officer. Reverend French wiped the sweat from his brow—Mrs. French was known to be wary of spending too much money. He'd catch an earful from Austa when get got home, no matter how much thanks he gave to God.

Every time a property came up, Doc Brisbane read the valuation, and the bidding would start, a flurry of hands raising the price in twenty or fifty dollar steps. In his jacket pocket, Robert had money they'd been saving from the store. The pile of seven hundred dollars from Charleston had already been spent, but he'd earned it back and kept that same amount carefully hidden. The price he'd had for his family. There was more besides, from the *Planter*'s prize money. He could have bought most of the houses already sold, and maybe even gone in with someone on a plantation. But he was only interested in one particular property.

He looked around the crowd, trying to guess which northerners might still have money in their pockets. Or maybe Prince Rivers. Hard to say. Working on the boats and at the store made Robert familiar with every face in that room.

"511 Prince Street. Valued at seven hundred dollars. Who will make an opening bid?"

"Six hundred fifty dollars," Robert boomed, using the same voice he used on the *Planter* to get the crew's attention. The crowd gave him half a step clearance. Every eye looked at him, and he looked them all right back, straight in the eyes. Didn't matter whether they were black or white, officers or clergymen. He fixed his scabbed face and swollen eyes on each of them. Which one of them would dare take away the closest thing he and his mother might have called a home?

Not one person raised a hand.

"Six hundred and fifty dollars," said Doc Brisbane, "to Mr. Smalls. Do I hear seven hundred?"

Still no one moved.

"Going once. Going twice. Sold to Mr. Smalls for six hundred and fifty dollars."

*****

As a child, Robert had fantasized about being free, about him and Mama having their own little house, but he'd never thought this one would be his very own. No matter how this war turned out, not one Negro would be the same—their dreams would be different from now on. If you wanted to keep people slaves, you had to whittle down their dreams, to where they spent their spare thoughts fantasizing about an afternoon out of the heat of the field, or away from the kitchen, a morning spent in church singing hymns, a meal that actually fills the belly, a month without the lash. They'd all have better, bigger dreams now.

In the front entranceway, they could see into the parlor on one side and the dining room on the other. The stairs led upstairs to the bedrooms that had been shared by old Mrs. McKee and Henry McKee and his wife, Jane. The children, Elizabeth Jane and baby Willie, slept in bedrooms on this floor, down the hall. The kitchen was out back, close to the slave quarters.

The bones of the house still looked the same, but the details of his memory didn't match the dimly lit room in front of him. The pink floral wallpaper had been replaced by the DeTrevilles with one patterned in grape vines. The Cotton Settlement Agents had confiscated every stick of fine furniture. The soldiers who had been living here on and off since the occupation had left behind a few broken chairs and a rickety table in the parlor. Otherwise it was empty, except for liquor bottles, cracked dirty dishes, a weathered boot missing a sole, a pile of newspapers, and a ten of spades playing card.

It didn't smell anything like his childhood. Mrs. McKee had always insisted on fresh flowers throughout the house, and the scent of baking bread and beef cooking in the kitchen usually wafted through the halls. Now it smelled like stale smoke, wet wool, and rotten food.

"We gon' need a broom and a bucket of hot water," Mama

Lydia said.

"It's a good house," Robert assured Hannah.

"Oh, I knows it," Hannah said. "I been seeing this place every day for a year, and always wondered what it look like inside."

"You should have seen it when Mama lived here. The McKees was very particular."

"I ain't worried. Me and Mama Lydia, we'll get this place to shine. It's ours now."

Mama Lydia wandered off through the parlor, muttering. "Never should have let the place sink this low. Look at these floors. No decency to people today."

"Going to have plenty of room for the new baby," Robert said, laying his hand on Hannah's belly.

She stepped closer and leaned against him. "Don't seem real, does it?"

"Not yet. But when we get some furniture in here, it will. Maybe we can save to buy a table and chairs for the dining room."

She laughed. "Dining room. I like the sound of that. Our own dining room."

"I'm making enough from piloting the *Planter*, we can hire you some help to keep the house. Hire someone to keep up the yard, too. Prune them trees and bushes. There's a hundred hands in Beaufort desperate for work right now."

"What people gon' think of us?"

"They gon' think: there's Robert and Hannah Smalls, respectable people about town. They must be something special."

She put her arm around his waist. "Maybe we is."

*****

Hannah and Mama Lydia were off exploring the kitchen, their very own kitchen, one designed to cook for a whole house of people. Robert stood in the slave quarters out back, where he used to sleep as a boy. It was painted white and built so it matched the rest of the main house in style, just a lot smaller. Mrs. McKee said she didn't want to be in her garden and have to look at a ramshackle shed like some of her neighbors kept for their slaves. Nothing ugly was allowed in her yard.

It started out as one room, but George built a wall out of salvaged lumber, to give a little privacy to Mama Lydia and her son. They were glad for it, especially because George was a fierce snorer. Some nights, Robert wondered if those snores might shake the whole place down.

The wall was still there. Maybe the DeTreville's slaves liked having separate spaces, too. With all the refugees in town, they were lucky there weren't squatters in here.

He could just tear it down. Borrow a sledgehammer and start swinging. Could have the whole place in splinters in no time. The place where he had been owned. Or maybe the place where he was made. Did his conception happen inside the main house, on one of the beds, or on the floor? Maybe it happened when everyone was gone but Mr. Henry and Lydia. Or maybe it was here in the slave house, and George was told to go take care of the horses in the stable, so they could be alone. Had she wanted it, or did Henry McKee force himself on her?

He'd never know because Mama would never tell him.

He was tempted to burn it all down. Leave nothing but ashes. Erase any trace of the past and start fresh. Build a new house, just for them.

But no. This wasn't the game they were playing. He owned this place now, fair and square. He owned himself now. That would be satisfaction enough.

CHAPTER 31

Port Royal buzzed with more activity than Robert had ever seen. And it wasn't just Port Royal, on every plantation on Hilton Head and St. Helena Island, troops drilled and practiced firing artillery. Rumors flew, but the one Robert believed was that they were going to make a land assault on Charleston. Usually the heat of a July afternoon would have everyone seeking the shade of trees, porches, or under the upper decks of the *Planter*, but he and the rest of the crew couldn't help standing near the rail, watching soldiers marching onto the nearby *Cossack*. They were from the 1st New York Volunteer Engineers and carried crates and carts of shovels, planks, and pumps.

It'd be the *Planter*'s time soon, once their new captain arrived. Captain Milton had taken over while Robert was on the *Keokuk*, and left shortly for a new assignment a few days ago, right after Robert returned from his injuries. The scars around Robert's eyes seemed to be mending, and a healer woman from Fripp Plantation had given him salve to put on them. He wouldn't have minded staying at the new house and helping Hannah settle in, but the call came for all hands and he wasn't about to let the *Planter* get into trouble without him.

They still had most of the same old crew, and a new chief engineer, Danielson, a jowly, pale, bulldog of a man from Connecticut who knew his way around a steam engine, but almost never spoke. He'd bark one word commands at Alfred—"Steam," "Wood," "Pressure," and expect him to fix whatever problem needed solving.

"They could just make you captain, Robert," Chisholm had suggested. They all laughed, even Robert, though not quite as hard as the rest. The navy had had plenty of chances to make him captain of the *Planter*. If anyone could have done it, Admiral DuPont would have been the one, but after the failed attack on Charleston, DuPont had faced a barrage of criticism from the press and the politicians in Washington. Robert had only seen the admiral in passing, and even a glimpse showed a distracted man who had grown old and pale.

A navy lieutenant wove his way between the lines of uniformed soldiers loading onto the *Cossack* and headed toward the *Planter*. A black porter in an old castoff uniform followed, pushing a cart with the lieutenant's steamer trunk, a chair, a pillow, and a seabag. The lieutenant, a tall blond man, who couldn't have been much older than Robert, stopped at the gangway to the *Planter*. He looked down at the papers in his hand, then at the side of the ship, and then back at the papers.

Robert walked over to him. "Can I help you, suh?"

The man's voice wasn't nearly as big as his body and he seemed genuinely confused. "I am looking for the *Planter*."

"You's found her. Not as new as she once was, but she can out haul most of these scows."

"But... this can't be the *Planter*."

"You can see it right there." Robert pointed to the name, "Planter," painted almost three feet high in the middle of the paddle wheel housing. Maybe this lieutenant wasn't as good of a reader as most of them.

"There isn't another?"

"Not that I know of."

"But this is a river boat. A paddle wheeler."

"Always has been. Best one anywhere."

The lieutenant made a face like he'd just taken a mouthful of vinegar. "Stay here," he instructed the porter, then strode away, disappearing towards headquarters.

"Hey, Hector," Robert asked the porter, "who that?"

STEERING TO FREEDOM

Hector shook his head sadly, "Nickerson. Cape Cod man. He your new captain."

*****

By the time Nickerson returned, Robert had the crew lined up on deck and had summoned Engineer Danielson from the engine room.

Nickerson stomped onto the deck and the men snapped to attention, with the exception of Danielson, who barely made an effort to stand a little straighter. Nickerson surveyed them, taking no effort to hide his disappointment.

"I'm Lieutenant John Nickerson and apparently I am to captain this vessel, such as it is. At least until they find me a ship that uses sails and is meant to traverse the sea instead of fetid rivers. Who are you?" he demanded of Danielson, who half closed a rheumy eye to get a better look at this new captain.

"Danielson."

"Your post?"

"Chief engineer."

"Is she seaworthy?"

"She'll do."

"Where's the first officer?" Nickerson demanded.

"Danielson's our only officer, besides yourself, suh," Robert volunteered. "Captain Milton took his with him. We ain't seen no one else."

"And you are?" asked Nickerson, moving to stand in front of Robert.

"Robert Smalls, suh. Pilot and crew chief."

"You're all Negroes."

Robert held back the impulse to laugh, and he desperately hoped Chisholm could do the same.

"Yessuh."

"And this is the entire crew?"

"Yessuh." Robert named them as they stood. "Assistant Engineer Alfred, cook and hand Jackson, fireman Chisholm,

281

fireman Pilgrim, fireman Johnny, and ship's boy Cesar. Every man a hard worker. We know how to get her loaded, running, and wherever she need to go. Don't you worry, suh."

Nickerson muttered half to himself, "A half broken down river barge full of Negroes. Thanks a lot, Uncle Jake.

"All right, then," he continued, this time to the crew. "We'll make the best of it. We have orders to transport a company of infantry from St. Helena to Folly Island, for a night landing. Do you think you can find it?" he asked Robert.

"With my eyes closed, suh."

"A 'yes, sir,' would do fine. No cockiness on board my ship. My ship. Hm. You," he pointed at Johnny. "Load my gear into my cabin. Bring the boy to help you unpack it. Engineer Danielson, how are we fixed for coal?"

"Coal?"

Robert wondered if Nickerson's face could turn any redder. "Are we sufficiently fueled with coal to reach and return from Lighthouse Inlet?"

"Wood."

"Excuse me?"

"Wood."

Robert jumped in to break the communication gap before Nickerson's frustration made the young officer explode into pieces. "The *Planter* has a wood-burning boiler, sir. She was built for hauling cotton up and down the rivers, where they's plenty of trees, but ain't much coal."

"Thank you for the geography and the history lesson, Mr. Smalls. Wood. Of course. Why not? That's how the day's been going. A wood propelled river barge. Mr. Danielson, are we fully loaded with wood?"

"Yes, sir."

"Excellent. Mr. Smalls, since you seem to be a fountain of knowledge, why don't you give me a tour of the ship, so I can discover what other surprises lie in store before we're neck deep in soldiers."

STEERING TO FREEDOM

*****

The tour of the ship was quick, but long enough for Robert to understand that the new captain had little affection for heat, rivers, steam ships, Negroes, Southerners, and whole host of other offending entities.

"Congratulations for keeping this tub intact for so long. Let's hope you can keep it afloat long enough for us to land it in Charleston," he said to Danielson. Maybe Nickerson knew more about the coming plans than he was saying.

Nickerson insisted on taking the wheel as they pulled away from the wharf into Port Royal Sound. Robert called out obstructions: "There's a sunken bar at ten o'clock. Watch out for Talley's Snag, up ahead on the starboard side. You'll want to drive her back to port and stay clear of this end of Middle's Island."

Nickerson seemed to at least have basic seamanship, and Robert was pretty sure that on a sailing vessel, the lieutenant could name every line and sheet. He had a bit of a quick hand at the wheel of the *Planter,* though. "She don't draw much, so she'll spin like a top if you give her too much wheel," Robert counseled, but Nickerson merely gave him a sour look.

They gave the hull a good rub on the bar off Parris Island, just enough to clean off a few barnacles. Then they were in deeper water around St. Helena Island, and Robert watched Nickerson experiment with the bell calls and the power on both paddlewheel engines.

*****

They docked at Frogmore Plantation to pick up the Tenth Connecticut, who waited impatiently at the crumbling wharf. As Johnnie and Chisholm tied up, the colonel in charge called out to Nickerson.

"What took you so long?"

"Technical issues. Everything should be fine now."

"We need to get loaded and out of here. Important that we

arrive on Folly Island before sun up. Understand?"

"We have everything under control, Colonel," Nickerson reassured him.

The soldiers streamed on board. Robert had heard stories about the 10th Connecticut—they'd seen a lot of action in North Carolina last year, giving some rare good news to the Union army.

When he'd heard they were moving troops from St. Helena Island, he'd hoped they were going to transport the 54th Massachusetts. They were around here somewhere, under the command of Colonel Robert Gould Shaw, the son of Francis Shaw, whom Robert had met while giving speeches in New York. He'd seen the 54th briefly when they'd first arrived down south in June and stayed in Beaufort a few days. Everyone in town had stopped to stare at the sight of a thousand carefully uniformed black soldiers.

They weren't much like the First South Carolina. The First South Carolina were mostly dark-skinned and rough around the edges—nearly every one had been a slave before the war. The 54th Massachusetts were light-skinned Negroes from the North, free men, many of whom could read and write. Robert had never seen a more serious bunch of soldiers. They marched up the street like they were one body in motion. Even the white soldiers in the street stopped and admired their precision. One or two white infantrymen had a smart remark or two about *here come the monkeys in uniform*, but the comments dried to dust. The soldiers of the 54th looked at every white man, every person they saw, with a ferocity that said, "I'm better than you."

With all this action coming up, maybe they'd have a chance to prove it.

Now, the *Planter* was filling with white soldiers, sweating rivers in their wool uniforms. One who'd been standing in the sun too long wobbled as he walked over the gangway and crashed flat on his face. The soldiers on either side quickly stripped him of his jacket and gratefully accepted a bucket of cool sea water from Chisholm. July heat in South Carolina laid

STEERING TO FREEDOM

Yankees low as fast as a rebel battery.

*****

They were ready to depart just as the sun was setting and the mosquitoes were getting serious. Mosquitoes were yet another Southern charm despised by Captain Nickerson, though from the look on his face, he didn't have great affection for infantrymen from Connecticut either.

At Nickerson's command, they cast off and rang the bells for the engine. The *Cossack*, another steamer, was making way out of Jenkins Creek as they started downstream. She gave a toot on her horn, and Nickerson swung the wheel too hard, then readjusted the wrong way, and rang the bell for slow, but accidentally rang it telling them to increase speed.

"There's a stretch of mud hard to port," Robert warned. They didn't want to get stranded in the muck with two hundred soldiers on board.

Nickerson adjusted too hard again, and they surged into the current wrapping around the bend, and straight towards the *Cossack*. The captain of the *Cossack* yanked hard on his whistle.

"Sir," Robert warned his new captain.

Nickerson wasn't used to river work in the dark, and he spun the *Planter* onto a collision course with the *Cossack*, at a good six knots, closing fast. Seventy yards. Fifty yards.

Robert gently but firmly grabbed the wheel and twisted it back to the left, while also ringing the bells to cut the port engine.

The soldiers on the deck below realized they were about to smack into another ship and rushed away from the rail, tipping the ship ever so slightly, which gave the starboard paddle a little less grab. Nickerson tried wrestling back control of the wheel, but Robert was stronger.

Thirty yards, twenty-five, ten.

The *Cossack* adjusted back towards shore, and the *Planter* spun into the current and slipped forward, passing within a foot of the other ship. Soldiers on both ships, suddenly realizing they weren't going to crash, leaned across the water and shook hands with each other, calling, "Race you to Charleston!"

The instant they were clear of the *Cossack*, Robert released his grip on the wheel and Nickerson grabbed it back, looking around, making sure no one had seen what happened. Many eyes from the deck looked up at the pilot house. The colonel was still sound asleep in the spare officer's cabin. His lieutenants would be well advised not to wake him, Robert thought. Bears don't like their sleep disturbed.

Nickerson focused on the dim waterway heading out to sea. The Carolina pine forest lay black and forbidding on either side of the entrance to St. Helena Sound. Robert knew there were four submerged islands and sandbars at the mouth of the sound.

"Don't ever do that again," Nickerson said, his voice low and hard.

"Sorry, suh. I knows you's new to the *Planter*. Didn't want your first day to end with a bang."

"You're lucky it was dark. Otherwise, you'd be riding to Folly Island in the water at the end of a rope. Do I make myself clear?"

"Yessuh."

"I'm going to check on our visiting officers. The helm is now yours. Take us to the south end of Folly Island."

"Aye, suh."

Robert watched Nickerson disappear in the ward rooms. Grabbing the wheel was wrong, but he'd never seen a captain about to plow into another ship and not know how to fix it. Nickerson had better figure out either how to steer the *Planter* or how to let Robert run her. Next time it might not be a near miss.

CHAPTER 32

Ten days later, they carried a load of fresh horses and mules from a staging area on the Edisto, listening to the rumble of artillery fire. The animals stood calmly, eating hay and drinking from barrels of fresh water hauled by their teamsters. If the attack on Morris Island succeeded, the teams would be used to haul material to newly captured works. If it was a failure, they would pull ambulance carts with bloody soldiers, maybe the same men from the Tenth Connecticut they'd dropped off at the start of the assault. Robert didn't figure the horses cared much either way, as long as they were fed and watered.

As they approached the end of Folly Island, Captain Nickerson was a lot more nervous than the horses. He paced the observation deck outside the pilot house, constantly bringing his spyglass up and down, like he had a nervous tic.

"They need to tell us where to go," Nickerson said, as Robert worked to keep the *Planter* steady in the current streaming through Lighthouse Inlet. Four ironclads, the *Catskill*, *Nahant*, *Montauk*, and *Weehawken*, lay anchored off shore, out of range of the guns of Battery Wagner, firing shot after shot into the Rebel lines on the southern end of Morris Island.

If the signal flags ordered them to land in Lighthouse Inlet, they might be in the middle of all sorts of bad luck.

Smoke drifted over the water. The sound of musket fire mixed with men shouting in triumph and screaming in agony. Drums and fife spurred men on to tear each other's guts out with bayonets. The blasting of cannon echoed from the ships off shore and the landside batteries—the Union had been

287

constructing secret gun placements on the Folly Island side of Lighthouse Inlet. Construction had been only done in absolute darkness, with tools muffled, not a word allowed, except for the whispers of the engineering officers. The slightest sound could have brought down a rain of fire from rebel guns on Morris Island and deep in the swampy woods of James Island. Apparently the silence and secrecy had worked, because he could see fire lighting up the shroud of smoke from the new batteries. The Rebel emplacements on the lower end of Morris Island seemed unusually quiet.

Finally, a new series of signal flags raised above the Union observation tower behind the Folly Island batteries.

"What they say?" Robert asked.

"Bring the cargo to Morris Island. They must have pushed the rebels out. Let's hope the guns from Wagner can't reach us."

*****

Abandoned landing boats lay scattered across the beach, like driftwood after a hurricane. A corps of engineers had already rowed over from Folly Island and set up a temporary pontoon wharf, where the *Planter* could tie up, alongside another steamer unloading a steady stream of soldiers.

The horses and mules didn't like the erratic rocking of the pontoon wharf under their hooves, but the teamsters snapped their whips and prodded them onto shore. A company of soldiers, soaked to the waist from landing in longboats, hurried after the horses and unloaded crates of provisions. Nickerson called down to their commanding officer, a lieutenant who took the time to brush the fine white sand from his uniform and straighten his mustache. Despite his fastidiousness, he egged his men on to unload the ship even faster.

"What news?" Nickerson asked.

The lieutenant looked up, his face radiant with victory. "General Strong made the push, and Chatfield broke around the end and flanked them. The Rebs are routed all the way back to

Battery Wagner. All of Morris Island should be ours soon enough. As soon as you're unloaded, you're to start ferrying men here from Folly Island. We'll need every man, especially in this blasted heat."

"We were supposed to return to Edisto for more supplies," Nickerson said. Robert knew the captain didn't like being close to artillery. A trip back to Edisto would keep them well away from trouble.

"Change of plans. Once the men are moved, we'll need those supplies. And there's more news, too. They found newspapers in the one of the camps. Grant has captured Vicksburg, and Meade has stopped General Lee at Gettysburg!"

At hearing the news again, the soldiers unloading stopped and shouted, "Victory is near! Victory!"

"Where's Gettysburg?" Robert asked Nickerson.

"Pennsylvania, I think. I was starting to think General Lee could never be defeated." He called down again, "Is Lee captured?"

"The old fox is too slick for that. But the Confederates lost thousands and thousands of men. The battle was enough to force the Rebel army back down South again."

"Send 'em all the way to the ocean," one soldier called.

"All the way to hell!" said another.

"Hell's too good for them. Ain't so hot in hell as it is in South Carolina."

From the east, the ironclads loosed another wave of shells at Battery Wagner. The fort ran low and strong all the way across Morris Island, almost two miles away. Robert didn't share the soldier's view that South Carolina was worse than hell, but for whoever was in Battery Wagner, hell was raining down one shell at a time.

*****

A week and a half later, Robert finally saw soldiers from the Massachusetts 54th again. Two companies from the 54th, about twenty men in tattered uniforms, were detailed to unload bales of canvas for tents and crates of shovels and empty sandbags off the *Planter*. The ship was tied at the new wharf, which was slightly sturdier than the pontoon dock, but not by much. Robert climbed down to the deck, to oversee his own crew and the men from the 54th.

He'd heard all about their late-night charge on Battery Wagner three days ago. Their beloved commander, Colonel Shaw, was killed as they reached the top of Wagner's ramparts. By the time they were driven back, the 54th Massachusetts had lost more than a third of its men. Robert had asked Nickerson to volunteer the *Planter* to return the wounded black soldiers to the Beaufort hospitals, but the captain declined. Instead the honor went to the *Alice Price*.

Now the same brave men who'd charged into the lion's teeth were unloading the *Planter*. He looked at one of them, a corporal, his face slack with fatigue, as he picked up one end of a roll of tents. A jagged red line ran down one of his cheeks, remnants of a near miss from a bullet or a bayonet.

Four more black soldiers came back for another load. Together with Johnny and Chisholm, they wrestled a gun carriage off the ship. If Battery Wagner couldn't be taken front on, the Union army would settle in for a siege. Shovels and sandbags didn't come all this way for no reason.

"We heard what y'all did at Wagner," Robert said to the men. "Some say it's the bravest thing they ever saw."

He wondered if he'd have it in him to run headlong at a fort full of guns, knowing that if things didn't go your way, you weren't coming back. Things had definitely not gone their way. It was one thing to take the *Keokuk* against Sumter—at least the *Keokuk* was covered with armor. It was something else to run out there, just you and a gun, versus a whole fort.

The men looked up and at first none spoke, but finally a tall, beanpole of a man, not so young as the others, said, "It was our turn to prove ourselves. No one on this beach has to ask whether we're men now, do they?"

Another soldier piped up. "Maybe you fellas ought to join

up. Used to be slaves, right? Give yourself a chance to prove you can do something."

"Shut up, Lance." A third said. "Don't you know nothing? This is the *Planter*."

Lance looked around, as if he'd suddenly woken up. "The *Planter*. The one with Robert Smalls?"

"Yeah. You so dumb your head's like an empty bucket with hair."

Johnny grunted as they finally settled the crate onto the cart. "That Robert, right there."

"No way."

Robert smiled. "Johnny and Chisholm was on the ship, too. Took her right out past Sumter. Got my chance to try to get back in again, on the *Keokuk*, but that didn't go so good. You all, in the 54th, y'all are something special."

They shook hands like men and settled against the rail for a break from the heat and to tell stories of their adventures, until Nickerson's voice called down from above. "Robert, Johnny, Chisholm, what are you doing? We need to get this ship unloaded and go back to pick up the rest. Stop loafing around."

"He don't like the sound of the guns. Sometimes we drop crates on the deck, just to see him jump," Robert whispered to the other men, as they returned to work. The guns were quiet today, while the commanders of the two sides met to exchange prisoners, but the firing would start again soon. Nickerson also didn't like it when anyone recognized Robert or the other crew or the *Planter*. Nickerson had no interest in their story and claimed to have never heard a thing about their escape from Charleston.

They unloaded for another hour, before Jackson snuck down from galley with a pot of beef and potatoes and bowls to go around. The men from the 54th requested permission from their sergeant, a stern, mud-colored man with a permanent frown, who made sure each of his men ate before he attacked his own bowl.

291

"Sure hope one of your ships brings more food as good as this," he growled. "Ain't nothin' to eat besides hard biscuits all week."

"I hear they got some fresh beef coming your way, waiting on Hilton Head right now," Robert assured them.

"Oh, sure," one of the men said. "They ship empty sandbags our way before sending us something to put in our bellies."

Robert heard a noise from offshore and looked up to see a single-paddle steamer working up Lighthouse Inlet. Heavy smoke gushed from her twin smokestacks, as she maneuvered around the reef, through the current, and tied up next to them.

The men of the 54th quickly gulped down the rest of their stew. "Sergeant. Permission requested to inquire of the *Alice Price* to see if there's any news."

The white officer with the companies, Lieutenant Michaels, was upstairs in the wardroom having lunch with Captain Nickerson. Sergeant Bolton looked at the upper deck, considered whether he needed to interrupt his commander, but decided against it. "Corporal Hewett, see if they have any word about our wounded in Beaufort."

Hewett was one of the youngest of the company. Generally, the men in the 54th were an older bunch than white soldiers. They were men instead of boys, men who'd lived some life, and had something to lose if they didn't make it home in one piece.

They returned to unloading, but each of them kept an eye out for Hewett.

"I'm guessing it might take him just as long to get back as it takes us to unload the rest of this, eh?" Chisholm suggested.

The men laughed, then one of them said, "That's why Sergeant sent Hewett. Any of the rest of us, that's how it would be. We're all plenty smart enough to get out of work. But Hewett's got a heart so shiny, you'll see him come back on a run."

And he did. Despite the burning heat, Corporal Hewett jogged off the *Alice Price* around the dock and up onto the

Planter.

He was panting by the time he got there.

"Don't knock yourself out in this heat, Corporal," Sergeant Bolton commanded.

"The officers is in Hospital Number 3. The enlisted went to Hospital 14."

"That's the Baptist Church. They'll take good care of them," Robert reassured the men.

"They didn't have much news about how they was doing. Private Parker wasn't looking so good when they off loaded him."

"How many men they send to Beaufort?" Robert asked.

"Seventy-six," replied Sergeant Bolton.

Seventy-six wounded men. That would just about fill the church to overflowing.

"The pilot on the *Alice Price* gave me message for Mr. Smalls, too. From his wife." Hewett produced a small envelope.

"Oh, love letters. Probably gets them from more than just his wife, being so famous and all," one of the soldiers teased.

"Oh, they come with perfume and locks of hair. I get them, too," said Chisholm. "Sealed with kisses."

They all laughed. Except Sergeant Bolton, who barked, "Companies F and K, get your lazy asses back to work."

Robert took the note from Hewett and retreated into the shade of the overhanging deck, gesturing for Chisholm to follow. Robert hadn't had any time to work on his reading, so it seemed unlikely Hannah was sending him love notes. He opened the folded paper and looked at the unsteady handwriting. "I don't think I'm seeing it right," he said to Chisholm as he handed it over.

Chisholm smiled, "Not sure I should be reading your love letters from Hannah."

"Read it."

Chisholm read it first to himself, and then hesitated. "Robert."

"Read it."

Not a speck of Chisholm's humor showed, as he read as slowly and clearly as he could, trying to cushion the impact of the words with his voice.

"Dear Robert, I don't know how to tell you this, but I don't know when I will see you next. Robert Junior and Lizzie both come down with the pox. Lizzie is strong, and I think she will be all right. Robert Junior fought as best he could, but the Lord took him from us on the 10th of July. I wished we could have waited to bury him until you got home to say good bye, but given the heat and sickness, we laid him to rest on the 14th. I am healthy in my body, but broken in my heart for our sweet, sweet boy. Stay safe, and come home to me when you can.

"Yours dearly. Hannah"

Robert's legs weakened, and he collapsed onto the deck. Every bit of strength fled. He felt like he could dissolve into a thick black puddle, slide over the deck, and vanish into the murky waves beneath the *Planter*. His boy, his only son. Once this war was over, he was supposed to sneak out from the store on slow days and teach Junior to sail, to fish. Teach him how to read the water, how to love it. Junior was going to learn to work hard, for himself. He was going to learn to think for himself. A free man. Now he was gone. Gone.

When he'd been home last, the little man couldn't stop looking at the wounds around Robert's eyes. Already, even at two and a half, he was about as big across as he was tall. You could tell he was Robert's son. He'd strut over and say, "Ow?"

"Nah. I heal fast. Gotta be tough."

"Tough."

"That's right. Strong. You be strong, just like daddy, right?"

"Just like daddy. All better? I make it all better."

And the little man got some of the salve and rubbed it onto the cuts. Gentle. Of course, the next minute, they were yelling at the boy to stop messing with Lizzie's doll and leave big sister alone, but Junior had a healing touch. Maybe he could have made himself a doctor. If the white Southern man rolled his eyes crazy at the thought of a Negro soldier, try a black doctor.

He was a squirmy child, like a basket of snakes when you picked him up and tickled. Robert liked to put him under his arm and pretend he forgot he was carrying the boy. "Daddy, daddy, put me down," laughing the whole time. Junior had a belly laugh so big you'd think it was coming out of a grown man.

To never hear that laugh again made his ears feel useless. All of him, useless.

Whole parts of Robert's body felt hollowed out. Like each member of his family was part of the stuffing that filled him up, and someone just scooped out everything that was Junior. If someone came and pressed his side, there'd be nothing under the skin but emptiness.

How was Hannah supposed to bury her boy on her own? How sick was Lizzie? What about the baby yet to come? Hannah was the strongest woman he ever met, but she loved that little boy. She'd carried him to freedom held close to her heart, braved death to escape with him. All of them were tied tightly together, and now the Lord had come and snipped some of the strings.

Darkness. Sheer darkness. Everywhere, all around him.

There was nothing he could have done to stop it. Plenty of soldiers died from the pox, though some cut themselves and rubbed old pox dust in the cuts to try to keep from catching it. Should he have tried it on Junior? If he had been there, he could not have stopped it. He could not have stopped it. If only he'd been there.

Chisholm sat by his side and, for once, kept his mouth shut. It helped, having someone there. The soldiers and the crew went back to loading, giving them room. All of them had lost friends, comrades, brothers, children of their own.

Robert tried to stand, but his legs were only water. Losing Junior was like losing his very bones.

Chisholm must have said something to someone, because Alfred came out and took Robert back into the engine room, where he could be away from everyone, where the engines and the steam could drown the sounds of grief that flowed out of Robert's chest and lungs.

*****

The bells rang in the engine room, and the boy, Cesar, came down with an urgent look on his face. "Where's Robert? Anyone seen Robert? Captain say time to go, but no Robert."

"Tell the captain that Robert is on his way," Alfred said, taking the boy by the shoulders and steering him out of the engine room. "Go on now."

Robert huddled in a dark corner, not wanting a single speck of light to touch him. That was the strangest part about war—it came with grief everlasting, but no space for mourning.

"You's ready," Alfred told him.

"My boy. Just a baby. He's gone, Alfred."

"And Hannah's a mother with a broken heart. Just like the mothers of all these boys out here who ain't gon' make it home."

"Just wish... I..." Even his voice wouldn't work anymore.

"You wish you could be there. For Hannah. And for Junior, to say goodbye. War takes away a lot of goodbyes that should be said. Lord knows. We'll find a way to get you home. But right now, you need to get us to the next stop without setting the *Planter* at the bottom of the ocean."

Robert took the strength he needed from Alfred's voice, from the hand gripped on his shoulder. A father's touch from a man who had no children, just the engines on this ship and his shipmates, helping a man who didn't have a father of his own, not one who would claim him anyways. Having Junior slip away without being there to claim him filled the hollow spaces in Robert with icy cold. He never wanted Junior to feel like he wasn't claimed by his own daddy.

For now, that empty space needed to be covered over. He

climbed out of the engine room up to the pilot house, where Nickerson waited on the observation deck. "Get us back to Hilton Head," Nickerson said, a little more gently than he might normally have done.

Robert put his trembling hands on the wheel and steered the *Planter* out into the current, pushing closer to home, knowing he wouldn't get there tonight. Maybe not for many nights to come.

*****

It was fifty-five miles from the supply depot at Hilton Head to Light House Inlet. Every day, Robert steered the ship back and forth between the two stops. He watched it load and unload when he should have been sleeping. Half slept when he should have been focusing on the water and the reefs, but his hands knew where to turn the wheel and when to ring the bells.

It took tons of provisions to feed and shelter the men who spent all day and all night digging trenches on Morris Island, like giant moles. They filled sandbags and dove into the fetid bottoms of the holes when lookouts called out, "Incoming!" as another shell arced its way from Battery Wagner or Fort Sumter or James Island.

If the generals would just charge the fort once and for all, Robert could go home, instead of being caught in a never ending loop on the ocean. Standing on the observation deck, while they loaded the ship in Hilton Head with timbers, food, rope, canvas, empty sandbags, stretchers, Robert would look up the Beaufort River and think of Hannah, trying to make her know he was thinking of her, trying to imagine the small hole in the ground, covered with sand, that held his son. Only fifteen miles upriver. He was tempted to take the *Planter* one more time. The first time was to set his son free, this time would be to say Goodbye.

The Union army had been digging for weeks and weeks. The soldiers who unloaded the *Planter* at the base of Morris Island were on a rotation. One day digging, one day unloading, half a day rest. That was the black soldiers. The white soldiers spent a lot more time on guard duty. Black soldiers were good for suicide rushes at forts and for digging ditches. They said the closer they got to the fort, the worse the water smelled in the trenches. The summer heat was melting the bodies buried from the attack on July 18 and they were oozing back through the sand.

Alfred had talked to Nickerson and asked if they might volunteer to take some of the wounded over to Beaufort, just once, so Robert might have a minute to get home. But nothing worked—they kept hauling crates of hard tack.

It took a month before they broke out of the loop. Finally, Nickerson gave Robert the order to take the *Planter* to Port Royal. The *Cape May* had broken down, and they were to retrieve the guns she'd been carrying to add to the new batteries being carved into the sand, ever closer to the walls of Battery Wagner.

As soon as they were tied up at the wharf in Port Royal, Robert turned to Captain Nickerson. The captain leaned against one of the deck posts and looked at Robert closely.

"You should get some sleep."

"How long until we need to leave?"

"General Gillmore wants these guns right away. As soon as they're loaded, we need to leave."

"We's low on firewood, too. And in this heat, if the men work too fast, they just gonna keel over." Beaufort was only four miles upstream. Did Nickerson intend to make him beg?

"The men are slow in the sun, you're right. Those guns are heavy, and there's paperwork." Nickerson pulled a silver watch on a chain out of his pocket. "You have six hours. Don't be late."

*****

Robert found a launch carrying naval officers to Beaufort. They knew him by sight and didn't hesitate to make a spot for him. In less than an hour, he stood on the doorstep of the house where he was born. His house. Their house.

The quiet hit him as soon as he walked through the door. When he'd left, the two children were still getting used to the house, running around and playing in every corner. Now it was silent.

"Hello?" he called cautiously.

"Up here," came Mama Lydia's voice from above.

In the upstairs bedroom, Mama Lydia sat next to Lizzie's bed. His daughter smiled a weak smile at him, and he had her in his arms before, "Hello, Daddy," was all the way out of her mouth.

Even though it was hot inside the house, she felt cool to his touch. He let himself take a look at her. She had a few pock marks around the edge of her face, but she'd been spared the heavy damage that came to so many victims of small pox. She still looked like his little girl, just a little thinner and paler.

"Hey, baby. How you doing? You listening to Gramma and Mama? You getting strong?"

"Yes, daddy. I been real sick, but I do like Gramma say."

"She been like a little angel," said Mama Lydia. "Glad you stayin' safe. They gon' need you more now than ever."

"I don't know how much longer we gon' stay on this duty, but that fort can't hold out forever. Then we get a little time to rest the men and the *Planter*, and I'll come home."

Mama Lydia looked smaller since he'd left, as if the grief and love she poured into Lizzie and Hannah had shrunk her. She'd put up with a lot in her life and could put a smile on her face for Lizzie without half thinking about it. Any woman born a slave in the South had a whole collection of masks for when she needed them. But Robert could tell this loss had hurt her more than he'd expected. Maybe it was harder to lose someone when you were free.

"Where's Hannah?"

"Kitchen. Maybe you be the salve she need. She need to get stronger for that new baby. She need you here."

299

"I only got an hour, maybe two."

"Then you best go see her. But you stop by and give us a proper goodbye when it time to go."

She ran a wrinkled hand along his shoulder, as if reassuring herself that her own son was still alive.

*****

Hannah was standing at the kitchen table, frozen in the midst of making biscuits, with a spoon in her hand, staring out the open window, as if she'd gotten stuck in time. How long had she been like that?

He called from the doorway, as gently as he could. "Hannah."

She turned towards him, her face gradually coming back to life, but cautiously, as if she couldn't be sure he was really there. He could see the bump of her belly under her apron, round and firm, but still small. With Lizzie and Junior, she had showed big. Maybe this was just going to be a small baby.

"Oh, Robert. Thank God you's here. Thank God."

In his arms, she allowed herself be held, like she barely even had the strength to put her arms around him. Her shoulders shook, but there was no sound, no tears. She was cried out, tapped dry. There were women like her all across the nation, souls left brittle at the never-ending loss of sons.

She leaned on him and he held her up, knowing she'd been strong for Lizzie, for Mama Lydia, even for all the sisters from the church who brought something to eat, or who came by the store with tears in their eyes. He could hold her, had to hold her, as long as she needed him. Even the lioness' heart breaks sometimes. He waited for a roar, but all he got was the sound of her trying to get some air in her lungs to push out the dust of death and loss.

"Oh, I missed you," she said.

"I tried so hard, but they wouldn't let me away."

"You home to stay?" There was faint note of hope in her

voice.

"Just a few hours. They need me back at the ship. Bringing guns up to Morris Island tonight."

Her breathing finally calmed, as she gathered strength, or merely withdrew, knowing she'd have to say goodbye again. He stepped back to look at her, a hand on her belly.

"Mama say you need to eat more."

Her face had been transformed by sorrow. She'd been growing plump before he left, finally having enough food for herself and her unborn child, for once in her life. Freedom had agreed with her. But anything extra she'd had on her body had melted away, buried along with Junior.

"I try." She attempted a smile and got it at halfway there. "I been trying so hard, for all of them, trying to act like..."

"It's all right. You keep trying. All right? It gon' be okay."

"Is it?" She looked straight into his eyes and it was everything he could do to hold his gaze steady, even as his reassurance felt like a lie.

"In time. You and me, our family, we gon' survive this. The Lord took Junior home with him, and he gon' help us learn to bear it."

"You ain't the boy I married no more," she said, stroking his cheek. "You a man, all the way through."

Was that it what it took? Not just a midnight run to freedom, not meeting with the president, not standing in the *Keokuk* as the fires of hell poured over them, but the loss of part of his soul. Face that and come out the other side, then he could be a man. Let white folks debate whether a Negro man was fully human, let one of them face the loss any slave had faced every day.

"Where did you bury him?"

"Out back. Some said to put him in the cemetery, but I couldn't bear to have him so far from me."

She took him by the hand and led him outside into the yard, under the magnolia tree, its blossoms spent from the last blast

301

of summer heat. A rectangle of yellowing sod lay ten feet out from the tree, collecting crisped, brown magnolia petals.

"I'm glad you brought him here."

"I'm sorry you didn't get to say goodbye."

He kept one hand in Hannah's, but the other he wrapped across his ribs, as if to keep his heart in his own chest. Part of that heart was buried now, under this tree. It would be there forever. In stories, sometimes a man could sail down the river of death, to the gates of heaven, and bring back the souls of the ones he loved. But as skilled a sailor as he was, Robert knew there was no voyage he could take that would unbury his boy.

Chapter 33

December opened with a misty, chilly dawn. It had been drizzling on and off all night, just enough to make everything on land slick and muddy. Robert hoped the soldiers would finish loading the pile of provisions before the fog burned off. Captain Nickerson was in his cabin, sulking. Until now, they'd run supplies from Hilton Head to Battery Delafield and Fort Green on Folly Island, or to the rickety temporary wharfs at the south end of Morris Island. After the fall of Battery Wagner, the need had grown for more supplies for the twenty thousand men scattered across the bloody sands, preparing for an assault on Charleston. Any day now.

They'd been saying that since September.

Getting food to the troops in the tiny marsh batteries and islands tucked between Morris Island and the rebel forts on James Island was no simple task. There was no way to haul any volume of supplies via land, because there was no land, only swamp crisscrossed with plank pathways, barely wide enough for an infantryman. River boats could navigate the marsh, but the Confederate batteries at Secessionville and along James Island, not to mention Fort Johnson, happily attempted to reduce any supplies to splinters. The last two ships to try the run were now playgrounds for shrimp and redfish.

Now it was the *Planter*'s turn.

The fore and aft decks were piled high with crates, reaching all the way to the base of the pilot house. The late fall harvest had come in strong at the plantations, and the farmers had taken time from planting cotton to pick cabbage, peppers, tomatoes, and every sort of green vegetable. Chickens squawked in crates, next to bleating goats. Casks of gunpowder and cases of bullets nestled amongst the provisions.

The load wasn't exactly a thousand bales of cotton, or dozens of heavy cannon, but it was heavy enough to press the *Planter* down into the water. If there was one time she needed to be kept out of the muck, this was it. The heavy load was going to make this mission a lot trickier.

"Cesar," Robert called. The boy ran over. "Tell Captain Nickerson we's loaded. We need to make way afore that fog burns off."

The young steward sprang away into the officer's quarters. He was a good kid, even younger than Alston, and just as eager to please. Smoked a pipe like a full-grown man, and they'd been teaching him to spit. He had a quick mind and watchful eyes. Always paying attention to how they ran the ship, how Robert navigated, and how Alfred worked the engines.

"Chisholm," he called down to the deck, "Make sure that those crates don't lean like that. We might get busy out there, and we don't need a cloud of chickens flying all over the ship."

Chisholm gave him a half-hearted wave and instructed the soldiers on loading detail to restack the crates. They were white boys from Pennsylvania, and not interested in instructions from a skinny Negro with bushy hair and rag tag uniform. But Chisholm grabbed some himself, to show them, and made some sort of joke, so they laughed and followed his lead.

After this run, Robert would find an excuse to get home. Hannah was close to having the new baby, if she hadn't had it already. He'd last seen her more than a week ago, when they'd stopped at Port Royal for minor repairs to the starboard paddle wheel. Looked like she was carrying a watermelon under her dress. She was more than ready for it to come out. He'd already talked to one of the doctors at the colored soldier's hospital and made sure he'd be there if Hannah needed him. Robert brought the doctor a bottle of whiskey to grab his attention, and told him there'd be a twenty dollar gold piece if he made sure

Hannah came through the delivery safely. This was a real doctor, not like in the old days, when the only white man who would doctor a Negro was the one who took care of cows and pigs and drank too much. Mama Lydia would be there to help and so would Lila. Hannah would be all right. That's what he kept telling himself.

Maybe she'd bring him a new boy. No one would replace Junior, but they sure as hell needed something new in that house. Even Lizzie seemed serious, like she felt the empty space left behind by Junior, and it was a burden to try to fill it on her own. Mama Lydia said the baby would be a girl, but Robert wasn't so sure. Must be a boy to kick like he did. Could just about see the movement in Hannah's belly all the way across the room, that baby kicked so hard.

Still no sign of Nickerson. Johnny and Chisholm climbed the stacks of crates and cages and ran canvas strapping across the top of the load. Robert could smell eggs and bacon and coffee from the galley, so Jackson was doing his job. They just needed Nickerson.

A whole mess of people hoped Nickerson would land a promotion and get assigned to a different ship. Nickerson made it clear that he deserved a better ship, which to him meant any ship other than the *Planter*. But Nickerson put on such a sour face that senior officers couldn't stand to be near him. As long as they kept delivering supplies and men where they needed to be, but without accomplishing anything spectacular, Nickerson would likely sit on the *Planter* for the rest of the war.

Good looking men like Nickerson, who got started with help from their uncles and cousins, didn't know how to make friends. If it had been Robert, he would have volunteered the *Planter* for extra duty all the time. Army officers were impressed by spit and polish and by risks and responsibility. There were more than enough officers out here who knew how to cover their asses. Show some spark and you'd get noticed.

Captain Nickerson finally arrived at the pilot house, just in time for the flood tide. Which was a good thing, because the only way they were going to get to the backside of Morris Island was to pass quickly through some awfully narrow creeks. Every inch of tide would help.

"Cast off!" Nickerson shouted to Johnny and Chisholm, loud enough for soldiers and officers to notice that there was a captain on board giving orders, but the men on the wharf were more interested in finding breakfast and keeping an ear open for the occasional shell lobbed by Fort Lamar. "Take us up Lighthouse Creek, Robert!"

"Aye, Captain."

And this time, just between them, Nickerson asked, "Are you certain you can get her through?"

"I been sailing these creeks since I was twelve years old. I don't usually have to bring a boat quite this big, quite this full, through a space quite so small, but she'll squeeze through."

"According to this chart, it looks like we have to pass within a quarter mile of Secessionville."

"Let's hope the fog holds and those Rebels like to sleep late. Should have arranged for them to find a case or two of whiskey washed up on shore, so they'd be hung over this morning."

Nickerson didn't smile. His face had grown a bit of flesh over the past few months. Jackson was too good of a cook for Nickerson. And maybe the man got lonesome. Anyone would, if his only dining companion was Chief Danielson. Of course, he could ask Robert to join him, but Robert hadn't heard anyone ordering ice skates for hell lately. "Let's get moving," Nickerson said.

"Those soldiers on Morris Island gon' be mighty glad to see all this food," Robert said. "Their officers will be all kinds of grateful. Even generals notice when they get a bit of fresh chicken on they plate."

"Let's make some speed while we can. If we can get the first mile or two behind us, we won't be stuck in the maze for quite so long."

"Aye, sir." Robert rang the bells and brought her up to

speed. This part of Lighthouse Creek was almost a thousand feet wide, but in half a mile it would choke down to a fraction of that. They'd have two options. Johnson Creek might do the trick, but Copeland's Bend might be a bit much when they were loaded this heavy. Sticking with Lighthouse Creek would give them speed but put them closer to the batteries in Secessionville and the Rebel lines along James Island. Robert wasn't sure which Nickerson would choose.

"Who is that coming in behind us?" Nickerson asked, as he stood out on the observation deck, looking back towards Fort Green. He raised his spyglass. "Did the *Commodore McDonough* say anything about providing support guns?"

"No, suh." The *Planter* was on an army mission, and half the time the army and navy were barely on speaking terms. The soldiers said General Gillmore and Admiral Dahlgren hated each other. It would be nice to have a support ship hanging back—the *Commodore McDonough* had half a dozen guns that could catch some attention. It was a ship made for ferry work up North, a double wheel paddle steamer about the same length as the *Planter*, with better armor. The *McDonough* drew twice as much water, so if it followed them, it was only coming as far as the northern bend on Lighthouse Creek.

"Chisholm!" Nickerson called. "Signal the *Commodore McDonough* to see if they're coming with us."

Chisholm climbed the crates and boxes up to the roof of the main cabin. Robert was glad to have him on board. They'd found a way to keep him sober most of the time, though sometimes they'd still catch him falling off the edge into the bottle.

Chisholm dropped down to the observation deck. "Yessuh. They plans to follow us up Lighthouse Creek. Must think we's too pretty to go walkin' through the swamp without an escort."

Nickerson finally showed a little light in his eyes. "Well, we might get there in one piece after all. Let's avoid Johnson Creek, so they can shadow us most of the way."

"Aye, suh," said Robert.

With any luck the mist would hold for another hour, and no one on the Rebel shore would take notice of the *Planter*. As long as the sailors on the *Commodore McDonough* didn't get too itchy for some action.

They just needed a little luck.

*****

The clouds feeding the drizzle blew off, and the mist evaporated in the morning sun just as they neared Copeland's Bend, giving them a clear view, over the waving swamp grass, of Fort Lamar and her guns. Also giving Lamar's rebel gunners a fine view of the *Planter*.

On the observation deck, Nickerson stiffened as much as a man could without splintering, and the crew seemed especially loose, as if in opposition. Jackson lingered with Robert in the pilot house, drinking coffee and smoking his pipe. Chisholm sat with Johnny on top of the stacks of crates and barrels on the foredeck, juggling heads of cabbage. Behind them, the *Commodore McDonough* chugged along.

Robert was trying to get a feel for the load—it wasn't as heavy as many he'd carried on the *Planter*, but it was uneven. The tide was nearing its height, and it'd swirl at the bend, as the tide met the water coming down the creek.

Maybe the Rebels were still drinking their morning coffee.

He rang the bell for more power on the port engine, to bring them around the wide right turn. This is where the *Commodore McDonough* would stop, if they had any sense. The next half mile was still a couple hundred feet wide, but it ran shallow.

One of Chisholm's juggled cabbages exploded at the top of its arc, followed by the sharp crack of the rifle that shot it. One of the barrels suddenly began to spray beer, followed by another, and another, as rifle fire pop, pop, popped against the *Planter's* armor.

The Rebels must have finished their breakfasts.

Captain Nickerson scrambled into the pilot house,

cramming himself next to Robert and Jackson. Down on deck, Johnny and Chisholm dove for cover between stacks of crates.

"Evade their fire, Smalls!" Nickerson shouted over the crackling gunshots. A bullet touched one of the lines leading from the pilot house to the smoke stack, pinging a tone like a hammer on a piano wire.

"Yessuh." There wasn't much Robert could do. The channel was going to get narrower as they steamed towards the tidal basin.

A puff of smoke rose from low walls of Fort Lamar, followed by the boom of a gun. They watched the shell on its path, soaring over them, then exploding in the swamp fifty yards past them, sending up a geyser of mud and water.

Suddenly thunder roared from behind them, as the *Commodore McDonough* opened up with two of its guns. One shell came up short in the water across the marsh, and another hit the narrow beach in front of the fort. They'd better find their range fast, or the *Planter* was in trouble.

Another shell from Fort Lamar arced over, this one hitting the water not twenty yards in front of the *Planter*, sending water all the way up to the pilot house. Nickerson squealed like a wounded animal and pressed his body even lower.

"Faster! Stay away from the shells. Evade their fire!"

Robert swung the wheel and tried to zig zag up the creek, staying mindful of the muck reaching out from the sides of the creek like grabbing fingers. There were no landmarks out here, no trees or humps, just flat swamp grass stretching for miles, and narrow channels that he hadn't seen since before the war.

The *Commodore McDonough* sent off another round of fire, three quick booms, with one of the shells striking the earthen ramparts of the fort, spraying sand and dirt, but not much more than that. At least the *McDonough* had caught their attention—the next set of rebel shells landed between the two ships, as if the Confederate artillerymen couldn't decide which ship was the better target.

A small orange speck drew Robert's eye from across the tidal basin, then four more. The rebels on James Island had been busy building batteries along the edge of the island, and now more guns opened on the *Planter*. Four balls of iron buried themselves in the mud, a hundred yards off the port bow. The *Planter* was out of range from the James Island guns, but to get into the basin and over to the Union soldiers on Morris Island they'd need to sail half a mile closer, into the teeth of the far batteries. And then make their way through a thin channel.

More explosions joined the growing symphony of cannon fire, this time from a mile off the starboard rail. The Union gunners in the marsh batteries wanted their supper and intended to let the rebels in Secessionville know about it.

"Goddamn it, what are they doing?" Nickerson shouted.

"Hard to say, suh. Maybe trying to keep them 'cesh gunners from getting too comfortable."

The top of the flagpole exploded into splinters as a shell from the Union marsh batteries misfired and barely passed over their heads. Nickerson shrieked again, though it was lost in the growing din. Jackson looked at Robert with alarm, and neither of them were sure what to do, as the captain squeezed himself against the back of the pilot house, eyes wide with terror.

"Get us out of here," Nickerson croaked.

"Working on it, suh." Robert pulled the line for more speed.

Shells from *Commodore McDonough* burst over the top of Fort Lamar. Robert hoped it was enough to send the gunners under cover, though another quick set of shells showed it'd take more than that to get the Confederates to hide their heads. The armor around the paddle wheel thunked and dinged, as it protected against shrapnel. By now, the enemy gunners had probably seen the *Planter*'s name through their spy glasses. There was no more appealing target to any Charleston-based soldier.

One of the crates of chickens burst into a mass of feathers, and they drifted serenely in the midst of chaos as another shot almost hit them. The power coming to the engine still wasn't what Robert wanted.

"We need more power, sir. Might need more fire. You should send Johnny to the engine room to feed wood."

"What? Yes. Send him. Send him."

Robert hoped Nickerson might at least give the order himself, but he wasn't moving from against the wall of the pilot house.

"I'll go, too," Jackson volunteered.

"Tell them we need to push faster. Get that fire hot. Send Cesar back with a report," Robert commanded.

"You got it." Jackson dashed from the pilot house into the interior cabins, where he could descend safely into the engine room.

Robert looked at Nickerson, who crouched closer to the floor, as another shell landed in the water close enough to push the prow to the right. The captain was officially useless. Robert leaned forward, out of the pilothouse and yelled, "Johnny! Go throw wood!"

Johnny looked up from his and Chisholm's protected space and waved. Another shell rained down fragments of metal over the decks, but mostly just made a mess on top of the cargo. Johnny emerged from the protected space and climbed quickly over the load, his arms and legs hugging the cargo like a giant black spider. He waved again and disappeared with a smile.

Chisholm looked up. "Where you want me?" he yelled.

Robert was trying to concentrate on where he was steering the ship, weaving across the channel to make it harder for the gunners to find the exact range. Hoping the Union marsh batteries wouldn't accidentally skip a shell over the mud and shatter a paddle wheel.

The ship suddenly rocked, as a cannon ball glanced off the top of the smokestack with a resounding "dong."

Robert's eyes focused ahead, completely aware of Nickerson cringing behind him. The opening to the mud flats was only a hundred yards away, and it was going to take some tricky maneuvering to get through without getting hung up. The rebel James Island batteries on the other side of the basin were starting to find their range.

"Captain Nickerson! What are your orders, sir? Captain. Captain, we need you up here, sir."

The urgency in his voice somehow picked Nickerson off the floor and brought him up to the window beside him. They looked out together at the smoky shoreline, over the eel grass and twisting maze of channels, at the cloud of weeds, muck, and water thrown up by shells, and gnat-like specks of iron flying back and forth between Fort Lamar and the *Commodore McDonough*.

Chisholm stood on the deck in behind a row of crates, looking up at them, waiting to be told where to go. Suddenly, his head and shoulder erupted into spray of blood and bone. The rest of his body dropped like discarded cargo into the supplies meant for hungry soldiers.

Robert's stomach lurched in horror and despair. Chisholm gone, destroyed in the space of a single heartbeat. Another soul reduced to nothingness by the angry hand of war.

"Beach the ship!" Nickerson shrieked.

Nickerson's high-pitched panic brought Robert back to the hard reality of the bridge. There would be time to mourn Chisholm later. "What?"

"Surrender. Beach her and get us the hell out of here. Find a white flag and surrender." Nickerson backed away from the window, his face speckled with mud and gore.

Robert gripped the wheel harder, watching the gap in the reeds that led to the flats. They were in the middle of nowhere. The *Commodore McDonough* was half a mile behind them. If they gave up the ship, the rebels from James Island would take her with their long boats and capture the captain and crew.

"White flag. Run up a white flag. Surrender. I'm telling you. Get it to stop!" Nickerson repeated.

"I can't beach her, sir. The crew is all escaped slaves. They'll kill us all." Robert had a five hundred dollar price on his head. If they didn't shoot him on sight, they'd hang him in the center of Charleston in front of the workhouse until his bones fell apart into a pile.

"They're going to blow us to bits. Beach her and run the white flag."

Cesar stood at the entrance to the pilot house, mouth agape. A bullet smashed into the roof of the deck, just over the boy's head, but none of them moved.

"I won't scuttle this ship, sir. Not for you. We can make it to Morris Island."

Nickerson looked at him, eyes bulging, the white around them reducing the black and blue to pinpricks of fear. Another shell from James Island hurled a wave of water over the bow. Robert gripped the wheel. He was taking her into the tidal basin, whether Nickerson wanted him to or not.

One, two, three more explosions, and suddenly Nickerson pushed past Cesar, sending the boy sprawling. The captain of the *Planter* disappeared into the cabins.

Cesar crawled into the pilothouse.

"Robert? Robert, what should I do?"

"Find where he went. If you see him trying to run up a white flag, get Jackson and tell him to stop him. Come back and tell me where the captain went, as fast as you can. This the most important thing you ever done in your life."

The boy ran after Nickerson, leaving Robert alone in the pilothouse. He felt like he was the only one in the ship, suspended in the smoking thunderous hell between Morris and James Island.

He felt if he raised his head and looked over the flat water of the basin, he would see the eyes of the Rebel gunners, taking aim right at the *Planter*. But he needed clear vision and a clear mind to make it through the channel into the tidal flats. If the Rebels had planted obstructions, they were finished. Nickerson would get what he wanted—the *Planter* would be destroyed and they'd all die. This channel was maybe seventy-five feet wide, and the *Planter* stretched thirty feet wide at the beam. Not much water to keep them afloat.

The fire from the *Commodore McDonough* and the marsh batteries increased. The *McDonough* finally found the range on her nine inch gun, and a big cloud of smoke, dirt, and brick erupted from one of the James Island batteries. Smoke from a fire in the fort began to smudge the sky.

Robert felt a rub on the port edge of the hull and he shivered her slightly to the center of the channel. He avoided the first open channel. He knew that one led into a spider web. The second channel, even though the mouth looked narrower, would carry them to deeper water.

Cesar appeared by his elbow. Robert could barely afford the time to look at him.

"Speak. Where is he?"

"Hiding in the firewood bunker. Keeps saying abandon ship, surrender, abandon ship."

"He tell that to Danielson?"

"Yessuh. Chief told him to go fuck himself and stay away from his goddamn engines."

"Danielson said all that?"

"Most words any of us ever heard from him."

Robert signaled the engine room for full stop on the starboard engine, as he racked the *Planter* to a halt, rotated her ninety degrees, and slipped her into the channel. They barely fit. In a lull between shells, he could hear the marsh grass swishing against the sides.

"Tell Jackson to keep the captain down below. And nobody get a white flag. We ain't about to surrender. If he don't want to hear the order from you, tell him to come up here and hear it from me himself. I'm running the ship now. You tell everyone that. I'm gon' get us to Morris Island in one piece, but they got to keep the engine running smooth. We gon' practically have to crawl over the mud to get there."

Cesar gaped at him, open mouthed.

"Go!"

The boy sped off below decks. In a world with less fire and iron filling the air, they'd have a man on the prow, signaling the twists and turns of the channel, but he didn't want another shattered body on deck. It was up to him to feel his way in.

The channel narrowed, and he could feel the muck pressing against the sides of the hull. He rang for more power, and pushed her through, the rear of the ship rising slightly as the paddles ground against the mud and grass.

Jackson appeared, soaking wet. Cesar right behind him.

"What's the report?"

"He's still in there, hiding behind the wood pile. Plumb out of his mind. Cesar say you in charge now."

"Someone got to be. Danielson still with us?"

"He'll do what it takes to keep this ship moving. We got a hole just below the rail, near the starboard engine. We taking water."

"Plug, it patch it, put something in it, even if it takes putting Nickerson's head in it. Get Johnny on the pumps."

"Where is Chisholm?"

"Dead on deck. Ain't much left of him." It pained Robert to even say it, but he didn't have time for pain now. He only had time to steer the *Planter* to safety.

"Oh, Lord."

"Get those pumps going, and Cesar, you start shoving wood into that boiler. We either make it this last half mile, or they gon' blow us to bits."

Jackson and the boy ran below. Robert stared ahead, trying to ignore the thunder. His back was exposed to the rebel guns now. He wished he had eyes in the back of his head, so he could track the incoming shells, but there was nothing to see but the twisting channel in front of them. Why had he thought he could get her through here?

The covering fire from the Union batteries grew closer. The shells barely passed overhead now. The tide allowed the *Planter* to float in this mess of a tidal flat, but it also drowned out the obvious channel edges at this point. He could only go by the silhouettes of the submerged weeds, and the ripples in the water from the currents and the wind. At least the Rebel guns were receding. Every fifty feet the *Planter* advanced made them harder to hit.

A thousand feet to go. He could see the soldiers lined up along a massive pile of sandbags running the length of the sandbar where they'd constructed their fort. The fort was so low to the water it was lucky to make it through any high tide. There was a slight deepening to the water in front of the battery where they'd set up a makeshift wharf.

The Union guns directly in front of them stopped firing and Robert said a prayer of thanks that they realized they were going to blow their own dinner out of the water. One or two rebel shells hit the channel beside them, but the firing was beginning to slow. Anything now was mostly for show. Back on Lighthouse Creek, the *Commodore McDonough* continued to send shots into James Island, and more into Secessionville, but even she was starting to relent.

He twisted the wheel back and forth, gliding the *Planter* into the channel that swept in front of the battery. A great cheer rose from the hundreds of men who had watched the fight. Robert took his hand off the wheel for a quick wave, and then pulled the signal lever to tell Alfred to power down the engines. He drifted her into the wharf, towards a landing party that stood ready to toss lines to a crew that was nowhere to be seen. Three short, two long chimes on the bell brought Jackson and Johnny out on deck, and they scrambled over splintered crates and barrels and landed the *Planter*.

Robert stood absolutely still. All the guns suddenly fell silent, even the engines of the *Planter* quieted to a neutral purr. He let his hands slip from the wheel. Any sense of triumph was completely snuffed out—his friend lay dead on the deck, his captain locked in the wood bin, his ship splintered.

CHAPTER 34

Soldiers crowded the end of the makeshift wharf, but made space for a small knot of officers—including a red-faced general with a pair of binoculars still gripped in his hands.

Robert signaled to Johnny and Jackson to join him, and they stood in a ragged line, facing the officers. Robert saluted, his hands trembling. Not twenty feet away, Chisholm's headless body lay in a gory pile under a blanket that Jackson had found. "The *Planter*," Robert said, barely able to speak. "The *Planter* is pleased to deliver food and supplies to your men, suh."

The black-bearded general stepped forward, flanked at each elbow by captains. Robert realized that this wasn't just any general, this was Major General Gillmore, department commander.

"That was an impressive bit of piloting. What's your name?"

"Robert Smalls."

"*The* Robert Smalls?" The general leaned forward, intrigued.

"Yessuh. We request permission to tend to our wounded and the ship, suh."

The general took a moment to survey the mess of the deck and the shrouded body behind them. He seemed like a man who didn't miss much. "Did you take many losses?"

"Lost one crew member, suh. These men here been below decks, manning the pumps." He turned to Jackson. "How much water are we taking?"

Jackson's voice barely rose to a whisper. "Alfred ran a fast

318

patch that should hold. Ain't that bad."

General Gillmore shifted impatiently, his eyes scanning the ship, and clearly aware of the impatient rumblings of the men behind him. "We're anxious to unload the cargo. And to assist with your casualties, too, of course. Who's your captain? Where is he?"

Robert hesitated. "Lieutenant Nickerson, suh. He, ah, well, he's below decks."

"I've been watching you all the way from the big bend. He left you on your own. Is he hurt?"

"He's hiding."

Gillmore's face reddened again. "What?"

"Panicked, suh. They said he in the wood bin."

"Take me to him. Captain Leonard, work with these men to unload this ship. Captain Miller, find a corpsman to handle the body." The general turned his fierce, hawk-like eyes to Robert and nodded sharply.

"Jackson. You stay here with Chisholm, all right?" Robert said. It felt wrong to leave their friend with strangers.

Robert led General Gillmore and his entourage through the narrow aisle between crates to the engine room, stepping over splintered crates and shredded cabbage, all speckled with mud and blood. Inside the ship, Cesar and Alfred still manned one of the pumps. A thin film of water covered the deck. A column of light streamed in from a hole punched through the ceiling. Danielson worked in the boiler room, in his undershirt, covered in grease and oil. He had a wrench in his hand and was busily adjusting valves and levers on the starboard boiler.

Alfred and Cesar stopped pumping at the sight of the officers and stood at attention. They were a mismatched pair, the old man and the boy. Danielson, who didn't have much hearing left after a lifetime in boiler rooms, didn't notice the parade of new arrivals until Alfred went and brought him away from the boiler to stand with them.

"What the hell?" Danielson growled as he turned around.

He barely straightened himself at the sight of the officers. "General."

General Gillmore's lip almost quivered into a smile at the sight of the hard-working engineers, but his anger quelled any appreciation. Robert had heard soldiers on Morris Island complain that Gillmore was more at home with engineers and artillery than fighting men. "Where's Lieutenant Nickerson?"

Danielson pointed a grubby finger towards the back corner of the firewood bunker, where firewood lay neatly stacked. "There." The soles of a pair of boots poked out from where the pile had been nearly emptied to feed the belly of the *Planter*.

In the murky lantern light, General Gillmore stomped over to the boots. "Nickerson! On your feet!"

The captain of the *Planter* twitched and pulled himself to standing. "Lieutenant John Nickerson, United States Navy. We surrender. We have one other white officer on board. As for the crew, I ask you to spare their lives. They're hard workers and will fetch a good price."

Gillmore slapped Nickerson, leaving a red mark on his cheek. "You're at the marsh battery, Lieutenant. This vessel remains in the hands of the United States of America. No thanks to you."

Nickerson shook his head, trying to rid himself of the cobwebs. Maybe he still heard the shells bursting around him. His eyes barely focused on the general. "Sorry, sir. My mistake."

"You are a betrayal of everything an officer should be, Nickerson. Consider yourself removed from command, for cowardice. These men risked their lives, gave their lives, while you crept down here like a dog. You'll be tried for dereliction of duty, and I'll see you scrubbing barnacles for the rest of your natural life."

"No! It... I wasn't... The shells just kept... It just wasn't possible for us to... When I gave the order to... I wasn't really..."

"I saw the whole thing. You're a disgrace. Captain Leonard, have Mr. Nickerson escorted from the ship and held in irons until he can be transported to a proper facility. Mr. Smalls, please oversee the unloading on deck. Major Nelson, may I have a word?"

Nickerson was led out of the engine room, strong hands on each of his arms. His face was drenched with sweat, from the heat of the engine room and from panic, and he continued to mumble to himself.

Robert whispered to Alfred, barely able to get the words out "Chisholm took a hit. Full on."

Alfred slumped against bulkhead. "No."

Any last scrap of joy from escaping the barrage flooded out of Robert, leaving him with the black absence left behind by the loss of their joker. It was his playfulness, in this very room, that had started them all on their way to freedom. Now he was gone.

*****

Out on deck, Robert, Jackson, Johnny, and Alfred gathered around what remained of Chisholm. Army corpsmen had already laid the various body parts under a sheet, now patterned with a lacework of dried blood, punctuated by flies searching for a fresh meal. Behind the gathering, soldiers unloaded the cargo, using a line of men that seemed to engage every soldier in the entire fort to carry the boxes, bales, and crates.

The world seemed entirely too quiet and a lot emptier.

"World gon' miss his laugh, that's fo' sure," Robert said.

"He really dead?" Johnny asked, wringing his hat in his hands.

"Yeah," said Jackson.

"Never thought he'd be the one to go," said Alfred, wiping his oil stained face with his bandanna.

"Don't know if anyone enjoyed his freedom much as Chisholm," Robert said.

They noticed a presence behind them. General Gillmore and his aides stood watching in a space that had been cleared on the deck. The men behind him seemed anxious to leave, but

Gillmore stood totally still, hat in hand, head slightly bowed.

"I'm sorry to disturb you," said General Gillmore. "We've all lost too many friends and brothers."

"Yessuh. Chisholm was a good man. Escaped to freedom with us on this very ship."

"We'll see he's buried with full honors."

"We'd like to bring him home with us to Beaufort. That's where he's from and he might find some rest there."

"Of course. Mr. Smalls, there are many men in this fort grateful for what you and your men have done here today. You've shown astounding strength of character. The command of the *Planter* is yours."

An aide to the general cleared his throat gently, "I'm, ah, not sure a Negro has been in command of an actual United States ship before, so there might be—"

Gillmore cut him off. "I don't care. I'll do the paperwork myself. I'll talk to Admiral Dahlgren, whoever else it takes. They won't say no. Now let's unload this ship and see to any injuries. Captain Smalls, I thank you."

The general shook Robert's hand with a strong grip. Shook hands with the new captain of the *Planter*.

*****

The trip out, made near midnight, came with a lot less fire and thunder. They brought the *Planter* home without another shell even fired in their direction. Robert feared that in the dark, he'd founder his new command in the swamp, but with Jackson and Johnny running hooded lamps on the bow, he snuck her out like a cat.

Now they stood at Chisholm's grave site, a plain pine coffin resting in a hole in Beaufort's colored cemetary. Hannah stood next to Robert, leaning against his shoulder, holding their newborn daughter, bundled thickly against the cool December air. Sarah had arrived in the world at almost the same instant Chisholm had left it.

STEERING TO FREEDOM

She was born free.

The rest of them had given birth to their own freedom. Every one who'd come to new life on board the *Planter* had found the power to midwive themselves to the light of day. Chisholm gave his life in the struggle that would devour thousands of the nation's sons. But it was their nation, too. The black men and women Robert saw all around him, each of them reaching down and tossing a handful of earth on the wooden box, their hands were stained with the soil, the blood of the land. They would not board ships to be shipped off to Africa, or South America, or Mexico. This was their home, fully paid for. Each of them would get back on the *Planter* tomorrow, and do their small part to win the battle for the soul of a nation.

Robert would do it as captain of the *Planter*.

EPILOGUE

APRIL 14, 1865

The *Planter* steamed into Charleston Harbor completely covered in humanity, as if she'd sprung a fur coat. Hundreds of former slaves filled the decks, even the engine room, covering the roof of the cabins and the pilot house. They were every shade of black and brown, every age, from a toothless four-day-old baby to a toothless old mammy. Some were almost skeletons held together by rags, after months of following armies, begging for scraps, severed from the land to which they'd once been bound, their homes and crops burned to ash.

Robert stood on the roof of the pilot house in his best dress uniform, taking it all in, while still trying to pay attention to where they were going. He shouted down an order down to Turno, who manned the helm. Johnny stood out from the crowd on the main deck, a head taller than the woolly scalps and bright turbans around him. Jackson had hidden himself in the galley, wanting to protect his space and equipment from the throng. Alfred was in the engine room, showing off the *Planter*'s refurbished engines and the new coal bins to anyone who asked. They'd taken her all the way up to the coast to Philadelphia last year to have her refitted. Some thought Robert could never get the riverboat across so much open ocean. Well, here he was, and the *Planter* was better than ever.

Even in the swarm of people, Robert still felt the absence of

Chisholm. He could pick out the exact spot where his blood had seeped into the deck. Chisholm would have loved the crowd, the laughter, the smiles so bright they were like a thousand new suns. The singing. It was like bringing a ship full of angels back home to heaven.

But Charleston was a far cry from heaven these days. The bombardment and fires had left her a broken shell of a city. Their old place over the stables was nothing but burnt timbers. The blocks around the Mill House Hotel were reduced to rubble. Robert had been on parade through the city with General Saxton and the Massachusetts 54th, shortly after the Confederates deserted the city in February. Those celebrations had been dampened by the knowledge that the war wasn't over yet. Today, nothing could hold anyone back. No shout, no song could be suppressed today. General Lee had surrendered to General Grant in Appomattox, Virginia. They said it was all just details now.

It was a giant birthday party. Four years to the day that the flag was lowered from Fort Sumter, they were here to put it back up.

None of them were the same. Turno had a wooden leg. Lost it last year on James Island. The changes in the rest of them were harder to see. Even Johnny would wake covered in sweat, taking cover from incoming fire under his blankets until they could bring him to his senses.

Hannah and the girls were right below, next to Turno in the pilot house. Mama Lydia, too. All their families. It was easy to look back at that night three years ago, and think of all that could have gone wrong. One missed connection, one wrong sound, and all of them might be dead. Or Hannah and Lizzie might be in the vast camps of refugees scattered across the South, looking for a home that didn't exist anymore. There would be no Sarah. And Junior? Would he still be gone?

"Hard to starboard, Turno!" Robert shouted, trying to get them through the flotilla, as they moved over the bar into the harbor. The water was thick with warships, river steamers, long boats, dinghies. The *Planter*'s goal was the wharf at Fort Sumter. He'd been invited to be part of the ceremony with all of the fancy white folks from up North. Reverend French was already there, and C.C. Leigh and Reverend Henry Ward Beecher from New York, and William Lloyd Garrison from Boston.

There'd been talk of President Lincoln coming to raise the stars and stripes over Fort Sumter himself. General Saxton promised Robert that if that happened, Mr. Lincoln would want to ride into Charleston Harbor on the prow of the *Planter*. Put two riverboat pilots together on the most famous riverboat of the war. But they'd kept the president up in Washington, saying it wasn't safe for him to come to the burnt out hornet's nest of the Confederacy.

Robert would have loved to see the old man again, but this group wasn't a bad replacement. There were scores of new black farmers from all around Port Royal, who had bought up chunks of the old plantations. They were free men now, who owned their own land, whose future finally rested in their own hands.

"Three cheers for Robert Smalls and the *Planter*," someone called from the *Chicora*, as they passed. Robert waved his cap, as he felt a scrape and sudden shake and he almost fell off the top of the pilot house. They were sliding alongside the *Alice Price* on the port side. "Bring us starboard, ring the port engine up a notch," he called down to Turno. The assembled mass of people on board gave a nervous laugh, not willing to panic quite yet. The *Planter* scooted ahead, then ground into the mud, not five hundred yards southeast of Sumter. Passengers grabbed on to each other to keep from being pitched over the side into the water.

They'd just grounded her in full view of a thousand boats filling the harbor.

Robert flushed, his face hot. He should have taken the wheel himself, not been busy waving to admirers. "Full stop!" he shouted to Turno. He grabbed the edge of the pilot house roof and swung down through the open window. Every reporter in Charleston would see the *Planter* stuck in the mud.

Turno looked at him sheepishly, maybe the first time Robert had ever seen anything close to an apology in the eyes of his friend. "They's so many damn boats out here. Can't go ten feet without trying not to hit one."

"Maybe you should try to hit one, and then maybe you'd miss," Robert said.

But the sight of Mama Lila and Hannah and all the children, drained Robert's anger. "This is the hardest place we ever tried to steer," he reassured Turno. He signaled the engine room to reverse. He'd just like to get them out of the mud on their own power. The *Planter* was so loaded down with people, it didn't make it any easier.

All the muscle of the *Planter* couldn't unloose her, and it took a cable from *Chicora* to pull her free. For a moment, Robert thought about keeping the wheel himself the rest of the narrow way in. But Turno was standing there, as strong and proud as ever, though not as straight, on the new leg. "You take the wheel," Robert said. "Let's get these folks to the party."

*****

Fort Sumter had been abandoned in February, left as not much more than a pile of rocks, only one face remaining slightly intact. But in the past two months, crews cleared some of the rubble and made it a secure fort again. For today, bleachers had been constructed in a circle around an enormous central flagpole, reaching high into the sky. People filled every possible seat, thousands of them. They were Negroes ferried over from the city and the plantations, white politicians and abolitionists come from up North, soldiers and sailors. They were a mass of folk who had lost part of their hearts on the day four years earlier when the flag was lowered and the war officially began. They had lost blood and brothers on the ships and the land, from Jacksonville to Gettysburg to the outer reaches of Texas. Robert stood on the edge of the central platform, in a place of honor, with Hannah on one side, Reverend French on the other. The girls stood with Mama Lydia at the front of the crowd. There were speeches from every important man eager to have his voice join the chime of victory over slavery, over dis-Union.

When the speeches finally died down, General Saxton introduced a silver-haired man in uniform. "Today, we bring forth the man who was here to witness the start of this terrible conflagration. General Anderson is here to raise the flag he lowered at this very spot four years ago."

General Anderson looked out over the crowd, his eyes weary from war and sorrow. Robert thought he wasn't as old as he looked. All of them had lost a lot more than four years since that flag had come down.

"After four long, long years of war, I restore to its proper place this flag which floated there in peace. I thank God I have lived to see this day."

The crowd fell silent as Anderson pulled the lanyard and raised the banner up the massive white flag staff, sending the stars and stripes flapping into the sky, so high on the pole that it almost looked like it flew there all on its own.

A great roar rose from the assembly, a mix of shouts of joy and exhalation of relief and anger and hope. Robert found himself crying with them, joining with every newly freed brother and every veteran and do-gooder, all sending voices ringing over the man-made island, as if their collective sound could purge the land of blood and hate.

He gripped tightly onto Hannah's hand, as she turned to him, tears streaming down her face, shining in the sun. All of them shouted to Heaven, in thanks for having lived, and in mourning for sons they'd lost.

*****

That night, Robert stood on the observation deck of the *Planter*. Hannah and the children were already in the tiny captain's cabin. He was grateful they had a covered place to sleep for the night.

He looked over his ship. He'd gotten her shot and splintered and stuck and bloody, but she'd never let him down. The stars above were the same ones they'd seen three years ago, on that fateful night. But the *Planter* wasn't quite the same anymore, none of them were.

On shore, bonfires and celebrations had been raging all night. They'd grown quieter lately, maybe having spent every last ounce of energy. But he noticed the flag on Sumter being lowered to half mast, just after a small steam launch had arrived.

He climbed over the sleeping forms that covered the deck, people with nowhere else to go, or waiting to return to Beaufort once the parties were over. He stood by the rail and shouted down to the launch as it passed by on its way back to Charleston, "What news? Why is the flag down?"

The answer floated thinly over the water. "The president is dead. Lincoln has been shot tonight."

Robert felt ice in his belly. The heat of the day's celebration suddenly felt cooled by the mist of death. A pall lay over the future.

He picked his way over the passengers and climbed up to his cabin. Inside, Hannah slept on the bunk, cradling Sarah against her bosom. Lizzie slept nestled in a pile of blankets, her face a look of pure peace.

Let them sleep. Let them all sleep and finish their night of happy dreams. Tomorrow, the news would come and the celebration would turn to mourning and the bunting replaced with black cloth.

The old man's eyes never lit up all the way with a smile, Robert remembered. There was always something remaining, deep down, that couldn't shake loose of the black dog of death. But Mr. Lincoln had helped guide them this far. Those that still lived would have to pilot themselves carefully in the currents leading to the future.

Robert walked back to the pilot house, held the wheel in his calloused palms, and looked out into the dark night. The sun would rise in the east tomorrow, over a nation nursing millions of broken hearts. Once the president was buried, they would all have a choice, a million choices. It was up to each of them to navigate a maze of branching channels. He would put every ounce of himself into steering his family, his Beaufort, his Carolina, down the right path.

THE END

About the Author

Patrick Gabridge

Patrick Gabridge is an award winning playwright, novelist, and screenwriter. His other novels include *Tornado Siren* and *Moving [a life in boxes]*. His plays have been staged in venues around the world, and his historical plays include work about the creation of the English Bible (*Fire on Earth*), the astronomers Kepler and Tycho (*Reading the Mind of God*), a volcanic eruption on Martinique (*The Prisoner of St. Pierre*), 19th century Boston publisher Daniel Sharp Ford (*None But the Best*), and the Boston Massacre (*Blood on the Snow*). His work for radio has been broadcast by NPR, Shoestring Radio Theatre, Playing on Air, and Icebox Radio Theatre. In his spare time, he likes to farm.

IF YOU ENJOYED THIS BOOK

Please write a review.

This is important to the author and helps to get the word out to others

Visit

PENMORE PRESS

www.penmorepress.com

All Penmore Press books are available directly through our website, amazon.com, Barnes and Noble and Nook, Sony Reader, Apple iTunes, Kobo books and via leading bookshops across the United States, Canada, the UK, Australia and Europe.

THE LAUNDRY ROOM

BY

LYNDA LIPPMAN-LOCKHART

The Laundry Room dramatizes a fascinating moment in the history of the founding of Israel as a self-ruling nation. Based on actual events, Lynda Lippmann-Lockhart follows the lives of several young Israelis as they found a kibbutz and run a clandestine ammunition factory, which supplied Israeli troops fighting against Arab forces following the end of British occupation in the late 1940s. Under British rule, it was illegal for Israelis to possess firearms, so it was necessary not only to create and stockpile bullets for the coming war, but to do so in secret.

The ingenuity, courage, and sheer audacity displayed by the members of the code-named "Ayalon Institute" as they operated their factory right under the noses of the British military make for an intriguing tale. Lippmann-Lockhart shows readers what it might have been like to be one of the young pioneers whose work shaped the outcome of Israel's fight for independence. The Ayalon Institute remains standing to this day, but the secret hidden under the kibbutz's laundry room was not revealed until the 1970s. It was made a National Historic Site in 1987 and is open to the public every day of the year except Yom Kippur.

PENMORE PRESS
www.penmorepress.com

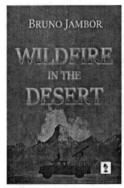

WILDFIRE IN THE DESERT

BY

BRUNO JAMBOR

Action Adventure, Crime, Mystery,
Southwest History

Highly entertaining, well researched and original:

A Navy veteran returns home to his ancestral land to escape the pace of modern life. His nephew begs him to hide the drugs he is transporting to escape his pursuers.

An astronomer trying to find a replacement for his estranged wife finds solace in his work with the stars.

Police and the drug cartel try to recover the missing shipment, regardless of consequences, ready to sacrifice any opponent.

The antagonists crisscross the desert of Southern Arizona in a chess game where the loser will be eliminated.

Unexpected help comes from a famous missionary who blazed new paths through the same desert three centuries ago.

The climactic resolution will captivate readers of this thriller with deep spiritual undertones.

PENMORE PRESS
www.penmorepress.com

ASSASSINS OF ALAMUT

BY

JAMES BOSCHERT

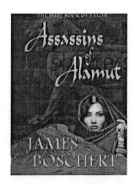

An Epic Novel of Persia and Palestine in the Time of the Crusades

The *Assassins of Alamut* is a riveting tale, painted on the vast canvas of life in Palestine and Persia during the 12th century.

On one hand, it's a tale of the crusades—as told from the Islamic side—where Shi'a and Sunni are as intent on killing Ismaili Muslims as crusaders. In self-defense, the Ismailis develop an elite band of highly trained killers called Hashshashin whose missions are launched from their mountain fortress of Alamut.

But it's also the story of a French boy, Talon, captured and forced into the alien world of the assassins. Forbidden love for a princess is intertwined with sinister plots and self-sacrifice, as the hero and his two companions discover treachery and then attempt to evade the ruthless assassins of Alamut who are sent to hunt them down.

It's a sweeping saga that takes you over vast snow-covered mountains, through the frozen wastes of the winter plateau, and into the fabulous cites of Hamadan, Isfahan, and the Kingdom of Jerusalem.

"A brilliant first novel, worthy of Bernard Cornwell at his best."—Tom Grundner

PENMORE PRESS
www.penmorepress.com

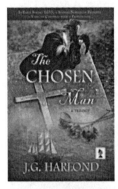

The Chosen Man

by

J. G Harlond

From the bulb of a rare flower bloom ambition and scandal

Rome, 1635: As Flanders braces for another long year of war, a Spanish count presents the Vatican with a means of disrupting the Dutch rebels' booming economy. His plan is brilliant. They just need the right man to implement it.

They choose Ludovico da Portovenere, a charismatic spice and silk merchant. Intrigued by the Vatican's proposal—and hungry for profit— Ludo sets off for Amsterdam to sow greed and venture capitalism for a disastrous harvest, hampered by a timid English priest sent from Rome, accompanied by a quick-witted young admirer he will use as a spy, and bothered by the memory of the beautiful young lady he refused to take with him.

Set in a world of international politics and domestic intrigue, *The Chosen Man* spins an engrossing tale about the Dutch financial scandal known as tulip mania—and how decisions made in high places can have terrible repercussions on innocent lives.

PENMORE PRESS
www.penmorepress.com

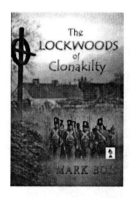

The Lockwoods

of Clonakilty

by

Mark Bois

Highly entertaining, well researched and original in thought. Lieutenant James Lockwood of the Inniskilling Regiment returns to his family in Clonakilty, Ireland, after being badly wounded at Waterloo. After three years on active service his return is a joyous occasion, but home is not the perfect refuge he craves.

Twenty years before, he had married Brigid O'Brian, a beautiful Irish Catholic woman of willful intelligence, an act that estranged him from his wealthy family. Their five children, especially their second daughter, Cissy, are especially and irritant to the other branches of the family, as the children balance their native Irish heritage against the expectations of the Anglo-Irish Lockwoods.

PENMORE PRESS
www.penmorepress.com

Penmore Press

Challenging, Intriguing, Adventurous, Historical and Imaginative

www.penmorepress.com